Robert Calkins
146 West Hampden
Englewood, Colorodo

Raise the TITANIC!

Stay clear
of icebergs.

Clive Cussler

10-76

Also by Clive Cussler

The Mediterranean Caper

Iceberg

Clive Cussler

Raise the TITANIC!

The Viking Press   New York

With gratitude to my wife, Barbara, Errol Beauchamp, Janet and Randy Richter, and Dick Clark.

First published in 1976 by The Viking Press
625 Madison Avenue, New York, N.Y. 10022

Published simultaneously in Canada by
The Macmillan Company of Canada Limited

LIBRARY OF CONGRESS CATALOGING IN PUBLICATION DATA
  Cussler, Clive.
    Raise the Titanic!
    1. Titanic (Steamship)—Fiction. I. Title.
  PZ4.C9856Rai [PS3553.U75]   813'.5'4   76-25871
  ISBN 0-670-58933-0

Printed in the United States of America

I am particularly indebted to G. J. Marcus, whose book *The Maiden Voyage* has been invaluable to me.   C.C.

Contents

Prelude

The man on Deck A, Stateroom 33, tossed and turned in his narrow berth, the mind behind his sweating face lost in the depths of a nightmare. He was small, no more than two inches over five feet, with thinning white hair and a bland face, whose only imposing feature was a pair of dark, bushy eyebrows. His hands lay entwined on his chest, his fingers twitching in a nervous rhythm. He looked to be in his fifties. His skin had the color and texture of a concrete sidewalk, and the lines under his eyes were deeply etched. Yet he was only ten days shy of his thirty-fourth birthday.

The physical grind and the mental torment of the last five months had exhausted him to the ragged edge of madness. During his waking hours, he found his mind wandering down vacant channels, losing all track of time and reality. He had to remind himself continually where he was and what day it was. He was going mad, slowly but irrevocably mad, and the worst part of it was that he knew he was going mad.

His eyes fluttered open and he focused them on the silent fan that hung from the ceiling of his stateroom. His hands traveled over his face and felt the two-week growth of beard. He didn't have to look at his clothes; he knew they were soiled and rumpled and stained with nervous sweat. He should have bathed and changed after he'd boarded the ship, but, instead, he'd taken to his berth and slept a fearful, obsessed sleep off and on for nearly three days.

It was late into Sunday evening, and the ship wasn't due to dock in New York until early Wednesday morning, slightly more than fifty hours hence.

He tried to tell himself he was safe now, but his mind refused to accept it, in spite of the fact that the prize that had cost so many lives was absolutely secure. For the hundredth time he felt the lump in his vest pocket. Satisfied that the key was still there, he rubbed a hand over his glistening forehead and closed his eyes once more.

He wasn't sure how long he'd dozed. Something had jolted him awake. Not a loud sound or a violent movement, it was more like a trembling motion from his mattress and a strange grinding noise somewhere far below his starboard stateroom. He rose stiffly to a sitting position and swung his feet to the floor. A few minutes passed and he sensed an unusual, vibrationless quiet. Then his befogged mind grasped the reason. The engines had stopped. He sat there listening, but the only sounds came from the soft joking of the stewards in the passageway, and the muffled talk from the adjoining cabins.

An icy tentacle of uneasiness wrapped around him. Another passenger might have simply ignored the interruption and quickly gone back to sleep, but he was within an inch of a mental breakdown, and his five senses were working overtime at magnifying every impression. Three days locked in his cabin, neither eating nor drinking, reliving the horrors of the past five months, served only to stoke the fires of insanity behind his rapidly degenerating mind.

He unlocked the door and walked unsteadily down the passageway to the grand staircase. People were laughing and chattering on their way from the lounge to their staterooms. He looked at the ornate bronze clock which was flanked by two figures in bas-relief above the middle landing of the stairs. The gilded hands read 11:51.

A steward, standing alongside an opulent lamp standard at the bottom of the staircase, stared disdainfully up at him, obviously annoyed at seeing so shabby a passenger wandering the first-class accommodations, while all the others strolled the rich oriental carpets in elegant evening dress.

"The engines . . . they've stopped," he said thickly.

"Probably for a minor adjustment, sir," the steward replied. "A new ship on her maiden voyage and all. There's bound to be a few bugs to iron out. Nothing to worry about. She's unsinkable, you know."

"If she's made out of steel, she can sink." He massaged his bloodshot eyes. "I think I'll take a look outside."

The steward shook his head. "I don't recommend it, sir. It's frightfully cold out there."

The passenger in the wrinkled suit shrugged. He was used to the cold. He turned, climbed one flight of stairs and stepped through a door that led to the starboard side of the boat deck. He gasped as though he'd been stabbed by a thousand needles. After lying for three days in the warm womb of his stateroom, he was rudely shocked by the thirty-one-degree temperature. There was not the slightest hint of a breeze, only a biting, motionless cold that hung from the cloudless sky like a shroud.

He walked to the rail and turned up the collar of his coat. He leaned over but saw only the black sea, calm as a garden pond. Then he looked fore and aft. The Boat Deck from the raised roof over the first-class smoking room to the wheelhouse forward of the officers' quarters was totally deserted. Only the smoke drifting lazily from the forward three of the four huge yellow and black funnels, and the lights shining through the windows of the lounge and reading room revealed any involvement with human life.

The white froth along the hull diminished and turned black as the massive vessel slowly lost her headway and drifted silently beneath the endless blanket of stars. The ship's purser came out of the officers' mess and peered over the side.

"Why did we stop?"

"We've struck something," the purser replied without turning.

"Is it serious?"

"Not likely, sir. If there's any leakage, the pumps should handle it."

Abruptly, an ear-shattering roar that sounded like a hundred Denver and Rio Grande locomotives thundering through a tunnel at the same time erupted from the eight exterior exhaust ducts. Even as he put his hands to his ears, the passenger recognized the cause. He had been around machinery long enough to know that the excess steam from the ship's idle reciprocating engines was blowing off through the bypass valves. The terrific blare made further speech with the purser impossible. He turned away and watched as other crew members appeared on the Boat Deck. A terrible dread spread through his stomach as he saw them begin stripping off the lifeboat covers and clearing away the lines to the davits.

He stood there for nearly an hour while the din from the exhaust ducts died slowly in the night. Clutching the handrail, oblivious to the cold, he barely noticed the small groups of passengers who had begun to wander the Boat Deck in a strange, quiet kind of confusion.

One of the ship's junior officers came past. He was young, in his early twenties, and his face had the typically British milky-white complexion and the typically British bored-with-it-all expression. He approached the man at the railing and tapped him on the shoulder.

"Beg your pardon, sir. But you must get your life jacket on."

The man slowly turned and stared. "We're going to sink, aren't we?" he asked hoarsely.

The officer hesitated a moment, then nodded. "She's taking sea faster than the pumps can keep up."

"How long do we have?"

"Hard to say. Maybe another hour if the water stays clear of the boilers."

"What happened? There was no other ship nearby. What did we collide with?"

"Iceberg. Slashed our hull. Damnable bit of bloody luck."

He grasped the officer's arm so hard the young man winced. "I must get into the cargo hold."

"Little chance of that, sir. The mailroom on F Deck is flooding and the luggage is already floating down in the hold."

"You must guide me there."

The officer tried to shake his arm loose, but it was held like a vise. "Impossible! My orders are to see to the starboard lifeboats."

"Some other officer can man the boats," the passenger said tonelessly. "You're going to show me the way to the cargo hold."

It was then that the officer noticed two discomforting things. First, the twisted, insane look on the passenger's face, and, second, the muzzle of the gun that was pressing against his genitals.

"Do as I ask," the man snarled, "if you wish to see grandchildren."

The officer stared dumbly at the gun and then looked up. Something inside him was suddenly sick. There was no thought of argument or resistance. The reddened eyes that burned into his, burned from within the depths of insanity.

"I can only try."

"Then try!" the passenger snarled. "And no tricks. I'll be at your back all the way. One stupid mistake and I'll shoot your spine in two at the base."

Discreetly, he shoved the gun into a coat pocket, keeping the barrel nudged against the officer's back. They made their way without difficulty through the milling throng of people who now cluttered the Boat Deck. It was a different ship now. No laughter or gaiety, no class distinction; the wealthy and the poor were joined by the common bond of fear. The stewards were the only ones smiling and making small talk as they handed out ghost-white life preservers.

The distress rockets soared into the air, looking small and vain under the smothering blackness, their burst of white sparkles seen by no one except those aboard the doomed ship. It provided an unearthly backdrop for the heart-rending good-bys, the forced expressions of hope in the men's eyes as they tenderly lifted their women and children into the lifeboats. The terrible unreality of the scene was heightened as the ship's eight-piece band assembled on the Boat Deck, incongruous with their instruments and pale life jackets. They began to play Irving Berlin's "Alexander's Ragtime Band."

The ship's officer, prodded by the gun, struggled down the main stairway against the wave of passengers who were surging up toward the lifeboats. The low angle of the bow was becoming more pronounced. Going down the steps, their stride was off-balance. At B Deck they commandeered an elevator and rode it down to D Deck.

The young officer turned and studied the man whose strange whim had inexorably bound him tighter in the grip of certain death. The lips were drawn back tightly over the teeth, the eyes glassy with a faraway look. The passenger glanced up and saw the officer staring at him. For a long moment their eyes locked.

"Don't worry . . ."

"Bigalow, sir."

"Don't worry, Bigalow. You'll make it before she goes."

"What section of the cargo hold do you want?"

"The ship's vault in number one cargo hold, G Deck."

"G Deck must surely be under water by now."

"We'll only know when we get there, won't we?" The passenger motioned with the gun in his coat pocket as the elevator doors opened. They moved out and pushed their way through the crowd.

Bigalow tore off his life belt and ran around the staircase leading to E Deck. There he stopped and looked down and saw the water crawling upward, inching its relentless path up the steps. Some of the lights still burned under the cold green water, giving off a haunting, distorted glow.

"It's no use. You can see for yourself."

"Is there another way?"

"The watertight doors were closed right after the collision. We might make it down one of the escape ladders."

"Then keep going."

The journey along the circuitous alleyways went rapidly through the unending steel labyrinth of passages and ladder tunnels. Bigalow halted and lifted a round hatch cover and peered into the narrow opening. Surprisingly, the water on the cargo deck beneath was only two feet deep.

"No hope," he lied. "It's flooded."

The passenger roughly shoved the officer to one side and looked for himself.

"It's dry enough for my purpose," he said slowly. He waved the gun at the hatch. "Keep going."

The overhead electric lights were still burning in the hold as the two men sloshed their way toward the ship's strong room. The dim rays glinted off the brass of a giant Renault town car blocked to the deck.

Both of them stumbled and fell in the icy water several times, numbing their bodies with the cold. Staggering like drunken men, they reached the vault at last. It was a cube in the middle of the cargo compartment. It measured eight feet by eight feet by eight feet; its sturdy walls were constructed of twelve-inch-thick Belfast steel.

The passenger produced a key from his vest pocket and inserted it in the slot. The lock was new and stiff, but finally the tumblers gave with an audible click. He pushed the heavy door open and stepped into the vault. Then he turned and smiled for the first time. "Thanks for your help, Bigalow. You'd better head topside. There's still time for you."

Bigalow looked puzzled. "You're staying?"

"Yes, I'm staying. I've murdered eight good and true men. I can't live with that." It was said flatly. The tone final. "It's over and done with. Everything."

Bigalow tried to speak, but the words would not come.

The passenger nodded in understanding and began pulling the door closed behind him.

"Thank God for Southby," he said.

And then he was gone, swallowed up in the black interior of the vault.

Bigalow survived.

He won his race with the rising water and managed to reach the Boat Deck and throw himself over the side only seconds before the ship took her plunge.

As the bulk of the great ocean liner sank from sight, her red pennant with the white star that had been hanging limply, high on the aft mastpeak under the dead calm of the night, suddenly unfurled when it touched the sea, as though in final salute to the fifteen hundred men, women, and children who were either dying of exposure or drowning in the frigid waters over the grave.

Blind instinct clutched at Bigalow and he reached out and seized the pennant as it slipped past. Before his mind could focus, before he knew the full danger of his foolhardy act, he found himself being pulled beneath the water. Yet he stubbornly held on, refusing to release his grip. He was nearly twenty feet below the surface when at last the pennant's grommets tore from the halyard and the prize was his. Only then did he struggle upward through the liquid blackness. After what seemed to him an eternity, he broke into the night air again, thankful that the expected suction from the sinking ship had not gotten him.

The twenty-eight-degree water nearly killed him. Given another ten minutes in its freezing grip, he would have simply been one more statistic of that terrible tragedy.

A rope saved him; his hand brushed against and grabbed a trailing rope attached to a capsized boat. With the last ounce of his ebbing strength, he pulled his nearly frozen body on board and shared with thirty other men the numbing ache of the cold until they were rescued by another ship four hours later.

The pitiful cries of the hundreds who died would forever linger in the minds of those who survived. But as he clung to the overturned, partly submerged lifeboat, Bigalow's thoughts were on another memory: the strange man sealed forever in the ship's vault.

Who was he?

Who were the eight men he claimed to have murdered?

What was the secret of the vault?

They were questions that were to haunt Bigalow for the next seventy-six years, right up to the last few hours of his life.

1

The Sicilian Project

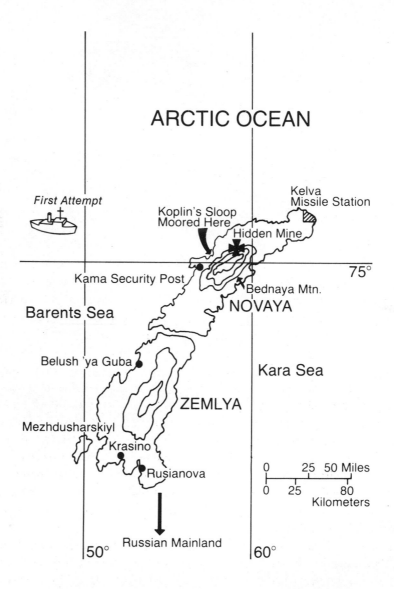

ARCTIC OCEAN

First Attempt

Kelva
Missile Station

Koplin's Sloop
Moored Here

Hidden Mine

Kama Security Post

75°

Bednaya Mtn.

Barents Sea

NOVAYA

Kara Sea

Belush 'ya Guba

ZEMLYA

Mezhdusharskiyl

Krasino

Rusianova

0		25	50 Miles
0	25		80

Kilometers

50°

Russian Mainland

60°

1

The President swiveled in his chair, clasped his hands behind his head, and stared unseeing out of the window of the Oval Office and cursed his lot. He hated his job with a passion. he hadn't thought possible. He had known the exact moment the excitement had gone out of it. He had known it the morning he had found it hard to rise from bed. That was always the first sign. A dread of beginning the day.

He wondered for the thousandth time since taking office why he had struggled so hard and so long for the damned, thankless job anyway. The price had been painfully high. His political trail was littered with the bones of lost friends and a broken marriage. And, he'd no sooner taken the oath of office when he had found his infant administration staggered by a Treasury Department scandal, a war in South America, a nationwide airlines strike, and a hostile Congress that had come to mistrust whoever resided in the White House. He threw in an extra curse for Congress. Its members had overridden his last two vetoes and the news didn't sit well with him.

Thank God, he would escape the bullshit of another election. How he'd managed to win two terms still mystified him. He had broken all the political taboos ever laid down for a successful candidate. Not only was he a divorced man but he was not a churchgoer, smoked cigars in public, and sported a large mustache besides. He had campaigned by ignoring his opponents and by hitting the voters solidly between the eyes with tough talk. And they had loved it. Opportunely, he had come along at a time when the average American was fed up with goody-goody candidates who smiled big and made love to the TV cameras, and who spoke trite, nothing sentences that the press couldn't twist or find hidden meanings to invent between the nouns.

Eighteen more months and his second term in office would be over. It was the one thought that kept him going. His predecessor had accepted the post of head regent at the University of California. Eisenhower had withdrawn to his farm in Gettysburg, and Johnson to his ranch in Texas. The President smiled to himself. None of that elder-statesman-on-the-sidelines crap for him. His plans called for self-exile to the South Pacific on a forty-foot ketch. There he would ignore every damned crisis that stirred the world while sipping rum and eyeing any pug-nosed, balloon-chested native girls who wandered within view. He closed his eyes and almost had the vision in focus when his aide eased open the door and cleared his throat.

"Excuse me, Mr. President, but Mr. Seagram and Mr. Donner are waiting."

The President swiveled back to his desk and ran his hands through a patch of thick silver-tinted hair. "Okay, send them in."

He brightened visibly. Gene Seagram and Mel Donner enjoyed immediate access to the President at any time, day or night. They were the chief evaluators for the Meta Section, a group of scientists who worked in total secrecy, researching projects that were as yet unheard of—projects that attempted to leapfrog current technology by twenty to thirty years.

Meta Section was the President's own brainchild. He had conceived it during his first year in office, connived and manipulated the unlimited secret funding, and personally recruited the small group of brilliant and dedicated men who comprised its core. He took great unadvertised pride in it. Even the CIA and the National Security Agency knew nothing of its existence. It had always been his dream to back a team of men who could devote their skills and talents to impossible schemes, fantasy schemes with one chance in a million for success. The fact that Meta Section was still batting zero five years after its inception bothered his conscience not at all.

There was no hand shaking, only cordial hello's. Then Seagram unlatched a battered leather briefcase and withdrew a folder stuffed with aerial photographs. He laid the pictures on the President's desk and pointed at several circled areas that were marked on transparent overlays.

"The mountain region on the upper island of Novaya Zemlya, north of the Russian mainland. All indications from our satellite sensors pinpoint this area as a slim possibility."

"Damn!" the President muttered softly. "Every time we discover something like this, it has to sit in the Soviet Union or in some other untouchable location." He scanned the photographs and then turned his eyes to Donner. "The earth is a big place. Surely there must be other promising areas?"

Donner shook his head. "I'm sorry, Mr. President, but geologists have been searching for byzanium ever since Alexander Beesley discovered its existence in 1902. To our knowledge, none has ever been found in quantity."

"It's radioactivity is so extreme," Seagram said, "it has long vanished from the continents in anything more than very minute trace amounts. The few bits and pieces we've gathered on this element have been gleaned from small, artifically prepared particles."

"Can't you build a supply through artificial means?" the President asked.

"No, sir," Seagram replied. "The longest-lived particle we managed to produce with a high-energy accelerator decayed in less than two minutes."

The President sat back and stared at Seagram. "How much of it do you need to complete your program?"

Seagram looked to Donner, then at the President. "Of course you realize, Mr. President, we're still in a speculative stage. . . ."

"How much do you need?" the President repeated.

"I should judge about eight ounces."

"I see."

"That's only the amount required to test the concept fully," Donner added. "It would take an additional two hundred ounces to set up the equipment on a fully operational scale at strategic locations around the nation's borders."

The President slumped in his chair. "Then I guess we scrap this one and go on to something else."

Seagram was a tall lanky man, with a quiet voice and a courteous manner, and, except for a large, flattened nose, he could almost have passed as an unbearded Abe Lincoln.

Donner was just the opposite of Seagram. He was short and seemed almost as broad as he was tall. He had wheat-colored hair, melancholy eyes, and his face always seemed to be sweating. He began talking at a machine-gun pace. "Project Sicilian is too close to reality to bury and forget. I strongly urge that we push on. We'd be playing for the inside straight to end inside straights, but if we succeed . . . my God, sir, the consequences are enormous."

"I'm open to suggestions," the President said quietly.

Seagram took a deep breath and plunged in. "First, we'd need your permission to build the necessary installations. Second, the required funds. And third, the assistance of the National Underwater and Marine Agency."

The President looked questioningly at Seagram. "I can understand the first two requests, but I don't grasp the significance of NUMA. Where does it fit in?"

"We're going to have to sneak expert mineralogists into Novaya Zemlya. Since it's surrounded by water, a NUMA oceanographic expedition nearby would make the perfect cover for our mission."

"How long will it take you to test, construct, and install the system?"

Donner didn't hesitate. "Sixteen months, one week."

"How far can you proceed without byzanium?"

"Right up to the final stage," Donner answered.

The President tilted back in his chair and gazed at a ship's clock that sat on his massive desk. He said nothing for nearly a full minute. Finally he said, "As I see it, gentlemen, you want me to bankroll you into building a multimillion-dollar, unproven, untested, complex system that won't operate because we lack the primary ingredient which we may have to steal from an unfriendly nation."

Seagram fidgeted with his briefcase while Donner merely nodded.

"Suppose you tell me," the President continued, "how I explain a maze of these installations stretching around the country's perimeters to some tight-fisted liberal in Congress who gets it in his head to investigate?"

"That's the beauty of the system," said Seagram. "It's small and it's compact. The computers tell us that a building constructed along the lines of a small power station will do the job nicely. Neither the Russian spy satellites nor a farmer living next door will detect anything out of the ordinary."

The President rubbed his chin. "Why do you want to jump the gun on the Sicilian Project before you're one-hundred-per-cent ready?"

"We're gambling, sir," said Donner. "We're gambling that in the next sixteen months we can either make a breakthrough and produce byzanium in the laboratory or find a deposit we can extract somewhere on earth."

"Even if it takes us ten years," Seagram blurted, "the installations would be in and waiting. Our only loss would be time."

The President stood up. "Gentlemen, I'll go along with your science-fiction scheme, but on one condition. You have exactly eighteen months and ten days. That's when the new man, whoever he may be, takes over my job. So if you want to keep your sugar daddy happy until then, get me some results."

The two men across the desk went limp.

At last Seagram managed to speak. "Thank you, Mr. President. Somehow, some way, the team will bring in the mother lode. You can count on it."

"Good. Now if you'll excuse me. I have to pose in the Rose Garden with a bunch of fat old Daughters of the American Revolution." He held out his hand. "Good luck, and remember, don't screw up your under-cover operations. I don't want another Eisenhower U-2 spy mission to blow up in my face. Understood?"

Before Seagram and Donner could answer, he had turned and walked out a side door.

Donner's Chevrolet was passed through the White House gates. He eased into the mainstream of traffic and headed across the Potomac into Virginia. He was almost afraid to look in the rearview mirror for fear that the President might change his mind and send a messenger to chase them down with a rejection. He rolled down the window and breathed in the humid summer air.

"We came off lucky," Seagram said. "I guess you know that."

"You're telling me. If he'd known we'd sent a man into Russian territory over two weeks ago, the fertilizer would have hit the windmill."

"It still might," Seagram mumbled to himself. "It still might if NUMA can't get our man out."

2

Sid Koplin was sure he was dying.

His eyes were closed and the blood from his side was staining the white snow. A burst of light whirled around in Koplin's mind as consciousness gradually returned, and a spasm of nausea rushed over him and he retched uncontrollably. Had he been shot once, or was it twice? He wasn't sure.

He opened his eyes and rolled up onto his hands and knees. His head pounded like a jackhammer. He put his hand to it and touched a congealed gash that split his scalp above the left temple. Except for the headache, there was no exterior sensation; the pain had been dulled by the cold. But there was no dulling of the agonizing burn on his left side, just below his rib cage, where the second bullet had struck, and he could feel the syruplike stickiness of the blood as it trickled under his clothing, over his thighs and down his legs.

A volley of automatic weapons fire echoed down the mountain. Koplin looked around, but all he could see was the swirling white snow that was whipped by the vicious arctic wind. Another burst tore the frigid air. He guessed that it came from only a hundred yards away. A Soviet patrol guard must be firing blindly through the blizzard in the random hope of hitting him again.

All thought of escape had vanished now. It was finished. He knew he could never make it to the cove where he'd moored the sloop. Nor was he in any condition to sail the little twenty-eight-foot craft across fifty miles of open sea to a rendezvous with the waiting American oceanographic vessel.

He sank back in the snow. The bleeding had weakened him beyond further physical effort. The Russians must not find him. That was part of the bargain with Meta Section. If he must die, his body must not be discovered.

Painfully, he began scraping snow over himself. Soon he would be only a small white mound on a desolate slope of Bednaya Mountain, buried forever under the constantly building ice sheet.

He stopped a moment and listened. The only sounds he heard were his own gasps and the wind. He listened harder, cupping his hands to his ears. Just audible through the howling wind he heard a dog bark.

"Oh God," he cried silently. As long as his body was still warm, the sensitive nostrils of the dog were sure to pick up his scent. He sagged in defeat. There was nothing left for him but to lie back and let his life ooze away.

But a spark deep inside him refused to dim and be extinguished. Merciful God, he thought deliriously, he couldn't just lie there waiting for the Russians to take him. He was only a professor of mineralogy, not a trained secret agent. His mind and forty-year-old body weren't geared to stand up under intensive interrogation. If he lived, they could tear the whole story from him in a matter of hours. He closed his eyes as the sickness of failure overcame all physical agony.

When he opened them again, his field of vision was filled with the head of an immense dog. Koplin recognized him as a komondor, a mighty beast standing thirty inches at the shoulder, covered by a heavy coat of matted white hair. The great dog snarled savagely and would have ripped Koplin's throat open if it hadn't been kept in check by the gloved hand of a Soviet soldier. There was an indifferent look about the man. He stood there and stared down at his helpless quarry, gripping the leash in his left hand while he steadied a machine pistol with his right. He looked fearsome in his huge greatcoat that came down to booted ankles, and the pale, expressionless eyes showed no compassion for Koplin's wounds. The soldier shouldered his weapon and reached down and pulled Koplin to his feet. Then without a word, the Russian began dragging the wounded American toward the island's security post.

Koplin nearly passed out from the pain. He felt as though he'd been dragged through the snow for miles when actually it was only a distance of fifty yards. That was as far as they'd got when a vague figure appeared through the storm. It was blurred by the wall of swirling white. Through the dim haze of near unconsciousness, Koplin felt the soldier stiffen.

A soft "plop" sounded over the wind, and the massive komondor fell noiselessly on its side in the snow. The Russian dropped his hold on Koplin and frantically tried to raise his gun, but the strange sound was repeated and a small hole that gushed red suddenly appeared in the middle of the soldier's forehead. Then the eyes went glassy and he crumpled beside the dog.

Something was terribly wrong; this shouldn't be happening, Koplin told himself, but his exhausted mind was too far gone to draw any valid conclusions. He sank to his knees and could only watch as a tall man in a gray parka materialized from the white mist and gazed down at the dog.

"A damned shame," he said tersely.

The man presented an imposing appearance. The oak-tanned face looked out of place for the Arctic. And the features were firm, almost cruel. Yet it was the eyes that struck Koplin. He had never seen eyes quite like them. They were a deep sea-green and radiated a penetrating kind of warmth, a marked contrast from the hard lines etched in the face.

The man turned to Koplin and smiled. "Dr. Koplin, I presume?" The tone was soft and effortless.

The stranger pushed a handgun with silencer into a pocket, knelt down to eye level, and nodded at the blood spreading through the material of Koplin's parka. "I'd better get you to where I can take a look at that." Then he picked Koplin up as one might a child and began trudging down the mountain toward the sea.

"Who are you?" Koplin muttered.

"My name is Pitt. Dirk Pitt."

"I don't understand . . . where did you come from?"

Koplin never heard the answer. At that moment, the black cover of unconsciousness abruptly lifted up, and he fell gratefully under it.

3

Seagram finished off a margarita as he waited in a little garden restaurant just off Capitol Street to have lunch with his wife. She was late. Never in the eight years they had been married had he known her to arrive anywhere on time. He caught the waiter's attention and gestured for another drink.

Dana Seagram finally entered and stood in the foyer a moment searching for her husband. She spotted him and began meandering between the tables in his direction. She wore an orange sweater and a brown tweed skirt so youthfully it made her seem like a coed in graduate school. Her hair was blond and tied with a scarf, and her coffee-brown eyes were funny and gay and quick.

"Been waiting long?" she said, smiling.

"Eighteen minutes to be precise," he said. "About two minutes, ten seconds longer than your usual arrivals."

"I'm sorry," she replied. "Admiral Sandecker called a staff meeting, and it dragged on later than I'd figured."

"What's his latest brainstorm?"

"A new wing for the Maritime Museum. He's got the budget and now he's making plans to obtain the artifacts."

"Artifacts?" Seagram asked.

"Bits and pieces salvaged from famous ships." The waiter came with Seagram's drink and Dana ordered a daiquiri. "It's amazing how little is left. A life belt or two from the *Lusitania,* a ventilator from the *Maine* here, an anchor from the *Bounty* there; none of it housed decently under one roof."

"I should think there are better ways of blowing the taxpayer's money."

Her face flushed. "What do you mean?"

"Collecting old junk," he said diffidently, "enshrining rusted and corroded bits of nonidentifiable trash under a glass case to be dusted and gawked at. It's a waste."

The battle flags were raised.

"The preservation of ships and boats provides an important link with man's historical past." Dana's brown eyes blazed. "Contributing to knowledge is an endeavor an asshole like you cares nothing about."

"Spoken like a true marine archaeologist," he said.

She smiled crookedly. "It still frosts your balls that your wife made something of herself, doesn't it?"

"The only thing that frosts my balls, sweetheart, is your locker-room language. Why is it every liberated female thinks it's chic to cuss?"

"You're hardly one to provide a lesson in savoir-faire," she said. "Five years in the big city and you still dress like an Omaha anvil salesman. Why can't you style your hair like other men? That Ivy League haircut went out years ago. I'm embarrassed to be seen with you."

"My position with the administration is such that I can't afford to look like a hippie of the sixties."

"Lord, lord." She shook her head wearily. "Why couldn't I have married a plumber or a tree surgeon? Why did I have to fall in love with a physicist from the farm belt?"

"It's comforting to know you loved me once."

"I still love you, Gene," she said, her eyes turning soft. "This chasm between us has only opened in the last two years. We can't even have lunch together without trying to hurt each other. Why don't we say to hell with it and spend the rest of the afternoon making love in a motel. I'm in the mood to feel deliciously sexy."

"Would it make any difference in the long run?"

"It's a start."

"I can't."

"Your damned dedication to duty again," she said, turning away. "Don't you see? Our jobs have torn us apart. We can save ourselves, Gene. We can both resign and go back to teaching. With your Ph.D. in physics and my Ph.D. in archaeology, along with our experience and credentials, we could write our own ticket with any university in the country. We were on the same faculty when we met, remember? Those were our happiest years together."

"Please, Dana, I can't quit. Not now."

"Why?"

"I'm on an important project—"

"Every project for the last five years has been important. Please, Gene, I'm begging you to save our marriage. Only you can make the first move. I'll go along with whatever you decide if we can get out of Washington. This town will kill any hope of salvaging our life together if we wait much longer."

"I need another year."

"Even another month will be too late."

"I am committed to a course that makes no conditions for abandonment."

"When will these ridiculous secret projects ever end? You're nothing but a tool of the White House."

"I don't need that bleeding-heart, liberal crap from you."

"Gene, for God's sake, give it up!"

"It's not for God's sake, Dana, it's for my country's sake. I'm sorry if I can't make you understand."

"Give it up," she repeated, tears forming in her eyes. "No one is indispensable. Let Mel Donner take your place."

He shook his head. "No," he said firmly. "I created this project from nothing. My gray matter was its sperm. I must see it through to completion."

The waiter reappeared and asked if they were ready to order.

Dana shook her head. "I'm not hungry." She rose from the table and looked down at him. "Will you be home for dinner?"

"I'll be working late at the office."

There was no stopping her tears now.

"I hope whatever it is you're doing is worth it," she murmured. "Because it's going to cost you a terrible price."

Then she turned and hurried away.

4

Unlike the Russian intelligence officer so often stereotyped in American motion pictures, Captain André Prevlov had neither bull-shoulders nor shaven head. He was a well-proportioned, handsome man who sported a layered hairstyle and a modishly trimmed mustache. His image, built around an orange Italian sports car and a plushly furnished apartment overlooking the Moscow River, didn't sit too well with his superiors in the Soviet Navy's Department of Foreign Intelligence. Yet, despite Prevlov's irritating leanings, there was little possibility of his being purged from his high position in the department. The reputation he had carefully constructed as the Navy's most brilliant intelligence specialist, and the fact that his father was number twelve man in the Party, combined to make Captain Prevlov untouchable.

With a practiced, casual movement, he lit a Winston and poured himself a shot glass of Bombay gin. Then he sat back and read through the stack of files that his aide, Lieutenant Pavel Marganin, had laid on his desk.

"It's a mystery to me, sir," Marganin said softly, "how you can take so easily to Western trash."

Prevlov looked up from a file and gave Marganin a cool, disdainful stare. "Like so many of our comrades, you are ignorant of the world at large. I think like an American, I drink like an Englishman, I drive like an Italian, and I live like a Frenchman. And do you know why, Lieutenant?"

Marganin flushed and mumbled nervously. "No, sir."

"To know the enemy, Marganin. The key is to know your enemy better than he knows you, better than he knows himself. Then do unto him before he has a chance to do unto you."

"Is that a quote from Comrade Nerv Tshetsky?"

Prevlov shrugged in despair. "No, you idiot; I'm bastardizing the Christian Bible." He inhaled and blew a stream of smoke through his nostrils and sipped the gin. "Study the Western ways, my friend. If we do not learn from them, then our cause is lost." He turned back to the files. "Now then, why are these matters sent to our department?"

"No reason other than that the incident took place on or near a seacoast."

"What do we know about this one?" Prevlov snapped open the next file.

"Very little. A soldier on guard patrol at the north island of Novaya Zemlya is missing, along with his dog."

"Hardly grounds for a security panic. Novaya Zemlya is practically barren. An outdated missile station, a guard post, a few fishermen—we have no classified installations within hundreds of miles of it. Damned waste of time to even bother sending a man and a dog out to patrol it."

"The West would no doubt feel the same way about sending an agent there."

Prevlov's fingers drummed the table as he squinted at the ceiling.

Finally, he said, "An agent? Nothing there . . . nothing of military interest . . . yet—" He broke off and flicked a switch on his intercom. "Bring me the National Underwater and Marine Agency's ship placements of the last two days."

Marganin's brows lifted. "They wouldn't dare send an oceanographic expedition near Novaya Zemlya. That's deep within Soviet waters."

"We do not own the Barents Sea," Prevlov said patiently. "It is international water."

An attractive blond secretary, wearing a trim brown suit, came into the room, handed a folder to Prevlov, and then left, closing the door softly behind her.

Prevlov shuffled through the papers in the folder until he found what he was looking for. "Here we are. The NUMA vessel *First Attempt,* last sighted by one of our trawlers three hundred and twenty-five nautical miles southwest of Franz Josef Land."

"That would put her close to Novaya Zemlya," Marganin said.

"Odd," Prevlov muttered. "According to the United States Oceanographic Ship Operating Schedule, the *First Attempt* should have been conducting plankton studies off North Carolina at the time of this sighting." He downed the remainder of the gin, mashed out the butt of his cigarette, and lit another. "A very interesting concurrence."

"What does it prove?" Marganin asked.

"It proves nothing, but it suggests that the Novaya Zemlya patrol guard was murdered and the agent responsible escaped, most likely rendezvoused with the *First Attempt*. It suggests that the United States is up to something when a NUMA research ship deviates from her planned schedule without explanation."

"What could they possibly be after?"

"I haven't the foggiest notion." Prevlov leaned back in his chair and smoothed his mustache. "Have the satellite photos enlarged of the immediate area at the time of the event in question."

The evening shadows were darkening the streets outside the office windows when Lieutenant Marganin spread the photo blowups on Prevlov's desk and handed him a high-powered magnifying glass.

"Your perceptiveness paid off, sir. We have something interesting here."

Prevlov intently studied the pictures. "I see nothing unusual about the ship; typical research equipment, no military-detection hardware in evidence."

Marganin pointed at a wide-angle photo that barely revealed a ship as a small white mark on the emulsion. "Please note the small shape about two thousand meters from the *First Attempt* in the upper-right corner."

Prevlov peered through the glass for almost a full half-minute. "A helicopter!"

"Yes, sir, that's why I was late with the enlargements. I took the liberty of having the photos analyzed by Section R."

"One of our Army security patrols, I imagine."

"No, sir."

Prevlov's brows raised. "Are you suggesting that it belongs to the American vessel?"

"That's their guess, sir." Marganin placed two more pictures in front of Prevlov. "They examined earlier photos from another reconnaissance satellite. As you can see by comparing them, the helicopter is flying on a course away from Novaya Zemlya toward the *First Attempt*. They judged its altitude at ten feet and its speed at less than fifteen knots."

"Obviously avoiding our radar security," Prevlov said.

"Do we alert our agents in America?" said Marganin.

"No, not yet. I don't want to risk their cover until we are certain what it is the Americans are after."

He straightened the photographs and slipped them neatly into a folder, then looked at his Omega wristwatch. "I've just time for a light supper before the ballet. Do you have anything else, Lieutenant?"

"Only the file on the Lorelei Current Drift Expedition. The American deep-sea submersible was last reported in fifteen thousand feet of water off the coast of Dakar."

Prevlov stood up, took the file and shoved it under his arm. "I'll study it when I get a chance. Probably nothing in it that concerns naval security. Still, it should make good reading. Leave it to the Americans to come up with strange and wonderful projects."

5

"Damn, damn, double damn!" Dana hissed. "Look at the crow's-feet coming in around my eyes." She sat at her dressing table and stared dejectedly at her reflection in the mirror. "Who was it who said old age is a form of leprosy?"

Seagram came up behind her, pulled back her hair, and kissed the soft, exposed neck. "Thirty-one on your last birthday and already you're running for senior citizen of the month."

She stared at him in the mirror, bemused at his rare display of affection. "You're lucky; men don't have this problem."

"Men also suffer from the maladies of age and crow's-feet. What makes women think we don't crack at the seams, too?"

"The difference is, you don't care."

"We're more prone to accept the inevitable," he said, smiling. "Speaking of the inevitable, when are you going to have a baby?"

"You bastard! You never give up, do you?" She threw a hairbrush on the dressing table, knocking a regiment of evenly spaced bottles of artificial beauty about the glass top. "We've been through all this a thousand times. I won't subject myself to the indignities of pregnancy. I won't swish crap-laden diapers around in a toilet bowl ten times a day. Let someone else populate the earth. I'm not about to split off my soul, like some damned amoeba."

"Those reasons are phony. You don't honestly believe them yourself."

She turned back to the mirror and made no reply.

"A baby could save us, Dana," he said gently.

She dropped her head in her hands. "I won't give up my career any more than you'll give up your precious project."

He stroked her soft golden hair and gazed at her image in the mirror. "Your father was an alcoholic who deserted his family when you were only ten. Your mother worked behind a bar and brought men home to earn extra drinking money. You and your brother were treated like animals until you were both old enough to run away from the garbage bin you called home. He turned crud and started holding up liquor stores and gas stations; a nifty little occupation that netted him a murder conviction and life imprisonment at San Quentin. God knows, I'm proud of how you lifted yourself from the sewer and worked eighteen hours a day to put yourself through college and grad school. Yes, you had a rotten childhood, Dana, and you're afraid of having a baby because of your memories. You've got to understand: your nightmare doesn't belong to the future; you can't deny a son or daughter their chance at life."

The stone wall remained unbreached. She shook off his hands and furiously began plucking her brows. The discussion was closed; she had shut him out as conclusively as if she had caused him to vanish from the room.

When Seagram emerged from the shower, Dana was standing in front of a full-length closet mirror. She studied herself as critically as a designer who was seeing a finished creation for the first time. She wore a simple white dress that clung tightly to her torso before falling away to the ankles. The décolletage was loose and offered a more than ample view of her breasts.

"You'd better hurry," she said casually. It was as though the argument had never happened. "We don't want to keep the President waiting."

"There will be over two hundred people there. No one will stick a black star on our attendance chart for being tardy."

"I don't care." She pouted. "We don't receive an invitation to a White

House party every night of the week. I'd at least like to create a good impression by arriving on time."

Seagram sighed and went through the ticklish ritual of tying a bow tie and then attaching his cuff links clumsily with one hand. Dressing for formal parties was a chore he detested. Why couldn't Washington's social functions be conducted with comfort in mind? It might be an exciting event to Dana, but to him it was a pain in the rectum.

He finished buffing his shoes and combing his hair and went into the living room. Dana was sitting on the couch, going over reports, her briefcase open on the coffee table. She was so engrossed she didn't look up when he entered the room.

"I'm ready."

"Be with you in a moment," she murmured. "Could you please get my stole?"

"It's the middle of summer. What in hell do you want to sweat in a fur for?"

She removed her horned-rimmed reading glasses and said, "I think one of us should show a little class, don't you?"

He went into the hall, picked up the telephone, and dialed. Mel Donner answered in the middle of the first ring.

"Donner."

"Any word yet?" Seagram asked.

"The *First Attempt*—"

"Is that the NUMA ship that was supposed to pick up Koplin?"

"Yeah. She bypassed Oslo five days ago."

"My God! Why? Koplin was to jump ship and take a commercial flight stateside from there."

"No way of knowing. The ship is on radio silence, per your instructions."

"It doesn't look good."

"It wasn't in the script, that's for sure."

"I'll be at the President's party till around eleven. If you hear anything, call me."

"You can count on it. Have fun."

Seagram was just hanging up when Dana came out of the living room. She read the thoughtful expression on his face. "Bad news?"

"I'm not sure yet."

She kissed him on the cheek. "A shame we can't live like normal people so you could confide your problems to me."

He squeezed her hand. "If only I could."

"Government secrets. What a colossal bore." She smiled slyly. "Well?"

"Well, what?"

"Aren't you going to be a gentleman?"

"I'm sorry, I forgot." He pulled her stole from the closet and slipped it over her shoulders. "A bad habit of mine, ignoring my wife."

Her lips spread in a playful grin. "For that, you will be shot at dawn."

Christ, he thought miserably, a firing squad might not be too far-fetched at that, if Koplin screwed up at Novaya Zemlya.

6

The Seagrams settled behind the crowd gathered at the entrance to the East Room and waited their turn in the receiving line. Dana had been in the White House before, but she was still impressed by it.

The President was standing smartly and devilishly handsome. He was in his early fifties and was definitely a very sexy man. The latter was supported by the fact that standing next to him, greeting every guest with the fervor of discovering a rich relative, was Ashley Fleming, Washington's most elegant and sophisticated divorcée.

"Oh shit!" Dana gasped.

Seagram frowned at her irritably. "Now what's your problem?"

"The broad standing beside the President."

"That happens to be Ashley Fleming."

"I know that," Dana whispered, trying to hide behind Seagram's reassuring bulk. "Look at her gown."

Seagram didn't get it at first, and then it hit him, and it was all he could do to suppress a boisterous laugh. "By God, you're both wearing the same dress!"

"It's not funny," she said grimly.

"Where did you get yours?"

"I borrowed it from Annette Johns."

"That lesbian model across the street?"

"It was given to her by Claude d'Orsini, the fashion designer."

Seagram took her by the hand. "If nothing else, it only goes to prove what good taste my wife has."

Before she could reply, the line joggled forward and they suddenly found themselves standing awkwardly in front of the President.

"Gene, how nice to see you." The President smiled politely.

"Thank you for inviting us, Mr. President. You know my wife, Dana."

The President studied her, his eyes lingering on her cleavage. "Of course. Charming, absolutely charming." Then he leaned over and whispered in her ear.

Dana's eyes went wide and she flushed scarlet.

The President straightened and said, "May I introduce my lovely hostess, Miss Ashley Fleming. Ashley, Mr. and Mrs. Gene Seagram."

"It's a great pleasure to meet you at last, Miss Fleming," Seagram murmured.

He might as well have been talking to a tree. Ashley Fleming's eyes were cutting apart Dana's dress.

"It seems apparent, Mrs. Seagram," Ashley said sweetly, "one of us will be searching for a new dress designer first thing in the morning."

"Oh, I couldn't switch," Dana replied innocently. "I've been going to Jacques Pinneigh since I was a little girl."

Ashley Fleming's penciled brows raised questioningly. "Jacques Pinneigh? I've never heard of him."

"He's more widely known as J. C. Penney," Dana smiled sweetly. "His downtown store is having a clearance sale next month. Wouldn't it be fun if we shopped together. That way we wouldn't wind up as look-a-likes."

Ashley Fleming's face froze in a mask of indignation as the President went into a coughing spasm. Seagram nodded weakly, grabbed Dana's arm, and quickly hustled her away into the mainstream of the crowd.

"Did you have to do that?" he growled.

"I couldn't resist it. That woman is nothing but a glorified hooker." Then Dana's eyes looked up at him in bewilderment. "He propositioned me," she said, unbelieving. "The President of the United States propositioned me."

"Warren G. Harding and John F. Kennedy were rumored to be swingers. This one is no different. He's only human."

"A lecher for a President. It's disgusting."

"Are you going to take him up on it?" Seagram grinned.

"Don't be ridiculous!" she snapped back.

"May I join the battle?" The request came from a little man with flaming red hair, nattily dressed in a blue dinner jacket. He had a precisely trimmed beard that matched the hair and complemented his piercing hazel eyes. To Seagram the voice seemed vaguely familiar, but he drew a blank on the face.

"Depends whose side you're on," Seagram said.

"Knowing your wife's fetish for Women's Lib," the stranger said, "I'd be only too happy to join forces with her husband."

"You know Dana?"

"I should. I'm her boss."

Seagram stared at him in amazement. "Then you must be—"

"Admiral James Sandecker," Dana cut in, laughing, "Director of the National Underwater and Marine Agency. Admiral, may I introduce my easily flustered husband, Gene."

"An honor, Admiral." Seagram extended his hand. "I've often looked forward to the opportunity of thanking you in person for that little favor."

Dana looked puzzled. "You two know each other?"

Sandecker nodded. "We've talked over the telephone. We've never met face-to-face."

Dana slipped her hands through the men's arms. "My two favorite people consorting behind my back. What gives?"

Seagram met Sandecker's eyes. "I once called the Admiral and requested a bit of information. That's all there was to it."

Sandecker patted Dana's hand and said, "Why don't you make an old man eternally grateful and find him a scotch and water."

She hesitated a moment, then kissed Sandecker lightly on the cheek and obediently began worming her way through the scattered groups of guests milling around the bar.

Seagram shook his head in wonder. "You have a way with women. If I had asked her to get me a drink, she'd have spit in my eye."

"I pay her a salary," Sandecker said. "You don't."

They made their way out on the balcony and Seagram lit a cigarette while Sandecker puffed to life an immense Churchill cigar. They walked in silence until they were alone beneath a tall column in a secluded corner.

"Any word on the *First Attempt* from your end?" Seagram asked quietly.

"She docked at our Navy's submarine base in the Firth of Clyde at thirteen hundred hours, our time, this afternoon."

"That's nearly eight hours ago. Why wasn't I notified?"

"Your instructions were quite clear," Sandecker said coldly. "No communications from my ship until your agent was safely back on U.S. soil."

"Then how? . . ."

"My information came from an old friend in the Navy. He phoned me only a half an hour ago, madder than hell, demanding to know where my skipper got off using naval facilities without permission."

"There's been a screw-up somewhere," Seagram said flatly. "Your ship was supposed to dock at Oslo and let my man come ashore. Just what in hell is she doing in Scotland?"

Sandecker gave Seagram a hard stare. "Let's get one thing straight, Mr. Seagram, NUMA is not an arm of the CIA, FBI, or of any other intelligence bureau, and I don't take kindly to risking my people's lives just so you can poke around Communist territory playing espionage games. Our business is oceanographic research. Next time you want to play James Bond, get the Navy or the Coast Guard to do your dirty work. Don't con the President into ordering out one of *my* ships. Do you read me, Mr. Seagram?"

"I apologize for your agency's inconvenience, Admiral. I meant nothing derogatory. You must understand my uneasiness."

"I'd like to understand." There was a slight softening in the admiral's face. "But you'd make things a damned sight simpler if you would take me into your confidence and tell me what it is you're after."

Seagram turned away. "I'm sorry."

"I see," Sandecker said.

"Why do you suppose the *First Attempt* bypassed Oslo?" Seagram said.

"My guess is that your agent felt it was too dangerous to catch a civilian plane out of Oslo and decided on a military flight instead. Our nuclear sub base on the Firth of Clyde has the nearest airfield, so he probably ordered the captain of my research vessel to skip Norway and head there."

"I hope you're right. Whatever the reason, I'm afraid that the deviation from our set plan can only spell trouble."

Sandecker spied Dana standing in the balcony doorway with a drink in one hand. She was searching for them. He waved and caught her eye, and she started to move toward them.

"You're a lucky man, Seagram. Your wife is a bright and lovely gal."

Suddenly, Mel Donner appeared, rushed past Dana, and reached them first. He excused himself to Admiral Sandecker.

"A naval transport landed twenty minutes ago with Sid Koplin on board," Donner said softly. "He's been taken to Walter Reed."

"Why Walter Reed?"

"He's been shot up pretty badly."

"Good God." Seagram groaned.

"I've got a car waiting. We can be there in fifteen minutes."

"Okay, give me a moment."

He spoke quietly to Sandecker and asked the admiral to see that Dana got home and to make his regrets to the President. Then he followed Donner to the car.

7

"I'm sorry, but he is under sedation and I cannot allow any visitors at this time." The aristocratic Virginia voice was quiet and courteous, but there was no hiding the anger that clouded the doctor's gray eyes.

"Is he able to talk?" Donner asked.

"For a man who regained consciousness only minutes ago, his mental faculties are remarkably alert." The cloud remained behind the eyes. "But don't let that fool you. He won't be playing any tennis for a while."

"Just how serious is his condition?" Seagram asked.

"His condition is just that: serious. The doctor who operated on him aboard the NUMA vessel did a beautiful job. The bullet wound in his left side will heal nicely. The other wound, however, left a neat little hairline crack in the skull. Your Mr. Koplin will be having headaches for some time to come."

"We must see him now," Seagram said firmly.

"As I've told you, I'm sorry, but no visitors."

Seagram took a step forward so that he was eye to eye with the doctor. "Get this into your head, Doctor. My friend and I are going into that room whether you like it or not. If you personally try to stop us, we'll put you on one of your own operating tables. If you yell for attendants, we'll shoot them. If you call the police, they will respect our credentials and do what we tell them." Seagram paused and his lips curled in a smug grin. "Now then, Doctor, the choice is yours."

Koplin lay flat on the bed, his face as white as the pillowcase behind his head, but his eyes were surprisingly bright.

"Before you ask," he said in a low rasp, "I feel awful. And that's true. But don't tell me I look good. Because that's a gross lie."

Seagram pulled a chair up to the bed and smiled. "We don't have much time, Sid, so if you feel up to it, we'll jump right in."

Koplin nodded to the tubes connected to his arm. "These drugs are fogging my mind, but I'll stay with you as long as I can."

Donner nodded. "We came for the answer to the billion-dollar question."

"I found traces of byzanium, if that's what you mean?"

"You actually found it! Are you certain?"

"My field tests were by no stroke of the imagination as accurate as lab analysis might have been, but I'm ninety-nine-per-cent positive it was byzanium."

"Thank God." Seagram sighed. "Did you come up with an assay figure?" he asked.

"I did."

"How much . . . how many pounds of byzanium do you reckon can be extracted from Bednaya Mountain?"

"With luck, maybe a teaspoonful."

At first Seagram didn't get it, then it sunk in. Donner sat frozen and expressionless, his hands clenched over the armrests of the chair.

"A teaspoonful," Seagram mumbled gloomily. "Are you certain?"

"You keep asking me if I'm certain." Koplin's drawn face reddened with indignation. "If you don't buy my word for it, send somebody else to that asshole of creation."

"Just a minute." Donner's hand was on Koplin's shoulder. "Novaya Zemlya was our only hope. You took more punishment than we had any right to expect. We're grateful, Sid, truly grateful."

"All hope isn't lost yet," Koplin murmured. His eyelids drooped.

Seagram didn't hear. He leaned over the bed. "What was that, Sid?"

"You've not lost yet. The byzanium was there."

Donner moved closer. "What do you mean, the byzanium *was* there?"

"Gone . . . mined. . . ."

"You're not making sense."

"I stumbled over the tailings on the side of the mountain." Koplin hesitated a moment. "Dug into them . . ."

"Are you saying someone has already mined the byzanium from Bednaya Mountain?" Seagram asked incredulously.

"Yes."

"Dear God." Donner moaned. "The Russians are on the same track."

"No . . . no . . ." Koplin whispered.

Seagram placed his ear next to Koplin's lips.

"Not the Russians—"

Seagram and Donner exchanged confused stares.

Koplin feebly clutched Seagram's hand. "The . . . the Coloradans . . ."

Then his eyes closed and he drifted into unconsciousness.

They walked through the parking lot as a siren whined in the distance. "What do you suppose he meant?" Donner asked.

"It doesn't figure," Seagram answered vaguely. "It doesn't figure at all."

8

"What's so important that you have to wake me on my day off?" Prevlov grunted. Without waiting for an answer, he shoved open the door and motioned Marganin into the apartment. Prevlov was wearing a silk Japanese robe. His face was drawn and tired.

As he followed Prevlov through the living room into the kitchen, Marganin's eyes traveled professionally over the furnishings and touched each piece. To someone who lived in a tiny six-by-eight-foot barracks room, the décor, the vastness of the apartment seemed like the interior east wing of Peter the Great's summer palace. It was all there, the crystal chandeliers, the floor to ceiling tapestries, the French furniture.

His eyes also noted two glasses and a half-empty bottle of Chartreuse on the fireplace mantel; and on the floor, beneath the sofa, rested a pair of women's shoes. Expensive, Western, by the look of them. He palmed a strand of hair and found himself staring at the closed bedroom door. She would have to be extremely attractive. Captain Prevlov had high standards.

Prevlov leaned into the refrigerator and lifted out a pitcher of tomato juice. "Care for some?"

Marganin shook his head.

"Mix it with the right ingredients," Prevlov muttered, "as the Americans do, and you have an excellent cure for a hangover." He took a sip of the tomato juice and made a face. "Now then, what do you want?"

"KGB received a communication from one of their agents in Washington last night. They had no clues as to its meaning and hoped that perhaps we might throw some light on it."

Marganin's face reddened. The sash on Prevlov's robe had loosened and he could see that the captain wore nothing beneath it.

"Very well." Prevlov sighed. "Continue."

"It said, 'Americans suddenly interested in rock collecting. Most secret operation under code name Sicilian Project.' "

Prevlov stared at him over his Bloody Mary. "What sort of drivel is that?" He finished the glass in one gulp and slammed it down on the sink counter. "Has our illustrious brother intelligence service, the KGB, become a house of fools?" The voice was the dispassionate, efficient voice of the official Prevlov—cold, and devoid of all inflection except bored irritation. "And you, Lieutenant? Why do you bother me with this childish riddle now? Why couldn't this have waited until tomorrow morning when I'm back in the office?"

"I . . . I thought perhaps it was important," Marganin stammered.

"Naturally." Prevlov smiled coldly. "Every time the KGB whistles, people jump. But veiled threats don't interest me. Facts, my dear Lieutenant, facts are what count. What do you feel is so important about this Sicilian Project?"

"It seemed to me the reference to rock collecting might tie in with the Novaya Zemlya files."

Perhaps twenty seconds elapsed before Prevlov spoke. "Possible, just possible. Still, we can't be certain of a connection."

"I . . . I only thought—"

"Please leave the thinking to me, Lieutenant." He tightened the sash on his robe. "Now, if you have run out of hare-brained witch hunts, I would like to get back to bed."

"But if the Americans are looking for something—"

"Yes, but what?" Prevlov asked dryly. "What mineral is so precious to them that they must look for it in the earth of an unfriendly country?"

Marganin shrugged.

"You answer that and you have the key." Prevlov's tone hardened almost imperceptibly. "Until then, I want solutions. Any peasant bastard can ask stupid questions."

Marganin's face reddened again. "Sometimes the Americans have hidden meanings to their code names."

"Yes," Prevlov said with mock solemnity. "They do have a penchant for advertising."

Marganin plunged forward. "I researched the American idioms that refer to Sicily, and the most prevalent seems to be their obsession with a brotherhood of hooligans and gangsters."

"If you had done your homework . . ." Prevlov yawned ". . . you'd have discovered it's called the Mafia."

"There is also a musical ensemble that refer to themselves as the Sicilian Stilettos."

Prevlov offered Marganin a glacial stare.

"Then there is a large food processor in Wisconsin who manufactures a Sicilian salad oil."

"Enough!" Prevlov held up a protesting hand. "Salad oil, indeed. I am not up to such stupidity so early in the morning." He gestured at the front door. "I trust you have other projects at our office that are more stimulating than rock collecting."

In the living room he paused before a table on which was a carved ivory chess set and toyed with one of the pieces. "Tell me, Lieutenant, do you play chess?"

Marganin shook his head. "Not in a long time. I used to play a little when I was a cadet at the Naval Academy."

"Does the name Isaak Boleslavski mean anything to you?"

"No, sir."

"Isaak Boleslavski was one of our greatest chess masters," Prevlov said, as if lecturing a schoolboy. "He conceived many great variations of the game. One of them was the Sicilian Defense." He casually tossed the black king at Marganin who deftly caught it. "Fascinating game, chess. You should take it up again."

Prevlov walked to the bedroom door and cracked it. Then he turned and smiled indifferently to Marganin. "Now, if you will excuse me. You may let yourself out. Good day, Lieutenant."

Once outside, Marganin made his way around the rear of Prevlov's apartment building. The door to the garage was locked, so he glanced furtively up and down the alley and then tapped a side window with his fist until it splintered. Carefully, he picked out the pieces until his hand could grope inside and unlatch the lock. One more look down the alley and he pushed up the window, climbed the sill, and entered the garage.

A black American Ford sedan was parked next to Prevlov's orange Lancia. Quickly, Marganin searched both cars and memorized the numbers on the Ford's embassy license plate. To make it look like the work of a burglar, he removed the windshield wipers—the theft of which was a national pastime in the Soviet Union—and then unlocked the garage door from the inside and walked out.

He hurried back to the front of the building and he had only to wait three minutes for the next electric bus. He paid the driver and eased into a seat and stared out the window. Then he began to smile. It had been a most profitable morning.

The Sicilian Project was the furthest thing from his mind.

2

The Coloradans

9

Mel Donner routinely checked the room for electronic eavesdropping equipment and set up the tape recorder. "This is a test for voice level." He spoke into the microphone without inflection. "One, two, three." He adjusted the controls for tone and volume, then nodded to Seagram.

"We're ready, Sid," Seagram said gently. "If it becomes tiring, just say so and we'll break off until tomorrow."

The hospital bed had been adjusted so that Sid Koplin sat nearly upright. The mineralogist appeared much improved since their last meeting. His color had returned and his eyes seemed bright. Only the bandage around his balding head showed any sign of injury. "I'll go until midnight," he said. "Anything to relieve the boredom. I hate hospitals. The nurses all have icy hands and the color on the goddamned TV is always changing."

Seagram grinned and laid the microphone in Koplin's lap. "Why don't you begin with your departure from Norway."

"Very uneventful," Koplin said. "The Norwegian fishing trawler *Godhawn* towed my sloop to within two hundred miles of Novaya Zemlya as planned. Then the captain fed the condemned man a hearty meal of roast reindeer with goat-cheese sauce, generously provided six quarts of aquavit, cast off the tow-hawser, and sent yours truly merrily on his way across the Barents Sea."

"Any weather problems?"

"None—your meteorological forecast held perfect. It was colder than a polar bear's left testicle, but I had fine sailing weather all the way." Koplin paused to scratch his nose. "That was a sweet little sloop your Norwegian friends fixed me up with. Was she saved?"

Seagram shook his head. "I'd have to check, but I'm certain it had to be destroyed. There was no way to take it on board the NUMA research vessel, and it couldn't be left to drift into the path of a Soviet ship. You understand."

Koplin nodded sadly. "Too bad. I became rather attached to her."

"Please continue," Seagram said.

"I raised the north island of Novaya Zemlya late in the afternoon of the second day. I had been at the helm for over forty hours, dozing off and on, and I began to find it impossible to keep my eyes open. Thank god for the aquavit. After a few swigs, my stomach was burning like an out-of-control forest fire and suddenly I was wide awake."

"You sighted no other boats?"

"None ever showed on the horizon," Koplin answered. Then he went on, "The coast proved to be a seemingly unending stretch of rocky cliffs. I saw no point in attempting a landing—it was beginning to get dark. So I turned out to sea, hove to, and sneaked a few hours sleep. In the morning I skirted the cliffs until I picked out a small sheltered cove and then went in on the auxiliary diesel."

"Did you use your boat for a base camp?"

"For the next twelve days. I made two, sometimes three field trips a day on cross-country skis, prospecting before returning for a hot meal and a good night's rest in a warm bunk."

"Up to now, you had seen no one?"

"I kept well clear of the Kelva missile station and the Kama security post. I saw no sign of the Russians until the final day of the mission."

"How were you discovered?"

"A Russian soldier on patrol; his dog must have crossed my trail and picked up my scent. Small wonder. I hadn't bathed in almost three weeks."

Seagram dropped a smile. Donner picked up the questioning more coldly, aggressively "Let's get back to your field trips. What did you find?"

"I couldn't cover the whole island on cross-country skis, so I concentrated on the promising areas that had been pinpointed by the satellite computer printouts." He stared at the ceiling. "The north island; the outer continuation of the Ural and Yugorski mountain chains, a few rolling plains, plateaus, and mountains—most of which are under a permanent ice sheet. Violent winds much of the time. The chill factor is murderous. I found no vegetation other than some rock lichen. If there were any warm-blooded animals, they kept to themselves."

"Let's stick to the prospecting," Donner said, "and save the travel lecture for another time."

"Just laying the groundwork." Koplin shot Donner a disapproving stare, his tone icy. "If I may continue without interruption—"

"Of course," Seagram said. He pulled his chair strategically between the bed and Donner. "It's your game, Sid. We'll play by your rules."

"Thank you." Koplin shifted his body. "Geographically, the island is quite interesting. A description of the faulting and uplifting of rocks that were once sediments formed under an ancient sea could fill several text books. Mineralogically, the magmatic paragenesis is barren."

"Would you mind translating that?"

Koplin grinned. "The origin and geological occurrence of a mineral is called its paragenesis. Magma, on the other hand, is the source of all matter; a liquid rock heated under pressure which turns solid to form igneous rock, perhaps better known as basalt or granite."

"Fascinating," Donner said dryly. "Then what you're stating is that Novaya Zemlya is void of minerals."

"You are singularly perceptive, Mr. Donner," Koplin said.

"But how did you find traces of byzanium?" Seagram asked.

"On the thirteenth day, I was poking around the north slope of Bednaya Mountain and ran onto a waste dump."

"Waste dump?"

"A pile of rocks that had been removed during the excavation of a mine shaft. This particular dump happened to have minute traces of byzanium ore."

The expressions on his interrogators' faces suddenly went sober.

"The shaft entrance was cunningly obscured," Koplin continued. "It took me the better part of the afternoon to figure which slope it was on."

"One minute, Sid." Seagram touched Koplin's arm. "Are you saying the entrance to this mine was purposely concealed?"

"An old Spanish trick. The opening was filled until it was even with the natural slope of the hill."

"Wouldn't the waste dump have been on a direct line from the entrance?" Donner asked.

"Under normal circumstances, yes. But in this case they were spaced over a hundred yards apart, separated by a gradual arc that ran around the mountain's slope to the west."

"But you *did* discover the entrance?" Donner went on.

"The rails and ties for the ore cars had been removed and the track bed covered over, but I managed to trace its outline by moving off about fifteen hundred yards and studying the mountain's slope through binoculars. What you couldn't see when you were standing on top of it became quite clear from that distance. The exact location of the mine was then easy to determine."

"Who would go to all that trouble to hide an abandoned mine in the Arctic?" Seagram asked no one in particular. "There's no method or logic to it."

"You're only half right, Gene," Koplin said. "The logic, I fear, remains an enigma; but the method was brilliantly executed by professionals—Coloradans." The word came slowly, almost reverently. "They were the men who excavated the Bednaya Mountain mine. The muckers, the blasters, the jiggers, the drillers, the Cornishmen, the Irishmen, Germans, and Swedes. Not Russians, but men who emigrated to the United States and became the legendary hard-rock miners of the Colorado Rockies. How they came to be on the icy slopes of Bednaya Mountain is anybody's guess, but these were the men who came and mined the byzanium and then vanished into the obscurity of the Arctic."

The sterile blankness of total incomprehension flooded Seagram's face. He turned to Donner and was met by the same expression. "It sounds crazy, absolutely crazy."

" 'Crazy'?" Koplin echoed. "Maybe, but no less true."

"You seem pretty confident," Donner muttered.

"Granted. I lost the tangible proof during my pursuit by the security guard; you have only my word on it, but why doubt it? As a scientist, I only report facts, and I have no devious motive behind a lie. So, if I were you, gentlemen, I would simply accept my word as genuine."

"As I said, it's your game." Seagram smiled faintly.

"You mentioned tangible evidence." Donner was calm and coldly efficient.

"After I penetrated the mine shaft—the loose rock came away in my hands, and I had only to scoop out a three-foot tunnel—the first thing my head collided with in the darkness was a string of ore cars. The strike of my fourth match illuminated an old pair of oil lamps. They both had fuel and lit on the third try." The faded blue eyes seemed to stare at something beyond the hospital room wall. "It was an unnerving scene that danced under the lamp's glow—mining tools neatly stacked in their racks, empty ore cars standing on rusting eight-gauge rails, drilling equipment ready to attack the rock—it was as though the mine was waiting for the incoming shift to sort the ore and run the waste to the dump."

"Could you say whether it looked as if someone left in a hurry?"

"Not at all. Everything was in its place. The bunks in a side chamber were made, the kitchen was cleared up, all the utensils were still on the shelves. Even the mules used to haul the ore cars had been taken to the working chamber and efficiently shot; their skulls each had a neat round hole in its center. No, I'd say the departure was very methodical."

"You have not yet explained your conclusion as to the Coloradans' identity," Donner said flatly.

"I'm coming to it now." Koplin fluffed a pillow and turned gingerly on his side. "The indications were all there, of course. The heavier equipment still bore the manufacturers' trademarks. The ore cars had been built by the Guthrie and Sons Foundry of Pueblo, Colorado; the drilling equipment came from the Thor Forge and Ironworks of Denver; and the small tools showed the names of the various blacksmiths who had forged them. Most had come from Central City and Idaho Springs, both mining towns in Colorado."

Seagram leaned back in his chair. "The Russians could have purchased the equipment in Colorado and then shipped it to the island."

"Possibly," Koplin said. "However, there were a few other bits and pieces that also led to Colorado."

"Such as?"

"The body in one of the bunks for one."

Seagram's eyes narrowed. "A body?"

"With red hair and a red beard," Koplin said casually. "Nicely preserved by the sub-zero temperature. It was the inscription on the wood above the bunk supports that proved most intriguing. It said, in English, I might add, 'Here rests Jake Hobart. Born 1874. A damn good man who froze in a storm, February 10, 1912.' "

Seagram rose from his chair and paced around the bed. "A name:

that at least is a start." He stopped and looked at Koplin. "Were there any personal effects left lying around?"

"All clothing was gone. Oddly, the labels on the food cans were French. But then there were about fifty empty wrappers of Mile-Hi Chewing Tobacco scattered on the ground. The last piece of the puzzle though, the piece that definitely ties it to the Coloradans, was a faded yellow copy of the *Rocky Mountain News,* dated November 17, 1911. It was this part of the evidence that I lost."

Seagram pulled out a pack of cigarettes and shook one loose. Donner held a lighter for him and Seagram nodded.

"Then there is a chance the Russians may not have possession of the byzanium," he said.

"There is one more thing," Koplin said quietly. "The top-right section of page three of the newspaper had been neatly snipped out. It may mean nothing, but, on the other hand, a check of the publisher's old files might tell you something."

"It might at that." Seagram regarded Koplin thoughtfully. "Thanks to you, we have our work laid out for us."

Donner nodded. "I'll reserve a seat on the next flight to Denver. With luck, I should come up with a few answers."

"Make the newspaper your first stop, then try and trace Jake Hobart. I'll make a check on old military records from this end. Also, contact a local expert on Western mining history, and run down the names of the manufacturers Sid gave us. However unlikely, one of them might still be in business."

Seagram stood up and looked down at Koplin. "We owe you more than we can ever repay," he said softly.

"I figure those old miners dug nearly half a ton of high grade byzanium from the guts of that bitch mountain," Koplin said, rubbing his hand through a month's growth of beard. "That ore has got to be stashed away in the world somewhere. Then again, if it hasn't emerged since 1912, it may be lost forever. But, if you find it, make that *when* you find it, you can say thanks by sending me a small sample for my collection."

"Consider it done."

"And while you're at it, get me the address of the fellow who saved my life so I can send him a case of vintage wine. His name is Dirk Pitt."

"You must mean the doctor on board the research vessel who operated on you."

"I mean the man who killed the Soviet patrol guard and his dog, and carried me off the island."

Donner and Seagram looked at each other thunderstruck.

Donner was the first to recover. "Killed a Soviet patrol guard!" It was more statement than question. "My God, that tears it!"

"But that's impossible!" Seagram finally managed to blurt. "When you rendezvoused with the NUMA ship, you were alone."

"Who told you that?"

"Well . . . no one. We naturally assumed—"

"I'm not Superman," Koplin said sarcastically. "The patrol guard picked up my trail, closed to within two hundred yards, and shot me twice. I was hardly in any condition to outrun a dog and then sail a sloop over fifty miles of open sea."

"Where did this Dirk Pitt come from?"

"I haven't the vaguest idea. The guard was literally dragging me off to his security post commander when Pitt appeared through the blizzard, like some vengeful Norse god, and calmly, as if he did it every day before breakfast, shot the dog and then the guard without so much as a how-do-you-do."

"The Russians will make propaganda hay with this." Donner groaned.

"How?" Koplin demanded. "There were no witnesses. The guard and his dog are probably buried under five feet of snow by now: they may never be found. And if they are, so what? Who's to prove anything? You two are pushing the panic button over nothing."

"It was a hell of a risk on that character's part," Seagram said.

"Good thing he took it," Koplin muttered. "Or instead of me lying here safe and snug in my sterile hospital bed, I'd be lying in a sterile Russian prison spilling my guts about Meta Section and byzanium."

"You have a valid point," Donner admitted.

"Describe him," Seagram ordered. "Face, build, clothing, everything you can remember."

Koplin did so. His description was sketchy in some areas, but in others his recollection of detail was remarkably accurate.

"Did you talk with him during the trip to the NUMA ship?"

"Couldn't. I blacked out right after he picked me up and didn't come to until I found myself here in Washington in the hospital."

Donner gestured to Seagram. "We'd better get a make on this guy, quick."

Seagram nodded. "I'll start with Admiral Sandecker. Pitt must have been connected with the research vessel. Perhaps someone in NUMA can identify him."

"I can't help wondering how much he knows," Donner said staring at the floor.

Seagram didn't answer. His mind had strayed to a shadowy figure on a snow-covered island in the Arctic. Dirk Pitt. He repeated the name in his mind. Somehow it seemed strangely familiar.

10

The telephone rang at 12:10 A.M. Sandecker popped open one eye and stared at it murderously for several moments. Finally, he gave in and answered it on the eighth ring.

"Yes, what is it?" he demanded.

"Gene Seagram here. Admiral. Did I catch you in bed?"

"Oh, hell no." Sandecker yawned. "I never retire before I write five chapters on my autobiography, rob at least two liquor stores, and rape a cabinet member's wife. Okay, what are you after, Seagram?"

"Something has come up."

"Forget it. I'm not endangering any more of my men and ships to bail your agents out of enemy territory." He used the word enemy as though the country were at war.

"It's not that at all."

"Then what?"

"I need a line on someone."

"Why come to me in the dead of night?"

"I think you might know him."

"What's the name?"

"Pitt. Dirk. The last name is Pitt, probably spelled P-i-t-t."

"Just to humor an old man's curiosity, what makes you think I know him?"

"I have no proof, but I'm certain he has a connection with NUMA."

"I have over two thousand people under me. I can't memorize all their names."

"Could you check him out? It's imperative that I talk to him."

"Seagram," Sandecker grunted irritably, "you're a monumental pain in the ass. Did it ever occur to you to call my personnel director during normal working hours?"

"My apologies," Seagram said. "I happened to be working late and—"

"Okay, if I dig up this character, I'll have him get in touch with you."

"I'd appreciate it." Seagram's tone remained impersonal. "By the way, the man your people rescued up in the Barents Sea is getting along nicely. The surgeon on the *First Attempt* did a magnificent job of bullet removal."

"Koplin, wasn't it?"

"Yes, he should be up and around in a few days."

"That was a near thing, Seagram. If the Russians had cottoned onto us, we'd have a nasty incident on our hands about now."

"What can I say?" Seagram said helplessly.

"You can say good night and let me get back to sleep," Sandecker snarled. "But first, tell me how this Pitt figures into the picture."

"Koplin was about to be captured by a Russian security guard when this guy appears out of a blizzard and kills the guard, carries Koplin across fifty miles of stormy water, not to mention stemming the blood flow from his wounds, and somehow deposits him on board your research vessel, ready for surgery."

"What do you intend to do when you find him?"

"That's between Pitt and myself."

"I see," Sandecker said. "Well, good night, Mr. Seagram."

"Thank you, Admiral. Good-by."

Sandecker hung up and then sat there a few moments, a bemused expression on his face. "Killed a Russian security guard and rescued an American agent. Dirk Pitt . . . you sly son of a bitch."

11

United's early flight touched down at Denver's Stapleton Airfield at eight in the morning. Mel Donner passed quickly through the baggage claim and settled behind the wheel of an Avis Plymouth for the fifteen-minute drive to 400 West Colfax Avenue and the *Rocky Mountain News*. As he followed the west-bound traffic, his gaze alternated between the windshield and a street map stretched open beside him on the front seat.

He had never been in Denver before, and he was mildly surprised to see a pall of smog hanging over the city. He expected to be confronted with the dirty brown and gray cloud over places like Los Angeles and New York, but Denver had always conjured up visions in his mind of a city cleansed by crystal clean air, nestled under the protective shadow of Purple Mountain Majesties. Even these were a disappointment; Denver sat naked on the edge of the great plains, at least twenty-five miles from the nearest foothills.

He parked the car and found his way to the newspaper's library. The girl behind the counter peered back at him through tear-shaped glasses and smiled an uneven-toothed, friendly smile.

"Can I help you?"

"Do you have an issue of your paper dated November 17, 1911?"

"Oh my, that does go back." She twisted her lips. "I can give you a photocopy, but the original issues are at the State Historical Society."

"I only need to see page three."

"If you care to wait, it'll take about fifteen minutes to track down the film of November 17, 1911, and run the page you want through the copy machine."

"Thank you. By the way, would you happen to have a business directory for Colorado?"

"We certainly do." She reached under the counter and laid a booklet on the smudged plastic top.

Donner sat down to study the directory as the girl disappeared to search out his request. There was no listing of a Guthrie and Sons Foundry in Pueblo. He thumbed to the T's. Nothing there either for the Thor Forge and Ironworks of Denver. It was almost too much to expect, he reasoned, for two firms still to be in business after nearly eight decades.

The fifteen minutes came and went, and the girl hadn't returned, so he idly leafed through the directory to pass the time. With the exception of Kodak, Martin Marietta, and Gates Rubber, there were very few companies he'd heard of. Then suddenly he stiffened. Under the J listings his eyes picked out a Jensen and Thor Metal Fabricators in Denver. He tore out the page, stuffed it in his pocket, and tossed the booklet back on the counter.

"Here you are sir," the girl said. "That'll be fifty cents."

Donner paid and quickly scanned the headline in the upper-right corner of the old newsprint's reproduction. The article covered a mine disaster.

"Is it what you were looking for?" the girl asked.

"It will have to do," he said as he walked away.

Jensen and Thor Metal Fabricators was situated between the Burlington-Northern rail yards and the South Platte River; a massive corrugated monstrosity that would have blotted any landscape except the one that surrounded it. Inside the work shed, overhead cranes shuffled enormous lengths of rusty pipe from pile to pile, while stamping machines pounded away with an intolerable clangor that made Donner's eardrums cringe from the attack. The main office sat off to one side behind sound-proofed aggregate concrete walls and tall arched windows.

An attractive, large-breasted receptionist escorted him down a shag-carpeted hall to a spacious paneled office. Carl Jensen, Jr., came around the desk and shook hands with Donner. He was young; no more than twenty-eight and wore his hair long. He had a neatly trimmed mustache and wore an expensive plaid suit. He looked for all the world like a UCLA graduate; Donner couldn't see him as anything else.

"Thank you for taking the time to see me, Mr. Jensen."

Jensen smiled guardedly. "It sounded important. A big man on the Washington campus and all. How could I refuse?"

"As I mentioned over the telephone, I'm checking on some old records."

Jensen's smile thinned. "You're not from the Internal Revenue, I hope."

Donner shook his head. "Nothing like that. The government's interest is purely historical. If you still keep them, I'd like to check over your sales records for July through November of 1911."

"You're putting me on." Jensen laughed.

"I assure you, it's a straight request."

Jensen stared at him blankly. "Are you sure you've got the right company?"

"I am," Donner said brusquely, "if this is a descendant of the Thor Forge and Ironworks."

"My great-grandfather's old outfit," Jensen admitted. "My father bought up the outstanding stock and changed the name in 1942."

"Would you still have any of the old records?"

Jensen shrugged. "We threw out the ancient history some time ago. If we'd saved every receipt of sale since great granddaddy opened his doors back in 1897, we'd need a warehouse the size of Bronco Stadium just to store them."

Donner pulled out a handkerchief and wiped the beads of sweat from his face. He sagged in his chair.

"However," Jensen continued, "and you can thank the foresight of Carl Jensen, Sr., we have all our past records down on microfilm."

"Microfilm?"

"The only way to fly. After five years, we film everything. Efficiency personified, that's us."

Donner couldn't believe his luck. "Then you *can* provide me with sales for the last six months of 1911?"

Jensen didn't answer. He leaned over the desk, spoke into his intercom, and then tilted back in his executive chair. "While we wait, can I get you a cup of coffee, Mr. Donner?"

"I'd prefer something with a little more snap."

"Spoken like a man from the big city." Jensen stood up and walked over to a mirrored bar from which he produced a bottle of Chivas Regal. "You'll find Denver quite gauche. A bar in an office is generally frowned upon here. The locals' idea of entertaining visiting firemen is to treat them to a large Coca-Cola and a lavish lunch at the Wiener-schnitzel. Fortunately for our esteemed out-of-town customers, I spent my business apprenticeship on Madison Avenue."

Donner took the offered glass and downed it.

Jensen looked at him appraisingly and then refilled the glass. "Tell me, Mr. Donner, just what is it you expect to find?"

"Nothing of importance," Donner said.

"Come now. The government wouldn't send a man across half the country to itemize seventy-six-year-old sales records strictly for laughs."

"The government often handles its secrets in a funny way."

"A classified secret that goes back to 1911?" Jensen shook his head in wonder. "Truly amazing."

"Let's just say we're trying to solve an ancient crime whose perpe-trator purchased your great-grandfather's services."

Jensen smiled and courteously accepted the lie.

A black-haired girl in long skirt and boots swiveled into the room, threw Jensen a seductive look, laid a Xerox paper on his desk, and retreated.

Jensen picked up the paper and examined it. "June to November must have been a recession year for my ancestor. Sales for those months were slim. Any particular entry you're interested in, Mr. Donner?"

"Mining equipment."

"Yes, this must be it . . . drilling tools. Ordered August tenth and picked up by the buyer on November first." Jensen's lips broke into a wide grin. "It would seem, sir, the laugh is on you."

"I don't follow."

"The buyer, or as you've informed me, the criminal . . ." Jensen paused for effect ". . . was the U.S. government."

12

The Meta Section headquarters was buried in a nondescript old cinder-block building beside the Washington Navy Yard. A large sign, its painted letters peeling under the double onslaught of the summer's heat and humidity, humbly advertised the premises as the Smith Van & Storage Company.

The loading docks appeared normal enough: packing crates and boxes were piled in strategic locations, and to passing traffic on the Suitland Parkway, the trucks parked around the yard behind a fifteen-foot-high chain-link fence looked exactly as moving vans should look. Only a closer inspection would have revealed old derelicts with missing engines and dusty, unused interiors. It was a scene that would have warmed the soul of a motion-picture set designer.

Gene Seagram read over the reports on the real-estate purchases for the Sicilian Project's installations. There were forty-six in all. The northern Canadian border numbered the most, followed closely by the Atlantic seaboard. The Pacific Coast had eight designated areas, while only four were plotted for the border above Mexico and the Gulf of Mexico. The transactions had gone off smoothly; the buyer in each case had gone under the guise of the Department of Energy Studies. There would be no cause for suspicion. The installations were designed, to all outward appearances, to resemble small relay power stations. To even the most wary of minds, there was nothing to suspect on the surface.

He was going over the construction estimates when his private phone rang. Out of habit, he carefully put the reports back in their folder and slipped it in a desk drawer, then picked up the phone. "This is Seagram."

"Hello, Mr. Seagram."

"Who's this?"

"Major McPatrick, Army Records Bureau. You asked me to call you at this number if I came up with anything on a miner by the name of Jake Hobart."

"Yes, of course. I'm sorry, my mind was elsewhere." Seagram could almost envision the man on the other end of the line. A West Pointer, under thirty—that much was betrayed by the clipped verbs and the youngish voice. Probably make general by the time he was forty-five, providing he made the right contacts while commanding a desk at the Pentagon.

"What do you have, Major?"

"I've got your man. His full name was Jason Cleveland Hobart. Born January 23, 1874, in Vinton, Iowa."

"At least the year checks."

"Occupation, too: he was a miner."

"What else?"

"He enlisted in the Army in May of 1898 and served with the First Colorado Volunteer Regiment in the Philippines."

"You did say Colorado?"

"Correct, sir." McPatrick paused and Seagram could hear the riffling of papers over the line. "Hobart had an excellent war record. Got promoted to sergeant. He suffered serious wounds fighting the Philippine insurrectionists and was decorated twice for meritorious conduct under fire."

"When was he discharged?"

"They called it 'mustering out' in those days," McPatrick said knowledgeably. "Hobart left the Army in October of 1901."

"Is that your last record of him?"

"No, his widow is still drawing a pension—"

"Hold on," Seagram interrupted. "Hobart's widow is still living?"

"She cashes her fifty dollars and forty cents' pension check every month, like clockwork."

"She must be over ninety years old. Isn't that a little unusual, paying a pension to the widow of a Spanish-American War veteran? You'd think most of them would be pushing up tombstones by now."

"Oh hell no, we still carry nearly a hundred Civil War widows on the pension rolls. None were even born when Grant took Richmond. May and December marriages between sweet young things and old toothless Grand Army of the Republic vets were quite ordinary in those days."

"I thought a widow was eligible for pension only if she was living at the time her husband was killed in battle."

"Not necessarily," McPatrick said. "The government pays widows' pensions under two categories. One is for service-oriented death. That, of course, includes death in battle, or fatal sickness or injury inflicted while serving between certain required dates as set by Congress. The second is nonservice death. Take yourself, for example. You served with the Navy during the Vietnam war between the required dates set for that particular conflict. That makes your wife, or any future wife, eligible for a small pension should you be run over by a truck forty years from now."

"I'll make a note of that in my will," Seagram said, uneasy in the knowledge that his service record was where any desk jockey in the Pentagon could lay his hands on it. "Getting back to Hobart."

"Now we come to an odd oversight on the part of Army records."

"Oversight?"

"Hobart's service forms fail to mention re-enlistment, yet he is recorded as 'died in the service of his country.' No mention of the cause, only the date . . . November 17, 1911."

Seagram suddenly straightened in his chair. "I have it on good authority that Jake Hobart died a civilian on February 10, 1912."

"Like I said, there's no mention of cause of death. But I assure you, Hobart died a soldier, not a civilian, on November 17. I have a letter in his file dated July 25, 1912, from Henry L. Stimson, Secretary of War under President Taft, ordering the Army to award Sergeant Jason Hobart's wife full widow's pension for the rest of her natural life. How

Hobart rated the personal interest of the Secretary of War is a mystery, but it leaves little doubt of our man's status. Only a soldier in high standing would have received that kind of preferential treatment, certainly not a coal miner."

"He wasn't a coal miner," Seagram snapped.

"Well, whatever."

"Do you have an address for Mrs. Hobart?"

"I have it here somewhere." McPatrick hesitated a moment. "Mrs. Adeline Hobart, 261-B Calle Aragon, Laguna Hills, California. She's in that big senior citizens development down the coast from L.A."

"That about covers it," Seagram said. "I appreciate your help in this matter, Major."

"I hate to say this, Mr. Seagram, but I think we've got two different men here."

"I think perhaps you're right," Seagram replied. "It looks as though I might be on the wrong track."

"If I can be of any further help, please don't hesitate to call me."

"I'll do that," Seagram grunted. "Thanks again."

After he hung up, he dropped his head in his hands and slouched in the chair. He sat that way not moving for perhaps two full minutes. Then he laid his hands on the desk and smiled a wide, smug grin.

Two different men very well could have existed with the same surname and birth year who worked in the same state at the same occupation. That part of the puzzle might have been a coincidence. But not the connection, the glorious 365-to-1-longshot connection that mysteriously tied the two men together and made them one; Hobart's recorded death and the old newspaper found by Sid Koplin in the Bednaya Mountain mine bore the same date: November 17, 1911.

He pushed the intercom switch for his secretary. "Barbara, put through a call to Mel Donner at the Brown Palace Hotel in Denver."

"Any message if he isn't in?"

"Just leave word for him to call me on my private line when he returns."

"Shall do."

"And one more thing, book me on United's early-morning flight tomorrow to Los Angeles."

"Yes, sir."

He clicked the switch to off and leaned back in the chair thoughtfully.

Adeline Hobart, over ninety years old. He hoped to God she wasn't senile.

13

Donner didn't normally stay in a downtown hotel. He preferred the more inconspicuous setting of a garden-variety motel closer to the suburbs, but Seagram had insisted on the grounds that local cooperation comes more easily to an investigator when he lets it be known that he has a room in the city's oldest and most prestigious building. Investigator, the word nauseated him. If one of his fellow professors on the University of Southern California campus had told him five years ago that his doctorate in physics would lead him to play such a clandestine role, he'd have choked laughing. Donner wasn't laughing now. The Sicilian Project was far too vital to the country's interests to risk a leak through outside help. He and Seagram had designed and created the project on their own, and it was agreed that they'd take it as far as they could alone.

He left his rented Plymouth with the parking attendant and walked across Tremont Place, through the hotel's old-fashioned revolving doors, and into the pleasantly ornate lobby, where the young mustachioed assistant manager gave him a message without so much as a smile. Donner took it without so much as a thank you, then made his way to the elevators and his room.

He slammed the door and threw the room key and Seagram's message on the desk and turned on the television. It had been a long and tiresome day, and his bodily systems were still operating on Washington, D.C., time. He dialed room service and ordered dinner, then kicked off his shoes, loosened his tie, and sagged onto the bed.

For perhaps the tenth time he began going over the photocopy of the old newspaper page. It made very interesting reading, if, that is, Donner's interest lay in advertisements for piano tuners, electric belts for rupture, and strange malady remedies, along with editorials on the Denver City Council's determination to clear such-and-such street of sinful houses of entertainment, or intriguing little inserts guaranteed to make feminine readers of the early 1900s gasp in innocent horror.

CORONER'S REPORT

Last week, the habitués of the Paris Morgue were greatly puzzled by a curious India-rubber leg that lay exposed for recognition on one of the slabs. It appears that the body of an elegantly dressed woman, apparently aged about 50, had been found in the Seine, but the body was so decomposed that it could not be kept. It was remarked, however, that the left leg, amputated at the thigh, had been replaced by an ingeniously constructed India-rubber leg, which was exhibited in the hope that it might lead to the identification of the owner.

Donner smiled at the quaint piece of history and turned his attention to the upper-right-hand section of the page, the part that Koplin had said was missing from the paper he'd discovered on Novaya Zemlya.

DISASTER AT THE MINES

Tragedy struck like a vengeful wraith early this morning when a dynamite blast set off a cave-in at the Little Angel Mine near Central City, trapping nine men of the first shift, including the well-known and respected mining engineer, Joshua Hays Brewster.

The weary and haggard rescue crews report that hope of finding the men alive is black indeed. Bull Mahoney, the intrepid foreman of the Satan Mine, made a herculean effort to reach the trapped miners, but was turned back by a wall of tidal water that inundated the main shaft.

"Them poor fellows is goners sure," Mahoney stated to reporters at the disaster scene. "The water has gushed up near two levels above where they was working. They surely was drowned like rats before they knew what hit them."

The silent and sorrowful throng milling around the mine entrance woefully bemoaned the chilling likelihood that this is one time when the bodies of the lost men will not be recovered and brought to the "grass" for decent burial.

It is reliably known that it was Mr. Brewster's intent to re-open the Little Angel Mine which had been closed since 1881. Friends and business associates say that Brewster often boasted that the original digging had missed the high-grade lode, and with luck and fortitude, he was going to be the discoverer.

When reached for comment, Mr. Ernest Bloeser, now retired and former owner of the Little Angel Mine, said on the front porch of his home in Golden, "That mine was dogged by bad luck from the day I opened it. All it ever turned out to be was a low-grade ore shoot which never did turn a profit." Mr. Bloeser further stated, "I think Brewster was dead wrong. There was never any indication of the mother lode. I am astounded that a man of his reputation could think so."

In Central City, the last message proclaimed that if the situation is in the eternal graces of the almighty, the opening will be sealed as a tomb and the missing men will rest in blackness through the ages, never again to see the "grass" or sunlight.

The grim reaper's list of the men caught up in this most terrible of disasters is as follows:

> Joshua Hays Brewster, Denver
> Alvin Coulter, Fairplay
> Thomas Price, Leadville
> Charles P. Widney, Cripple Creek
> Vernon S. Hall, Denver
> John Caldwell, Central City
> Walter Schmidt, Aspen
> Warner E. O'Deming, Denver
> Jason C. Hobart, Boulder

May God watch over these brave toilers of the mountains.

No matter how many times Donner's eyes traveled over the old news type, they always came back to the last name among the missing miners. Slowly, like a man in a trance, he laid the paper in his lap, picked up the phone and dialed long distance.

14

"The Monte Cristo!" Harry Young exclaimed delightedly. "I heartily endorse the Monte Cristo. The Roquefort dressing is also excellent. But first, I'd like a martini, very dry, with a twist."

"Monte Cristo sandwich and Roquefort on your salad. Yes, sir," the young waitress repeated, bending over the table so that her short skirt rode up to reveal a pair of white panties. "And you, sir?"

"I'll take the same." Donner nodded. "Only I'll start with a Manhattan on the rocks."

Young peered over the top of his glasses as the waitress hurried to the kitchen. "If only someone would give me that for Christmas," he said, smiling.

Young was a skinny little man. In decades past he would have been called an overdressed, silly old fool. Now he was an alert, eager-faced seventy-eight-year-old *bon vivant* with a practiced eye for beauty. He sat across the booth table from Donner in a blue turtleneck and patterned, double-knit sportscoat.

"Mr. Donner!" he said happily. "This is indeed a pleasure. The Broker is my favorite restaurant." He waved his hand at the walnut-paneled walls and booths. "This was once a bank vault, you know."

"So I noticed when I had to duck through the five-ton door."

"You should come here for dinner. They give you an enormous tray of shrimp for an appetizer." He fairly beamed at the thought.

"I'll bear that in mind on my next visit."

"Well, sir." Young looked at him steadily. "What's on your mind?"

"I have a few questions."

Young's eyebrows raised above his glasses. "Oh my, now you *have* tickled my curiosity. You're not with the FBI are you? Over the phone, you simply said you were with the federal government."

"No, I'm not with the FBI. And I'm not on the payroll of Internal Revenue, either. My department is welfare. It's my job to track down the authenticity of pension claims."

"Then how can I help you?"

"My particular project at the moment is the investigation of a seventy-six-year-old mining accident that took the lives of nine men. One of the victim's descendants has filed for a pension. I'm here to check the validity of the claim. Your name, Mr. Young, was recommended to me by the State Historical Society, which glowingly described you as a walking encyclopedia on Western mining history."

"A bit of an exaggeration," Young said, "but I'm flattered, nonetheless."

The drinks arrived and they sipped them for a minute. Donner took the time to study the pictures of turn-of-the-century Colorado silver kings that hung on the walls. Their faces all projected the same intense stare, as if they were trying to melt the camera lens with their wealth-fortified arrogance.

"Tell me, Mr. Donner, how can anyone file a pension claim on a seventy-six-year-old accident?"

"It seems the widow didn't receive all she was entitled to," Donner said, skating onto unsure ice. "Her daughter is demanding the back pay, so to speak."

"I see," Young said. He stared across the table speculatively and then began idly tapping his spoon against a plate. "Which of the men who were lost in the Little Angel disaster are you interested in?"

"My compliments," Donner said, avoiding the stare and unfolding his napkin self-consciously. "You don't miss a trick."

"It's nothing, really. A seventy-six-year-old mining accident. Nine men missing. It could only be the Little Angel disaster."

"The man's name was Brewster."

Young stared at him an extra moment, then stopped the plate-tapping and banged his spoon against the table top. "Joshua Hays Brewster," he murmured the name. "Born to William Buck Brewster and Hettie Masters in Sidney, Nebraska, on April 4 . . . or was it April 5, 1878."

Donner's eyes opened wide. "How could you possibly know all that?"

"Oh, I know that and much more." Young smiled. "Mining engineers, or the Lace-Boot Brigade, as they were once known, are a rather cliquish group. It's one of the few professions where sons follow fathers and also marry sisters or daughters of other mining engineers."

"Are you about to say that you were related to Joshua Hays Brewster?"

"My uncle." Young grinned.

The ice parted and Donner fell through.

"You look like you could stand another drink, Mr. Donner." Young signaled to the waitress for another round. "Needless to say, there is no daughter who is seeking a claim to a pension; my mother's brother died a childless bachelor."

"Liars never prosper," Donner said with a thin smile. "I'm sorry if I've embarrassed you by foolishly painting myself into a corner."

"Can you enlighten me?"

"I would prefer not to."

"You *are* from the government?" Young asked.

Donner showed him his credentials.

"Then, may I ask why you're investigating my long-dead uncle?"

"I would prefer not to," Donner repeated. "Not at this time, at any rate."

"What do you wish to know?"

"Whatever you can tell me about Joshua Hays Brewster and the Little Angel accident."

The drinks came along with the salad. Donner agreed that the dressing was excellent. They ate in silence. When Young had finished and wiped his tiny white mustache, he took a deep breath and relaxed against the backrest of the booth.

"My uncle was typical of the men who developed the mines in the early nineteen hundreds; white, eager, and middle class, and except for his small size—he stood only five feet two—he could easily have passed for what the novelists of the day vividly depicted as a gentlemanly, two-fisted, devil-may-care, adventurous mining engineer, complete with shining boots, jodhpurs, and a Smokey-the-Bear ranger hat."

"You make him sound like a hero from an old Saturday-matinee serial."

"A fictional hero could never have measured up," Young said. "The field is highly specialized today, of course, but an engineer of the old school had to be as tough as the rock he mined, and he had to be versatile—mechanic, electrician, surveyor, metallurgist, geologist, lawyer, arbitrator between penny-pinching management and muscle-brained workers—this was the kind of man it took to run a mine. This was Joshua Hays Brewster."

Donner kept silent, slowly swirling the liquor around in his glass.

"After my uncle graduated from the School of Mines," Young continued, "he followed his profession in the Klondike, Australia, and Russia before returning to the Rockies in 1908 to manage the Sour Rock and Buffalo, a pair of mines at Leadville owned by a group of French financiers in Paris who never laid eyes on Colorado."

"The French owned mining claims in the States?"

"Yes. Their capital flowed heavily throughout the West. Gold and silver, cattle, sheep, real estate; you name it, they had a finger in it."

"What possessed Brewster to reopen the Little Angel?"

"That's a strange story in itself," Young said. "The mine was worthless. The Alabama Burrow, three hundred yards away, coughed up two million dollars in silver before the water in the lower levels began running ahead of the pumps. That was the shaft that hit the high-grade lode. The Little Angel never came close." Young paused to sip at his drink and then stared at it as though he were seeing a vague image in the ice cubes. "When my uncle advertised his intentions to reopen the mine to anyone who would listen, people who knew him well were shocked. Yes, Mr. Donner, shocked. Joshua Hays Brewster was a cautious man, a man of painstaking detail. His every move was carefully calculated in terms of success. He never played the odds unless they were steeply in his favor. For him to publicly announce such a hare-brained scheme was unthinkable. The mere act was considered by all to be that of a madman."

"Maybe he found some clue the others had missed."

Young shook his head. "I've been a geologist for over sixty years, Mr. Donner, and a damned good one. I've re-entered and examined the Little Angel down to the flooded levels, and analyzed every accessible inch of the Alabama Burrow, and I'm telling you positively and un-equivocally: there is no untapped vein of silver down there now, nor was there one in 1911."

The Monte Cristo sandwiches came and the salad plates were whisked away.

"Are you suggesting your uncle went insane?"

"The possibility has occurred to me. Brain tumors were generally undiagnosed in those days."

"So were nervous breakdowns."

Young wolfed the first quarter of his sandwich and drained his second martini. "How is your Monte Cristo, Mr. Donner?"

Donner forced a few bites. "Excellent, and yours?"

"Grandly delicious. Would you like my private theory? Don't bother to be polite; you can laugh without embarrassment. Everyone else does when they hear it."

"I promise you I won't laugh," Donner said, his tone dead serious.

"Be sure to dip your Monte Cristo in the grape jam, Mr. Donner. It heightens the pleasure. Now then, as I've mentioned, my uncle was a man of great detail, a keen observer of his work, his surroundings and accomplishments. I've collected most of his diaries and notebooks; they fill a goodly portion of my study's bookshelves. His remarks concerning the Sour Rock and the Buffalo mines, for example, take up five hundred and twenty-seven pages of exacting sketches and neatly legible handwriting. The pages in the notebook that come under the heading of the 'Little Angel Mine,' however, are totally blank."

"He left nothing behind regarding the Little Angel, not even a letter, perhaps?"

Young shrugged and shook his head. "It was as though there was nothing to record. It was as though Joshua Hays Brewster and his eight-man crew went down into the bowels of the earth never intending to return."

"What are you suggesting?"

"Ridiculous as it seems," Young admitted, "the thought of mass suicide once darted through my mind. Extensive research showed me that all nine men were either bachelors or widowers. Most were itinerant loners who drifted from digging to digging, looking for any excuse to move on when they became bored or disenchanted with the foreman or mine management. They had little to live for once they became too old to work the mines."

"But Jason Hobart had a wife," Donner said.

"What? What's that?" Young's eyes widened. "I found no record of a wife for any of them."

"Take my word for it."

"God in heaven! If my uncle had known that, he'd never have recruited Hobart."

"Why is that?"

"Don't you see: he needed men he could trust implicitly, men who had no close friends or relatives to ask questions should they vanish."

"You're not making sense," Donner said flatly.

"Simply put, the reopening of the Little Angel Mine and the subsequent tragedy was a sham, a pretext, a hoax. I'm convinced my uncle was going mad. How or what caused his mental illness will never be known. His character altered drastically, even to the point of producing a different man."

"A split personality?"

"Exactly. His moral values changed; his warmth and love for friends disappeared. When I was younger, I talked to people who remembered him. They all agreed on one thing: the Joshua Hays Brewster they all knew and loved died months before the Little Angel disaster."

"How does this lead to a hoax?"

"Insanity aside, my uncle was still a mining engineer. Sometimes he could tell within minutes whether a mine would pay or not. The Little Angel was a bust, he knew that. He never had any intention of finding a high-grade lode. I don't have the vaguest idea of what his game was, Mr. Donner, but one thing I'm certain of, whoever pumps the water from the lower levels of that old shaft will find no bones."

Donner finished off his Manhattan and looked quizzically at Young. "So you think the nine men who went into the mine escaped?"

Young smiled. "Nobody actually saw them enter, Mr. Donner. It was assumed, and reasonably so, that they died down there in the black waters because they were never heard from again."

"Not enough evidence," Donner said.

"Oh, I have more, lots more," Young replied enthusiastically.

"I'm listening."

"Item One: The Little Angel's lowest working chamber was a good hundred feet above the mean water level. At worst, the walls leaked only moderately from surface accumulations. The lower shaft levels were already flooded because the water had gradually built up during the years the mine was originally shut down. Therefore, there was no way a dynamite blast could have unleashed a tidal wave of water over my uncle and his crew.

"Item Two: The equipment supposedly found in the mine after the accident was old, used junk. Those men were professionals, Mr. Donner. They'd never have gone below the surface with second-rate machinery.

"Item Three: Though he made it known to everyone that he was reopening the mine, my uncle never once consulted or discussed the project with Ernest Bloeser, the man who owned the Little Angel. In short, my uncle was claim-jumping. An unthinkable act to a man of his moral reputation.

"Item Four: The first warning of possible disaster didn't come until the next afternoon, when the foreman of the Satan Mine, one Bill Mahoney, found a note under his cabin door that said, 'Help! Little Angel Mine. Come Quick!' A most strange method to sound an alarm, don't you think? Naturally, the note was unsigned.

"Item Five: The sheriff in Central City stated that my uncle had given him a list of the crew's names with the request that he give it to the newspapers in case of a fatal accident. An odd premonition, to say the least. It was as if Uncle Joshua wanted to be certain there was no mistaking the victims' identities."

Donner pushed back his plate and drank a glass of water. "I find your theory intriguing, but not fully convincing."

"Ah, but finally, perhaps above all, Mr. Donner, I have saved the piece de resistance until last.

"Item Six: Several months after the tragedy, my mother and father, who were on a tour through Europe, saw my uncle standing on the boat-train platform in Southampton, England. My mother often related how she went up to him and said, 'God in heaven, Joshua, is it really you?' The face that stared back at her was bearded and deathly white, the eyes glassy. 'Forget me,' he whispered and then turned and ran. My father chased him down the platform but soon lost him in the crowd."

"The logical answer is a simple case of mistaken identity."

"A sister who doesn't know her own brother?" Young said sarcastically. "Come now, Mr. Donner, surely you could pick your brother out of a crowd?"

" 'Fraid not. I was an only child."

"A shame. You missed one of life's great joys."

"At least I didn't have to share my toys." The check arrived and Donner threw a credit card on the tray. "So what you're saying is that the Little Angel disaster was a cover-up."

"That's my theory." Young patted his mouth with his napkin. "No way of proving it, of course, but I've always had a haunting feeling that the Société des Mines de Lorraine was in back of it."

"Who were they?"

"They were and still are to France what Krupp is to Germany, what Mitsubichi is to Japan, what Anaconda is to the United States."

"Where does the Société—whatever you call it—fit in?"

"They were the French financiers who hired Joshua Hays Brewster as their engineer-manager of exploration. They were the only ones with enough capital to pay nine men to vanish off the face of the earth."

"But why? Where is the motive?"

Young gestured helplessly. "I don't know." He leaned forward and his eyes seemed to burn. "But I do know that whatever the price, whatever the influence, it took my uncle and his eight-man crew to some unnamed hell outside the country."

"Until the bodies are recovered, who's to say you're wrong."

Young stared at him. "You are a courteous man, Mr. Donner. I thank you."

"For what? a free lunch at the government's expense?"

"For not laughing," Young said softly.

Donner nodded and said nothing. The man across the table had just spliced one tiny strand of the frayed puzzle to the red-bearded bones in the Bednaya Mountain mine. There was nothing to laugh about, nothing to laugh about in the least.

15

Seagram returned the farewell smile from the stewardess, stepped off the United jet, and prepared himself for the quarter-mile trip to the street entrance of the Los Angeles International Airport. He finally reached the front lobby, and unlike Donner, who had rented his car from No. 2, Seagram preferred dealing with No. 1 and signed out a Lincoln from Hertz. He turned onto Century Boulevard, and within a few blocks entered the on-ramp south to the San Diego Freeway. It was a cloudless day and the smog was surprisingly light, allowing a hazy view of the Sierra Madre mountains. He drove leisurely in the right-hand lane of the freeway at sixty miles an hour, while the mainstream of local traffic sped by the Lincoln doing seventy-five and eighty with routine indifference to the posted fifty-five miles an hour limit. He soon left the chemical refineries of Torrance and the oil derricks around Long Beach behind and entered the vastness of Orange County where the terrain suddenly flattened out and gave way to a great, unending sea of tract homes.

It took him a little over an hour to reach the turn-off for Leisure World. It was an idyllic setting: golf courses, swimming pools, stables, neatly manicured lawns and park areas, golden-tanned senior citizens on bicycles.

He stopped at the main gate and an elderly guard in uniform checked him through and gave him directions to 261-B Calle Aragon. It was a picturesque little duplex tucked neatly on the slope of a hill overlooking an immaculate park. Seagram parked the Lincoln against the curb, walked through a small courtyard patio filled with rose bushes, and poked the doorbell. The door opened and his fears vanished; Adeline Hobart was definitely not the senile type.

"Mr. Seagram?" The voice was light and cheerful.

"Yes. Mrs. Hobart?"

"Please come in." She extended her hand. The grip was as firm as a man's. "Goodness, nobody's called me that in over seventy years. When I received your long-distance call regarding Jake, I was so surprised I almost forgot to take my Geritol."

Adeline was stout, but she carried her extra pounds easily. Her blue eyes seemed to laugh with every sentence and her face carried a warm, gentle look. She was everyone's idea of a sweet little old snow-haired lady.

"You don't strike me as the Geritol type," he said.

She patted his arm. "If that is meant as flattery, I'll buy it." She motioned him to a chair in a tastefully furnished living room. "Come and sit down. You will stay for lunch, won't you?"

"I'd be honored, if it's no trouble."

"Of course not. Bert is off chasing around the golf course, and I appreciate the company."

Seagram looked up. "Bert?"

"My husband."

"But I was under the impression—"

"I was still Jake Hobart's widow," she finished his sentence, smiling innocently. "The truth of the matter is, I became Mrs. Bertram Austin sixty-two years ago."

"Does the Army know?"

"Oh heavens, yes. I wrote letters to the War Department notifying them of my marital status a long time ago, but they simply sent polite, noncommittal replies and kept mailing the checks."

"Even though you'd remarried?"

Adeline shrugged. "I'm only human, Mr. Seagram. Why argue with the government. If they insist on sending money, who's to tell them they're crazy?"

"A lucrative little arrangement."

She nodded. "I won't deny it, particularly when you include the ten thousand dollars I received at Jake's death."

Seagram leaned forward, his eyes narrowed. "The Army paid you a ten-thousand-dollar indemnity? Wasn't that a bit steep for 1912?"

"You couldn't be half as surprised as I was then," she said. "Yes, that amount of money was a small fortune in those days."

"Was there any explanation?"

"None," she replied. "I can still see the check after all these years. All it said was 'Widow's Payment' and it was made out to me. That's all there was to it."

"Perhaps we can start at the beginning."

"When I met Jake?"

Seagram nodded.

Her eyes looked beyond him for a few moments. "I met Jake during the terrible winter of 1910. It was in Leadville, Colorado, and I had just turned sixteen. My father was on a business trip to the mining fields to investigate possible investment in several claims, and since it was close to Christmas, and I had a few days vacation from school, he relented and took mother and me along. The train barely made it into Leadville station when the worst blizzard in forty years struck the high country of Colorado. It lasted for two weeks, and believe me, it was no picnic, especially when you consider that the altitude of Leadville is over ten thousand feet."

"It must have been quite an adventure for a sixteen-year-old girl."

"It was. Dad paced the hotel lobby like a trapped bull while Mother just sat and worried, but I thought it was marvelous."

"And Jake?"

"One day, Mother and I were struggling across the street to the general store—an ordeal when you are lashed by fifty-mile-an-hour winds at twenty degrees below zero—when out of nowhere this giant brute of a man picks each of us up under one arm and carries us through the snowdrifts and deposits us on the doorstep of the store, just as sassy as you please."

"It was Jake?"

"Yes," she said distantly, "it was Jake."

"What did he look like?"

"He was a large man, over six feet, barrel-chested. He'd worked in the mines in Wales when he was a boy. Anytime you saw a crowd of men a mile away, you could easily pick Jake out. He was the one with the bright red hair and beard who was always laughing."

"Red hair and beard?"

"Yes, he was quite proud of the fact that he stood out from the rest."

"All the world loves a man who laughs."

She smiled broadly. "It certainly wasn't love at first sight on my part, I can tell you. To me, Jake looked like a big uncouth bear. He was hardly the type to tickle a young girl's fancy."

"But you married him."

She nodded. "He courted me all during the blizzard, and when the sun finally broke through the clouds on the fourteenth day, I accepted his proposal. Mother and Dad were distraught, of course, but Jake won them over, too."

"You couldn't have been married long?"

"I saw him for the last time a year later."

"The day he and the others were lost in the Little Angel." It was more statement than question.

"Yes," she said wistfully. She avoided his stare and looked nervously toward the kitchen. "My goodness, I'd better fix us some lunch. You must be starving, Mr. Seagram."

But Seagram's business-like expression faded and his eyes came alight with sudden excitement. "You heard from Jake after the Little Angel accident, didn't you, Mrs. Austin?"

She seemed to retreat into the cushions of her chair. Apprehension spread across her gentle face. "I don't know what you mean."

"I think you do," he said softly.

"No . . . no, you're mistaken."

"Why are you afraid?"

Her hands were trembling now. "I've told you all I can."

"There's more, much more, Mrs. Austin." He reached over and took her hands. "Why are you afraid?" he repeated.

"I'm sworn to secrecy," she murmured.

"Can you explain?"

She said, hesitantly, "You're with the government, Mr. Seagram. You know what it is to keep a secret."

"Who was it? Jake? Did he ask you to remain silent?"

She shook her head

"Then who?"

"Please believe me," she pleaded. "I can't tell you . . . I can't tell you anything."

Seagram stood up and looked down on her. She seemed to have aged, the wrinkles etched more deeply in her ancient skin. She had withdrawn into a shell. It would take a mild form of shock treatment to get her to open up.

"May I use your telephone, Mrs. Austin?"

"Yes, of course. You'll find the nearest extension in the kitchen."

It was seven minutes before the familiar voice came through the earpiece. Quickly, Seagram explained the situation and made his request. Then he turned back to the living room. "Mrs. Austin. Can you come here a moment?"

Timidly, she approached him.

He handed her the receiver. "Here is someone who wishes to speak to you."

Cautiously, she took it from his hands. "Hello," she muttered, "this is Adeline Austin."

For a brief instant, an expression of confusion was mirrored in her eyes, then it was slowly transformed and froze into genuine astonishment. She kept nodding, saying nothing, as though the detached voice over the line was standing before her.

Finally, at the end of the one-sided conversation, she managed to utter a few words: "Yes sir . . . I will. Good-by."

Slowly, she replaced the receiver and stood in a trancelike bewilderment. "Was . . . was that really the President of the United States?"

"It was. You can verify it if you wish. Call long distance and ask for the White House. When they answer, talk to Gregg Collins. He's the President's chief aide. It was he who passed along my call."

"Just imagine, the President asked me to help him." She shook her head dazedly. "I can't believe it really happened."

"It happened, Mrs. Austin. Believe me, any information you can give us concerning your first husband and the strange circumstances surrounding his death would be of great benefit to the nation. I know that sounds like a trite way of stating it, but . . ."

"Who can turn down a President?" The sweet smile was back. The tremor was gone from Adeline's hands. She was back on balance, outwardly, at least.

Seagram took her arm and gently guided her back to her chair in the living room. "Now then, tell me about Jake Hobart's relationship with Joshua Hays Brewster."

"Jake was an explosives specialist, a blaster, one of the best in the fields. He knew dynamite like a blacksmith knew his forge, and since Mr. Brewster insisted on only the top men to make up his mining crews, he often hired Jake to handle the blasting."

"Did Brewster know Jake was married?"

"Odd you should ask that. We had a little house in Boulder, away from the mining camps, because Jake didn't want it known he had a wife. He claimed that mine foremen wouldn't hire a blaster who was married."

"So naturally, Brewster, unaware of Jake's marital status, paid him to blast in the Little Angel mine."

"I know what was printed in the newspapers, Mr. Seagram, but Jake never set foot in the Little Angel mine, nor did the rest of the crew."

Seagram pulled his chair closer so that they were almost touching knees. "Then the disaster *was* a hoax," he said hoarsely.

She looked up. "You know . . . you know that?"

"We suspected, but have no proof."

"If it's proof you want, Mr. Austin, I'll get it for you." She rose to her feet, shrugging off Seagram's attempts to help her, and disappeared into another room. She returned carrying an old shoebox, which she proceeded to open reverently.

"The day before he was to enter the Little Angel, Jake took me down to Denver and we went on a shopping spree. He bought me fancy clothes, jewelry, and treated me to champagne at the finest restaurant in town. We spent our last night together in the honeymoon suite of the Brown Palace Hotel. Do you know of it?"

"I have a friend staying there right now."

"In the morning, he told me not to believe what I heard or read in the newspapers about his death in a mining accident, and that he would be gone for several months on a job somewhere in Russia. When he returned, he said we would be rich beyond our dreams. Then he mentioned something I've never understood."

"What was that?"

"He said the Frenchies were taking care of everything and that when it was all over, we would live in Paris." Her face took on a dreamlike quality. "In the morning he was gone. On his pillow was a note that simply said, 'I love you, Ad' and an envelope containing five thousand dollars."

"Do you have any idea where the money came from?"

"None. We only had about three hundred dollars in the bank at the time."

"And that was the last you heard from him?"

"No." She handed Seagram a faded postcard with a tinted photograph of the Eiffel Tower on the front. "This came in the mail about a month later."

Dear Ad, The weather is rainy here and the beer awful. Am fine and so is the other boys. Don't fret. As you can tell I ain't dead by a long shot. You know who.

The handwriting was obviously from a heavy hand. The postmark on the card was dated Paris, December 1, 1911.

"It was followed in a week by a second card," Adeline said as she handed it to Seagram. It depicted Sacré Coeur but was postmarked Le Havre.

Dear Ad, We're headin for the arctic. This will be my last message for some time. Be brave. The Frenchies are treating us right. Good food, good ship. You know who.

"You're certain it's Jake's handwriting?" Seagram asked.

"Absolutely. I have other papers and old letters of Jake's. You can compare them if you wish."

"That won't be necessary, Ad." She smiled when she heard her nickname. "Was there any further communication?"

She nodded. "The third and last. Jake must have stocked up on picture postcards of Paris. This one shows the Sainte-Chapelle, but it was mailed from Aberdeen, Scotland, on April 4, 1912."

Dear Ad, This is a frightful place. The cold is fearsome. We don't know if we will survive. If I can somehow get this to you, you will be taken care of. God Bless. Jake.

Along the side, another hand had written in:

Dear Mrs. Hobart. We lost Jake in a storm. We gave him a Christian readin. We're sorry. V.H.

Seagram took out the list of the crew's names that Donner had read him over the phone.

"V. H. must have been Vernon Hall," he said.

"Yes, Vern and Jake were good friends."

"What happened after that? Who swore you to secrecy?"

"About two months later, I think it was early in June, a Colonel Patman or Patmore—I can't remember which—came to the house in Boulder and told me it was imperative that I never reveal any contact from Jake after the Little Angel mine affair."

"Did he give any reason?"

She shook her head. "No, he simply said it was in the interest of the government to remain silent, and then he handed me the check for ten thousand dollars and departed."

Seagram sagged in his chair as though a great weight had been lifted from his shoulders. It didn't seem possible that this little ninety-three-year-old woman should have the key to a lost billion-dollar ore cache, but she did.

Seagram looked at her and smiled. "That offer of lunch is beginning to sound awfully good about now."

She grinned back and he could see the mischief in her eyes. "As Jake would have said, to hell with lunch. Let's have a beer first."

16

The crimson rays of the sunset were still lingering on the western horizon when the first rumble of distant thunder signaled the approach of a lightning storm. The air was warm and the gentle offshore breeze felt good on Seagram's face as he sat on the terrace of the Balboa Bay Club and sipped his after-dinner cognac.

It was eight o'clock, the hour when the fashionable residents of Newport Beach began their evening socializing. Seagram had taken a dip in the club pool and then eaten early. He sat there listening to the grumbling of the nearing storm. The air became thick and charged with electricity, but there was no sign of rain or wind. In the photographic flash of the lightning he could see pleasure boats cruising up the bay, showing red and green navigation lights, their white paint giving them the appearance of silent gliding ghosts. Lightning stabbed the night air again, a jagged fork splitting the clouded sky. He watched it strike somewhere behind the Balboa Island rooftops, and in almost the same instant, the roar of the thunder thrust against his eardrums like a cannon barrage.

Everyone else had nervously moved inside the dining room, and Seagram soon found the terrace deserted. He stayed, enjoying mother nature's display of fireworks. He finished off the cognac and leaned back in his chair, watching for the next flash of lightning. It soon came and illuminated a figure standing beside his table. In that instant of light, he made out a tall man with black hair and rugged features staring down at him through cool, piercing eyes. Then the stranger blended into the darkness again.

As the thunder rumbled away, a seemingly disembodied voice asked, "Are you Gene Seagram?"

Seagram hesitated, waiting for his eyes to readjust themselves to the dark that followed the flash. "I am."

"I believe you've been looking for me."

"At the moment, you have the advantage."

"My apologies. I'm Dirk Pitt."

The skies lit up again and Seagram was relieved to see a smiling face. "It would seem, Mr. Pitt, that dramatic entrances are a habit with you. Did you also conjure up this electrical storm?"

Pitt's answering laugh came to the accompaniment of a clap of thunder.

"I haven't mastered that feat yet, but I am making progress at parting the Red Sea."

Seagram gestured to an empty chair. "Won't you sit down?"

"Thank you."

"I'd offer you a drink, but my waiter apparently has a fear of lightning."

"The worst of it is passing," Pitt said, looking skyward. The voice was quiet and controlled.

"How did you find me?" Seagram asked.

"A step-by-step process," Pitt replied. "I called your wife in Washington, and she said you were on a business trip to Leisure World. Since it's only a few miles from here, I checked with the guard at the gate. He told me he had admitted a Gene Seagram who was okayed for entry by a Mrs. Bertram Austin. She in turn mentioned she had recommended the Balboa Bay Club when you stated a desire to postpone your flight back to Washington and lay over until tomorrow. The rest was easy."

"I should feel flattered by your persistent style."

Pitt nodded. "All very elementary."

"A fortunate circumstance that we happened to be in the same neck of the woods," Seagram said.

"I always like to take a few days off and go surfing about this time of year. My parents have a house just across the bay. I could have contacted you sooner, but Admiral Sandecker said there was no hurry."

"You know the Admiral?"

"I work for him."

"Then you're with NUMA?"

"Yes, I'm the agency's special projects director."

"I thought your name sounded vaguely familiar. My wife has mentioned you."

"Dana?"

"Yes, have you worked with her?"

"Only once. I flew in supplies to Pitcairn Island last summer when she and her NUMA archaeological team were diving for artifacts from the *Bounty*."

Seagram looked at him. "So Admiral Sandecker told you there was no hurry to contact me."

Pitt smiled. "From what I gather, you rubbed him wrong with a middle-of-the-night phone call."

The black clouds had rolled seaward and the lightning was stabbing at Catalina across the channel.

"Now that you have me in your sights," Pitt said, "what can I do for you?"

"You can begin by telling me about Novaya Zemlya."

"Not much to tell," Pitt said casually. "I was in charge of the expedition to pick up your man. When he didn't show on schedule, I borrowed the ship's helicopter and made a reconnaissance flight toward the Russian island."

"You took a chance. Soviet radar might have picked you up on their scopes."

"I took that possibility into consideration. I stayed within ten feet of the water and kept my air speed down to fifteen knots. Even if I had been spotted, my radar blip would have read as a small fishing boat."

"What happened after you reached the island?"

"I cruised the shoreline until I found Koplin's sloop moored in a cove. I set the copter down on the beach nearby and began searching for him. It was then I heard shots through a wall of swirling snow that had been kicked up by a gust of wind."

"How was it possible to run onto Koplin and the Russian patrol guard? Finding them in the middle of a snowstorm is akin to stumbling on a needle in a frozen haystack."

"Needles don't bark," Pitt answered. "I followed the sound of a dog on the hunt. It led me to Koplin and the guard."

"The latter, of course, you murdered," Seagram said.

"I suppose a prosecuting attorney might suggest that." Pitt gestured airily. "On the other hand, it seemed the thing to do at the time."

"What if the guard had been one of my agents also?"

"Comrades-in-arms don't sadistically drag each other through the snow by the scruff of the neck, especially when one of them is seriously wounded."

"And the dog, did you have to kill the dog?"

"The thought occurred to me that left to his own devices, he might have led a search patrol back to his master's body. As it is, chances are neither will be discovered, ever."

"Do you always carry a gun with a silencer?"

"This wasn't the first time Admiral Sandecker called upon me for a dirty job outside my normal duties," Pitt said.

"Before you flew Koplin to your ship, I take it you destroyed his sloop," Seagram said.

"Rather cleverly, I think," Pitt replied. There was no inflection of conceit in his tone. "I bashed a hole in the hull, raised the sail, and sent her on her way. I should judge that she found a watery grave about three miles from shore."

"You were far too confident," Seagram said testily. "You dared to meddle in something that didn't concern you. You flaunted Russian vigilance by taking a grave risk without authority. And, you cold-bloodedly murdered a man and his animal. If we were all like you, Mr. Pitt, this would be a sorry nation indeed."

Pitt rose and leaned across the table until he was eyeball to eyeball with Seagram. "You don't do me justice," he said, his eyes cold as glaciers. "You left out the best parts. It was I who gave your friend Koplin two pints of blood during his operation. It was I who ordered the ship to bypass Oslo and lay a course for the nearest U.S. military airfield. And it was I who talked the base commander out of his private transport plane for Koplin's flight back to the States. In conclusion, Mr. Seagram, bloodthirsty, mad-dog Pitt pleads guilty . . . guilty of salvaging the broken pieces of your sneaky little spy mission in the Arctic. I didn't expect a ticker-tape parade down Broadway or a gold medal; a simple thank you would have done nicely. Instead, your mouth flows with a diarrheal discharge of rudeness and sarcasm. I don't know what your hang-up is, Seagram, but one thing comes through loud and clear. You are a Grade-A asshole. And, as kindly as I can put it, you can go fuck yourself."

With that, Pitt turned and walked into the shadows and was gone.

17

Professor Peter Barshov pushed a leathery hand through his graying hair and pointed the stem of his meerschaum pipe across the desk at Prevlov.

"No, no, let me assure you, Captain, that the man I sent to Novaya Zemlya is not subject to hallucinations."

"But a mine tunnel. . . ." Prevlov muttered incredulously. "An unknown, unrecorded mine tunnel on Russian soil? I wouldn't have thought it possible."

"But nonetheless a fact," Barshov replied. "Indications of it first appeared on our aerial contour photos. According to my geologist, who gained entrance, the tunnel was very old, perhaps between seventy and eighty years."

"Where did it come from?"

"Not where, Captain. The question is who. Who excavated it and why?"

"You say the Leongorod Institute of Geology has no record of it?" Prevlov asked.

Barshov shook his head. "Not a word. However, you might find a trace of it in the old Okhrana files."

"Okhrana . . . oh yes, the secret police of the czars." Prevlov paused a moment. "No, not likely. Their sole concern in those days was revolution. They wouldn't have bothered with a clandestine mining operation."

"Clandestine? You can't be sure of that."

Prevlov turned and gazed out the window. "Forgive me, Professor, but in my line of work, I attach Machiavellian motives to everything."

Barshov removed the pipe from between his stained teeth and tamped its bowl. "I have often read of ghost mines in the Western Hemisphere, but this is the first such mystery I've heard of in the Soviet Union. It is almost as if this quaint phenomenon was a gift of the Americans."

"Why do you say that?" Prevlov turned and faced Barshov again. "What have they got to do with it?"

"Perhaps nothing, perhaps everything. The equipment found inside the tunnel was manufactured in the United States."

"Hardly proof positive," Prevlov said skeptically. "The equipment could merely have been purchased from the Americans and used by other parties."

Barshov smiled. "A valid assumption, Captain, except for the fact that the body of a man was discovered in the tunnel. I have it on reliable authority that his epitaph was written in the American vernacular."

"Interesting," Prevlov said.

"I apologize for not providing you with more in-depth data," Barshov said. "My remarks, you understand, are purely secondhand. You will have a detailed report on your desk in the morning concerning our findings at Novaya Zemlya, and my people will be at your disposal for any further investigation."

"The Navy is grateful for your cooperation, Professor."

"The Leongorod Institute is always at the service of our country." Barshov rose and gave a stiff bow. "If that is all for now, Captain, I will get back to my office."

"There is one more thing, Professor."

"Yes?"

"You didn't mention whether your geologists found any trace of minerals?"

"Nothing of value."

"Nothing at all?"

"Trace elements of nickel and zinc, plus slight radioactive indications of uranium, thorium, and byzanium."

"I'm not familiar with the last two."

"Thorium can be converted into nuclear fuel when bombarded by neutrons," Barshov explained. "It's also used in the manufacture of different magnesium alloys."

"And byzanium?"

"Very little is known about it. None has ever been discovered in enough quantity to conduct constructive experiments." Barshov tapped his pipe in an ashtray. "The French are the only ones who have shown interest in it over the years."

Prevlov looked up. "The French?"

"They have spent millions of francs sending geological expeditions around the world looking for it. To my knowledge, none of them was successful."

"It would seem then that they know something our scientists do not."

Barshov shrugged. "We do not lead the world in every scientific endeavor, Captain. If we did, we, and not the Americans, would be driving autos over the moon's surface."

"Thank you again, Professor. I look forward to your final report."

18

Four blocks from the Naval Department building, Lieutenant Pavel Marganin relaxed on a park bench, casually reading a book of poems. It was noontime and the grassy areas were crowded with office workers eating their lunch beneath the evenly spaced rows of trees. Every so often he looked up and cast an appraising eye on the occasional pretty girl who wandered by.

At half past twelve, a fat man in a rumpled business suit sat down on the other end of the bench and began unwrapping a small roll of black bread and a cup of potato soup. He turned to Marganin and smiled broadly.

"Will you share a bit of bread, sailor?" the stranger said jovially. He patted his paunch. "I have more than enough for two. My wife always insists on feeding me too much and keeping me fat so the young girls won't chase after me."

Marganin shook his head no, and went back to his reading.

The man shrugged and seemed to bite off a piece of the bread. He began chewing vigorously, but it was an act; his mouth was empty.

"What have you got for me?" he murmured between jaw movements.

Marganin stared into his book, raising it slightly to cover his lips. "Prevlov is having an affair with a woman who has black hair, shortly cropped, wears expensive, size six low-heeled shoes, and is partial to Chartreuse liqueur. She drives an American embassy car, license number USA–one-four-six."

"Are you sure of your facts?"

"I don't create fiction," Marganin muttered while nonchalantly turning a page. "I suggest you act on my information immediately. It may be the wedge we have been looking for."

"I will have her identified before sunset." The stranger began slurping his soup noisily. Anything else?"

"I need data on the Sicilian Project."

"I never heard of it."

Marganin lowered the book and rubbed his eyes, keeping a hand in front of his lips. "It's a defense project connected somehow with the National Underwater and Marine Agency."

"They may prove fussy about leaks on defense projects."

"Tell them not to worry. It will be handled discreetly."

"Six days from now. The men's toilet of the Borodino Restaurant. Six-forty in the evening." Marganin closed his book and stretched.

The stranger slurped another spoonful of soup in acknowledgment and totally ignored Marganin, who rose and strolled off in the direction of the Soviet Naval Building.

19

The President's secretary smiled courteously and got up from behind his desk. He was tall and young, and had a friendly, eager face.

"Mrs. Seagram, of course. Please step this way."

He led Dana to the White House elevator and stood aside for her to enter. She put on a show of indifference, staring straight ahead. If he knew or suspected anything, he'd be mentally stripping her to the skin. She sneaked a quick glance at the secretary's face; his eyes remained inscrutably locked on the blinking floor lights.

The doors opened and she followed him down the hall and into one of the third-floor bedrooms.

"There it is on the mantel," the secretary said. "We found it in the basement in an unmarked crate. A beautiful piece of work. The President insisted we bring it up where it can be admired."

Dana's eyes narrowed as she found herself looking at the model of a sailing ship that rested in a glass case above the fireplace.

"He was hoping you might be able to shed some light on its history," the secretary continued. "As you can see, there is no indication of a name either on the hull or the dust case."

She moved uncertainly toward the fireplace for a closer look. She was confused; this was hardly what she had expected. Over the telephone earlier that morning, the secretary had simply said, "The President wonders if it would be convenient for you to drop by the White House about two o'clock?" A strange sensation passed through her body. She wasn't sure if it was a feeling of letdown or relief.

"Early-eighteenth-century merchantman by the look of her," she said. "I'd have to make some sketches and compare them with old records in the Naval Archives."

"Admiral Sandecker said if anybody could identify her, you could."

"Admiral Sandecker?"

"Yes, it was he who recommended you to the President." The secretary moved toward the doorway. "There is a pad and pencil on the nightstand beside the bed. I have to get back to my desk. Please feel free to take as much time as you need."

"But won't the President? . . ."

"He's playing golf this afternoon. You won't be bothered. Just take the elevator down to the main floor when you're finished." Then, before Dana could reply, the secretary turned and left.

Dana sat heavily on the bed and sighed. She had rushed home after the phone call, taken a perfumed bath, and carefully donned a girlish, virginal white dress over black lingerie. And it had all been for nothing. The President didn't want sex; he simply wanted her to put the make on some damned old ship's model.

Utterly defeated, she went into the bathroom and checked her face. When she came out, the bedroom door was closed and the President was standing by the fireplace, looking tanned and youthful in a polo shirt and slacks.

Dana's eyes flew wide. For a moment she couldn't think of anything to say. "You're supposed to be golfing," she finally said stupidly.

"That's what it says in my appointment book."

"Then this model ship business . . ."

"The brig *Roanoke* out of Virginia," he said, nodding at the model. "Her keel was laid in 1728, and she went on the rocks off Nova Scotia in 1743. My father built the model from scratch about forty years ago."

"You went to all this trouble just to get me alone?" she said dazedly.

"That's obvious, isn't it?"

She stared at him. He met her eyes steadily and she blushed.

"You see," he went on, "I wanted to have a little informal chat, just the two of us, without interference or interruption from the hassles of my office."

The room reeled about her. "You . . . you just want to talk?"

He looked at her curiously for a moment and then he began to chuckle. "You flatter me, Mrs. Seagram. It was never my intent to seduce you. I fear my reputation as a ladies' man is somewhat exaggerated."

"But at the party—"

"I think I understand." He took her by the hand and led her to a chair. "When I whispered, 'I must meet you alone,' you took it as a proposition from a lecherous old man. Forgive me, that was not my intent."

Dana sighed. "I wondered what a man who could have any one of a hundred million women just by snapping his fingers could possibly see in a drab, married, thirty-one-year-old marine archaeologist."

"You don't do yourself justice," he said, suddenly serious. "You are really quite lovely."

Again she found herself blushing. "No man has made a pass at me in years."

"Perhaps it is because most honorable men do not make passes at married women."

"I'd like to think so."

He pulled up a chair and sat opposite her. She sat primly, her knees pressed together, hands in lap. The question, when it came, caught her totally unprepared.

"Tell me, Mrs. Seagram, are you still in love with him?"

She stared at him, incomprehension written in her eyes. "Who?"

"Your husband, of course."

"Gene?"

"Yes, Gene," he said, smiling. "Unless you have another spouse hidden away somewhere."

"Why must you ask that?" she said.

"Gene is cracking at the seams."

Dana looked puzzled. "He works hard, but I can't believe he is on the verge of a mental breakdown."

"Not in the strict clinical sense, no." The President's expression was grim. "He is, however, under enormous pressure. If he is faced with serious marital problems on top of his workload, he might fall over the brink. I cannot allow that to happen, not yet, not until he completes a highly secret project that is vital to the nation."

"It's that very damned secret project that's come between us," she burst out angrily.

"That and a few other problems—such as your refusal to bear children."

She looked at him thunderstruck. "How could you possibly know all this?"

"The usual methods. It makes no difference how. What matters is that you stick with Gene for the next sixteen months and give him all the tender loving care you can find in your soul to give."

Nervously, she folded and unfolded her hands. "It's that important?" she asked in a faint voice.

"It's that important," he said. "Will you help me?"

She nodded silently.

"Good." He patted her hands. "Between us, maybe we can keep Gene on the track."

"I'll try, Mr. President. If it means so much, I'll try. I can promise no more."

"I have complete confidence in you."

"But I draw the line at having a baby," she said defiantly.

He grinned the famous grin so often captured by photographers. "I can order a war, and I can order men to die, but not even the President of the United States has the power to order a woman to become pregnant."

For the first time, she laughed. It seemed so strange, talking intimately with a man who wielded such incredible power. Power was indeed an aphrodisiac and she began to feel the bitter disappointment of not being taken to bed.

The President rose and took her arm. "I must go now. I have a meeting with my economic advisers in a few minutes." He began guiding her toward the door. Then he stopped and drew her face to his and she felt the firmness of his lips. When he let her go, he looked into her eyes and said, "You are a very desirable woman, Mrs. Seagram. Don't you forget that."

He escorted her to the elevator.

20

Dana was waiting on the concourse when Seagram departed his plane.

"What gives?" He eyed her questioningly. "You haven't met me at the airport in ages."

"An overwhelming impulse of affection." She smiled.

He claimed his luggage and they walked to the parking lot. She held his arm tightly. The afternoon seemed a faraway dream now. She had to keep reminding herself that another man had found her alluring and had actually kissed her.

She took the wheel and drove onto the highway. The last of the rush-hour traffic had faded away, and she made good time through the Virginia countryside.

"Do you know Dirk Pitt?" he asked, breaking the silence.

"Yes, he's Admiral Sandecker's special projects director. Why?"

"I'm going to burn the bastard's ass," he said.

She glanced at him in astonishment. "What's your connection with him?"

"He screwed up an important part of the project."

Her hands tightened on the wheel. "You'll find him a tough ass to burn," she said.

"Why do you say that?"

"He's considered a legend around NUMA. His list of achievements since he joined the agency is second only to his outstanding war record."

"So?"

"So, he's Admiral Sandecker's fair-haired boy."

"You forget, I carry more weight with the President than Admiral Sandecker."

"More weight than Senator George Pitt of California?" she said flatly.

He turned and looked at her. "They're related?"

"Father and son."

He slouched in a morose silence for the next several miles.

Dana put her right hand on his knee. When she stopped at a red light, she leaned over and kissed him.

"What was that for?"

"That's a bribe."

"How much is it going to cost me?" he grumbled.

"I have this great idea," she announced. "Why don't we take in that new Brando film, and afterward we can have a scrumptious lobster dinner at the Old Potomac Inn, then go home, turn out the lights and—"

"Take me to the office," he said. "I have work to do."

"Please, Gene, don't push yourself," she pleaded. "There's time for your work tomorrow."

"No, now!" he said.

The chasm between them was uncrossable, and from now on, things would never be the same again.

21

Seagram looked down at the metal attaché case on his desk, then up at the colonel and the captain who were standing across from him. "There's no mistake on this?"

The colonel shook his head. "Researched and verified by the Director of Defense Archives, sir."

"That was fast work. Thank you."

The colonel made no attempt to leave. "Sorry, sir, I am to wait and return to the Department of Defense with the file on my person."

"By whose orders?"

"The Secretary," the colonel answered. "Defense Department policy dictates that all material classified as Code Five Confidential must be kept under surveillance at all times."

"I understand," Seagram said. "May I study the file alone?"

"Yes, sir. My aide and I will wait outside, but I must respectfully request that no one be allowed to enter or leave your office while the file is in your possession."

Seagram nodded. "All right, gentlemen, make yourselves comfortable. My secretary will be at your service for coffee and refreshments."

"Thank you for your courtesy, Mr. Seagram."

"And, one more thing," Seagram said, and smiled faintly. "I have my own private bathroom, so don't expect to see me for a while."

Seagram sat motionless for several moments after the door closed. The final vindication of five years work lay before his eyes. Or did it? Maybe the documents within the case would only lead to another mystery, or, worse yet, a dead end. He inserted the key into the case and opened it. Inside there were four folders and a small notebook. The labels on the folders read:

CD5C	7665	1911	Report on the scientific and monetary value of the rare element byzanium.
CD5C	7687	1911	Correspondence between Secretary of War and Joshua Hays Brewster examining the possible acquirement of byzanium.

| CD5C | 7720 | 1911 | Memorandum by Secretary of War to the President regarding funds for Secret Army Plan 371-990-R85. |
| CD5C | 8039 | 1912 | Report of closed investigation into the circumstances surrounding the disappearance of Joshua Hays Brewster. |

The notebook was simply entitled: "Journal of Joshua Hays Brewster."

Logic dictated that Seagram study the folders first, but logic was set aside as he settled back in his chair and opened the journal.

Four hours later, he stacked the book neatly on top of the folders and pushed a button on the side of his intercom. Almost immediately a recessed panel in a side wall swung open and a man in a white technician's coat entered.

"How soon can you copy all this?"

The technician thumbed through the book and peeked in the folders. "Give me forty-five minutes."

Seagram nodded. "Okay, get right on it. There's someone in my outer office who's waiting for the originals."

After the panel closed, Seagram pushed himself wearily from his chair and staggered into the bathroom. He closed the door and leaned against it, his face twisted in a grotesque mask.

"Oh God, no," he moaned. "It's not fair, it's not fair."

Then he leaned over the sink and vomited.

22

The President shook hands with Seagram and Donner in the doorway of his study at Camp David.

"Sorry to ask you up here at seven in the morning, but it's the only time I could squeeze you in."

"No problem, Mr. President," said Donner. "I'm usually out jogging about this time anyway."

The President stared at Donner's rotund frame with amused eyes. "Who knows? I may have saved you from a coronary." He laughed at Donner's woeful expression and motioned them into the study. "Come, come, sit down and make yourselves at home. I've ordered a light breakfast."

They grouped themselves about on a sofa and chair in front of a spacious picture window overlooking the Maryland hills. Coffee came with a tray of sweet rolls and the President passed them around.

"Well, Gene, I hope the news is good for a change. The Sicilian Project is our only hope of stopping this crazy arms race with the Russians and Chinese." The President rubbed his eyes wearily. "It has to be the greatest display of stupidity since the dawn of man, particularly when you consider the tragic and absurd fact that we can each blow the other's country to ashes at least five times over." He gestured helplessly. "So much for the sad facts of life. Suppose you tell me where we stand."

Seagram looked bleary-eyed across the coffee table, holding the copy of the Defense Archive file. "You are, of course, Mr. President, aware of our progress to date."

"Yes, I've studied the reports of your investigation."

Seagram handed the President a copy of Brewster's journal. "I think you'll find this an absorbing account of early-twentieth-century intrigue and human suffering. The first entry is dated July 8, 1910, and opens with Joshua Hays Brewster's departure from the Taimyr mountains near the north coast of Siberia. There, he spent nine months opening a lead mine under contract with his employer, the Société des Mines de Lorraine, for the czar of Russia. He then goes on to tell how his ship, a small coastal steamer bound for Archangel, became lost in fog and ran aground on the upper island of Novaya Zemlya. Fortunately, the ship held together and the survivors managed to exist within its freezing steel hull until they were rescued by a Russian naval frigate nearly a month later. It was during this sojourn that Brewster spent his time prospecting the island. Sometime during the eighteenth day, he stumbled on an outcropping of strange rock on the slopes of Bednaya Mountain. He had never seen that type of composition before, so he took several samples back with him to the United States, finally reaching New York sixty-two days after he left the Taimyr Mine."

"So now we know how the byzanium was discovered," the President said.

Seagram nodded and continued. Brewster turned all his samples over to employer save one; that he kept purely as a souvenir. Some months later, having heard nothing, he asked the United States director of the Société des Mines de Lorraine what had become of his Bednaya Mountain ore samples. He was told they had assayed out as worthless and had been thrown away. Suspicious, Brewster took the remaining sample to the Bureau of Mines in Washington for analysis. He was astounded when he learned it was byzanium, hitherto a virtually unknown element, seen only rarely through a high-powered microscope."

"Had Brewster informed the Société as to the location of the byzanium outcropping?" the President asked.

"No, he played it shrewd and merely gave them vague directions to the site. In fact, he even suggested that it lay on the lower island of Novaya Zemlya, many miles to the south."

"Why the subterfuge?"

"A common tactic among prospectors," Donner answered. "By withholding the exact location of a promising find, the discoverer can negotiate a higher percentage of the profits against the day the mine becomes operational."

"Makes sense," the President murmured. "But what incited the French to secrecy back in 1910? What could they possibly have seen in byzanium that no one else saw for the next seventy years?"

"Its similarity to radium, for one thing," Seagram said. "The Société des Mines passed Brewster's samples on to the Radium Institute in Paris, where their scientists found that certain properties of byzanium and radium were identical."

"And since it cost fifty thousand dollars to process one gram of radium," Donner added, "the French government suddenly saw a chance to corner the world's only known supply of a fantastically expensive element. Given enough time, they could have realized hundreds of millions of dollars on a few pounds of byzanium."

The President shook his head in disbelief. "My God, if I remember my weights and measures correctly, there are about twenty-eight grams to the ounce."

"That's right, sir. One ounce of byzanium was worth one million four hundred thousand dollars. And that's at 1910 prices."

The President slowly stood up and gazed out the window. "What was Brewster's next move?"

"He turned over his information to the War Department." Seagram pulled out the folder on the funds for Secret Army Plan 371-990-R85 and opened it. "If they knew the full story, the boys over at CIA would be proud of their ancestor organization. Once the generals of the old Army Intelligence Bureau saw what Brewster was onto, they dreamed up the grandest double-cross of the century. Brewster was ordered to inform the Société des Mines that he had identified the ore samples and bluff them into thinking he was going to form a mining syndicate and go after the byzanium on his own. He had the Frenchies by the balls, and they knew it. By this time, they'd figured that his directions to the outcropping were off the mark. No Brewster, no byzanium. It was that simple. They had no choice but to sign him on as chief engineer for a piece of the profits."

"Why couldn't our own government have backed a mining operation?" the President asked. "Why let the French into the picture?"

"Two reasons," Seagram replied. "First, since the byzanium was on foreign soil, the mine would have to be operated in secret. If the miners were caught by the Russians, the French government would get the blame, not the Americans. Second, the Congress in those days penny-pinched the Army to death. There were simply not enough funds to include a mining venture in the Arctic, regardless of the potential profit."

"It would seem the French were playing against a stacked deck."

"It was a two-way street, Mr. President. There was no doubt in Brewster's mind that once he opened the Bednaya Mountain Mine and began shipping the ore, he and his crew of men would be murdered by paid assassins of the Société des Mines de Lorraine. That was obvious from the Société's fanatical insistence on secrecy. And one other little matter. It was the French and not Brewster who masterminded the Little Angel Mine tragedy."

"You have to give them credit for playing a good game," said Donner. "The Little Angel hoax was the perfect cover for eventually killing off Brewster and his entire crew. After all, how could anyone be accused of murdering nine men in the Arctic when it was a matter of public record that they had all died six months earlier in a Colorado mining accident?"

Seagram continued, "We're reasonably certain that the Société des Mines spirited our heroes to New York in a private railroad car. From there, they probably took passage on a French ship under assumed names."

"One question I wish you'd clear up," the President said. "In reading over your report, Donner here stated that the mining equipment found at Novaya Zemlya was ordered through the U.S. government. That piece doesn't fit."

"Again, a cover story by the French," Seagram replied. "The Jensen and Thor files also showed that the drilling equipment was paid for by a check drawn on a Washington, D.C., bank. The account, as it turns out, was under the name of the French ambassador. It was simply one more ruse to cloud the true operation."

"They didn't miss a trick, did they?"

Seagram nodded. "They planned well, but, for all their insight, they had no idea they were being led down the garden path."

"After Paris, then what?" the President persisted.

"The Coloradans spent two weeks at the Société office, ordering supplies and making final preparations for the dig. When at last all was in readiness, they boarded a French naval transport in Le Havre and slipped into the English Channel. It took twelve days for the ship to pick its way through the Barents Sea ice floes before it finally anchored off Novaya Zemlya. After the men and equipment were safely ashore, Brewster shifted the Secret Army Plan into first gear and ordered the captain of the supply ship not to return for the ore until the first week in June, nearly seven months away."

"The plan being that the Coloradans and the byzanium would be long gone by the time the Société des Mines ship returned."

"Exactly. They beat the deadline by two months. It took only five months for the gang to pry the precious element from the bowels of that icy hell. It was body-breaking work, drilling, blasting, and digging through solid granite while stabbed by fifty-degree-below-zero temperatures. Never, during the long winter months high along the Continental Divide of the Rockies, had they ever experienced anything like the frigid winds that howled down across the sea from the great polar ice cap to the north; winds that paused only long enough to deposit the terrible cold and replenish Bednaya Mountain's permanent ice sheet before sweeping on toward the Russian coast just over the horizon to the south. It took a frightful toll on the men. Jake Hobart died from exposure when he became lost in a snowstorm, and the others all suffered terribly from fatigue and frostbite. In Brewster's own words, 'it was a frozen purgatory, not fit to waste good spit on.' "

"It's a miracle they didn't all die," the President said.

"Good old hardy guts saw them through," Seagram said. "In the end they beat the odds. They had wrested the world's rarest mineral from that wasteland, and they had pulled off the job without detection. It had been a classic operation of stealth and engineering skill."

"They escaped the island with the ore, then?"

"Yes, Mr. President." Seagram nodded. "Brewster and his crew covered over the waste dump and ore-car tracks and concealed the entrance to the mine. Then they hauled the byzanium to the beach, where they loaded it on board a small three-masted steamer dispatched by the War Department under the guise of a polar expedition. The ship was under the command of a Lieutenant Pratt of the United States Navy."

"How much ore did they take?"

"According to Sid Koplin's estimates, about half a ton of extremely high-grade ore."

"And when processed . . . ?"

"A rough guess at best would put it in the neighborhood of five hundred ounces."

"More than enough to complete the Sicilian Project," the President said.

"More than enough," Donner acknowledged.

"Did they make it back to the States?"

"No, sir. Somehow the French had figured the game and were patiently waiting for the Americans to do the dangerous dirty work before stepping on the stage and snatching the prize. A few miles off the southern coast of Norway, before Lieutenant Pratt could set a course east onto the shipping lane for New York, they were attacked by a mysterious steam cutter that bore no national flag."

"No identification, no international scandal," the President said. "The French covered every avenue."

Seagram smiled. "Except this time, if you'll pardon the pun, they missed the boat. Like most Europeans, they underestimated good old Yankee ingenuity; our War Department had also covered every contingency. Before the French could pump a third shot into the American ship, Lieutenant Pratt's crew had dropped the sides on a phony deckhouse and were blasting back with a concealed five-inch gun."

"Good, good," the President said. "As Teddy Roosevelt might have said, 'Bully for our side.' "

"The battle lasted until almost dark," Seagram went on. "Then Pratt got a shot into the Frenchman's boiler and the cutter burst into flames. But the American vessel was hurt, too. Her holds were taking water, and Pratt had one killed and four of his crew seriously wounded. After a consultation, Brewster and Pratt decided to head for the nearest friendly port, set the injured men ashore, and ship the ore on to the States from there. By dawn, they limped past the breakwater at Aberdeen, Scotland."

"Why couldn't they have simply transported the ore to an American warship? Surely that would have been safer than shipping it by commercial means?"

"I can't be certain," Seagram replied. "Apparently, Brewster was afraid the French might then demand the ore through diplomatic channels, thereby forcing the Americans into admitting the theft and giving up the byzanium. As long as he kept it in his possession, our government could claim ignorance of the whole affair."

The President shook his head. "Brewster must have been a lion of a man."

"Oddly enough," Donner said, "he was only five-feet-two."

"Still, an amazing man, a great patriot to go through all that hell with no personal profit motive in mind. You can't help but wish to God he'd made it home free."

"Sadly, his odyssey wasn't finished." Seagram's hands began to tremble. "The French consulate in the port city blew the whistle on the Coloradans. One night, before they could unload the byzanium onto a truck, the French agents struck without warning from the shadows of the landing dock. No shots were fired. It was fists and knives and clubs. The hard-rock men from the legendary towns of Cripple Creek, Leadville, and Fairplay were no strangers to violence. They gave better than they took, tossing six bodies into the black waters of the harbor before the rest of their assailants melted into the night. But it was only the beginning. Crossroad after crossroad, from one village to the next, on city streets, and from behind every tree and doorway it seemed, the piratical attacks continued until the running flight across Britain had bloodied the landscape with a score of dead and wounded. The battles took on the aspects of a war of attrition; the men from Colorado were up against a massive organization which threw in five men for every two the miners eliminated. The attrition began to tell. John Caldwell, Alvin Coulter, and Thomas Price died outside of Glasgow. Charles Widney fell at Newcastle, Walter Schmidt near Stafford, and Warner O'Deming at Birmingham. One by one, the tough old miners were whittled away, their gore staining the cobblestone streets far from home. Only Vernon Hall and Joshua Hays Brewster lived to set the ore on the Ocean Dock at Southampton."

The President clenched his lips and tightened his fists. "Then the French won out."

"No, Mr. President. The French never touched the byzanium." Seagram picked up Brewster's journal and thumbed to the back. "I'll read the last entry. It's dated April 10, 1912:

'The deed is only a eulogy now, for I am but dead. Praise God, the precious ore we labored so desperately to rape from the bowels of that cursed mountain lies safely in the vault of the ship. Only Vernon will be left to tell the tale, for I depart on the great White Star steamer for New York within the hour. Knowing the ore is secure. I leave this journal in the care of James Rodgers, Assistant United States Consul in Southampton, who will see that it reaches the proper authorities in the event I am also killed. God rest the men who have gone before me. How I long to return to Southby.' "

A cold silence fell on the study. The President turned from the window and settled in his chair once more. He sat there a moment, saying nothing. Then he spoke: "Can it mean the byzanium is in the United States? Is it possible that Brewster? . . ."

"I'm afraid not, sir," Seagram murmured, his face pale and beaded with sweat.

"Explain yourself!" the President demanded.

Seagram took a deep breath. "Because, Mr. President, the only White Star steamship that departed Southampton, England, on April the tenth, 1912, was the R.M.S. *Titanic.*"

"The *Titanic!*" The President looked as if he had been shot. The truth had suddenly hit him. "It fits," he said tonelessly. "It would explain why the byzanium has been lost all these years."

"Fate dealt the Coloradans a cruel hand," Donner muttered. "They bled and died only to send the ore on a ship that was destined to sink in the middle of the ocean."

Another silence, deeper even than the one that had gone before.

The President sat granite-faced. "What do we do now, gentlemen?"

There was a pause of perhaps ten seconds, then Seagram rose unsteadily to his feet and stared down at the President. The strain of the past days, plus the agony of defeat, swept over him. There was no other door open to them; they had no choice but to see it through to the finish. He cleared his throat. "We raise the *Titanic,*" he mumbled.

The President and Donner looked up.

"Yes, by God!" Seagram said, his voice suddenly hard and determined. "We raise the *Titanic!*"

3

The Black Abyss

23

The forbidding beauty of pure, absolute black pressed against the view-port and blotted out all touch with earthly reality. The total absence of light, Albert Giordino judged, took only a few minutes to shift the human mind into a state of confused disorder. He had the impression of falling from a vast height with his eyes closed on a moonless night; falling through an immense black void without the tiniest fragment of sensation.

Finally, a bead of sweat trickled over his brow and dropped into his left eye, stinging it. He shook off the spell, wiped a sleeve across his face, and gently eased a hand over the control panel immediately in front of him, touching the various and familiar protrusions until his probing fingers reached their goal. Then he flicked the switch upward.

The lights attached to the hull of the deep-sea submersible flashed on and cut a brilliant swath through the eternal night. Although the narrow sides of the beam abruptly turned a blackish-blue, the tiny organisms floating past the direct glare reflected the light for several feet above and below the area around the viewport. Turning his face so as not to fog the thick Plexiglas, Giordino expelled a heavy sigh and then leaned back against the soft padding of the pilot's chair. It was nearly a full minute before he bent over the control console and began bringing the silent craft to life again. He studied the rows of dials until the wavering needles were calibrated to his satisfaction, and he scanned the circuit lights, making certain they all blinked out their green message of safe operation before he re-engaged the electrical systems of the *Sappho I*.

The *Sappho I*. He swung the chair and gazed idly down the center passageway toward the stern. It might have been the newest and largest research submersible in the world to the National Underwater and Marine Agency, but, to Al Giordino, the first time he set eyes on it, the general design looked like a giant cigar on an ice skate.

The *Sappho I* wasn't built to compete with military submarines. She was functional. Scientific survey of the ocean bottom was her game, and her every square inch was utilized to accommodate a seven-man crew and two tons of oceanographic research instruments and equipment. The *Sappho I* would never fire a missile or cut through the sea at seventy knots, but then she could operate where no other submarine had ever dared to go: 24,000 feet below the ocean's surface. Yet Giordino was never totally at ease. He checked the depth gauge, wincing at the reading of almost 12,500 feet. The pressure of the sea increases at the rate of fifteen pounds per square inch for every thirty feet. He winced again when his mental gymnastics gave him an approximate answer of nearly 6200 pounds per square inch, the pressure which at that moment was pushing against the red paint on the *Sappho I*'s thick titanium skin.

"How about a cup of fresh sediment?"

Giordino looked up into the unsmiling face of Omar Woodson, the photographer on the mission. Woodson was carrying a steaming mug of coffee.

"The chief valve- and switch-pusher should have had his brew exactly five minutes ago," said Giordino.

"Sorry. Some idiot turned out the lights." Woodson handed him the mug. "Everything check out?"

"Okay across the board," Giordino answered. "I gave the aft battery section a rest. We'll juice off the center section for the next eighteen hours."

"Lucky we didn't drift into a rock outcropping when we shut down."

"Surely you jest." Giordino slid down in his seat, squinted his eyes and yawned with effortless finesse. "Sonar hasn't picked out anything larger than a baseball-size rock in the last six hours. The bottom here is as flat as my girl friend's stomach."

"You mean chest," Woodson said. "I've seen her picture." Woodson was smiling, which was rare for him.

"Nobody's perfect," Giordino conceded. "However, considering the fact her father is a wealthy liquor distributor, I can overlook her bad points—"

He broke off as Rudi Gunn, the commander of the mission, leaned into the pilot's compartment. He was short and thin, and his wide eyes, magnified by a pair of horn-rimmed glasses, peered intently over a large Roman nose, giving him the look of an undernourished owl about to strike. Yet his appearance was deceiving. Rudi Gunn was warm and kind. Every man who ever served under his command respected him enormously.

"You two at it again?" Gunn smiled tolerantly.

Woodson looked solemn. "The same old problem. He's getting horny for his girl again."

"After fifty-one days on this drifting closet, even his grandmother would forgive the gleam in his eye." Gunn leaned over Giordino and gazed through the viewport. For a few seconds only a dim blue filled his eyes, then gradually, just below the *Sappho I,* he could make out the reddish ooze of the top layer of bottom sediment. For a brief moment a bright red shrimp, barely over an inch long, floated across the beam of the light before it vanished into the darkness.

"Damned shame we can't get out and walk around," Gunn said as he stepped back. "No telling what we might find out there."

"Same thing you'd find in the middle of the Mojave Desert," Giordino grunted. "Absolutely zilch." He reached up and tapped a gauge. "Colder temperature though. I read a rousing thirty-four-point-eight degrees Fahrenheit."

"A great place to visit," Woodson said, "but you wouldn't want to spend your golden years there."

"Anything show on sonar?" Gunn asked.

Giordino nodded at a large green screen in the middle of the panel. The reflected pattern of the terrain was flat. "Nothing ahead or to the sides. The profile hasn't wavered for several hours."

Gunn wearily removed his glasses and rubbed his eyes. "Okay, gentlemen, our mission is as good as ended. We'll give it another ten hours, then we surface." Almost as a reflex action, he looked up at the overhead panel. "Is Mother still with us?"

Giordino nodded. "Mother is hanging in there."

He needed only to glance at the fluctuating needle on the transducer instrument to know that the mother ship, a surface support tender, was continuously tracking the *Sappho I* on sonar.

"Make contact," Gunn said, "and signal Mother that we'll begin our ascent at oh-nine hundred hours. That should leave them plenty of time to load us aboard and take the *Sappho I* in tow before sunset."

"I've almost forgotten what a sunset looks like," Woodson murmured. "It's off to the beach to recapture a suntan and ogle all those gorgeous bikini-clad honeys for Papa Woodson. No more of these deep-sea funny farms for me."

"Thank God, the end is in sight," Giordino said. "Another week cooped up in this overgrown wiener and I'll start talking to the potted plants."

Woodson looked at him. "We don't have any potted plants."

"You get the picture."

Gunn smiled. "Everybody deserves a good rest. You men have put on a fine show. The data we've compiled should keep the lab boys busy for a long time."

Giordino turned to Gunn, gave him a long look, and spoke slowly: "This has been one hell of a weird mission, Rudi."

"I don't get your meaning," Gunn said.

"A poorly cast drama is what I mean. Take a good look at your crew." He gestured to the four men working in the aft section of the submersible—Ben Drummer, a lanky Southerner with a deep Alabama drawl; Rick Spencer, a short, blond-haired Californian who whistled constantly through clenched teeth; Sam Merker, as cosmopolitan and citified as a Wall Street broker, and Henry Munk, a quiet, droopy-eyed wit who clearly wished he were anywhere but on the *Sappho I*. "Those clowns aft, you, Woodson, and myself; we're all engineers, nuts-and-bolts mechanics. There isn't a Ph.D. in the lot."

"The first men on the moon weren't intellectuals, either," Gunn countered. "It takes the nuts-and-bolts mechanics to perfect the equipment. You guys have proven the *Sappho I*; you've demonstrated her capabilities. Let the next ride go to the oceanographers. As for us, this mission will go down in the books as a great scientific achievement."

"I am not," Giordino declared pontifically, "cut out to be a hero."

"Neither am I, pal," Woodson added. "But you've got to admit it beats hell out of selling life insurance."

"The drama of it all escapes him," Gunn said. "Think of the stories you can tell your girl friends. Think of the enraptured looks on their pretty faces when you tell them how you unerringly piloted the greatest undersea probe of the century."

"Unerringly?" Giordino said. "Then suppose you tell me why I'm running this scientific marvel around in circles five hundred miles off our scheduled course?"

Gunn shrugged. "Orders."

Giordino stared at him. "We're supposed to be under the Labrador Sea. Instead, Admiral Sandecker changes our course at the last minute and makes us chase all over the abyssal plains below the Grand Banks of Newfoundland. It doesn't make sense."

Gunn smiled a sphinxlike smile. For several moments none of the men spoke, but Gunn didn't require a concentrated dose of ESP to know the questions that were running through their minds. They were, he was certain, thinking what he was thinking. Like himself, they were three months back in time and two thousand miles in distance at the headquarters of the National Underwater and Marine Agency in Washington, D.C., where Admiral James Sandecker, chief director of the agency, was describing the most incredible undersea operation of the decade.

"God damn," Admiral Sandecker had thundered. "I'd give up a year's salary if I could join you men."

A figure of speech, Giordino reflected. Next to Sandecker, Ebenezer Scrooge spent money like a drunken sailor. Giordino relaxed in a deep leather sofa and tuned into the admiral's briefing, while idly blowing smoke rings between puffs on a giant cigar, lifted from a box on Sandecker's immense desk when everyone's attention was focused on a wall map of the Atlantic Ocean.

"Well, there she is." Sandecker rapped the pointer loudly on the map for the second time. "The Lorelei Current. She's born off the western tip of Africa, follows the mid-Atlantic ridge north, then curves easterly between Baffin Island and Greenland, and then dies in the Labrador Sea."

Giordino said: "I don't hold a degree in oceanography, Admiral, but it would seem that the Lorelei converges with the Gulf Stream."

"Not hardly. The Gulf Stream is surface water. The Lorelei is the coldest, heaviest water in the world's oceans, averaging fourteen thousand feet in depth."

"Then the Lorelei crosses under the Gulf Stream," Spencer said softly. It was the first time in the briefing he had spoken.

"That seems reasonable." Sandecker paused, smiled benevolently, then continued: "The ocean is basically made up of two layers—a surface or upper layer, heated by the sun and thoroughly churned by winds, and a cold, very dense layer consisting of intermediate, deep and bottom water. And the two never mix."

"Sounds very dull and forbidding," Munk said. "The mere fact that some character with a black sense of humor named the current after a Rhine nymph who lured sailors onto the rocks makes it the last place I'd want to visit."

A grim smile crawled slowly over Sandecker's griffin face. "Get used to the name, gentlemen, because deep in the Lorelei's gut is where we're going to spend fifty days. Where *you're* going to spend fifty days."

"Doing what?" Woodson asked defiantly.

"The Lorelei Current Drift Expedition is exactly what it sounds like. You men will descend in a deep-water submersible five hundred miles northwest of the coast of Dakar and begin a submerged cruise in the current. Your main job will be to monitor and test the sub and its equipment. If there are no malfunctions that would necessitate cutting short the mission, you should surface around the middle of September in the approximate center of the Labrador Sea."

Merker cleared his throat softly. "No submersible has stayed that long that deep."

"You want to back out, Sam?"

"Well . . . no."

"This is a volunteer expedition. Nobody is twisting your arm to go."

"Why us, Admiral?" Ben Drummer uncoiled his lean frame from the floor where he had been comfortably stretched. "Ah'm a marine engineer. Spencer here is an equipment engineer. And Merker is a systems expert. Ah can't see where we fit in."

"You're all professionals in your respective capacities. Woodson is also a photographer. The *Sappho I* will be carrying a number of photographic systems. Munk is the best instrument-component man in the agency. And, you'll all be under the command of Rudi Gunn, who has captained, at one time or another, every research ship in NUMA."

"That leaves me," Giordino said.

Sandecker glared at the cigar jutting from Giordino's mouth, recognized it as one from his private brand, and gave him a withering look that was completely ignored. "As assistant projects director for the agency, you'll be in over-all charge of the mission. You can also make yourself useful by piloting the craft."

Giordino smiled devilishly and stared back. "My pilot's license authorizes me to fly airplanes not submarines."

The admiral stiffened ever so slightly. "You'll just have to trust my judgment, won't you?" Sandecker said coldly. "Besides, what matters most is that you're the best crew I've got on hand at the moment. You all worked together on the Beaufort Sea Expedition. You are men with heavy experience and records of ability and ingenuity. You can operate every instrument, every piece of oceanographic equipment yet invented —we'll let the scientists analyze the data you bring back—and, as I mentioned, naturally you're all volunteers."

"Naturally," Giordino echoed, his face deadpan.

Sandecker went back behind his desk. "You will assemble and begin procedure training at our Key West port facility the day after tomorrow. The Pelholme Aircraft Company has already run extensive diving tests on the submersible, so you need only concern yourselves with familiarization of the equipment and instruction on the experiments you'll conduct during the expedition."

Spencer whistled through his teeth. "An aircraft company? Holy God, what do they know about designing a deep-sea submersible?"

"For your peace of mind," Sandecker said patiently, "Pelholme turned its aerospace technology toward the sea ten years ago. Since then, they've constructed four underwater environmental laboratories and two extremely successful submersibles for the Navy."

"They'd best have built this one good," Merker said. "I'd be most distressed to find that it leaked at fourteen thousand feet."

"Scared shitless, you mean," Giordino mumbled.

Munk rubbed his eyes, then stared at the floor, as though he saw the bottom of the sea in the carpet. When he spoke, his words came very slowly: "Is this trip really necessary, Admiral?"

Sandecker nodded solemnly. "It is. Oceanographers need a picture of the structure of the Lorelei's flow pattern to improve their knowledge of deep-ocean circulation. Believe me, this mission is as important as the first manned orbit around the earth. Besides testing the world's most advanced submersible, you'll be visually recording and mapping an area never before seen by man. Forget your doubts. The *Sappho I* has every safety feature built into her hull that science can devise. You have my personal guarantee of a safe and comfortable voyage."

That's easy for him to say, Giordino thought idly. He won't be there.

24

Henry Munk shifted his muscular frame to a different position on a long vinyl pad, stifled a yawn, and continued to stare out the *Sappho I*'s aft viewport. The flat, unending sediment was about as interesting as a book without printed pages, but Munk took delight in the knowledge that every tiny mound, every rock or occasional denizen of the deep that passed beneath the thick Plexiglas had never before been seen by man. It was a small but satisfying reward for the long, boring hours he'd spent scanning an array of detection instruments mounted on both sides above the pad.

Reluctantly, he forced his eyes from the viewport and focused them on the instruments: the S-T-SV-D sensor had been operating constantly during the mission, measuring the outside salinity, temperature, sound velocity, and depth pressure on a magnetic tape; the sub-bottom profiler that acoustically determined the depth of the top sediments and provided indications of the underlying structure of the sea floor's surface; the gravimeter that ticked off the gravity readings every quarter mile; the current sensor that kept its sensitive eye on the speed of the Lorelei Current and direction; and the magnetometer, a sensor for measuring and recording the bottom's magnetic field, including any deviations caused by localized metal deposits.

Munk almost missed it. The movement of the stylus on the magnetometer's graph was so slight, barely a tiny millimeter of a squibble, that he would have missed it completely if his eyes hadn't locked on the recording mark at exactly the right moment. Quickly, he threw his face against the viewport and peered at the sea floor. Then he turned and yelled at Giordino, who sat at the pilot's console only ten feet away, "All stop!"

Giordino spun around and stared aft. All he could see were Munk's legs; the rest of him was buried among the instruments. "What do you read?"

"We just passed over something that's metallic. Back her up for a closer look."

"Easing her back," Giordino said loudly so Munk could hear.

He engaged the two motors mounted on each side of the hull amidships, and set them at half-speed in reverse. For ten seconds, the *Sappho I* caught in the two-knot force of the current hung suspended, reluctant to move on her own. Then she began to forge backward very slowly against the relentless flow. Gunn and the others crowded around Munk's instrument tunnel.

"Make out anything?" Gunn asked.

"Not sure," Munk answered. "There's something sticking up from the sediment about twenty yards astern. I can only see a vague shape under the stern lights."

Everyone waited.

It seemed an eternity before Munk spoke again: "Okay, I've got it."

Gunn turned to Woodson. "Activate the two stereo bottom cameras and strobes. We should have this on film."

Woodson nodded and moved off toward his equipment.

"Can you describe it?" Spencer asked.

"It looks like a funnel sticking upright in the ooze." Munk's voice came through the instrument tunnel disembodied, but even the reverberated tone could not disguise the excitement behind it.

Gunn's expression went skeptical. "Funnel?".

Drummer leaned over Gunn's shoulder. "What kind of funnel?"

"A funnel with a hollow cone tapering to a point that you pour stuff through, you dumb rebel," Munk replied irritably. "It's passing under the starboard hull now. Tell Giordino to hold the boat stationary the second it appears under the bow viewports."

Gunn stepped over to Giordino. "Can you hold our position?"

"I'll give it a go, but if the current starts swinging us broadside, I won't be able to keep precise control and we'll lose visual contact with whatever that thing is out there."

Gunn moved to the bow and lay down on the rubber-sheathed floor. He stared out of one of the four forward viewports together with Merker and Spencer. They all saw the object almost immediately. It was as Munk had described it: simply an inverted bell-shaped funnel about five inches in diameter, its tip protruding from the bottom sediment. Surprisingly, its condition was good. The exterior surface of the metal was tarnished, to be sure, but it appeared to be sound and solid, with no indication of flaking or heavy rust layers.

"Holding steady," Giordino said, "but I can't guarantee for how long."

Without turning from the viewport, Gunn motioned to Woodson, who was bent over a pair of cameras, zooming their lenses toward the object on the sea floor. "Omar?"

"Focused and shooting."

Merker twisted around and looked at Gunn. "Let's make a grab for it."

Gunn remained silent, his nose almost touching the port. He seemed lost in concentration.

Merker's eyes narrowed questioningly. "What about it, Rudi? I say let's grab it."

The words finally penetrated Gunn's thoughts. "Yes, yes, by all means," he mumbled vaguely.

Merker unhooked a metal box that was attached to the forward bulkhead by a five-foot cable and positioned himself at the center viewport. The box contained a series of toggle switches that surrounded a small circular knob. It was the control unit for the manipulator, a four-hundred-pound mechanical arm that hung grotesquely from the lower bow of the *Sappho I*.

Merker pushed a switch that activated the arm. Then he deftly moved his fingers over the controls as the mechanism hummed and the arm extended to its full seven-foot reach. It was eight inches shy of the funnel in the sediment outside.

"I need another foot," Merker said.

"Get ready," Giordino replied. "The forward movement may break my position."

The funnel seemed to pass with agonizing slowness under the manipulator's stainless-steel claw. Merker gently eased the pincers over the lip of the funnel, and then he pressed another switch and they closed, but his timing was off; the current clutched the submersible and began swinging it broadside. The claw missed by no more than an inch and its pincers came together empty.

"She's breaking to port," Giordino yelled, "I can't hold her."

Quickly, Merker's fingers danced over the control box. He would have to try for a second grab on the fly. If he missed again, it would be next to impossible to relocate the funnel under the limited visibility. Sweat began erupting on his brow, and his hands grew tense.

He bent the arm against its stop and turned the claw six degrees to starboard, compensating for the opposite swing of the *Sappho*. He flipped the switch again and the claw dropped, and the pincers closed in almost the same motion. The lip of the funnel rested between them.

Merker had it.

Now he eased the arm upward, gradually easing the funnel from its resting place in the sediment. The sweat was rolling into his eyes now, but he kept them open. There could be no hesitating: one mistake and the object would be lost on the sea floor forever. Then the slimy ooze relinquished its hold and the funnel came free and rose up toward the viewports.

"My God!" Woodson whispered. "That's no funnel."

"It looks like a horn," Merker said.

Gunn shook his head. "It's a cornet."

"How can you be sure?" Giordino had left the pilot's console and was peering over Gunn's shoulder through the port.

"I played one in my high-school band."

The others recognized it now, too. They could readily make out the flaring mouth of the bell and behind it, the curved tubes leading to the valves and mouthpiece.

"Judging from the look of it," Merker said, "I'd say it was brass."

"That's why Munk's magnetometer barely picked it up on the graph," Giordino added. "The mouthpiece and the valve pistons are the only parts that contain iron."

"Ah wonder how long it's been down here?" Drummer asked no one in particular.

"It'd be more intriguing to know where it came from," said Merker.

"Obviously thrown overboard from a passing ship," Giordino said carelessly." Probably by some kid who hated music lessons."

"Maybe its owner is somewhere down here, too." Merker spoke without looking up.

Spencer shivered. "There's a chilling thought for you."

The interior of the *Sappho I* fell silent.

25

The antique Ford trimotor aircraft, famed in aviation history as the *Tin Goose,* looked too awkward to fly, and yet she banked as gracefully and majestically as an albatross when she lined up for her final approach to the runway of the Washington National Airport.

Pitt eased back the three throttles and the old bird touched down with all the delicacy of an autumn leaf kissing high grass. He taxied over to one of the NUMA hangars at the north end of the airport, where his waiting maintenance crew chocked the wheels and made the routine throat-cutting sign. Flipping off the ignition switches, he watched the silver-bladed propellers gradually slow their revolutions and come to rest, gleaming in the late afternoon sun. Then he removed the head-phones, draped them on the control column, undid the latch on his side window and pushed it open.

A bewildered frown slowly creased Pitt's forehead and hung there in the tanned, leathery skin. A man was standing on the asphalt below, frantically waving his hands.

"May I come aboard?" Gene Seagram shouted.

"I'll come down," Pitt yelled back.

"No, please stay where you are."

Pitt shrugged and leaned back in his seat. It took Seagram only a few seconds to climb aboard the trimotor and push open the cockpit door. He wore a stylish tan suit with vest, but his well-tailored appearance was diluted by a sea of wrinkles that creased the material, making it obvious that he hadn't seen a bed for at least twenty-four hours.

"Where did you ever find such a gorgeous old machine?" Seagram asked.

"I ran across it at Keflavík, Iceland," Pitt replied. "Managed to buy it at a fair price and have it shipped back to the States."

"She's a beauty."

Pitt motioned Seagram to the empty copilot's seat. "You sure you want to talk in here? In a few minutes the sun will make this cabin feel like the inside of an incinerator."

"What I have to say won't take long." Seagram eased into the seat and let out a long sigh.

Pitt studied him. He looked like a man who was unwilling and trapped . . . a proud man who had placed himself in an uncompromising position.

Seagram did not face Pitt when he spoke, but stared nervously through the windshield. "I suppose you're wondering what I'm doing here," he said.

"The thought crossed my mind."

"I need your help."

That was it. No mention of the harsh words from the past. No preliminaries; only a straight-to-the-gut request.

Pitt's eyes narrowed. "For some strange reason I had the feeling that my company was about as welcome to you as a dose of syphilis."

"Your feelings, my feelings, they don't matter. What does matter is that your talents are in desperate demand by our government."

"Talents . . . desperate demand . . ." Pitt did not disguise his surprise: "You're putting me on, Seagram."

"Believe me, I wish I was, but Admiral Sandecker assures me that you're the only man who stands a remote chance of pulling off a ticklish job."

"What job?"

"Salvaging the *Titanic*."

"Of course! Nothing like a salvage operation to break the monotony of—" Pitt broke off in mid-sentence; his deep green eyes widened and the blood rose to his face. "What ship did you say?" His voice came in a hoarse murmur this time.

Seagram looked at him with an amused expression. "The *Titanic*. Surely you've heard of it?"

Perhaps ten seconds ticked by in utter silence while Pitt sat there stunned. Then he said, "Do you know what you're proposing?"

"Absolutely."

"It can't be done!" Pitt's expression was incredulous, his voice still the same hoarse murmur. "Even if it were technically possible, and it isn't, it would take hundreds of millions of dollars . . . and then there's the unending legal entanglement with the original owners and the insurance companies over salvage rights."

"There are over two hundred engineers and scientists working on the technical problems at this moment," Seagram explained. "Financing will be arranged through secret government funding. And as far as legal rights go, forget it. Under international law, once a vessel is lost with no hope of recovery, it becomes fair game for anybody who wishes to spend the money and effort on a salvage operation." He turned and stared out the windshield again. "You can't know, Pitt, how important this under-taking is. The *Titanic* represents much more than treasure or historic value. There is something deep within its cargo holds that is vital to the security of our nation."

"You'll forgive me if I say that sounds a bit farfetched."

"Perhaps, but underneath the flag-waving, the facts hold true."

Pitt shook his head. "You're talking sheer fantasy. The *Titanic* lies in nearly two and a half miles of water. The pressure at those depths runs several thousand pounds to the square inch, Mr. Seagram; not square foot or square yard, but square inch. The difficulties and barriers are staggering. No one has ever seriously attempted to raise the *Andrea Doria* or the *Lusitania* from the bottom . . . and they both lie only three hundred feet from the surface."

"If we can put men on the moon, we can bring the *Titanic* up to the sunlight again," Seagram argued.

"There's no comparison. It took a decade to set a four-ton capsule on lunar soil. Lifting forty-five thousand tons of steel is a different proposi-tion. It may take months just to find her."

"The search is already under way."

"I heard nothing—"

"About a search effort?" Seagram finished. "Not likely that you should. Until the operation becomes unwieldy in terms of security, it will remain secret. Even your assistant special projects director, Albert Giordano—"

"Giordino."

"Yes, Giordino, thank you. He is at this very moment piloting a search probe across the Atlantic sea floor in total ignorance of his true mission."

"But the Lorelei Current Expedition . . . the *Sappho I*'s original mission was to trace a deep ocean current."

"A timely coincidence. Admiral Sandecker was able to order the submersible into the area of the *Titanic*'s last-known position barely hours before the sub was scheduled to surface."

Pitt turned and stared at a jet airliner that was lifting from the airport's main runway. "Why me? What have I done to deserve an invitation to what has to be the biggest hare-brained scheme of the century?"

"You are not simply to be a guest, my dear Pitt. You are to command the over-all salvage operation."

Pitt regarded Seagram grimly. "The question still stands. Why me?"

"Not a selection that excites me, I assure you," Seagram said. "However, since the National Underwater and Marine Agency is the nation's largest acknowledged authority on oceanographic science, and since the leading experts on deep-water salvage are members of their staff, and since you are the agency's Special Projects Director, you were elected."

"The fog begins to lift. It's a simple case of my being in the wrong occupation at the wrong time."

"Read it as you will," Seagram said wearily. "I must admit, I found your past record of bringing incredibly difficult projects to successful conclusions most impressive." He pulled out a handkerchief and dabbed his forehead. "Another factor that weighed heavily in your favor, I might add, is that you are considered somewhat of an expert on the *Titanic*."

"Collecting and studying *Titanic* memorabilia is a hobby with me, nothing more. It hardly qualifies me to oversee her salvage."

"Nonetheless, Mr. Pitt, Admiral Sandecker tells me you are, to use his words, a genius at handling men and coordinating logistics." He gazed over at Pitt, his eyes uncertain. "Will you take the job?"

"You don't think I can pull it off, do you, Seagram?"

"Frankly, no. But when one dangles over the cliff by a thread, one has little say about who comes to the rescue."

A faint smile edged Pitt's lips. "Your faith in me is touching."

"Well?"

Pitt sat lost in thought for several moments. Finally, he gave an almost imperceptible nod and looked squarely into Seagram's eyes. "Okay, my friend, I'm your boy. But don't count your chickens until that rusty old hulk is moored to a New York dock. There isn't a betmaker in Las Vegas who'd waste a second computing odds on this crazy escapade. When we find the *Titanic,* if we find the *Titanic,* her hull may be too far gone to raise. But then nothing is absolutely impossible, and though I can't begin to guess what it is that's so valuable to the government that warrants the effort, I'll try, Seagram. Beyond that, I promise nothing."

Pitt broke into a wide grin and climbed from the pilot's seat. "End of speech. Now then, let's get out of this hot box and find a nice cool air-conditioned cocktail lounge where you can buy me a drink. It's the least you can do after pulling off the con job of the year."

Seagram just sat there, too drained to do anything except shrug in helpless acquiescence.

26

At first John Vogel treated the cornet as simply another restoration job. There was no rarity suggested by its design. There was nothing exceptional about its construction that would excite a collector. At the moment it could excite nobody. The valves were corroded and frozen closed; the brass was discolored by an odd sort of accumulated grime; and a foul, fishlike odor emanated from the mud that clogged the interior of its tubes.

Vogel decided the cornet was beneath him; he would turn it over to one of his assistants for the restoration. The exotics, those were the instruments that Vogel loved to bring back to their original newness: the ancient Chinese and Roman trumpets, with the long, straight tubes and the ear-piercing tones; the battered old horns of the early jazz greats; the instruments with a piece of history attached—these, Vogel would repair with the patience of a watchmaker, toiling with exacting craftsmanship until the piece gleamed like new and played brilliantly clear tones.

He wrapped the cornet in an old pillowcase and set it against the far wall of his office.

The Executone on his desk uttered a soft bong. "Yes, Mary, what is it?"

"Admiral James Sandecker of the National Underwater and Marine Agency is on the phone." His secretary's voice scratched over the intercom like fingernails over a blackboard. "He says it's urgent."

"Okay, put him on." Vogel lifted the telephone. "John Vogel here."

"Mr. Vogel, this is James Sandecker."

The fact that Sandecker had dialed his own call and didn't bluster behind his title impressed Vogel.

"Yes, Admiral, what can I do for you?"

"Have you received it yet?"

"Have I received what?"

"An old bugle."

"Ah, the cornet," Vogel said. "I found it on my desk this morning with no explanation. I assumed it was a donation to the museum."

"My apologies, Mr. Vogel. I should have forewarned you, but I was tied up."

A straightforward excuse.

"How can I help you, Admiral?"

"I'd be grateful if you could study the thing and tell me what you know about it. Date of manufacture and so on."

"I'm flattered, sir. Why me?"

"As chief curator for the Washington Museum's Hall of Music, you seemed the logical choice. Also, a mutual friend said that the world lost another Harry James when you decided to become a scholar."

My God, Vogel thought, the President. Score another point for Sandecker. He knew the right people.

"That's debatable," Vogel said. "When would you like my report?"

"As soon as it's convenient for you."

Vogel smiled to himself. A polite request deserved extra effort. "The dipping process to remove the corrosion is what takes time. With luck, I should have something for you by tomorrow morning."

"Thank you, Mr. Vogel," Sandecker said briskly. "I'm grateful."

"Is there any information concerning how or where you found the cornet that might help me?"

"I'd rather not say. My people would like your opinions entirely without prompting or direction on our part."

"You want to compare my findings with yours, is that it?"

Sandecker's voice carried sharply through the earpiece. "We want you to confirm our hopes and expectations, Mr. Vogel, nothing more."

"I shall do my best, Admiral. Good-by."

"Good luck."

Vogel sat for several minutes staring at the pillowcase in the corner, his hand resting on the telephone. Then he pressed the Executone. "Mary, hold all calls for the rest of the day, and sent out for a medium pizza with Canadian bacon and a half gallon of Gallo burgundy."

"You going to lock yourself in that musty old workship again?" Mary's voice scratched back.

"Yes," Vogel sighed. "It's going to be a long day."

First, Vogel took several photos of the cornet from different angles. Then he noted the dimensions, general condition of the visible parts, and the degree of tarnish and foreign matter that coated the surfaces, recording each observation in a large notebook. He regarded the cornet with an increased level of professional interest. It was a quality instrument; the brass was of good commercial grade, and the small bores of the bell and the valves told him that it was manufactured before 1930. He discovered that what he had thought to be corrosion was only a hard crust of mud that flaked away under light pressure from a rubber spoon.

Next, he soaked the instrument in diluted Calgon water softener, gently agitating the liquid and changing the tank every so often to drain away the dirt. By midnight, he had the cornet completely disassembled. Then he started the tedious job of swabbing the metal surfaces with a mild solution of chromic acid to bring out the shine of the brass. Slowly, after several rinsings, an intricate scroll pattern and several ornately scripted letters began to appear on the bell.

"By God!" Vogel blurted aloud. "A presentation model."

He picked up a magnifying glass and studied the writing. When he set the glass down and reached for a telephone, his hands were trembling.

27

At precisely eight o'clock, John Vogel was ushered into Sandecker's office on the top floor of the ten-story solar-glassed building that housed the national headquarters of NUMA. His eyes were bloodshot and he made no effort to conceal a yawn.

Sandecker came out from behind his desk and shook Vogel's hand. The short, banty admiral had to lean backward and look up to meet the eyes of his visitor. Vogel was six foot five, a kindly faced man with puffs of unbrushed white hair edging a bald head. He gazed through brown Santa Claus eyes, and flashed a warm smile. His coat was neatly pressed, but his pants were rumpled and stained with a myriad of blotches below the knees. He smelled like a wino.

"Well," Sandecker greeted him. "It's a pleasure to meet you."

"The pleasure is mine, Admiral." Vogel set a black trumpet case on the carpet. "I'm sorry I appear so slovenly."

"I was going to say," Sandecker answered, "it seems you've had a difficult night."

"When one loves one's work, time and inconvenience have little meaning."

"True." Sandecker turned and nodded to a little gnomelike man who was standing in one corner of the office. "Mr. John Vogel, may I present Commander Rudi Gunn."

"Of course, Commander Gunn," Vogel said, smiling. "I was one of the many millions who followed your Lorelei Current Expedition every day in the newspapers. You're to be congratulated, Commander. It was a great achievement."

"Thank you," Gunn said.

Sandecker gestured to another man sitting on the couch. "And my Special Projects Director, Dirk Pitt."

Vogel nodded at the swarthy face that crinkled into a smile. "Mr. Pitt."

Pitt rose and nodded back. "Mr. Vogel."

Vogel sat down and pulled out a battered old pipe. "Mind if I smoke?"

"Not at all." Sandecker lifted one of his Churchill cigars out of a humidor and held it up. "I'll join you."

Vogel puffed the bowl into life and then sat back and said, "Tell me, Admiral, was the cornet discovered on the bottom of the North Atlantic?"

"Yes, just south of the Grand Banks off Newfoundland." He stared at Vogel speculatively. "How did you guess that?"

"Elementary deduction."

"What can you tell us about it?"

"A considerable amount, actually. To begin with, it is a high-quality instrument, crafted for a professional musician."

"Then it's not likely it was owned by an amateur player?" Gunn said, remembering Giordino's words on the *Sappho I*.

"No," Vogel said flatly. "Not likely."

"Could you determine the time and place of manufacture?" Pitt asked.

"The approximate month was either October or November. The exact year was 1911. And it was manufactured by a very reputable and very fine old British firm by the name of Boosey-Hawkes."

There was respect written in Sandecker's eyes. "You've done a remarkable job, Mr. Vogel. Quite frankly, we doubted whether we would ever know the country of origin, much less the actual manufacturer."

"No investigative brilliance on my part, I assure you," Vogel said. "You see, the cornet was a presentation model."

"A presentation model?"

"Yes. Any metal product that takes a high degree of craftsmanship to construct, and is highly prized as a possession, is often engraved to commemorate an unusual event or outstanding service."

"A common practice among gunmakers," Pitt commented.

"And also creators of fine musical instruments. In this instance, it was presented to an employee by his company in recognition of his service. The presentation date, the manufacturer, the employee, and his company are all beautifully engraved on the cornet's bell."

"You can actually tell who owned it?" Gunn asked. "The engraving is readable?"

"Oh my, yes." Vogel bent down and opened the case. "Here, you can read it for yourself."

He set the cornet on Sandecker's desk. The three men stared at it silently for a long time—a gleaming instrument whose golden surface reflected the morning sun that was streaming in the window. The cornet looked brand-new. Every inch was buffed to a high shine and the intricate engraving of sea waves that curled around the tube and bell were as clear as the day they were etched. Sandecker gazed over the cornet at Vogel, his brows lifted in doubt.

"Mr. Vogel, I think you fail to see the seriousness of the situation. I don't care for jokes."

"I admit," Vogel snapped back, "that I fail to see the seriousness of the situation. What I do see is a moment of tremendous excitement. And believe me, Admiral, this is no joke. I have spent the best part of the last twenty-four hours restoring your discovery." He threw a bulky folder on the desk. "Here is my report, complete with photographs and my step-by-step observations during the restoration procedure. There are also envelopes containing the different types of residue and mud that I removed, and also the parts that I replaced. I overlooked nothing."

"I apologize," Sandecker said. "Yet it seems inconceivable that the instrument we sent you yesterday, and the instrument on the desk are one and the same." Sandecker paused and exchanged glances with Pitt. "You see, we . . ."

". . . thought the cornet had rested on the sea bottom for a long time," Vogel finished the sentence. "I'm fully aware of what you're driving at, Admiral. And I confess I'm at a loss as to the instrument's remarkable condition, too. I've worked on any number of musical instruments which have been immersed in salt water for only three to five years that were in far worse shape than this one. I'm not an oceanographer so the solution to the puzzle eludes me. However, I can tell you to the day how long that cornet has been beneath the sea and how it came to be there."

Vogel reached over and picked up the horn. Then he slipped on a pair of rimless glasses and began reading aloud. " 'Presented to Graham Farley in sincere appreciation for distinguished performance in the entertainment of our passengers by the grateful management of the White Star Line.' " Vogel removed his glasses and smiled benignly at Sandecker. "When I discovered the words White Star Line, I got a friend out of bed early this morning to do a bit of research at the Naval Archives. He called only a half hour before I left for your office." Vogel paused to remove a handkerchief from his pocket and blew his nose. "It seems Graham Farley was a very popular fellow throughout the White Star Line. He was solo cornetist for three years on one of their vessels . . . I believe it was called the *Oceanic*. When the company's newest luxury liner was about to set sail on her maiden voyage, the management selected the outstanding musicians from their other passenger ships and formed what was considered at the time the finest orchestra on the seas. Graham, of course, was one of the first musicians chosen. Yes, gentlemen, this cornet has rested under the Atlantic Ocean for a very long time . . . because Graham Farley was playing it on the morning of April 15, 1912, when the waves closed over him and the *Titanic*."

The reactions to Vogel's sudden revelation were mixed. Sandecker's face turned half-somber, half-speculative; Gunn's went rigid; while Pitt's expression was one of casual interest. The silence in the room became intense as Vogel stuffed his glasses back in a breast pocket.

" '*Titanic*.' " Sandecker repeated the word slowly, like a man savoring a beautiful woman's name. He gazed penetratingly at Vogel, wonder mingled with doubt still mirrored in his eyes. "It's incredible."

"A fact nonetheless," Vogel said casually. "I take it, Commander Gunn, that the cornet was discovered by the *Sappho I*?"

"Yes, near the end of the voyage."

"It would appear that your undersea expedition stumbled on a bonus. A pity you didn't run onto the ship herself."

"Yes, a pity," Gunn said, avoiding Vogel's eyes.

"I'm still at a loss as to the instrument's condition," Sandecker said. "I hardly expected a relic sunk in the sea for seventy-five years to come up looking little the worse for wear."

"The lack of corrosion does pose an interesting question," Vogel replied. "The brass most certainly would weather well, but, strangely, the parts containing ferrous metals survived in a remarkable virgin state. The original mouthpiece, as you can see, is near-perfect."

Gunn was staring at the cornet as if it was the holy grail. "Will it still play?"

"Yes," Vogel answered. "Quite beautifully, I should think."

"You haven't tried it?"

"No . . . I have not." Vogel ran his fingers reverently over the cornet's valves. "Up to now, I have always tested every brass instrument my assistants and I have restored for its brilliance of tone. This time I cannot."

"I don't understand," Sandecker said.

"This instrument is a reminder of a small, but courageous act performed during the worst sea tragedy in man's history," Vogel replied. "It takes very little imagination to envision Graham Farley and his fellow musicians while they soothed the frightened ship's passengers with music, sacrificing all thought of their own safety, as the *Titanic* settled into the cold sea. The cornet's last melody came from the lips of · a very brave man. I feel it would border on the sacrilegious for anyone else ever to play it again."

Sandecker stared at Vogel, examining every feature of the old man's face as if he were seeing it for the first time.

" 'Autumn,' " Vogel was murmuring, almost rambling to himself. " 'Autumn,' an old hymn. That was the last melody Graham Farley played on his cornet."

"Not 'Nearer My God to Thee'?" Gunn spoke slowly.

"A myth," said Pitt. " 'Autumn' was the final tune that was heard from the *Titanic*'s band just before the end."

"You seem to have made a study of the *Titanic*," Vogel said.

"The ship and her tragic fate is like a contagious disease," Pitt replied. "Once you become interested, the fever is tough to break."

"The ship itself holds little attraction for me. But as a historian of musicians and their instruments, the saga of the *Titanic*'s band has always gripped my imagination." Vogel set the cornet in the case, closed the lid, and passed it across the desk to Sandecker. "Unless you have more questions, Admiral, I'd like to grab a fattening breakfast and fall into bed. It was a difficult night."

Sandecker stood. "We're in your debt, Mr. Vogel."

"I was hoping you might say that," the Santa Claus eyes twinkled slyly. "There is a way you can repay me."

"Which is?"

"Donate the cornet to the Washington Museum. It would be the prize exhibit of our Hall of Music."

"As soon as our lab people have studied the instrument and your report, I'll send it over to you."

"On behalf of the museum's directors, I thank you."

"Not as a gift donation, however."

Vogel stared uncertainly at the Admiral.

"I don't follow."

Sandecker smiled. "Let's call it a permanent loan. That will save hassle in case we ever have to borrow it back temporarily."

"Agreed."

"One more thing," Sandecker said. "Nothing has been mentioned to the press about the discovery. I'd appreciate it if you went along with us for the time being."

"I don't understand your motives, but of course I'll comply."

The towering curator bid his farewells and departed.

"Damn!" Gunn blurted out a second after the door closed. "We must have passed within spitting distance of the *Titanic*'s hulk."

"You were certainly in the ball park," Pitt agreed. "The *Sappho*'s sonar probed a radius of two hundred yards. The *Titanic* must have rested just outside the fringe of your range."

"If only we'd had more time. If only we'd known what in hell we were looking for."

"You forget," Sandecker said, "that testing the *Sappho I* and conducting experiments on the Lorelei Current were your primary objectives, and on that you and your crew did one hell of a job. Oceanographers will be sifting the data you brought back on deep-water currents for the next two years. My only regret is that we couldn't let you in on what we were up to, but Gene Seagram and his security people insist that we keep a tight lid on any information regarding the *Titanic* until we're far along on the salvage operation."

"We won't be able to keep it quiet for long," Pitt said. "All the news media in the world will soon smell a story on the greatest historical find since the opening of King Tut's tomb."

Sandecker rose from behind his desk and walked over to the window. When he spoke, his words came very softly, sounding almost as if they were carried over a great distance by the wind. "Graham Farley's cornet."

"Sir?"

"Graham Farley's cornet," Sandecker repeated wistfully. "If that old horn is any indication, the *Titanic* may be sitting down there in the black abyss as pretty and preserved as the night she sank."

28

To a chance observer standing on the shore or to anyone out for a leisurely cruise up the Rappahannock River, the three men slouched in a dilapidated old rowboat looked like a trio of ordinary weekend fishermen. They were dressed in faded shirts and dungarees, and sported hats festooned with the usual variety of hooks and flies. It was a typical scene, down to the six-pack of beer trapped in a fishnet dangling in the water beside the boat.

The shortest of the three, a red-haired, pinched-faced man, lay against the stern and seemed to be dozing, his hands loosely gripped around a fishing pole that was attached to a red and white cork bobbing a bare two feet from the boat's waterline. The second man simply slouched over an open magazine, while the third fisherman sat upright and mechanically went through the motions of casting a silver lure. He was large, with a well-fed stomach that blossomed through his open shirt, and he gazed through lazy blue eyes set in a jovial round face. He was the perfect image of everyone's kindly old grandfather.

Admiral Joseph Kemper could afford to look kindly. When you wielded the almost incredible authority that he did, you didn't have to squint through hypnotic eyes or belch fire like a dragon. He looked down and offered a benevolent expression to the man who was dozing.

"It strikes me, Jim, that you're not deeply into the spirit of fishing."

"This has to be the most useless endeavor ever devised by man," Sandecker replied.

"And you, Mr. Seagram? You haven't dropped a hook since we anchored."

Seagram peered at Kemper over the magazine. "If a fish could survive the pollution down there, Admiral, he'd have to look like a mutant out of a low-budget horror movie, and taste twice as bad."

"Since it was you gentlemen who invited me here," Kemper said, "I'm beginning to suspect a devious motive."

Sandecker neither agreed nor disagreed. "Just relax and enjoy the great outdoors, Joe. Forget for a few hours that you're the Navy's Chief of Staff."

"That's easy when you're around. You're the only one I know who talks down to me."

Sandecker grinned. "You can't go through life with the whole world kissing your ass. Simply look upon me as good therapy."

Kemper sighed. "I had hoped I'd gotten rid of you once and for all when you retired from the service. Now it seems you've come back to haunt me as a god-damned feather merchant."

"I understand they were dancing in the corridors of the Pentagon when I left."

"Let's just say there were no tears shed at your departure." Kemper slowly reeled his lure in. "Okay, Jim, I've known you too many years not to smell a squeeze play. What do you and Mr. Seagram have on your minds?"

"We're going after the *Titanic*," Sandecker replied casually.

Kemper went on reeling. "Indeed?"

"Indeed."

Kemper cast again. "What for? To take a few photographs for publicity's sake?"

"No, to raise her to the surface."

Kemper stopped reeling. He turned and stared at Sandecker. "You did say the *Titanic*?"

"I did."

"Jim, my boy, you've really slipped your moorings this time. If you expect me to believe—"

"This isn't a fairy tale," Seagram interrupted. "The authority for the salvage operation comes straight from the White House."

Kemper's eyes studied Seagram's face. "Then am I to assume that you represent the President?"

"Yes, sir. That is correct."

Kemper said, "I must say you have a rather strange way of doing business, Mr. Seagram. If you will give me the courtesy of an explanation . . ."

"That's why we're here, Admiral, to explain."

Kemper turned to Sandecker. "Are you in the game too, Jim?"

Sandecker nodded. "Let's just say that Mr. Seagram speaks softly and carries one hell of a big stick."

"Okay, Seagram, the podium is yours. Why the subterfuge and why the urgency to raise an old derelict?"

"First things first, Admiral. To begin with, I am head of a highly secret department of the government called Meta Section."

"Never heard of it," Kemper said.

"We are not listed in any journal on federal offices. Not even the CIA, the FBI, nor the NSA has any records of our operation."

"An undercover think-tank," Sandecker said curtly.

"We go beyond the ordinary think-tank," Seagram said. "Our people devise furturistic concepts and then attempt to construct them into successful functioning systems."

"That would cost millions of dollars," Kemper said.

"Modesty forbids me to mention the exact amount of our budget, Admiral, but ego compels me to admit that I have slightly over ten figures to play with."

"My Lord!" Kemper muttered under his breath. "Over a billion dollars to play with, you say. An organization of scientists that nobody knows exists. You stir my interest, Mr. Seagram."

"Mine too," Sandecker said acidly. "Up until now, you've sought NUMA's assistance through White House channels by passing yourself off as a Presidential aide. Why the Machiavellian Routine?"

"Because the President ordered strict security, Admiral, in the event of a leak to Capitol Hill. The last thing his administration needed was a congressional witch hunt into Meta Section's finances."

Kemper and Sandecker looked at each other and nodded. They looked at Seagram, waiting for the rest of it.

"Now then," he continued, "Meta Section has developed a defense system with the code name of the Sicilian Project. . . ."

"The Sicilian Project?"

"We named it after a chess strategy known as the Sicilian Defense. The project is devised around a variant of the maser principle. For example, if we push a sound wave of a certain frequency through a medium containing excited atoms, we can then stimulate the sound to an extremely high state of emission."

"Similar to a laser beam," Kemper commented.

"To some degree," Seagram answered. "Except a laser emits a narrow beam of light energy, while our device emits a broad, fanlike field of sound waves."

"Besides breaking a bevy of eardrums," Sandecker said, "what purpose does it serve?"

"As you recall from your elementary-school studies, Admiral, sound waves spread in circular waves much like ripples in a pond after a pebble is dropped in it. In the instance of the Sicilian Project, we can multiply the sound waves a million times over. Then, when this tremendous energy is released, it spreads out into the atmosphere, pushing air particles ahead of its unleashed force, condensing them until they combine to form a solid, impenetrable wall hundreds of square miles in diameter." Seagram paused to scratch his nose. "I won't bore you with equations and technical details concerning the actual instrumentation. The particulars are too complicated to discuss here, but you can easily see the potential. Any enemy missile launched against America coming into contact with this invisible protective barrier would smash itself into oblivion long before it entered the target area."

"Is . . . is this system for real?" Kemper asked hesitantly.

"Yes, Admiral. I assure you it can work. Even now, the required number of installations to stop an all-out missile attack are under construction."

"Jesus!" Sandecker burst out. "The ultimate weapon."

"The Sicilian Project is not a weapon. It is purely a scientific method of protecting our country."

"It's hard to visualize," Kemper said.

"Just imagine a sonic boom from a jet aircraft amplified ten million times."

Kemper seemed lost by it all. "But the sound—wouldn't it destroy everything on the ground?"

"No, the energy force is aimed into space and builds during its journey. To someone standing at sea level it would merely have the same harmless impact of distant thunder."

"What does all this have to do with the *Titanic*?"

"The element required to stimulate the optimum level of sound emission is byzanium, and therein lies the grabber, gentlemen, because the world's only known quantity of byzanium ore was shipped to the United States back in 1912 on board the *Titanic*."

"I see." Kemper nodded. "Then salvaging the ship is your last-ditch attempt at making your defense system operational?"

"Byzanium's atomic structure is the only one that will work. By programing its known properties into our computers, we were able to project a thirty-thousand-to-one ratio in favor of success."

"But why raise the entire ship?" Kemper asked. "Why not just tear out its bulkheads and bring up the byzanium."

"We'd have to blast our way into the cargo hold with explosives. The danger of destroying the ore forever is too great. The President and I agree that the added expense of raising the hull far outweighs the risk of losing it."

Kemper tossed out his lure again. "You're a positive thinker, Seagram. I grant you that. But what makes you think the *Titanic* is in any condition to be brought up in one piece. After seventy-five years on the bottom, she may be nothing but an immense pile of rusty junk."

"My people have a theory on that," said Sandecker. He put his fishing pole aside, opened his tackle box and pulled out an envelope. "Take a look at these." He handed Kemper several four-by-five photographs.

"Looks like so much underwater trash," Kemper commented.

"Exactly," Sandecker answered. "Every so often the cameras on our submersibles stumble on debris tossed overboard from passing ships." He pointed to the top photo. "This is a galley stove found at four thousand feet off Bermuda. Next is an automobile engine block photographed at sixty-five hundred feet off the Aleutians. No way to date either of these. Now, here is a Grumman F4F World War II aircraft discovered at ten thousand feet, near Iceland. We dug up a record on this one. The plane was ditched in the sea without injury by a Lieutenant Strauss when he ran out of fuel on March 17, 1946."

Kemper held out the next photo at arm's length. "What in hell is this thing?"

"That was taken at the moment of discovery by the *Sappho I* during the Lorelei Current Expedition. What at first looked like an ordinary kitchen funnel turned out to be a horn." He showed Kemper a shot of the instrument taken after Vogel's restoration.

"That's a cornet," Kemper corrected him. "You say the *Sappho I* brought this up?"

"Yes, from twelve thousand feet. It had been lying on the bottom since 1912."

Kemper's eyebrows raised. "Are you going to tell me it came from the *Titanic*?"

"I can show you documented evidence."

Kemper sighed and handed the pictures back to Sandecker. His shoulders sagged, the weary, fatigued droop of a man no longer young, a man who had been carrying a heavy burden for too long a time. He pulled a beer from the fish net and popped the tab. "What does any of this prove?"

Sandecker's mouth tightened into a slight grin. "It was right in front of us for two years—that's how long ago the aircraft was discovered—but we completely overlooked the possibilities. Oh sure, there were remarks about the plane's excellent condition, yet none of my oceanographers really grasped the significance. It wasn't until the *Sappho 1* brought up the horn that the true implications came home."

"I'm not following you," Kemper said tonelessly.

"First of all," Sandecker continued, "ninety per cent of that F4F is made out of aluminum, and as you know, salt water eats the hell out of aluminum. Yet that plane, after sitting down there in the sea for over forty years, looks like the day it came out of the factory. Same with the horn. It's been underwater crowding eighty years, and it shined up like a newborn baby's ass."

"Have you any explanation?" Kemper asked.

"Two of NUMA's ablest oceanographers are now running data through our computers. The general theory at the moment is that it's a combination of factors: the lack of damaging sea life at great depths, the low salinity or salt content of bottom water, the freezing temperatures of the deep, and a lower oxygen content that would slow down oxidation of metal. It could be any one or all of these factors that delays deterioration of deep-bottom wrecks. We'll know better if and when we get a look at the *Titanic*."

Kemper thought for a moment. "What do you want from me?"

"Protection," Seagram answered. "If the Soviets get wind of what we're up to, they'll try everything short of war to stop us and grab the byzanium for themselves."

"Put your mind at rest on that score," Kemper said, his voice suddenly hard. "The Russians will think twice before they bloody their noses on our side of the Atlantic. Your salvage operations on the *Titanic* will be protected, Mr. Seagram. You have my iron-clad guarantee on that."

A faint grin touched Sandecker's face. "While you're in a generous mood, Joe, what're the chances of borrowing the *Modoc*?"

"The *Modoc*?" Kemper repeated. "She's the finest deep-water salvage vessel the Navy's got."

"We could also use the crew that comes with her," Sandecker pushed on.

Kemper rolled the beer can's cool surface across his sweating forehead. "Okay, you've got yourselves the *Modoc* and her crew, plus whatever extra men and equipment you need."

Seagram sighed. "Thank you, Admiral. I'm grateful."

"You're straddling an interesting concept," Kemper said. "But one fraught with problems."

"Nothing comes easy," Seagram replied.

"What's your next step?"

Sandecker answered that one. "We send down television cameras to locate the hull and survey the damage."

"God only knows what you'll find—" Kemper stopped abruptly and pointed at Sandecker's jerking bobber. "By God, Jim, I believe you've caught a fish."

Sandecker leaned lazily over the side of the boat. "So I have," he said smiling. "Let's hope the *Titanic* is just as cooperative."

"I am afraid that that hope may prove to be an expensive incentive," Kemper said, and there was no answering smile on his lips.

Pitt closed Joshua Hays Brewster's journal and looked across the conference table at Mel Donner. "That's it then."

"The whole truth and nothing but the truth," Donner said.

"But wouldn't this byzanium, or whatever you call it, lose its properties after being immersed in the sea all these years?"

Donner shook his head. "Who's to say? No one has ever had a sufficient quantity in their hands to know for sure how it reacts under any conditions."

"Then it may be worthless."

"Not if it's locked securely in the *Titanic*'s vault. Our research indicates that the strong room is watertight."

Pitt leaned back and stared at the journal. "It's a hell of a gamble."

"We're aware of that."

"It's like asking a gang of kids to lift a Patton tank out of Lake Erie with a few ropes and a raft."

"We're aware of that," Donner repeated.

"The cost alone of raising the *Titanic* is beyond comprehension," Pitt said.

"Name a figure."

"Back in 1974 the CIA paid out over three hundred million dollars just to raise the bow off a Russian submarine. I couldn't begin to fathom what it would run to salvage a passenger liner that grosses forty-six thousand tons from twelve thousand feet of water."

"Take a guess then."

"Who bankrolls the operation?"

"Meta Section will handle the finances," Donner said. "Just look upon me as your friendly neighborhood banker. Let me know what you think it will take to get the salvage operation off the ground, and I'll see to it the funds are secretly transferred into NUMA's annual operating budget."

"Two hundred and fifty million ought to start the ball rolling."

"That's somewhat less than our estimates," Donner said casually. "I suggest that you not limit yourself. Just to be on the safe side, I'll arrange for you to receive an extra five."

"Five million?"

"No." Donner smiled. "Five hundred million."

After the guard passed him out through the gate, Pitt pulled up at the side of the road and gazed back through the chain-link fence at the Smith Van and Storage Company. "I don't believe it," he said to no one. "I don't believe any of it." Then slowly, with much difficulty, as if he were fighting the commands of a hypnotist, Pitt dropped the shift lever into "Drive" and made his way back to the city.

29

It had been a particularly grueling day for the President. There were seemingly endless meetings with opposition-party congressmen; meetings in which he had struggled, vainly in most cases, to persuade them to support his new bill for the modification of income-tax regulations. Then there had been a speech at the convention of near hostile state governors, followed later in the afternoon by a heated session with his aggressive, overbearing secretary of state.

Now, just past ten o'clock, with one more unpleasant involvement to reckon with, he sat in an overstuffed chair holding a drink in his right hand while his left scratched the long ears of his sad-eyed basset hound.

Warren Nicholson, the director of the CIA, and Marshall Collins, his chief Kremlin security adviser, sat opposite him on a large sectional sofa.

The President took a sip from the glass and then stared grimly at the two men. "Do either of you have the vaguest notion of what you're asking of me?"

Collins shrugged nervously. "Quite frankly, sir, we don't. But this is clearly a case of the end justifying the means. I personally think Nicholson here has one hell of a scheme going. The payoff in terms of secret information could be nothing less than astonishing."

"It will cost a heavy price," the President said.

Nicholson leaned forward. "Believe me, sir, the cost is worth it."

"That's easy for you to say," the President said. "Neither of you has the slightest hint as to what the Sicilian Project is all about."

Collins nodded. "No argument there, Mr. President. Its secret is well kept. That's why it came as a shock when we discovered its existence through the KGB instead of our own security forces."

"How much do you think the Russians know?"

"We can't be absolutely certain at this point," Nicholson answered, "but the few facts we have in hand indicate the KGB possesses only the code name."

"Damn!" the President muttered angrily. "How could it have possibly leaked out?"

"I'd venture to guess that it was an accidental leak," Collins said. "My people in Moscow would smell something if Soviet intelligence analysts thought they were onto an ultrasecret American defense project."

The President looked at Collins. "What makes you sure it has to do with defense?"

"If security surrounding the Sicilian Project is as tight as you suggest, then a new military weapon emerges as the obvious theory. And there is no doubt in my mind that the Russians will soon come up with the same conclusion."

"I would have to go along with Collins' line of thinking," Nicholson concurred.

"All of which plays right into our hands."

"Go on."

"We feed Soviet Naval Intelligence data on the Sicilian Project in small doses. If they take the bait . . ." Nicholson's hands gestured like the closing of a trap, ". . . then we literally own one of the Soviets' top intelligence-gathering services."

Bored by the human talk, the President's basset hound stretched out and peacefully dozed off. The President looked thoughtfully at the animal for several moments, weighing the odds. The decision was a painful one. He felt as though he was stabbing all his friends from Meta Section in the back.

"I'll have the man who is heading the project draw up an initial report," he said finally. "You, Nicholson, will tell me where and how you want it delivered so the Russians do not suspect the deception. You will go through me, and only me, for any further information concerning the Sicilian Project. Is that clear?"

Nicholson nodded. "I will arrange the channels myself."

The President seemed to wither and shrink into the chair. "I don't have to impress upon you gentlemen," he said wearily, "the sorry fact that if we're found out, we'll all be branded as traitors."

30

Sandecker leaned over a large, contoured map of the North Atlantic Ocean floor, his hand toying with a small pointer. He looked at Gunn, then at Pitt standing on the other side of the miniaturized seascape. "I can't understand it," he said after a moment's silence. "If that horn is any indication, the *Titanic* doesn't lie where she's supposed to."

Gunn took a felt-tipped pen and made a tiny mark on the map. "Her last reported position just before she sank was here, at 41°46′N–50°14′W."

"And you found the horn where?"

Gunn made another mark. "The exact position of the *Sappho I*'s mother ship on the surface at the time we discovered Farley's cornet put us here, about six miles to the southeast."

"A six-mile discrepancy. How is that possible?"

"There was a conflict of evidence concerning the position of the *Titanic* when she went down," Pitt said. "The skipper of one of the rescue ships, the *Mount Temple,* put the liner much farther to the east, and his reading was based on a sun-sighting, far more accurate than the dead-reckoning position figured by the *Titanic*'s fourth officer right after she struck the iceberg."

"But the ship that picked up the survivors, the *Carpathia,* I believe it was," Sandecker said, "steamed on a course toward the position given by the *Titanic*'s wireless operator and came in direct contact with the lifeboats within four hours."

"There is some doubt that the *Carpathia* actually traveled as far as her captain assumed," Pitt replied. "If so, the sighting of the wreckage and the lifeboats could have occurred several miles southeast of the *Titanic*'s wirelessed position."

Sandecker idly tapped the pointer against the map railing. "This puts us between the devil and the deep blue sea, so to speak, gentlemen. Shall we conduct our search efforts in the exact area of 41°64′N–50°14′W? Or do we bet our money on Graham Farley's horn six miles to the southeast? If we lose, God only knows how many acres of Atlantic Ocean real estate we'll have to drag underwater television cameras over before we stumble on the wreck. What do you say, Rudi?"

Gunn did not hesitate. "Since our search pattern with the *Sappho I* failed in and around the *Titanic*'s advertised position, I say we drop the TV cameras in the vicinity where we picked up Farley's cornet."

"And you, Dirk?"

Pitt was silent a few moments. Then he spoke, "My vote goes for a delay of forty-eight hours."

Sandecker stared across the map speculatively. "We can't afford one hour, much less forty-eight."

Pitt stared back at him. "I suggest that we skip the TV cameras and leapfrog to the next step."

"Which is?"

"We send down a manned submersible."

Sandecker shook his head. "No good. A TV camera sled towed by a surface vessel can cover five times the area in half the time it would take a slow-moving submersible."

"Not if we pinpoint the gravesite in advance."

Sandecker's expression darkened. "And how do you propose to pull off that minor miracle?"

"We gather every shred of knowledge concerning the *Titanic*'s final hours—glean all records for speed, conflicting position reports, water currents, the angle she slid beneath the waves, throw in the cornet's resting place—everything, and program it through NUMA's computers. With luck, the readout data should point directly to the *Titanic*'s front yard."

"It's the logical approach," Gunn admitted.

"In the meantime," Sandecker said, "we lose two days."

"We lose nothing, sir. We gain," Pitt said earnestly. "Admiral Kemper has loaned us the *Modoc*. She's docked at Norfolk right now, fitted out and ready to sail."

"Of course!" Gunn blurted. "The *Sea Slug*."

"Precisely," Pitt replied. "The *Sea Slug* is the Navy's latest-model submersible, designed and constructed especially for deep-water salvage and rescue, and she's sitting on the *Modoc*'s afterdeck. In two days, Rudi and I can have both vessels over the general area of the wreck, ready to begin the search operation."

Sandecker rubbed the pointer across his chin. "And then, if the computers do their job, I feed you the corrected position of the wreck site. Is that the picture?"

"Yes, sir, that's the picture."

Sandecker moved away from the map and eased into a chair. Then he looked up into the determined faces of Pitt and Gunn. "Okay, gentlemen, it's your ball game."

31

Mel Donner leaned on the doorbell of Seagram's house in Chevy Chase and stifled a yawn.

Seagram opened the door and stepped out onto the front porch. They nodded silently without the usual early-morning pleasantries and walked to the curb and Donner's car.

Seagram sat and gazed dully out the side window, his eyes ringed with dark circles. Donner slipped the car into gear.

"You look like Frankenstein's monster before he came alive," Donner said. "How late did you work last night?"

"Actually came home early," Seagram replied. "Bad mistake; should have worked late. Simply gave Dana and me more time to fight. She's been so damned condescending lately, it drives me up the wall. I finally got pissed and locked myself in the study. Fell asleep at my desk. I ache in places I didn't know existed."

"Thank you," Donner said, smiling.

Seagram turned, puzzled. "Thank you for what?"

"For adding another brick under my determination to remain single."

They were both silent while Donner eased through Washington's rush-hour traffic.

"Gene," Donner said at last, "I know this is a touchy subject; put me on your shit list if you will, but you're beginning to come across like a self-tortured cynic."

There was no reaction from Seagram, so Donner forged ahead. "Why don't you take a week or two off and take Dana to a quiet, sunny beach somewhere. Get away from Washington for a while. The defense-installation construction is going off without a hitch, and there's nothing we can do about the byzanium except sit back and pray that Sandecker's boys at NUMA salvage it from the *Titanic*."

"I'm needed now, more than ever," Seagram said flatly.

"You're only kidding yourself into an ego trip. At the moment, everything is out of our hands."

A grim smile touched Seagram's lips. "You're closer to the truth than you can imagine."

Donner glanced at him. "What do you mean?"

"It's out of our hands," Seagram repeated vacantly. "The President ordered me to leak the Sicilian Project to the Russians."

Donner pulled over to the curb and looked at Seagram dumfounded. "My God, why?"

"Warren Nicholson over at CIA has convinced the President that by feeding bits of hard data on the project to the Russians, he can get control of one of their top intelligence networks."

"I don't believe a word of it," Donner said.

"It makes no difference what you believe," Seagram said brusquely.

"If what you say is true, what good will the Russians get out of bits and scraps? Without the necessary detailed equations and calculations, it would take them at least two years to put a workable theory on paper. And without byzanium, the whole concept is worthless."

"They could build a working system within thirty months if they get their hands on the byzanium first."

"Impossible. Admiral Kemper would never permit it. He'd send the Russians packing in a hurry if they tried to pirate the *Titanic*."

"Suppose," Seagram murmured softly, "just suppose Kemper was ordered to lay back and do nothing."

Donner leaned over the wheel and rubbed his forehead in disbelief. "Are you asking me to believe the President of the United States is working with the Communists?"

Seagram shrugged wearily and said, "How can I ask you to believe anything when I don't know what to believe myself?"

32

Pavel Marganin, tall and authoritative in his white naval uniform, took a deep breath of the evening air and turned into the ornate lobby of the Borodino Restaurant. He gave his name to the maître d' and followed him to Prevlov's customary table. The captain sat there reading a thick sheath of papers bound in a file folder. His eyes came up briefly and acknowledged Marganin with a bored glance before they flicked back to the contents of the file.

"May I sit down, Captain?"

"Unless you wish to place a towel over your arm and clear away the dishes," Prevlov said, still engrossed in his reading. "By all means."

Marganin ordered a vodka and waited for Prevlov to initiate the conversation. After nearly three full minutes, the captain finally laid the file aside and lit a cigarette.

"Tell me, Lieutenant, have you followed the Lorelei Current Drift Expedition?"

"Not in detail. I merely scanned the report before passing it along to your attention."

"A pity," Prevlov said loftily. "Think of it, Lieutenant, a submersible capable of moving fifteen hundred miles along the ocean floor without surfacing once in almost two months. Soviet scientists would do well to be half as imaginative."

"Frankly, sir, I found the report rather dull reading."

"Dull reading, indeed! If you had studied it during one of your rare fits of conscientious dedication, you would have discerned a strange course deviation during the expedition's final days."

"I fail to see a hidden meaning in a simple course change."

"A good intelligence man looks for the hidden meaning in everything, Marganin."

Properly rebuked, Marganin nervously checked his watch and stared in the direction of the men's room.

"I think we should investigate whatever it is the Americans find so interesting off the Newfoundland Grand Banks," Prevlov continued. "Since that Novaya Zemlya business, I want a close look into every operation undertaken by the National Underwater and Marine Agency, beginning six months ago. My intuition tells me the Americans are up to something that spells trouble for Mother Russia." Prevlov motioned to a passing waiter and pointed at his empty glass. He leaned back and sighed. "Things are never what they seem, are they? We are in a strange and baffling business when you consider that every comma, every period on a scrap of paper can possess a vital blueprint to an extraordinary secret. It is the least obvious direction that holds the answers."

The waiter came with Prevlov's cognac and he emptied the glass, swishing the liquor around in his mouth before downing it in one swallow.

"Will you excuse me a moment, sir?"

Prevlov looked up and Marganin nodded in the direction of the men's room.

"Of course."

Marganin stepped into the high-ceilinged, tiled bathroom and stood in front of the urinal. He was not alone. A pair of feet with the trousers draped about the ankles showed under a toilet stall. He stood there, taking his time, until he heard the toilet flush. Then he moved over to the washbasin and rinsed his hands slowly, watching in the mirror as the same fat man from the park bench hitched up his belt and approached him.

"Pardon me, sailor," the fat man said. "You dropped this on the floor."

He handed Marganin a small envelope.

Marganin took it without hesitation and slipped it into his tunic. "Oh, how careless of me. Thank you."

The fat man then leaned over the basin as Marganin turned away for a towel. "You have explosive information in that envelope," said the fat man softly. "Do not treat it lightly."

"It will be handled delicately."

33

The letter was resting neatly centered on Seagram's desk in the study. He turned on the lamp, sagged into the chair, and began reading.

Dear Gene,

I love you. It must seem like a banal way to begin, but it is true. I still love you with all my heart.

I have tried desperately to understand and comfort you during these months of stress. How I have suffered waiting for you to accept my love and attention, hoping for nothing in return except a small sign of your affection. I am strong in many respects, Gene, but I do not have the strength and patience to fight indifferent neglect. No woman does.

I long for our early days, the gentle days when our concern for one another far outweighed the demands of our professional lives. It was simpler then. We taught our classes at the university, we laughed and made love as though each time were our last. Perhaps I drove the wedge between us for not wanting children. Perhaps a son or a daughter might have bound us tighter together. I don't know. I can only regret the things I did not do.

I only know that it will be best for both of us if I set time and space between us for a while, for at present our living under the same roof seems to bring out a meanness and selfishness neither of us knew we possessed.

I have moved in with Marie Sheldon, a marine geologist with NUMA. She has been kind enough to loan me a spare room in her Georgetown house until I can untangle my mental cobwebs. Please do not try to contact me. It would only result in more ugly words. Give me time to work things out, Gene. I implore you.

They say time heals all wounds. Let us pray this is so. I do not mean to desert you, Gene, when you feel you need me most. I believe it will relieve one more burden from the heavy pressures of your position.

Forgive my feminine frailty, but from the other side of the coin,

*my side, it is as though you drove me away. Let us hope the future
will allow our love to endure.*
Again, I love you.

Dana

Seagram reread the letter four times, his eyes refusing to turn from the
neatly scripted pages. Finally, he clicked off the light and sat there in the
darkness.

34

Dana Seagram stood in front of her closet going through the feminine
ritual of deciding what to wear when a knock sounded on the bedroom
door.

"Dana? You almost ready?"

"Come on in, Marie."

Marie Sheldon opened the door and leaned into the bedroom. "Good
lord, sweetie, you're not even dressed yet."

Marie's voice came from deep within her throat. She was a small,
thin, vital woman with vivid blue eyes, a pert bobbed nose, and a mass
of bleached blond hair shaped in a shag style. She might have been very
provocative except for her square-cut chin.

"I go through this every morning," Dana said irritably. "If only I
could get organized and lay things out the night before, but I always
wait until the last moment."

Marie moved beside Dana. "How about the blue skirt?"

Dana slipped the skirt off the hanger and then threw it down on the
carpet. "Damn! I sent the matching blouse to the cleaners."

"If you're not careful, you'll start foaming at the mouth."

"I can't help it," Dana said. "Nothing seems to go right lately."

"Since you walked out on your husband, you mean."

"The last thing I need now is a sermon."

"Settle down, sweetie. If you want to take out your wrath on somebody, then stand in front of a mirror."

Dana stood, tense as a toy doll whose spring has been wound too
tightly. Marie could see an emotional crying jag coming on and beat a
strategic retreat.

"Relax. Take your time. I'll go down and warm up the car."

Dana waited until Marie's footsteps died before she went into the bathroom and downed two Librium capsules. As soon as the tranquilizer began to take effect, she calmly slipped on a turquoise linen dress, straightened her hair, pulled on a pair of flat-heeled shoes, and headed downstairs.

On the way to NUMA headquarters, Dana sat bright and perky while tapping her foot to the music from the car radio.

"One pill or two?" Marie said casually.

"Umm?"

"I said, one pill or two. It's a safe bet that when you instantly transform from a bitch into a Miss Goody Two-Shoes, you've been popping pills."

"I meant it about the sermon."

"Okay, but a warning, old roommate. If I find you flaked out on the floor some dark night from an overdose, I'm going to quietly fold my tent and silently steal off into the night. I can't stand traumatic death scenes."

"You're exaggerating."

Marie looked at her. "Am I? You've been hitting that stuff like a health nut gobbles vitamins."

"I'm all right," Dana said defiantly.

"Like hell you are. You're a classic case of an emotionally depressed and frustrated female. The worst kind, I might add."

"It takes time for the ragged edges to dull."

"Ragged edges, my ass. You mean it dulls your guilt."

"I won't delude myself into believing I did the best thing by leaving Gene. But I'm convinced I did the right thing."

"Don't you think he needs you?"

"I used to hope he would reach out to me, yet every time we're together, we fight like alley cats. He's closed me out, Marie. It's the same old tired story. When a man like Gene becomes a slave to the demands of his work, he throws up a wall that can't be breached. And the stupid reason, the incredibly stupid reason, is because he imagines that sharing his problems automatically throws me on the firing line, too. A man accepts the thankless burden of responsibility. We women do not. To us, life is a game we play one day at a time. We never plan ahead like men." Her face became sad and drawn. "I can only wait and come back after Gene falls wounded in his private battle. Then, and only then, am I certain he'll welcome a return of my company."

"It may be too late," Marie said. "From your description of him, Gene sounds like a prime candidate for a mental breakdown or a massive coronary. If you had an ounce of guts, you'd stick it out with him."

Dana shook her head. "I can't cope with rejection. Until we can get together peacefully again, I'm going to make another life."

"Does that include other men?"

"Platonic love only." Dana forced a smile. "I'm not about to play the liberated female and jump onto every penis that wanders across my path."

Marie grinned slyly. "It's one thing to be picky and play lip service to high standards, sweetie, but quite another matter in actual practice. You forget, this is Washington, D.C. We outnumber the men eight to one. They're the lucky ones who can afford to be choosy."

"If something happens, then something happens. I'm not going out and look for an affair. Besides, I'm out of practice. I've forgotten how to flirt."

"Seducing a man is like riding a bicycle," Marie said, laughing. "Once learned, never forgotten."

She parked in the vast open lot of the NUMA headquarters building. They walked up the steps into the lobby, where they joined the stream of other staff members who were hurrying down the halls and up the elevators to their offices.

"How about meeting me for lunch?" Marie said.

"Fine."

"I'll bring a couple of male friends for you to exercise your latent charms on."

Before Dana could protest, Marie had melted into the crowd. As she stood in the elevator, Dana noted with a curious sense of detached pleasure that her heart was thumping.

35

Sandecker pulled his car into the parking lot of the Alexandria College of Oceanography, climbed out from under the wheel, and walked over to a man standing beside an electric golf cart.

"Admiral Sandecker?"

"Yes."

"Dr. Murray Silverstein." The round, balding little man stuck out his hand. "Glad you could come, Admiral. I think we've got something that will prove helpful."

Sandecker settled into the cart. "We're grateful for every scrap of useful data you can give us."

Silverstein took the tiller and guided them down an asphalt lane. "We've run an extensive series of tests since last night. I can't promise anything mathematically exact, mind you, but the results are interesting, to say the least."

"Any problems?"

"A few. The main snag that throws our projections from the precise side of the scale to the approximate is a lack of solid facts. For instance, the direction of the *Titanic*'s bow when she went down was never established. This unknown factor alone could add four square miles to the search area."

"I don't understand. Wouldn't a forty-five-thousand-ton steel ship sink in a straight line?"

"Not necessarily. The *Titanic* corkscrewed and slid under the water at a depressed angle of roughly seventy-eight degrees, and, as she sank, the weight of the sea filling her forward compartments pulled her into a headway of between four and five knots. Next, we have to consider the momentum caused by her tremendous mass and the fact that she had to travel two and a half miles before she struck bottom. No, I'm afraid she landed on a horizontal line a fair distance from her original starting point on the surface."

Sandecker stared at the oceanographer. "How could you possibly know the precise angle of descent when the *Titanic* sank? The survivors' descriptions were on the whole unreliable."

Silverstein pointed to a huge concrete tower off to his right. "The answers are in there, Admiral." He stopped the cart at the front entrance of the building. "Come along and I'll give you a practical demonstration of what I'm talking about."

Sandecker followed him through a short hallway and into a room with a large acrylic plastic window at one end. Silverstein motioned for the admiral to move closer. A diver wearing scuba equipment waved from the other side of the window. Sandecker waved back.

"A deep-water tank," Silverstein said matter-of-factly. "The interior walls are made of steel and rise two hundred feet high with a diameter of thirty feet. There is a main pressure chamber for entering and exiting the bottom level and five air locks stationed at intervals along the side to enable us to observe our experiments at different depths."

"I see," Sandecker said slowly. "You've been able to simulate the *Titanic*'s fall to the sea floor."

"Yes, let me show you." Silverstein lifted a telephone from a shelf under the observation window. "Owen, make a drop in thirty seconds."

"You have a scale model of the *Titanic*?"

"Not exactly a prize exhibit for a maritime museum of course," Silverstein said, "but, for a scaled-down version of the ship's general configuration, weight, and displacement, it's a near-perfect, balanced replica. The potter did a damned fine job."

"The potter?"

"Ceramics," Silverstein said waving his hand in a vague gesture. "We can mold and fire twenty models in the time it would take us to fabricate a metal one." He laid a hand on Sandecker's arm and pulled him toward the window. "Here she comes."

Sandecker looked up and saw an oblong shape about four feet in length falling slowly through the water, preceded by what looked to be a shower of marbles. He could see that there had been no attempt to authenticate detail. The model looked like a smooth lump of unglazed clay: rounded at one end, narrowed at the other, and topped by three tubes, representing the *Titanic*'s smokestacks. He heard a distinct clink through the observation window as the model's bow struck the bottom of the tank.

"Wouldn't your calculations be thrown off by a flaw in the model's configuration?" Sandecker asked.

"Yes, a mistake could make a difference." Silverstein looked at him. "But I assure you, Admiral, we missed nothing!"

Sandecker pointed at the model. "The real *Titanic* had four funnels; yours has only three."

"Just before the *Titanic*'s final plunge," Silverstein said, "her stern rose until she was completely perpendicular. The strain was too much for the guy wires supporting the number one funnel. They snapped and it toppled over the starboard side."

Sandecker nodded. "My compliments, Doctor. I should have known better than to question the thoroughness of your experiment."

"It's nothing, really. It gives me a chance to show off my expertise." He turned and motioned a thumbs-up sign through the window. The diver tied the model onto a line that traveled toward the top of the tank. "I'll run the test again and explain how we arrived at our conclusions."

"You might begin by explaining the marbles."

"They act the role of the boilers," Silverstein said.

"The boilers?"

"Perfect simulation, too. You see, while the *Titanic*'s stern was pointing at the sky, her boilers broke loose from their cradle mounts and hurtled through the bulkheads toward the bows. Massive things they were—twenty-nine, all told; some of them were nearly sixteen feet in diameter and twenty feet long."

"But your marbles fell outside the model."

"Yes, our calculations indicate that at least nineteen of the boilers smashed their way through the bows and dropped to the bottom separately from the hull."

"How can you be sure?"

"Because if their fall had been contained, the tremendous shift in ballast caused by their journey from amidships to the forward section of the ship would have pulled the *Titanic* on a ninety-degree course straight downward. However, the reports of the survivors watching from the lifeboats—for once, most all tend to agree—state that soon after the earsplitting rumble from the boilers' crazy stampede had died away, the ship settled back a bit at the stern before sliding under. This fact indicates to me, at any rate, that the *Titanic* vomited her boilers and once free of this superincumbency, righted herself slightly to attain the seventy-eight-degree slant I mentioned previously."

"And the marbles bear out this theory?"

"To the letter." Silverstein picked up the telephone again. "Ready whenever you are, Owen." He replaced the receiver on its cradle. "Owen Dugan, my assistant above. About now he'll be setting the model in the water directly over that plumb line you see in the water off to one side of the tank. As the water begins coming in through holes drilled strategically in the bows of the model, she'll begin to go down by the head. At a certain angle the marbles will roll to the bow and a spring-loaded door will allow them to fall free."

As if on cue, the marbles began falling to the floor of the tank, followed closely by the model. It struck about twelve feet from the plumb line. The diver made a tiny mark on the bottom of the tank and held up his thumb and index finger, indicating one inch.

"There you have it, Admiral, a hundred and ten drops and she's never touched down outside a four-inch radius."

Sandecker stared into the tank for a long moment, then turned to Silverstein. "So where do we search?"

"After a few dazzling computations by our physics department," said Silverstein, "their best guess is thirteen hundred yards south of east from the point the *Sappho I* discovered the cornet, but at that, it's still a guess."

"How can you be certain the horn didn't fall on an angle, too?"

Silverstein feigned a hurt look. "You underestimate my genius for perfection, Admiral. Our evaluations here would be worthless without a clear-cut picture of the cornet's path to the sea floor. Included in my expense vouchers you will find a receipt from Moe's Pawnshop for two cornets. After a series of tests in the tank, we took them two hundred miles off Cape Hatteras and dropped them in twelve thousand feet of water. I can show you the charts from our sonar. They each landed within fifty yards of their vertical departure line."

"No offense," Sandecker said equably. "I have a sinking feeling, if you'll pardon the pun, that my lack of faith is going to cost me a case of Robert Mondavi Chardonnay 1984."

"1981," Silverstein said, grinning.

"If there's one thing I can't stand, it's a schmuck with good taste."

"Think how common the world would be without us."

Sandecker made no reply. He moved up to the window and stared inside the tank at the ceramic model of the *Titanic*. Silverstein moved up behind him. "She's a fascinating subject, no doubt of it."

"Strange thing about the *Titanic*," Sandecker said softly. "Once her spell strikes, you can think of nothing else."

"But why? What is there about her that grips the imagination and won't let go?"

"Because she's the wreck that puts all the others to shame," Sandecker said. "She's modern history's most legendary yet elusive treasure. A simple photograph of her is enough to pump the adrenalin. Knowing her story, the crew who sailed her, the people who walked her decks in the few short days she lived, that's what fires the imagination, Silverstein. The *Titanic* is a vast archive of an era we'll never see again. God only knows if it is within our power to bring the grand old dame into daylight again. But, by heaven, we're going to try."

36

The submersible *Sea Slug* looked aerodynamically clean and smooth from her outside, but to Pitt, as he contorted his six-foot-two frame into the pilot's chair, the interior seemed a claustrophobic nightmare of hydraulic plumbing and electrical circuitry. The craft was twenty feet long and tubular in shape, with rounded ends like its lethargic namesake. It was painted bright yellow and had four large portholes set in pairs on its bow, while mounted along the top, like small radar domes, were two powerful high-intensity lights.

Pitt completed the checklist and turned to Giordino, who sat in the seat to his right.

"Shall we make a dive?"

Giordino flashed a toothy smile. "Yes, let's."

"How about it, Rudi?"

Gunn looked up from his prone position behind the lower viewports and nodded. "Ready when you are."

Pitt spoke into a microphone and watched the small television screen above the control panel as it showed the *Modoc*'s derrick lift the *Sea Slug* from her deck cradle and gently swing her over the side and into the water. As soon as a diver had disconnected the lift cable, Pitt cracked the ballast valve and the submersible began to sink slowly under the rolling, deep-troughed waves.

"Life-support timer on," Giordino announced. "An hour to the bottom, ten hours for the search, two hours for surfacing, leaving us a reserve of five hours just in case."

"We'll use the reserve time for the search," Pitt said.

Giordino knew well the facts of the situation. If the unthinkable happened, an accident at twelve thousand feet, there would be no hope of rescue. A quick death would be the only prayer against the appalling suffering of slow asphyxiation. He found himself actually amused at wishing he was back on board the *Sappho I,* enjoying the uncramped comfort of open space and the security of her eight-week life-support system. He sat back and watched the water darken as the *Sea Slug* buried her hull in the depths, his thoughts drifting to the enigmatic man who was piloting the craft.

Giordino went back with Pitt to their high-school days, when they had built and raced hot rods together down the lonely farm roads behind Newport Beach, California. He knew Pitt better than any man alive; any woman, for that matter. Pitt possessed in a sense, two separate inner identities, neither directly related to the other. There was the congenial Dirk Pitt, who rarely deviated from the middle of the road, and was humorous, unpretentious, and radiated an easygoing friendliness with everyone he met. Then there was the other Dirk Pitt, the coldly efficient machine who seldom made a mistake and who often withdrew into himself, remote and aloof. If there was a key that would unlock the door between the two, Giordino had yet to discover it.

Giordino turned his attention back to the depth gauge. Its needle indicated twelve hundred feet. Soon they passed the two-thousand-foot mark and entered a world of perpetual night. From this point downward, as far as the human eye was concerned, there was only pure blackness. Giordino pushed a switch and the outside lights burst on and sliced a reassuring path through the darkness.

"What do you think our chances are of finding her on the first try?" he asked.

"If the computer data Admiral Sandecker sent us holds true, the *Titanic* should lie somewhere within a hundred-and-ten-degree arc, thirteen hundred yards southeast of the spot where you reclaimed the cornet."

"Oh, great," Giordino mumbled sarcastically. "That narrows it down from looking for a toenail in the sands of Coney Island to searching for an albino boll weevil in a cotton field."

"There he goes again," Gunn said, "offering his negative thought for the day."

"Maybe if we ignore him," Pitt laughed, "he'll go away."

Giordino grimaced and motioned into the watery void.

"Oh sure, just drop me off at the next corner."

"We'll find the old girl," Pitt said resolutely. He pointed at the illuminated clock on the control panel. "Let's see, it's oh-six-forty now. I predict we'll be over the *Titanic*'s decks before lunch, say about eleven-forty."

Giordino gave Pitt a sideways look. "The great soothsayer has spoken."

"A little optimism never hurts," Gunn said. He adjusted the exterior camera housings and triggered the strobe. It flashed blindingly for an instant like a shaft of lightning, reflecting millions of planktonic creatures that hung in the water.

Ten thousand feet and forty minutes later, Pitt reported to the *Modoc,* giving the depth and the water temperature: thirty-five degrees. The three men watched fascinated as a small angler fish, ugly in its stubby appearance, slowly swept past the viewports; the tiny luminous bulb that protruded from the top of its head glowed like a lonely beacon.

At 12,375 feet the sea floor came into view, moving up to meet the *Sea Slug* as though she were standing still. Pitt turned on the propulsion motors and adjusted the altitude angle, gently stopping the *Sea Slug*'s descent and turning her on a level course across the bleak red clay that carpeted the ocean floor.

Gradually, the ominous silence was broken by the rhythmic hum that came from the *Sea Slug*'s electric motors. At first, Pitt had difficulty distinguishing rises and gradual drops on the bottom; there was nothing to indicate a three-dimensional scale. His eyes saw only a flatness that stretched beyond the reach of the lights.

There was no life to be seen. And yet, evidence proved otherwise. Scattering tracks from the depth's habitants meandered and zigzagged in every direction through the sediment. One might have guessed that they were made only recently, but the sea can be misleading. The footprints from deep-dwelling sea spiders, sea cucumbers, or starfish might have been made several minutes ago or hundreds of years past, because the microscopic animal and plant remains that comprise the deep-ocean ooze filters down from above at the rate of only one or two centimeters every thousand years.

"There's a lovely creature," Giordino said pointing.

Pitt's eye followed Giordino's finger and picked out a strange blue-black animal that seemed a cross between a squid and an octopus. It had eight tentacles linked together like the webbed foot of a duck, and it stared back at the *Sea Slug* through two large globular eyes that formed nearly a third of its body.

"A vampire squid," Gunn informed them.

"Ask her if she's got relatives in Transylvania?" Giordino grinned.

"You know," Pitt said, "that thing out there sort of reminds me of your girl friend."

Gunn jumped in. "You mean the one with no boobs?"

"You've seen her?"

"Rave on, envious rabble," Giordino grumbled. "She's mad about me and her father keeps me floating in quality booze."

"Some quality," Pitt snorted. "Old Cesspool Bourbon, Attila the Hun Gin, Tijuana Vodka. Who the hell ever heard of those labels?"

Throughout the next few hours, the wit and the sarcasm bounced off the walls of the *Sea Slug*. Actually, it was put on; a defense mechanism to relieve the gnawing pangs of monotony. Unlike romanticized fiction, wreck-hunting in the depths can be a grueling and tedious job. Add to that the aggravated discomfort of the cramped quarters, the high humidity and chilling temperatures inside the submersible, and you have the ingredients for provoking an accident through human error that could prove both costly and fatal.

Pitt's hands stayed rock-steady as they handled the controls, guiding the *Sea Slug* a scant four feet above the bottom. Giordino's concentration was nailed to the life-support systems, while Gunn kept his eyes skinned on the sonar and magnetometer. The long hours of planning were over. It was now a case of patience and persistence, mixed with that peculiar blend of eternal optimism and love of the unknown shared by all treasure seekers.

"Looks like a pile of rocks up ahead," Pitt said.

Giordino stared up through the viewports. "They're just sitting there in the ooze. I wonder where they came from."

"Perhaps ballast thrown overboard from an old windjammer."

"More likely came from icebergs," Gunn said. "Many rocks and bits of debris are carried over the sea and then dropped to the floor when the icebergs melt—" Gunn broke off in the middle of his lecture. "Hold on . . . I'm getting a strong response on the sonar. Now the magnetometer is picking it up, too."

"Where away?" Pitt asked.

"On a heading of one-three-seven."

"One-three-seven it is," Pitt repeated. He swept the *Sea Slug* into a graceful bank, as though she was an airplane, and headed on the new course. Giordino peered intently over Gunn's shoulder at the green circles of light on the sonarscope. A small dot of pulsating brightness indicated a solid object three hundred yards beyond their range of vision.

"Don't get your hopes up," Gunn said quietly. "The target reads too small for a ship."

"What do you make of it?"

"Hard to say. No more than twenty or twenty-five feet in length, about two stories high. Might be anything. . . ."

"Or it might be one of the *Titanic*'s boilers," Pitt cut in. "The sea floor should be littered with them."

"You move to the head of the class," Gunn said, excitement creeping into his tone. "I have an identical reading, bearing one-one-five. And here comes another at one-six-zero. The last has an indicated length of approximately seventy feet."

"Sounds like one of her smokestacks," Pitt said.

"Lord!" Gunn murmured hoarsely. "It's beginning to read like a junkyard down here."

Suddenly, in the gloom at the outer edge of the blackness, a rounded object became visible, haloed in the eerie light like an immense tombstone. Soon the three pairs of eyes inside the submersible could distinguish the furnace gratings of the great boiler, and then the row upon row of rivets along the iron seams and the torn, jagged tentacles of what was left of its steam tubing.

"How would you like to have been a stoker in those days and fed that baby?" Giordino muttered.

"I've picked up another one," Gunn said. "No, wait . . . the pulse is getting stronger. Here comes the length. One hundred feet . . . two . . ."

"Keep coming, sweetheart," Pitt prayed.

"Five hundred . . . seven . . . eight hundred feet. We got her! We've got her!"

"What course?" Pitt's mouth was as dry as sand.

"Bearing zero-nine-seven," Gunn replied in a whisper.

They spoke no more for the next few minutes as the *Sea Slug* closed the distance. Their faces were pale and strained with anticipation. Pitt's heart was pounding painfully in his chest, and his stomach felt as if it had a great iron weight in it and a huge hand crushing it from the outside. He became aware that he was allowing the submersible to creep too close to the ooze. He pulled back the controls and kept his eyes trained through the viewport. What would they find? A rusty old hulk far beyond hope of salvaging? A shattered, broken hull buried to its superstructure in the muck? And then his straining eyes caught sight of a massive shadow looming up ominously in the darkness.

"Christ almighty!" Giordino mumbled in awe. "We've struck her fair on the bows."

As the range narrowed to fifty feet, Pitt slowed the motors and turned the *Sea Slug* on a parallel course with the ill-fated liner's waterline. The mere size of the wreck when viewed from alongside her steel plates was a staggering sight. Even after nearly eighty years, the sunken ship proved to be surprisingly free of corrosion; the gold band that encompassed the 882-foot black hull glistened under the high-intensity lights. Pitt eased the submersible upward past the eight-ton portside anchor until they could all clearly make out the three-foot-high golden letters that still proudly proclaimed her as the **Titanic.**

Spellbound, Pitt picked the microphone from its cradle and pressed the transmit button. *"Modoc, Modoc.* This is *Sea Slug* . . . do you read?"

The radio operator on the *Modoc* answered almost immediately. "This is *Modoc, Sea Slug.* We read you. Over."

Pitt adjusted the volume to minimize the background crackle. *"Modoc,* notify NUMA headquarters that we have found the Big T. Repeat, we have found the big T. Depth twelve thousand three hundred and forty feet. Time, eleven-forty-two hours."

"Eleven-forty-two?" Giordino echoed. "You cocky bastard. You only missed by two minutes."

Regenesis

The *Titanic* lay cloaked by the eerie stillness of the black deep and bore the grim scars of her tragedy. The jagged wound from her collision with the iceberg stretched from the starboard forepeak to the No. 5 boiler room nearly three hundred feet down her hull, while the gaping holes in her bows below the waterline betrayed the shattering impact made by her boilers when they tore from her bowels and smashed their way through bulkhead after bulkhead until they plunged free into the sea.

She sat heavily in the ooze with a slight list to port, her forecastle set on a southerly course, as if she were still pathetically struggling to reach

out and touch the waters of a port she had never known. The lights from
the submersible danced over her ghostlike superstructure, casting long
spectral shadows across her long teak decks. Her portholes, some open,
some closed, marched in orderly rows along the broad expanse of her
sides. She presented an almost modern, streamlined appearance now that
her funnels were gone; the forward three were nonexistent, two probably
having been carried away by her dive to the bottom, while number four
lay fallen across the After Boat Deck. And, except for the scattered
strands of rusty, disconnected funnel rigging that snaked over the railings, her Boat Deck showed only a few hulking air vents standing silent
guard above the vacant Welin davits that had once held the great liner's
lifeboats.

There was a morbid beauty about her. The men inside the submersible could almost see her dining saloons and staterooms flooded with
lights and crowded with hundreds of light-hearted and laughing passengers. They could visualize her libraries stacked with books, her smoking
rooms filled with the blue haze of gentlemen's cigars, and hear the music
of her band playing turn-of-the-century ragtime. The passengers walked
her decks: the wealthy, the famous, men in immaculate evening dress,
women in colorful ankle-length gowns, nannies with children clutching
favorite toys, the Astors, the Guggenheims, and the Strauses in first
class; the middle-class, the school teachers, the clergymen, the students,
and the writers in second; the immigrants, the Irish farmers and their
families, the carpenters, the bakers, the dressmakers, and the miners
from remote villages of Sweden, Russia, and Greece in steerage. Then
there were the almost nine hundred crew members, from the ship's
officers to the caterers, the stewards, the lift boys, and the engine-room
men.

Great opulence lay in the darkness beyond the doors and portholes.
What would the swimming pool, the squash court, and the Turkish baths
look like? Was there a rotten remnant of the great tapestry still hanging
in the reception room? What of the bronze clock on the grand staircase,
or the crystal chandeliers in the elegant Café Parisien, or the delicately
ornate ceiling above the first-class dining saloon? Would, perhaps the
bones of Captain Edward J. Smith remain somewhere within the shadows of the bridge? What mysteries were there to be discovered within
this once colossal floating palace if and when she ever greeted the sun
again?

The strobe light on the submersible's cameras seemed to flash endlessly as the tiny intruder circled the immense hulk. A large two-foot, rat-tailed fish with huge eyes and a heavy armored head skittered over the slanting decks, showing total unconcern for the exploding beams of light.

After what seemed like hours, the submersible, the faces of its crew still glued to the viewports, rose over the first-class lounge roof, hovered for a few moments, then deposited a small electronic-signal capsule. Its low-frequency impulses would now provide a traceable guideline for future dives to the wreck. Then the submersible made a gliding turn upward, her lights blinked out, and she melted back into the darkness from whence she had come.

Except for the few sparks of marine life that had somehow managed to adapt to survival in the black, bitter-cold environment, the *Titanic* was alone once more. But soon other submersibles would come and she would feel the tools of man working on her steel skin again, as she had so many years ago at the great slipways of the Harland and Wolff shipbuilding firm in Belfast.

Then, perhaps, just perhaps, she would make her first port after all.

4

The TITANIC

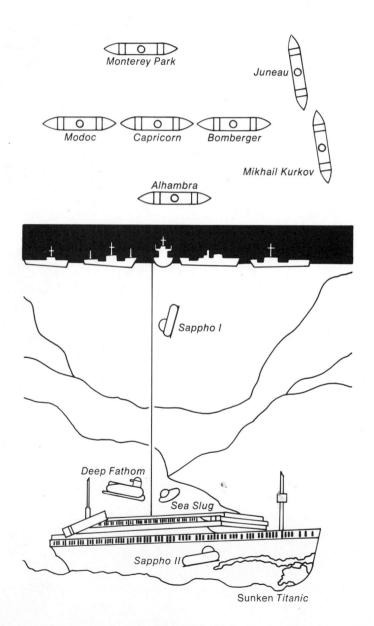

Monterey Park

Juneau

Modoc   Capricorn   Bomberger

Mikhail Kurkov

Alhambra

Sappho I

Deep Fathom

Sea Slug

Sappho II

Sunken *Titanic*

37

In a measured and precise manner, the Soviet General Secretary, Georgi Antonov, lit his pipe and surveyed the other men seated around the long mahogany conference table.

To his right sat Admiral Boris Sloyuk, director of Soviet Naval Intelligence, and his aide, Captain Prevlov. Opposite them were Vladimir Polevoi, Chief of the Foreign Secrets Direction of the KGB, and Vasily Tilevitch, Marshal of the Soviet Union and chief director of Soviet Security.

Antonov came straight to the point: "Well now, it seems the Americans are determined to raise the *Titanic* to the surface." He studied the papers sitting before him a few moments before continuing. "An extensive effort by the look of it. Two supply ships, three tenders, four deep-sea submersibles." He looked up at Admiral Sloyuk and Prevlov. "Do we have an observer in the area?"

Prevlov nodded. "The oceanographic research vessel *Mikhail Kurkov,* under the command of Captain Ivan Parotkin, is cruising the salvage perimeter."

"I know Parotkin personally," Sloyuk added. "He is a good seaman."

"If the Americans are spending hundreds of millions of dollars in an attempt to salvage a seventy-six-year-old piece of scrap," Antonov said, "there must be a logical motivation."

"There is a motivation," Admiral Sloyuk said gravely. "A motivation that threatens our very security." He nodded to Prevlov, who began passing out a red folder marked "Sicilian Project" to Antonov and the men across the table. "That is why I requested this meeting. My people have discovered outline plans for a new secret American defense system. I think you will find it a shocking, if not terrifying, study."

Antonov and the others opened the folders and began reading. For perhaps five minutes, the Soviet General Secretary read, occasionally glancing in Sloyuk's direction. Antonov's face went through a wide range of expressions, beginning with professional interest to frank bewilderment, to astonishment, and, finally, stunned realization.

"This is incredible, Admiral Sloyuk, absolutely incredible."

"Is such a defense system possible?" Marshal Tilevitch asked.

"I have put the same question to five of our most respected scientists. They all agreed, theoretically, that such a system is feasible, provided a strong enough power source is available."

"And you assume this source lies in the cargo holds of the *Titanic*?" Tilevitch put to him.

"We are certain of it, Comrade Marshal. As I mentioned in the report, the vital ingredient needed for the completion of the Sicilian Project is a little-known element called byzanium. We now know the Americans stole the world's only supply from Russian soil seventy-six years ago. Fortunately for us, they had the ill luck to transport it on a doomed ship."

Antonov shook his head in utter incomprehension. "If what you say in your report is true, then the Americans have the potential to knock down our intercontinental missiles as effortlessly as a goatherd swats flies."

Sloyuk nodded solemnly. "I am afraid that is the fearful truth."

Polevoi leaned across the table, his face a mask of suspicious consternation. "You state here that your contact is a high-level aide in the United States Department of Defense."

"That is correct." Prevlov nodded respectfully. "He became disillusioned with the American government during the Watergate affair and has since sent me whatever material he deems important."

Antonov stared piercingly into Prevlov's eyes. "Do you think they can do it, Captain Prevlov?"

"Raise the *Titanic*?"

Antonov nodded.

Prevlov stared back. "If you will recall the Central Intelligence Agency's successful recovery of one of our Soviet nuclear submarines in seventeen thousand feet of water off Hawaii in 1974—I believe the CIA referred to it as Project Jennifer—there is little doubt that the Americans have the technical capability to put the *Titanic* in New York harbor. Yes, Comrade Antonov, I firmly believe they will do it."

"I do not share your opinion," said Polevoi. "A vessel the size of the *Titanic* is a far cry from a submarine."

"I have to throw in my lot with Captain Prevlov," Sloyuk argued. "The Americans have an annoying habit of accomplishing what they set out to do."

"And what of this Sicilian Project?" Polevoi persisted. "The KGB has received no detailed data concerning its existence except the code name. How do we know the Americans have not created a mythical project to play a bluffing hand at the negotiations to limit strategic nuclear-delivery systems?"

Antonov rapped his knuckles on the tabletop. "The Americans do not bluff. Comrade Khrushchev found that out twenty-five years ago during the Cuban missile crisis. We cannot ignore any possibility, however remote, that they are on the verge of making this defense system operational as soon as they salvage the byzanium from the hull of the *Titanic*." He paused to suck on his pipe stem. "I suggest that our next thoughts be directed toward a course of action."

"Quite obviously we must see to it that the byzanium never reaches the United States," Marshal Tilevitch said.

Polevoi drummed his fingers on the Sicilian Project file. "Sabotage. We must sabotage the salvage operation. There is no other way."

"There must be no incident with international repercussions," Antonov said firmly. "There can be no suggestion of interference through overt military action. I do not want Soviet-United States relations jeopardized during yet another bad crop year. Is that clear?"

"We can do nothing unless we penetrate the salvage area," Tilevitch persisted.

Polevoi stared across the table at Sloyuk. "What steps have the Americans taken to protect the operation?"

"The nuclear-powered guided-missile cruiser *Juneau* is patrolling within sight of the salvage ships on a twenty-four-hour basis."

"May I speak?" Prevlov asked almost condescendingly. He did not wait for an answer. "With due consideration, comrades, the penetration has already taken place."

Antonov looked up. "Please explain yourself, Captain."

Prevlov took a side glance at his superior. Admiral Sloyuk acknowledged him with a faint nod.

"We have two undercover operatives working as members of the NUMA salvage crew," Prevlov elucidated. "An exceptionally talented team. They have been relaying important American oceanographic data to us for two years."

"Good, good. Your people have done well, Sloyuk," Antonov said, but there was no warmth in his tone. His gaze came back to Prevlov. "Are we to assume, Captain, that you have devised a plan?"

"I have, comrade."

Marganin was in Prevlov's office when he returned, casually sitting behind the captain's desk. There was a change about him. No longer did he seem like the common, bootlicking aide that Prevlov had left only a few hours ago. There was something about him that was more certain, more self-assured. It seemed to be in his eyes. Those insecure eyes now mirrored the confident look of a man who knew what he was about.

"How did the conference go, Captain?" Marganin asked without rising.

"I think I can safely say the day will soon come when you will be addressing me as Admiral."

"I must confess," Marganin said coolly, "your fertile mind is surpassed only by your ego."

Prevlov was caught off guard. His face paled with controlled anger, and, when he spoke, it required no acute sense of hearing or imagination to detect the emotion in his voice. "You dare to insult me?"

"Why not. You undoubtedly sold Comrade Antonov on the fact that it was your genius that arrived at the purpose of the Sicilian Project and the *Titanic* salvage operation, when, in reality, it was *my* source who passed along the information. And you also most likely told them about your wonderful plan to wrest the byzanium from the Americans' hands. Again, stolen from me. In short, Prevlov, you are nothing but an untalented thief."

"That will do!" Prevlov was pointing a finger at Marganin, his tone glacial. Suddenly, he stiffened and was completely under control again, intent, urbane, the true professional. "You will burn for your insubordination, Marganin," he said pleasantly. "I will see to it that you burn a thousand deaths before this month is through."

Marganin said nothing. He only smiled a smile that was as cold as a tomb.

38

"So much for secrecy," Seagram said, dropping a newspaper on Sandecker's desk. "That's this morning's paper. I picked it up from a newsstand not fifteen minutes ago."

Sandecker turned it around and looked at the front page. He didn't have to look farther, it was all there.

" 'NUMA TO RAISE *Titanic*,' " he read aloud. "Well, at least we don't have to pussyfoot around any more. 'Multimillion dollar effort to salvage ill-fated liner.' You have to admit, it makes for fascinating reading. 'Informed sources said today that the National Underwater and Marine Agency is conducting an all-out salvage attempt to raise the R.M.S. *Titanic*, which struck an iceberg and sank in the mid-Atlantic on April 15, 1912, with a loss of over fifteen hundred lives. This tremendous undertaking heralds a new dawn in deep-sea salvage that is without parallel in the history of man's search for treasure.' "

"A multimillion-dollar treasure hunt," Seagram frowned darkly. "The President will love that."

"Even has a picture of me," Sandecker said. "Not a good likeness. Must be a stock photo from their files, taken maybe five or six years ago."

"It couldn't have come at a worse time," Seagram said. "Three more weeks . . . Pitt said he would try to lift her in three more weeks."

"Don't hold your breath. Pitt and his crew have been at it for nine months; nine grueling months of battling every winter storm the Atlantic could throw at them, tackling every setback and technical adversity as it came up. It's a miracle they've accomplished so much in so little time. And yet, a thousand and one things can still go wrong. There may be hidden structural cracks that might split the hull wide open when it breaks from the sea floor, or then again, the enormous suction between the keel and the bottom ooze might never release its grip. If I were you, Seagram, I wouldn't get a glow on until you see the *Titanic* being towed past the Statue of Liberty."

Seagram looked wounded. The admiral grinned at his stricken expression and offered him a cigar. It was refused.

"On the other hand," Sandecker said comfortingly, "she may rise to the surface as pretty as you please."

"That's what I like about you, Admiral, your on-again, off-again optimism."

"I like to prepare myself for disappointments. It helps to ease the pain."

Seagram didn't reply. He was silent for a minute. Then he said, "So we worry about the *Titanic* when the time comes. But we still have the problem of the press to consider. How do we handle it?"

"Simple," Sandecker said airily. "We do what any red-blooded, grass-roots politician would do when his shady record is laid bare by scandal-hungry reporters."

"And that is?" Seagram asked warily.

"We call a press conference."

"That's madness. If Congress and the public ever got wind of the fact that we've poured over three-quarters of a billion dollars into this thing, they'll be on us like a Kansas tornado."

"So we play liar's poker and slice the salvage costs in half for publication. Who's to know? There's no way the true figure can be uncovered."

"I still don't like it." Seagram said. "These Washington reporters are master surgeons when it comes to dissecting a speaker at a press conference. They'll carve you up like a Thanksgiving turkey."

"I wasn't thinking of me," Sandecker said slowly.

"Then who? Certainly not me. I'm the little man who isn't here, remember?"

"I had someone else in mind. Someone who is ignorant of our behind-the-scenes skulduggery. Someone who is an authority on sunken ships and whom the press would treat with the utmost courtesy and respect."

"And where are you going to find this paragon of virtue?"

"I'm awfully glad you used the word virtue," Sandecker said slyly. "You see, I was thinking of your wife."

39

Dana Seagram stood confidently at the lectern and deftly fielded the questions put to her by the eighty-odd reporters seated in the NUMA headquarters auditorium. She smiled continuously, with the happy look of a woman who is enjoying herself and who knows she would be approved of. She wore a terra-cotta color wrap skirt and a deeply V'd sweater, neatly accented by a small mahogany necklace. She was tall, appealing, and elegant; an image that immediately put her inquisitors at a disadvantage.

A white-haired woman on the left side of the room rose and waved her hand. "Dr. Seagram?"

Dana nodded gracefully.

"Dr. Seagram, the readers of my paper, the *Chicago Daily,* would like to know why the government is spending millions to salvage an old rusty ship. Why wouldn't the money be better spent elsewhere, say for welfare or badly needed urban renewal?"

"I'll be happy to clear the air for you," Dana said. "To begin with, raising the *Titanic* is not a waste of money. Two hundred and ninety million dollars have been budgeted, and so far we are well below that figure; and, I might add, ahead of schedule."

"Don't you consider that a lot of money?"

"Not when *you* consider the possible return. You see, the *Titanic* is a veritable storehouse of treasure. Estimates run over three hundred million dollars. There are many of the passengers' jewels and valuables still on board: a quarter of a million dollars' worth in one stateroom alone. Then there are the ship's fittings, as well as the furnishings and the precious décor, some of which may have survived. A collector would gladly pay anywhere from five hundred to a thousand dollars for one piece of china or a crystal goblet from the first-class dining room. No, ladies and gentlemen, this is one time when a federal project is not, if you'll pardon the expression, a taxpayer ripoff. We will show a profit in dollars and a profit in historical artifacts of a bygone era, not to mention the tremendous wealth of data for marine science and technology."

"Dr. Seagram?" This from a tall, pinch-faced man in the rear of the auditorium. "We haven't had time to read the press release you passed out earlier, so could you please enlighten us as to the mechanics of the salvage?"

"I'm glad you asked me that." Dana laughed. "Seriously, I apologize for the old cliché, but your question, sir, is the cue for a brief slide presentation that should help explain many of the mysteries regarding the project." She turned to the wings of the stage. "Lights, please."

The lighting dimmed and the first slide marched onto a wide screen above and behind the lectern.

"We begin with a composite of over eighty photographs pieced together to show the *Titanic* as she rests on the sea floor. Fortunately, she's sitting upright with a light list to port which conveniently puts the hundred-yard-long gash she received from the iceberg in an accessible position to seal."

"How is it possible to seal an opening that size at that enormous depth?"

The next slide came on and showed a man holding what looked like a large blob of liquid plastic.

"In answer to that question," Dana said, "this is Dr. Amos Stannford demonstrating a substance he developed called 'Wetsteel.' As the name suggests, Wetsteel though pliable in air, hardens to the rigidity of steel ninety seconds after coming in contact with water, and it can bond itself to a metal object as though it were welded."

This last statement was followed by a wave of murmurs throughout the room.

"Ball-shaped aluminum tanks, ten feet in diameter, that contain Wetsteel have been dropped at strategic spots around the vessel," Dana continued. "They are designed so that a submersible can attach itself to the tank, not unlike the docking procedure of a shuttle rocket with a space laboratory, and then proceed to the working area where the crew can aim and expel the Wetsteel from a specially designed nozzle."

"How is the Wetsteel pumped from the tank?"

"To illustrate with another comparison, the great pressure at that depth compresses the aluminum tank much like a tube of toothpaste, squeezing the sealant through the nozzle and into the opening to be covered."

She signaled for a new slide.

"Now here we see a cut-away drawing of the sea, depicting the supply tenders on the surface and the submersibles clustered around the wreck on the bottom. There are four manned underwater vehicles involved in the salvage operation. The *Sappho I,* which you may recall was the craft used on the Lorelei Current Drift Expedition, is currently engaged in patching the damage caused by the iceberg along the starboard side of the hull and also the bows, where they were shattered by the *Titanic's* boilers. The *Sappho II,* a newer and more advanced sister ship, is sealing the smaller openings, such as the air vents and portholes. The Navy's submersible, the *Sea Slug,* has the job of cutting away unnecessary debris, including the masts, rigging, and the aft funnel which fell across the After Boat Deck. And finally, the *Deep Fathom,* a submersible belonging to the Uranus Oil Corporation, is installing pressure relief valves on the *Titanic's* hull and superstructure."

"Could you please explain the purpose of the valves, Dr. Seagram?"

"Certainly," Dana replied. "When the hulk begins its journey to the surface, the air that has been pumped into her interior will begin to expand as the pressure of the sea lessens against her exterior. Unless this inside pressure is continuously bled, the *Titanic* could conceivably blow herself to pieces. The valves, of course, are there to prevent this disastrous occurrence."

"Then NUMA intends to use compressed air to lift the derelict?"

"Yes, the support tender, *Capricorn,* has two compressor units capable of displacing the water in the *Titanic's* hull with enough air to raise her."

"Dr. Seagram?" came another disembodied voice, "I represent *Science Today,* and I happen to know that the water pressure where the *Titanic* lies is upwards of six thousand pounds per square inch. I also know that the largest available air compressor can only put out four thousand pounds. How do you intend to overcome this differential?"

"The main unit on board the *Capricorn* pumps the air from the surface through a reinforced pipe to the secondary pump, which is stationed amidships of the wreck. In appearance, this secondary pump looks like a radial aircraft engine with a series of pistons spreading from a central hub. Again, we utilized the sea's great abyssal pressures to activate the pump, which is also assisted by electricity and the air pressure coming from above. I am sorry I can't give you an in-depth description, but I am a marine archaeologist, not a marine engineer. However, Admiral Sandecker will be available later in the day to answer your technical questions in greater detail."

"What about suction?" the voice of *Science Today* persisted. "After sitting imbedded in the silt all these years, won't the *Titanic* be fairly well glued to the bottom?"

"She will indeed." Dana gestured for the lights. They came on and she stood blinking in the glare for a few moments until she could distinguish her inquirer. He was a middle-aged man, with long brown hair and large wire-rimmed glasses.

"When it is calculated that the ship has enough air to lift her mass toward the surface, the air pipe will be disconnected from the hull and converted to inject an electrolyte chemical, processed by the Myers-Lentz Company, into the sediment surrounding the *Titanic*'s keel. The resulting reaction will cause the molecules in the sediment to break down and form a cushion of bubbles that will erase the static friction and allow the great hulk to wrest herself free from the suction."

Another man raised his hand.

"If the operation is successful and the *Titanic* begins floating toward the surface, isn't there a good chance she could capsize? Two and a half miles is a long way for an unbalanced object of forty-five thousand tons to remain upright."

"You're right. There is the possibility she might capsize, but we plan to leave enough water in her lower holds to act as ballast and offset this problem."

A young, mannish-looking woman rose and waved her hand.

"Dr. Seagram! I am Connie Sanchez of *Female Eminence Weekly,* and my readers would be interested in learning what defense mechanisms you have personally developed for competing on a day-to-day basis in a profession dominated by egotistic male pigheads."

The audience of reporters greeted the question with uneasy silence. God, Dana thought to herself, it had to come sooner or later. She stepped alongside the lectern and leaned on it in a negligent, almost sexy attitude.

"My reply, Ms. Sanchez, is strictly off the record."

"Then you're copping out," said Connie Sanchez with a superior grin.

Dana ignored the jab. "First, I find that a defense mechanism is hardly necessary. My masculine colleagues respect my intelligence enough to accept my opinions. I don't have to go bra-less or spread my legs to get their attention. Second, I prefer standing on my own home ground and competing with members of my own sex, not a strange stance when you consider the fact that out of five hundred and forty scientists on the staff of NUMA, a hundred and fourteen are women. And third, Ms. Sanchez, the only pigheads it's been my misfortune to meet during my life have not been men, but rather the female of the species."

For several moments, a stunned silence gripped the room. Then, suddenly, shattering the embarrassed quiet, a voice burst from the audience. "Atta girl, Doc," yelled the little white-haired lady from the *Chicago Daily*. "That's putting her down."

A sea of applause rippled and then roared, sweeping the auditorium in a storm of approval. The battle-hardened Washington correspondents offered her their respect with a standing ovation.

Connie Sanchez sat in her seat and stared coldly in flushed anger. Dana saw Connie's lips form the word "bitch" and she returned a smug, derisive kind of smile that only women do so well. Adulation, Dana thought, how sweet it is.

40

Since early morning the wind had blown steadily out of the northeast. By later afternoon it had increased to a gale of thirty-five knots, which in turn threw up mountainous seas that pitched the salvage ships about like paper cups in a dishwasher. The tempest carried with it a numbing cold borne of the barren wastes above the Arctic Circle. The men dared not venture out onto the icy decks. It was no secret that the greatest barrier against keeping warm was the wind. A man could feel much colder and more miserable at twenty degrees above zero Fahrenheit with a thirty-five knot wind than at twenty degrees below zero with no wind. The wind steals the body heat as quickly as it can be manufactured—a nasty situation known as *chill factor*.

Joel Farquar, the *Capricorn*'s weatherman, on loan from the Federal Meteorological Services Administration, seemed unconcerned with the storm snapping outside the operations room as he studied the instrumentation that tied into the National Weather Satellites and provided four space pictures of the North Atlantic every twenty-four hours.

"What does your prognosticating little mind see for our future?" Pitt asked, bracing his body against the roll.

"She'll start easing in another hour," Farquar replied. "By sunrise tomorrow the wind should be down to ten knots."

Farquar didn't look up when he spoke. He was a studious, little red-faced man with utterly no sense of humor and no trace of friendly warmth. Yet, he was respected by every man on the salvage operation 'because of his total dedication to the job, and the fact that his predictions were uncannily accurate.

" 'The best laid plans . . . ' " Pitt murmured idly to himself. "Another day lost. That's four times in one week we've had to cast off and buoy the air line."

"Only God can make a storm," Farquar said indifferently. He nodded toward the two banks of television monitors that covered the forward bulkhead of the *Capricorn*'s operations room. "At least they're not bothered by it all."

Pitt looked at the screens which showed the submersibles calmly working on the wreck twelve thousand feet below the relentless sea. Their independence from the surface was the saving grace of the project. With the exception of the *Sea Slug,* which only had a down-time of eighteen hours and was now securely tied on the *Modoc*'s deck, the other three submersibles could be scheduled to stay down on the *Titanic* for five days at a stretch before they returned to the surface to change crews. He turned to Al Giordino, who was bent over a large chart table.

"What's the disposition of the surface ships?"

Giordino pointed at the tiny two-inch models scattered about the chart. "The *Capricorn* is holding her usual position in the center. The *Modoc* is dead ahead, and the *Bomberger* is trailing three miles astern."

Pitt stared at the model of the *Bomberger*. She was a new vessel. constructed especially for deep-water salvage. "Tell her captain to close up to within one mile."

Giordino nodded toward the bald radio operator, who was moored securely to the slanting deck in front of his equipment. "You heard the man, Curly. Tell the *Bomberger* to come up to one mile astern."

"How about the supply ships?" Pitt asked.

"No problem there. This weather is duck soup to big ten-tonners the likes of these two. The *Alhambra* is in position to port, and the *Monterey Park* is right where she's supposed to be to starboard."

Pitt nodded at a small red model. "I see our Russian friends are still with us."

"The *Mikhail Kurkov*?" Giordino said. He picked up a blue replica of a warship and placed it next to the red model. "Yeah, but she can't be enjoying the game. The *Juneau,* that Navy guided-missile cruiser, hangs on like glue."

"And the wreck buoy's signal unit?"

"Serenely beeping away eighty feet beneath the uproar," Giordino announced. "Only twelve hundred yards, give or take a hair, bearing zero-five-nine, southwest that is."

"Thank God we haven't been blown off the homestead." Pitt sighed.

"Relax." Giordino grinned reassuringly. "You act like a mother with a daughter out on a date after midnight every time there's a little breeze."

"The mother-hen complex becomes worse the closer we get," Pitt admitted. "Ten more days. Al. If we can get ten calm days, we can wrap it up."

"That's up to the weather oracle." Giordino turned to Farquar. "What about it, O Great Seer of Meteorological Wisdom?"

"Twelve hours' advance notice is all you'll get out of me," Farquar grunted, without looking up. "This is the North Atlantic. She's the most unpredictable of any ocean in the world. Hardly one day is ever the same. Now, if your precious *Titanic* had gone down in the Indian Ocean, I could give you your ten-day prediction with an eighty-per-cent chance of accuracy."

"Excuses, excuses," Giordino replied. "I bet when you make love to a woman, you tell her going in that there's a forty-per-cent chance she'll enjoy it."

"Forty per cent is better than nothing," Farquar said casually.

Pitt caught a gesture by the sonar operator and moved over to him. "What have you got?"

"A strange pinging noise over the amplifier," the sonar man replied. He was a pale-faced man, about the size and shape of a gorilla. "I've picked it up off and on during the last two months. Strange sort of sound, kind of like somebody was sending messages."

"Make anything of it?"

"No, sir. I had Curly listen to it, but he said it was pure gibberish."

"Most likely a loose object on the wreck that's being rattled about by the current."

"Or maybe it's a ghost," the sonar man said.

"You don't believe in them, but you're afraid of them, is that it?"

"Fifteen hundred souls went down with the *Titanic,*" the sonar man said. "It's not unlikely that at least one came back to haunt the ship."

"The only spirits I'm interested in," Giordino said from the chart table, "are the kind you drink. . . ."

"The interior cabin camera of *Sappho II* just blacked out." This from the sandy-haired man seated at the TV monitors.

Pitt was immediately behind him, staring at the blackened monitor. "Is the problem at this end?"

"No, sir. All circuits here and on the buoy's relay panel are operable. The problem must be on the *Sappho II*. It just seemed like somebody hung a cloth over the camera lens."

Pitt swung to face the radio operator. "Curly, contact *Sappho II* and ask them to check their cabin TV camera."

Giordino picked up a clipboard and checked the crew schedule. "Omar Woodson is in command of the *Sappho II* this shift."

Curly pressed the transmit switch. *"Sappho II,* hello *Sappho II,* this is *Capricorn.* Please reply."* Then he leaned forward, pressing his headset tighter to his ears. "The contact is weak, sir. Lots of interference. The words are very broken. I can't make them out."

"Turn on the speaker," Pitt ordered.

A voice rattled into the operations room, muffled behind a wave of static.

"Something is jamming the transmission," said Curly. "The relay unit on the air-line buoy should be picking them up loud and clear."

"Give your volume everything it's got. Maybe we can make some sense out of Woodson's reply."

"Sappho II, could you repeat please. We cannot read you. Over."

As soon as Curly turned up the speaker, the explosion of ear-splitting crackle made everyone jump.

"————corn, We———— —ou —lear. —ver."

Pitt grabbed the microphone. "Omar, this is Pitt. "Your cabin TV camera is out. Can you repair? We will await your reply. Over."

Every eye in the operations room locked on the speaker as though it were alive. Five interminable minutes dragged by while they patiently waited for Woodson's report. Then Woodson's fragmented voice hammered through the loudspeaker again.

"Hen—— Munk ————. ————est per————on ——sur————."

Giordino twisted his face, puzzled. "Something about Henry Munk. The rest is too garbled to comprehend."

"They're back on monitor." Not every eye had been aimed at the speaker. The young man at the TV monitors had never taken his off *Sappho II*'s screen. "The crew looks like they're grouped around someone lying on the deck."

Like spectators at a tennis match, every head turned in unison to the TV monitor. Figures were moving to and fro in front of the camera, while in the background three men could be seen bent over a body stretched grotesquely on the submersible's narrow cabin deck.

"Omar, listen to me," Pitt snapped into the microphone. "We do not understand your transmissions. You are back on TV monitor. I repeat, you are back on TV monitor. Write your message and hold it up to the camera. Over."

They watched one of the figures detach itself from the rest and lean over a table for a few moments writing and then approach the TV camera. It was Woodson. He held up a scrap of paper whose rough printing read, "Henry Munk dead. Request permission to surface."

"Good God!" Giordino's expression was one of pure astonishment. "Henry Munk dead? It can't be true."

"Omar Woodson isn't noted for playing games," Pitt said grimly. He began to transmit again. "Negative, Omar. You cannot surface. There is a thirty-five-knot gale up here. The sea is turbulent. I repeat, you cannot surface."

Woodson nodded that he understood. Then he wrote something else, looking over his shoulder furtively every so often. The note said: "I suspect Munk murdered!"

Even Farquar's usually inscrutable face had gone pale. "You'll have to let them surface now," he whispered.

"I will do what I have to do." Pitt shook his head decisively. "My feelings will have to look elsewhere. There are five men still alive and breathing inside *Sappho II*. I won't risk bringing them up only to lose them all under a thirty-foot wave. No, gentlemen, we will just have to sit it out until sunrise to see what there is to see inside the *Sappho II*."

41

Pitt had the *Capricorn* home in on the signal-relay buoy as soon as the wind dropped to twenty knots. Once again they connected the air line running from the ship's compressor to the *Titanic* and then waited for the *Sappho II*'s emergence from the deep. The eastern sky was beginning to brighten when final preparations were made to receive the submersible. Divers made ready to drop in position around the *Sappho II* and secure safety lines to prevent her from capsizing in the heavy seas; the winches and cables were set to haul her from the water and into the open stern of the *Capricorn;* down in the galley the cook began making an urn of coffee and a hearty breakfast to greet the crew of the submersible when they arrived. When all was in readiness, the scientists and engineers stood quietly shivering in the early morning cold, wondering about Henry Munk's death.

It was 0610 when the submersible popped into the marching swells one hundred yards off the port stern of the *Capricorn*. A line was run out by boat, and within twenty minutes the *Sappho II* was winched onto the stern ramp of her tender. As soon as she was blocked and secured into place, the hatch was opened and Woodson pulled himself out, followed by the four surviving members of his crew.

Woodson climbed to the top deck, where Pitt was waiting for him. His eyes were red with sleeplessness and his face stubble-bearded and gray, but he managed a thin smile as Pitt shoved a steaming mug of coffee into his hand. "I don't know which I'm happier to see, you or the coffee," he said.

"Your message mentioned murder," Pitt said, ignoring any word of greeting.

Woodson sipped at the coffee for a moment and looked back at the men who were gently lifting Munk's body through the submersible's hatch. "Not here," he said quietly.

Pitt motioned toward his quarters. Once the door was closed, he wasted no time. "Okay, let's have it."

Woodson dropped heavily onto Pitt's bunk and rubbed his eyes. "Not much to tell. We were hovering about sixty feet above the sea floor sealing off the starboard ports on C Deck when I got your message about the TV camera. I went aft to check it out and found Munk lying on the deck with his left temple caved in."

"Any sign of what caused the blow?"

"As plain as the nose on Pinocchio's face," Woodson answered. "Bits of skin, blood, and hair were stuck on the corner of the alternator housing cover."

"I'm not that familiar with the *Sappho II*'s equipment. How is it mounted?"

"On the starboard side, about ten feet from the stern. The housing cover is raised about six inches off the deck so the alternator below is easily accessible for maintenance."

"Then it might have been an accident. Munk could have stumbled and fallen, striking his head on the edge."

"He could have, except his feet were facing the wrong way."

"What do his feet have to do with it?"

"They were pointed toward the stern."

"So?"

"Don't you get it?" Woodson said impatiently. "Munk must have been walking toward the bow when he fell."

The fuzzy picture in Pitt's mind began to clear. And he saw the piece of the puzzle that didn't belong. "The alternator housing is on the starboard side so it should have been Munk's right temple that was smashed, not his left."

"You got it."

"What caused the TV camera to malfunction?"

"No malfunction. Somebody hung a towel over the lens."

"And the crew? Where was each member positioned?"

"I was working the nozzle while Sam Merker acted as pilot. Munk had left the instrument panel to go to the head which is located in the stern. We were the second watch. The first watch included Jack Donovan—"

"A young blond fellow; the structural engineer from Oceanic Tech?"

"Right. And, Lieutenant Leon Lucas, the salvage technician on assignment from the Navy, and Ben Drummer. All three men were asleep in their bunks."

"It doesn't necessarily follow that any one of them killed Munk," Pitt said. "What was the reasoning? You don't just kill someone in an unescapable situation twelve thousand feet under the sea without one hell of a motive."

Woodson shrugged. "You'll have to call in Sherlock Holmes. I only know what I saw."

Pitt continued to probe: "Munk could have twisted as he fell."

"Not unless he had a rubber neck that could turn a hundred and eighty degrees backward."

"Let's try another puzzler. How do you kill a two-hundred-pound man by knocking his head against a metal corner that's only six inches off the floor? Swing him by the heels like a sledge hammer?"

Woodson threw out his hands in a helpless gesture. "Okay, so maybe I got carried away and began seeing homicidal maniacs where none exist. God knows, that wreck down there gets to you after a while. It's weird. There are times I could have sworn I even saw people walking the decks, leaning over the rails, and staring at us." He yawned and it was evident that he was fighting to keep his eyes open.

Pitt made for the door and then turned. "You better get some sleep. We'll go over this later."

Woodson needed no further urging. He was peacefully gone to the world before Pitt was halfway to the sick bay.

Dr. Cornelius Bailey was an elephant of a man, broad-shouldered, and had a thrusting, square-jawed face. His sandy hair was down to his collar and the beard on the great jaw was cut in an elegant Van Dyke. He was popular among the salvage crews and could outdrink any five of them when he felt in the mood to prove it. His hamlike hands turned Henry Munk's body over on the examining table as effortlessly as if it was a stick doll, which indeed it very nearly was, considering the advanced stage of rigor mortis.

"Poor Henry," he said. "Thank God, he wasn't a family man. Healthy specimen. All I could do for him on his last examination was clean out a little wax from his ears."

"What can you tell me about the cause of death?" Pitt asked.

"That's obvious," Bailey said. "First, it was due to massive damage of the temporal lobe—"

"What do you mean by first?"

"Just that, my dear Pitt. This man was more or less killed twice. Look at this." He pulled back Munk's shirt, exposing the nape of the neck. There was a large purplish bruise at the base of the skull. "The spinal cord just below the medulla oblongata has been crushed. Most likely by a blunt instrument of some kind."

"Then Woodson was right; Munk *was* murdered."

"Murdered, you say? Oh yes, of course, no doubt of it." Bailey said calmly, as though homicide were an everyday shipboard occurrence.

"Then it would seem the killer struck Munk from behind and then rammed his head against the alternator housing to make it look like an accident."

"That's a fair assumption."

Pitt laid a hand on Bailey's shoulder. "I'd appreciate it if you kept your discovery quiet for a while, Doc."

"Mum's the word; my lips are sealed and all that crap. Don't waste another thought on it. My report and testimony will be here when you need it."

Pitt smiled at the doctor and left the sick bay. He made his way aft to where the *Sappho II* sat dripping salt water on the stern ramp, climbed up the hatch ladder, and dropped down inside. An instrument technician was checking the TV camera.

"How does it look?" Pitt asked.

"Nothing wrong with this baby," the technician replied. "As soon as the structural crew checks out the hull, you can send her back down."

"The sooner, the better," Pitt said. He moved past the technician to the after end of the submersible. The gore from Munk's injuries had already been cleaned from the deck and the corner of the alternator housing.

Pitt's mind was whirling. Only one thought broke away and uncoiled. Not a thought really, rather an unreasoning certainty that something would point an accusing finger towards Munk's murderer. He figured it would take him an hour or more, but the fates were kind. He found what he knew he must find within the first ten minutes.

42

"Let me see if I understand you," Sandecker said, glaring across his desk. "One of the members of my salvage crew has been brutally murdered and you're asking me to sit idle and do nothing about it while the killer is allowed to roam loose?"

Warren Nicholson shifted uneasily in his chair and avoided Sandecker's blazing eyes. "I realize that it's difficult to accept."

"That's putting it mildly," Sandecker snorted. "Suppose he takes it in his head to kill again?"

"That's a calculated risk we have considered."

" 'We have considered'?" Sandecker echoed. "It's simple for you to sit up there at CIA headquarters and say that. You're not down there, Nicholson, trapped in a submersible thousands of feet below the sea, wondering whether the man standing next to you is going to bash your brains out."

"I am certain it won't happen again," Nicholson said impassively.

"What makes you so sure?"

"Because professional Russian agents do not commit murder unless it is absolutely necessary."

"Russian agents—" Sandecker stared at Nicholson in startled and total disbelief. "What in God's name are you talking about?"

"Just that. Henry Munk was killed by an operative working for the Soviet Naval Intelligence Department."

"You can't be positive. There is no proof. . . ."

"Not one hundred per cent, no. It might have been someone else with a grudge against Munk. But the facts point to a Soviet-paid operative."

"But why Munk?" Sandecker asked. "He was an instrument specialist. What possible threat could he have been to a spy?"

"I suspect that Munk saw something he shouldn't have and had to be silenced," Nicholson said. "And that's only the half of it, in a manner of speaking. You see, Admiral, there happen to be not one, but two Russian agents who have infiltrated your salvage operation."

"I don't buy that."

"We're in the business of espionage, Admiral. We find out these things."

"Who are they?" Sandecker demanded.

Nicholson shrugged helplessly. "I'm sorry, that's all I can give you. Our sources reveal that they go under the code names of Silver and Gold. But as to their true identities, we have no idea."

Sandecker's eyes were grim. "And if my people discover who they are?"

"I hope you will cooperate, at least for the time being, and order them to remain silent and take no action."

"Those two could sabotage the entire salvage operation."

"We're banking heavily on the assumption that their orders do not include destruction."

"It's madness, pure madness," Sandecker murmured. "Do you have any idea of what you're asking of me?"

"The President put the same question to me some months ago, and my answer is still the same. No, I don't. I'm aware that your efforts go beyond mere salvage, but the President has not seen fit to make me privy to the real reason behind your show."

Sandecker's teeth were clenched. "And, if I should go along with you? What then?"

"I will keep you posted as to any new developments. And when the time comes, I will give you the green light to take the Soviet agents into custody."

The admiral sat silent for a few moments and, when he finally spoke, Nicholson noted his deadly serious tone.

"Okay, Nicholson, I'll string along. But God help you if there is a tragic accident or another murder down there. The consequences will be more terrible than you can possibly imagine."

43

Mel Donner came through Marie Sheldon's front door, his suit splattered from a spring rain.

"I guess this will teach me to carry an umbrella in the car," he said, taking out a handkerchief and brushing away the dampness.

Marie closed the front door and stared up at him curiously. "Any port in a storm. Is that it, handsome?"

"I beg your pardon?"

"From the look of you," Marie said, her voice soft and slurry, "you needed a roof until the rain let up, and the fates kindly led you to mine."

Donner's eyes narrowed for a moment, but only a moment. Then he smiled. "I'm sorry, my name is Mel Donner. I'm an old friend of Dana's. Is she at home?"

"I knew a strange man begging on my doorstep was too good to be true." She smiled. "I'm Marie Sheldon. Sit down and make yourself comfortable while I call Dana and get you a cup of coffee."

"Thank you. The coffee sounds like a winner."

Donner appraised Marie's backside as she swiveled toward the kitchen. She wore a short white tennis skirt, a sleeveless knit top, and her feet were bare. The taut swing of her hips flipped the skirt to and fro in a pert, seductive sort of way.

She returned with a cup of coffee. "Dana is lazy on weekends. She seldom rolls out of the sack before ten. I'll go upstairs and speed things up."

While he waited, Donner studied the books on the shelves beside the fireplace. It was a game he often practiced. Book titles seldom failed to unlock the door to their owner's personality and tastes.

The selections ran the usual gamut for the single female: there were several books of poetry, *The Prophet, The New York Times Cookbook,* and the usual sprinkling of gothics and best sellers. But it was the arrangement that interested Donner. Interwoven among *Physics of Intercontinental Laval Flows* and *Geology of Underwater Canyons,* he found *Explanation of Sexual Fantasies of the Female,* and *The Story of O.* He was just reaching for the latter when he heard the sound of feet coming down the stairs. He turned as Dana entered the room.

She came forward and embraced him. "Mel, how wonderful to see you."

"You look great," he said. The months of strain and anguish had been erased. She seemed more at ease and she smiled without tenseness.

"How's the swinging bachelor?" she asked. "Which line are you using on poor innocent girls this week, the brain surgeon or the astronaut?"

He patted his paunch. "I've retired the astronaut story until I can shed a few pounds. Actually, because of the publicity you people are getting on the *Titanic,* I can do no wrong by telling the little lovelies crowded around the Washington singles' bars that I'm a deep-sea diver."

"Why don't you simply tell the truth. After all, as one of the country's leading physicists, you have nothing to be ashamed of."

"I know, but somehow playing the real me takes the fun out of it. Besides, women love a lover who's phony."

She nodded at his cup. "Can I get you more coffee?"

"No thanks." He smiled, and then his expression became serious. "You know why I'm here."

"I guessed."

"I'm worried about Gene."

"So am I."

"You could go back to him . . ."

Dana met Mel's eyes evenly. "You don't understand. When we are together, it only makes things worse."

"He's lost without you."

She shook her head. "His job is his mistress. I was only a whipping post for his frustrations. Like most wives, I'm not geared to take the anguish that goes hand in hand with a husband's insensibility when he's overburdened with on-the-job stress. Don't you see, Mel? I had to leave Gene before we destroyed each other." Dana turned and held her face in her hands, then quickly composed herself. "If only he could quit and go back to teaching, then things would be different."

"I shouldn't be telling you this," Donner said, "but the project will be completed in another month if all goes according to plan. Then Gene will have nothing to keep him in Washington. He'll be free to return to the university."

"But what about your contracts with the government?"

"Finished. We enlisted for a specific project, and when it's finished, so are we. Then all of us take a bow and head back to whatever campus we originally came from."

"He may not even want me."

"I know Gene," Donner said. "He's a one-woman man. He'll be waiting . . . unless, of course, you're involved with another man."

She looked up surprised. "Why do you say that?"

"I happened to be in Webster's Restaurant last Wednesday night."

Oh God! Dana thought. One of her few dates since leaving Gene had come back to haunt her already. It had been a foursome with Marie and two biologists from the NUMA marine sciences laboratory, a friendly, comfortable evening. That was all, nothing had happened.

She stood up and glared down at Donner. "You, Marie, and yes, even the President, all expect me to go crawling back to Gene like some damned old security blanket he can't sleep without. But not one of you has even bothered to ask how *I* feel. What emotions and frustrations do I face? Well, to hell with all of you. I am my own woman, to do with my life as I please. I'll go back to Gene if and when I damn-well feel like it. And, if I feel in the mood to go out with other men and get laid, so be it."

She spun and left Donner sitting there stunned and embarrassed. Up the stairs and into the bedroom where she threw herself on the bed. She had mouthed nothing but mere words. There would never be another man in her life but Gene Seagram, and some day, soon, she was sure she would return to him. But now the tears came until there were none left.

Imbedded in one of the mirrored walls, a phonograph record, watched over by a female disc jockey, thundered through four huge quad speakers. The postage-stamp dance floor was jammed, and a thick haze of cigarette smoke filtered the brightly colored lights that exploded on the ceiling of the discothèque. Donner sat at the table alone, idly watching the couples gyrate to the blaring music.

A petite blonde wandered up to him and suddenly stopped. "The rainmaker?"

Donner looked up. He laughed and got to his feet. "Miss Sheldon."

"Marie," she said pleasantly.

"Are you alone?"

"No, I'm the third wheel with a married couple."

Donner's eyes followed her gesture, but it was impossible to tell who she meant amid the jumbled bodies on the dance floor. He pulled back a chair for her. "Consider yourself escorted."

A cocktail waitress happened by and Donner shouted an order above the din. He turned to find Marie Sheldon studying him approvingly. "You know, Mr. Donner, for a physicist, you're not a bad-looking man."

"Damn! I had hoped to be a CIA agent tonight."

She grinned. "Dana told me about a few of your escapades. Leading poor innocent girls astray. For shame."

"Don't believe all you hear. Actually, I'm shy and introverted when it comes to women."

"Oh really?"

"Scout's honor." He lit her cigarette. "Where's Dana tonight?"

"Very sly of you. You tried to zing one over on me."

"Not really. I just—"

"It's none of your prying business, of course, but Dana is on a ship somewhere in the North Atlantic Ocean about now."

"A vacation will do her good."

"You do have a way of milking a poor girl for information," Marie said. "Just for the record, so you can inform your pal Gene Seagram, she's not on holiday, but playing den mother to a regiment of news correspondents who demanded to be on the scene when the *Titanic* is raised next week."

"I guess I asked for that."

"Good. I'm always impressed by a man who admits the folly of his ways." She tilted her eyes at him in a kind of mocking amusement. "Now that that's settled, why don't you propose to me?"

Donner's brows knitted. "Isn't the coy maiden the one who's supposed to say, 'But sir, I hardly know you'?"

She took his hand and stood up. "Come on then."

"May I ask where?"

"To your place," she said with a mischievous grin.

"My place?" Events were clearly moving too fast for Donner.

"Sure. We have to make love, don't we? How else can two people who are engaged to be married get to know each other?"

44

Pitt slouched in his train seat and idly watched the Devon countryside glide past the window. The tracks curved along the coastline at Dawlish. In the Channel he could see a small fleet of fishing trawlers heading out for the morning's catch. Soon a misting rain streaked the glass and blurred his view, so he turned once more to the magazine on his lap and thumbed the pages without really seeing them.

If they had told him two days ago that he'd take a temporary leave from the salvage operation, he'd have thought them stupid. And, if they'd suggested that he'd travel to Teignmouth, Devonshire, population 12,260, a small picturesque resort town on the southeast coast of England, to interview a dying old man, he'd have thought them downright insane.

He had Admiral James Sandecker to thank for this pilgrimage, and that is exactly what the admiral had called it when he had ordered Pitt back to NUMA headquarters in Washington. A pilgrimage to the last surviving crew member of the *Titanic*.

"There's no use in arguing the matter any further," Sandecker said unequivocally. "You're going to Teignmouth."

"None of this adds up." Pitt was pacing the floor nervously, his equilibrium struggling to forget the months of endless pitching and rolling of the *Capricorn*. "You order me ashore during a crucial moment of the salvage and tell me I have two Russian agents, identities unknown, who have carte blanche to go about murdering my crew under the personal protection of the CIA, and then in the same breath, you calmly order me to England to take down the deathbed testimony of some ancient limey."

"That 'ancient limey' happens to be the only member of the *Titanic*'s crew who hasn't been buried."

"But what of the salvage operation," Pitt persisted. "The computers indicate the *Titanic*'s hull might break loose from the bottom any time after the next seventy-two hours."

"Relax, Dirk. You should be back on the decks of the *Capricorn* by tomorrow evening. Plenty of time before the main event. Meanwhile, Rudi Gunn can handle any problems that come up during your absence."

"You don't offer me much choice." Pitt gestured in defeat.

Sandecker smiled benevolently. "I know what your're thinking . . . that you're indispensable. Well, I've got news for you. That's the best salvage crew in the world out there. I feel confident that somehow they'll struggle through the next thirty-six hours without you."

Pitt smiled, but there was no humor in his face. "When do I leave?"

"There is a Lear jet waiting at the NUMA hangar at Dulles. It will take you to Exeter. You can catch a train from there for Teignmouth."

"Afterward, shall I report to you back here in Washington?"

"No, you can report to me aboard the *Capricorn*."

Pitt looked up. "The *Capricorn*?"

"Certainly. Just because you're relaxing in the English countryside, you don't expect me to miss out on seeing the *Titanic*'s regenesis in case she decides to come up ahead of schedule, do you?"

Sandecker grinned satanically. He could afford that as it was all he could do to keep from laughing at the aggrieved and crest-fallen expression on Pitt's face.

Pitt climbed into a cab at the railroad station and rode along a narrow road beside the river estuary to a small cottage overlooking the sea. He paid the cab driver, went through a vine-covered gate, and up a walk bordered by rose bushes. His knock was answered by a girl with absorbing violet eyes framed by neatly brushed red hair and a soft voice that was touched by a Scot's accent.

"Good morning, sir."

"Good morning," he said with a slight nod. "My name is Dirk Pitt, and—"

"Oh yes, Admiral Sandecker's cable said you were coming. Please come in. The commodore is expecting you."

She was dressed in a neatly pressed white blouse and a green wool sweater and matching skirt. He followed her into the living room of the cottage. It was cozy and comfortable; a fire was burning brightly in the fireplace, and if Pitt had not known that the owner was a retired mariner, he could have easily guessed it by the décor. Ships' models filled every available shelf, while framed prints of famous sailing vessels graced all four walls. A great brass telescope was mounted in front of the window facing the Channel, and a ship's wheel, its wood gleaming from hours of hand-waxed care, stood in one corner of the room as if awaiting a momentary turn from some long-forgotten helmsman.

"You look like you've had a very uncomfortable night," the girl said. "Would you like some breakfast?"

"Courtesy urges me to decline, but my stomach rumbles for me to accept."

"Americans are famous for hearty appetites. I would have been disappointed if you had shattered the myth."

"Then I'll do my best to uphold Yankee tradition, Miss . . ."

"Please forgive me. I'm Sandra Ross, the commodore's great-granddaughter."

"You look after him, I take it."

"When I can. I'm a flight attendant with Bristol Airlines. A village lady sees to him when I have a flight." She motioned him down a hallway. "While you're waiting for a bite to eat, you'd best talk to Grandfather. He's very, very old, but he's dying to hear—He's anxious to hear all about your efforts to raise the *Titanic.*"

She knocked lightly on a door and opened it a crack. "Commodore, Mr. Pitt is here to see you."

"Well, get him in here," a voice rasped back, "before I founder on the reef."

She stood aside and Pitt entered the bedroom.

Commodore Sir John L. Bigalow, K.B.E., R.D., R.N.R. (Retired) sat propped up in a bunklike bed and studied Pitt through deep blue eyes, eyes that had the dreamlike quality of another age. The few strands of hair on his head were pure white, as was his beard, and his face showed the ruddy, weathered look of a seafaring man. He wore a tattered turtleneck sweater over what looked to be a Dickens'-style nightshirt. He held out a leathery hand that was as steady as a rock.

Pitt took it and marveled at the firm grip. "This is indeed an honor, Commodore. I have often read of your heroic escape from the *Titanic.*"

"So much rot," he grumbled. "I was torpedoed and cast adrift in both

World Wars, and all anybody ever asks me about is the night of the *Titanic*." He motioned to a chair. "Don't stand there like a beardless lad on his first trip to sea. Sit down. Sit down."

Pitt did as he was told.

"Now tell me about the ship. What does she look like after all these years? I was a young man when I served on her, but I still remember her every deck."

Pitt reached into the breast pocket of his coat and handed Bigalow an envelope of photographs. "Perhaps these can give you some idea of her present condition. They were taken by one of our submersibles just a few weeks ago."

Commodore Bigalow slipped on a pair of reading glasses and studied the pictures. Several minutes ticked off a ship's clock beside the bed while the old mariner became lost in the memories of another time. Then he looked up wistfully. "She was in a class all by herself, she was. I know. I sailed them all: the *Olympic* . . . *Aquitania* . . . *Queen Mary.* Sure they were elaborate and modern for their time, but they couldn't touch the care and craftsmanship that went into the *Titanic*'s furnishings: her wonderful paneling and her marvelous staterooms. Aye, she still casts a heavy spell, she does."

"She grows ever more bewitching with the years," Pitt agreed.

"Here, here," Bigalow said as he pointed excitedly to a photo, "by the port ventilator on the roof over the officers' quarters. This is where I was standing when she sank beneath my feet and I was washed into the sea." The long decades seemed to melt away from his face. "Oh, but the sea was cold that night. Four degrees below freezing it was."

For the next ten minutes he talked of swimming in the icy water; miraculously finding a rope that led to an overturned lifeboat; the awful mass of struggling people; the pitiful cries that pierced the night air and then slowly died out; the long hours spent clutching the keel of the boat, huddled against the cold with thirty other men; the excitement when the Cunard liner *Carpathia* hove into view and made the rescue. Finally, he sighed and peered over the tops of his glasses at Pitt. "Am I boring you, Mr. Pitt?"

"Not in the least," Pitt answered. "Listening to someone who actually lived the event seems almost like living it myself."

"Then I'm going to give you another story to try on for size," Bigalow said. "Until now I never told a soul about my last minutes before the ship went down. I never mentioned a word in any of my interrogations about the sinking; not to the United States Senate inquiry or to the British Court of Inquiry. Nor, did I ever breathe a syllable to the newspaper reporters or writers who were forever researching books on the tragedy. You, sir, are the first and will be the last to hear it from my lips."

Three hours later, Pitt was on the train back to Exeter, neither tired nor worn. He did feel a kind of excitement. The *Titanic,* along with the strange enigma locked within the vault of cargo hold No. 1, G Deck, beckoned to him now more than ever. Southby, he wondered? How did Southby fit in the picture? For perhaps the fiftieth time he looked down at the package that Commodore Bigalow had given him. And he was not sorry that he had come to Teignmouth.

45

Dr. Ryan Prescott, chief of the NUMA Hurricane Center in Tampa, Florida, had had every intention of getting home on time for once and spending a quiet evening with his wife playing cribbage. But at ten minutes before midnight he was still at his desk staring tiredly at the satellite photos spread before him.

"Just when we think we've learned all there is to know about storms," he said querulously, "one pops out of nowhere and breaks the mold."

"A hurricane in the middle of May," his female assistant replied between yawns. "It's one for the record book all right."

"But why? The hurricane season normally extends from July to September. What caused this one to materialize two months early?"

"Beats me," the woman answered. "Where do you figure our pariah is headed?"

"Too early to predict with any certainty," Prescott said. "Her birth followed the normal patterns, true enough: vast low-pressure area fed by moist air, swirling counter-clockwise due to the earth's rotation. But here the difference ends. It usually takes days, sometimes weeks, for a storm four-hundred miles wide to build up. This baby pulled off the trick in less than eighteen hours."

Prescott sighed, rose from his desk, and walked to a large wall chart. He consulted a pad covered with scribbles, noting the known position, atmospheric conditions and speed. Then he began drawing a predicted track westerly from a point a hundred and fifty miles northeast of Bermuda, a track that gradually curved northward toward New-foundland.

"Until she gives us a hint of her future course, that's the best I can do." He paused as if waiting for confirmation. When none came, he asked, "Is that how you see it?"

Still receiving no reply, he turned to repeat the question but the words never came. His assistant had fallen asleep, her head cradled in her arms upon the desk. Gently he shook her shoulder until the green eyes fluttered open.

"There's nothing more we can do here," he said softly. "Let's go home and get some sleep." He glanced warily back at the wall chart. "Chances are it's a thousand-to-one fluke that will dissipate before morning and relapse into a minor localized storm." He spoke with some authority, but there was no conviction in his tone.

What he did not notice was that the line on the chart representing his predicted course for the hurricane traveled precisely over 41°46′ North by 50°14′ West.

46

Commander Rudi Gunn stood on the bridge of the *Capricorn* and watched a tiny blue speck far to the west materialize out of the diamond-clear sky. For a few minutes it seemed to hang there, neither changing shape nor growing larger; a dark blue dot suspended above the horizon, and then, almost all at once, it enlarged and took on the shape of a helicopter.

He made his way to the landing pad aft of the superstructure and stood waiting as the craft approached and hovered above the ship. Thirty seconds later the skids kissed the flight pad, the whine of the turbines died away, and the blades slowly idled to a stop.

Gunn moved in closer as the right-hand door opened and Pitt stepped out.

"Good trip?" Gunn asked.

"Interesting," Pitt replied.

Pitt read the strain in Gunn's face. The lines around the little man's eyes were set tight and his face was grim. "You look like a kid who just had his Christmas presents stolen, Rudi. What's the problem?"

"The Uranus Oil sub, the *Deep Fathom*. She's trapped on the wreck."

Pitt was silent for a moment. Then he asked simply, "Admiral Sandecker?"

"He set up his headquarters on the *Bomberger*. Since it was the *Deep Fathom*'s tender, he thought it would be better to conduct the rescue mission from there until you returned."

"You say *was,* as if the sub is as good as lost."

"It doesn't look good. Come topside and I'll fill you in on the details."

There was an air of tension and despair in the *Capricorn*'s operations room. The usually gregarious Giordino simply nodded at Pitt's arrival, totally bypassing any word of greeting. Ben Drummer was on the microphone, talking to the crew of the *Deep Fathom,* encouraging them with a show of forced cheer and optimism that was betrayed by the dread in his eyes. Rick Spencer, the salvage operations equipment engineer, was gazing in mute concentration at the TV monitors. The other men in the room went about their business quietly, their faces pensive.

Gunn began explaining the situation. "Two hours before she was to ascend and change crews, the *Deep Fathom,* manned by engineers Joe Kiel, Tom Chavez, and Sam Merker—"

"Merker was with you on the Lorelei Current Expedition," Pitt interrupted.

"So was Munk." Gunn nodded solemnly. "It would seem we're a cursed crew."

"Go on."

"They were in the midst of installing a pressure bleed valve on the starboard side of the *Titanic*'s forecastle deck bulkheads when their stern brushed against a forward cargo crane. The corroded mounts broke loose and the derrick section fell across the sub's buoyancy tanks, rupturing them. More than two tons of water poured through the opening and pinned her hull to the wreck."

"How long ago did it happen?" Pitt asked.

"About three and a half hours ago."

"Then why all the gloom? You people act as if there wasn't a prayer. The *Deep Fathom* carries enough oxygen in her reserve system to support a crew of three for over a week. Plenty of time for *Sappho I* and *II* to seal the air tanks and pump clear the water."

"It's not all that simple," Gunn said. "Six hours is all we've got."

"How do you figure a six-hour margin?"

"I left the worst part for last." Gunn stared bleakly at Pitt. "The impact from the falling crane cracked a welded seam on the *Deep Fathom*'s hull. It's only a tiny pinhole, but the tremendous pressure at that depth is forcing the sea into the cabin at the rate of four gallons a minute. It's a miracle the seam hasn't burst, collapsing the hull and crushing those guys to jelly." He tilted his head toward the clock over the computer panel. "Six hours is all they've got before the water fills the cabin and they drown . . . and there's not a damned thing we can do about it."

"Why not plug the leak from the outside with Wetsteel?"

"Easier said than done. We can't get at it. The section of the hull's seam that contains the leak is jammed against the *Titanic*'s forecastle bulkhead. The admiral sent down the other three submersibles in the hope that their combined power could move the *Deep Fathom* just enough to reach and repair the damage. It was no-go."

Pitt sat down in a chair, picked up a pencil, and began making notations on a pad. "The *Sea Slug* is equipped with cutting equipment. If she could attack the derrick—"

"Negative." Gunn shook his head in frustration. "During the tugging operation, the *Sea Slug* broke her manipulator arm. She's back on the *Modoc*'s deck now and the Navy boys say its impossible to repair the arm in time." Gunn slammed his fist down on the chart table. "Our last hope was the winch on the *Bomberger*. If it was possible to attach a cable to the derrick, we might have pulled it free of the sub."

"End of rescue," Pitt said. "The *Sea Slug* is the only submersible we've got that's equipped with a heavy-duty manipulator arm, and without it, there is no way of making a hookup with the cable."

Gunn rubbed his eyes wearily. "After thousands of man-hours poured into the planning and construction of every back-up safety system conceivable, and the calculating of concise emergency procedures for every predictable contingency, the unforeseen rose up and smacked us below the belt with a beyond-the-bounds-of-probability, million-to-one accident the computers didn't count on."

"Computers are only as good as the data fed into them," Pitt said.

He moved over to the radio and took the microphone from Drummer's hand. *"Deep Fathom,* this is Pitt. Over."

"Nice to hear your cheery voice again," Merker came over the speaker as calmly as if he were on the telephone lying at home in bed. "Why don't you drop down and make up a fourth for bridge?"

"Not my game," Pitt answered matter-of-factly. "How much time left before the water reaches your batteries?"

"At the rate she's rising, approximately another fifteen to twenty minutes."

Pitt turned to Gunn and said what needed no saying. "When their batteries go, they'll be out of communication."

Gunn nodded. "The *Sappho II* is standing by to keep them company. That's about all we can do."

Pitt pressed the mike button again. "Merker, how about your life-support system?"

"What life-support system? That crapped out half an hour ago. We're existing on bad breath."

"I'll send you down a case of Certs."

"Better make it fast. Chavez has a malignant case of halitosis." Then a trace of doubt surfaced in Merker's tone. "If the worst happens and we don't see you guys again, at least we'll be surrounded by good company down here."

Merker's abrupt reference to the *Titanic*'s dead left every man in the operations room a shade paler; every man that is, except Pitt. He touched the transmit button. "Just see to it you leave a clean ship. We may want to use it again. Pitt out."

It was interesting to see the reaction to Pitt's seemingly callous remark. Giordino, Gunn, Spencer, and the others just stared at him. Only Drummer displayed an expression of anger.

Pitt touched Curly, the radio operator, on the shoulder. "Patch me into the admiral on the *Bomberger,* but use a different frequency."

Curly looked up. "You don't want those guys on the *Deep Fathom* to hear?"

"What they don't know won't hurt them," said Pitt coldly. "Now hurry it up."

Moments later Sandecker's voice boomed over the speaker. *"Capricorn,* this is Admiral Sandecker. Over."

"Pitt here, Admiral."

Sandecker wasted no time on niceties. "You're aware of what we're up against?"

"Gunn has briefed me," Pitt replied.

"Then you know we have exhausted every avenue. No matter how you slice it, time is the enemy. If we could stall the inevitable for another ten hours, we'd have a fighting chance of saving them."

"There's one other way," Pitt said. "The odds are high but mathematically, it's possible."

"I'm open to suggestions."

Pitt hesitated. "To begin with, we forget the *Deep Fathom* for the moment and turn our energies in another direction."

Drummer came close to him. "What are you saying Pitt? What goes on here? 'Forget the *Deep Fathom.*' " he shouted through twitching lips. "Are you mad?"

Pitt smiled a disarming smile. "The last desperate roll of the dice, Drummer. You people failed, and failed miserably. You may be God's gift to the world of marine salvage, but as a rescue force, you come off like a bunch of amateurs. Bad luck compounded your mistakes, and now you sit around whining that all is lost. Well all is not lost, gentlemen. We're going to change the rules of the game and put the *Deep Fathom* on the surface before the six-hour deadline, which, if my watch serves me, is now down to five hours and forty-three minutes."

Giordino looked at Pitt. "Do you really think it can be done?"

"I really think it can be done."

47

The structural engineers and the marine scientists huddled around in small circles, mumbling to themselves as they frantically shoved their slide rules back and forth. Every so often, one of them would break away and walk over to the computers and check the readout sheets. Admiral Sandecker, who had just arrived from the *Bomberger,* sat behind a desk gripping a mug of coffee and shaking his head.

"This will never be written into the textbooks on salvage," he murmured. "Blowing a derelict off the bottom with explosives. God, it's insane."

"What other choice do we have?" Pitt said. "If we can kick the *Titanic* out of the mud, the *Deep Fathom* will be carried up with her."

"The whole idea is crazy," Gunn muttered. "The concussion will only expand the cracked seam in the submersible's hull and cause instant implosion."

"Maybe. Maybe not," Pitt said. "But even if that occurs, it's probably best that Merker, Kiel, and Chavez die instantly from the sea's crush than suffer the prolonged agony of slow suffocation."

"And what about the *Titanic*?" Gunn persisted. "We could blow everything we've worked for all these months all over the abyssal landscape."

"Score that as a calculated risk," Pitt said. "The *Titanic*'s construction is of a greater strength than most ships afloat today. Her beams, girders, bulkheads, and decks are as sound as the night she sank. The old girl can take whatever we dish out. Make no mistake about it."

"Do you honestly think it will work?" Sandecker asked.

"I do."

"I could order you not to do this thing. You know that."

"I know that," Pitt replied. "I'm banking on you to keep me in the ball game until the final inning."

Sandecker rubbed his hand across his eyes, then shook his head slowly as if to clear it. Finally he said, "Okay, Dirk, it's your baby."

Pitt nodded and turned away.

There were just five hours and ten minutes to go.

Two and a half miles below, the three men in the *Deep Fathom,* cold and alone in a remote, uncharitable environment, watched the water creep up the cabin walls inch by inch until it flooded the main circuitry and shorted out the instruments, throwing the interior of the cabin into blackness. Then they began to feel the sting of the thirty-four-degree water in earnest as it swirled around their legs. Standing there shivering under the torment of certain death, they still nurtured the spark to survive.

"As soon as we get topside," Kiel murmured, "I'm going to take a day off, and I don't care who knows it."

"Come again?" Chavez said in the darkness.

"They can fire me if they want to, but I'm sleeping in tomorrow."

Chavez groped for and found Kiel's arm, gripping it roughly. "What are you babbling about?"

"Take it easy," Merker said. "With the life-support system gone, the carbon-dioxide buildup is getting to him. I'm beginning to feel a bit giddy myself."

"Foul air on top of everything else," Chavez grumbled. "If we don't drown, we get crushed when the hull bursts, and if we don't get mashed like eggshells, we suffocate on our own air. Our future looks none too bright."

"You left out exposure," Merker added sardonically. "If we don't climb above this freezing water, we won't get a chance at the other three."

Kiel said nothing but limply allowed Chavez to shove him into the uppermost sleeping bunk. Then Chavez followed and sat on the edge, his feet dangling over the side.

Merker struggled through the crotch-deep water to the forward view-port and looked out. He could see only the haloed outline of the *Sappho II* through the blinding glare of her lights. Even though the other craft hovered only ten feet away, there was nothing she could do for the stricken *Deep Fathom* while they were both surrounded by the relentless pressure of the hostile deep. As long as she is still there, Merker thought, they haven't written us off. He took no small consolation in the fact that they were not alone. It wasn't much to lean on, but it was all they had.

On board the supply ship *Alhambra,* camera crews from the three major networks, swept up in the swirling tide of expectation, feverishly struggled to get their equipment into action. Along every available foot of starboard-deck railing, wire-service reporters peered through binoculars in hypnotic concentration at the *Capricorn* floating two miles away, while photographers aimed their telephoto lenses on the surface of the water between the ships. Trapped in one corner of a makeshift press-room, Dana Seagram pulled a foul-weather jacket tightly around her shoulders and gamely stood up to the dozen news people armed with tape recorders who were pushing microphones toward her face as though they were lollipops.

"Is it true, Ms. Seagram, that attempting to raise the *Titanic* three days ahead of schedule is in reality a last-ditch attempt to save the lives of the men trapped below?"

"It is only one of several solutions," Dana replied.

"Are we to understand that all other attempts have failed?"

"There have been complications," Dana admitted.

Inside one of the jacket's pockets, Dana nervously twisted a handkerchief until her fingers turned sore. The long months of give-and-take with the men and women of the press were beginning to tell.

"Since the loss of communications with the *Deep Fathom,* how can you know for certain whether the crew is still alive?"

"Computer data assure us that their situation will not turn critical for another four hours and forty minutes."

"How does NUMA intend to bring up the *Titanic* if the electrolyte chemical is not fully injected into the silt around the hull?"

"I can't answer that," Dana said. "Mr. Pitt's last message from the *Capricorn* only stated that they were going to raise the wreck in the next few hours. He did not offer details regarding the method."

"What if it's too late? What if Kiel, Chavez, and Merker are already dead?"

Dana's expression went rigid. "They are not dead," she said with eyes blazing. "And, the first one of you who reports such a cruel and inhuman rumor before it's a proven fact will get their ass kicked off this ship, credentials and Nielsen ratings be damned. Do you understand?"

The reporters stood there a moment in mute surprise at Dana's sudden display of anger, and then slowly and silently they began to lower the microphones and melt toward the deck outside.

Rick Spencer unrolled a large piece of paper on the chart table and anchored it down with several half-empty coffee mugs. It was an overhead drawing that depicted the *Titanic* and her position in relation to the sea floor. He began pointing a pencil at various spots about the hulk that were marked with tiny crosses.

"Here's the way it shapes up," he explained. "According to the computer data, we set eighty charges, each containing thirty pounds of explosives, at these key points in the sediment along the *Titanic*'s hull."

Sandecker leaned over the drawing, his eyes scanning the crosses. "I see that you've staggered them in three rows on each side."

"That's right, sir," Spencer said. "The outside rows are set sixty yards away; the middle, forty; and the inner rows are just twenty yards from the ship's plates. We'll detonate the starboard outer row first. Then eight seconds later we fire the port outer row. Another eight seconds and we repeat the procedure with the middle rows, and so on."

"Kind of like rocking a car back and forth that's stuck in the mud," Giordino volunteered.

Spencer nodded. "You might say that's a fair comparison."

"Why not jolt her out of the silt with one big bang?" Giordino asked.

"It's possible a sudden shock might do it, but the geologists are in favor of separate overlapping shock waves. It's vibration we're after."

"Have we the explosives?" Pitt asked.

"The *Bomberger* carries nearly a ton for seismic-research purposes," Spencer replied. "The *Modoc* has four hundred pounds in her stores for underwater salvage blasting."

"Will it do the trick?"

"Border line," Spencer admitted. "Another three hundred pounds would have given us a more acceptable margin for success."

"We could have it flown from the mainland by jet and air-dropped," Sandecker suggested.

Pitt shook his head. "By the time the explosives arrived, and were loaded in a sub and planted on the sea floor, it would be two hours too late."

Then we'd best get on with it," Sandecker said brusquely. "We have a tight deadline to meet." He turned to Gunn. "How soon can the explosives be set in place?"

"Four hours," Gunn said unhesitatingly.

Sandecker's eyes narrowed. "That's cutting it pretty thin. That only leaves a leeway of fourteen minutes."

"We'll make it," Gunn said. "However, there is one condition."

"What is it?" Sandecker snapped impatiently.

"It will take every operational submersible we've got."

"That means pulling the *Sappho II* from its station beside the *Deep Fathom*," Pitt said. Those poor bastards down there will think we're deserting them."

"There's no other way," Gunn said helplessly. "There's simply no other way."

Merker had lost all track of time. He stared at the luminous dial on his watch but his eyes couldn't focus on the glowing numbers. How long since the derrick had fallen across their buoyancy tanks, he wondered— five hours—ten—was it yesterday? His mind was sluggish and confused.

He could only sit there without moving a muscle, breathing shallowly and slowly, each breath seemingly taking a lifetime. Gradually, he became aware of a movement. He reached out and touched Kiel and Chavez in the darkness, but they made no sound, no response; they had fallen into a lethargic stupor.

Then he became aware of it again, a minute but perceptible something that was not where it was supposed to be. His mind turned over as though it were immersed in syrup. But at last he had it. Except for the relentless rise of the water, there was no change, no sign of physical motion inside the flooding cabin; it was the angle of the *Sappho II*'s light beam through the forward viewports that had dimmed.

He dropped off the bunk into the water—it came up to his chest now—and almost as if in a nightmare, he struggled toward the upper front ports and peered into the depths outside.

Suddenly, his numbed senses were gripped by a fear such as he had never known before. His eyes widened and glazed, his hands clenched in futility and despair.

"Oh God!" he cried aloud. "They're leaving us. They've given us up."

Sandecker twisted the huge cigar he had just lit and continued to pace the deck. The radio operator raised his hand and the admiral turned in mid-step and came up behind him.

"The *Sappho I* reporting, sir," Curly said. "She's finished positioning her charges."

"Tell her to head topside as fast as her buoyancy tanks will take her. The higher she goes, the less pressure on her hull when the explosives detonate." The admiral swung and faced Pitt, who was keeping a watchful eye on the four monitors, whose cameras and floodlights were mounted in strategic spots around the *Titanic*'s superstructure. "How does it look?"

"So far, so good," Pitt answered. "If the Wetsteel pressure seals hold up against the concussions, we'll stand a fighting chance."

Sandecker stared at the color images and his brow furrowed as he perceived great streams of bubbles issuing from the liner's hulk. "She's losing a lot of air," he said.

"Excess pressure escaping through the bleeder valves," Pitt said tonelessly. "We switched from the electrolyte pumps back to the compressors in order to cram as much extra air as we can into the upper compartments." He paused to fine-tune a picture and then continued. "The *Capricorn*'s compressors put out ten thousand cubic feet of air an hour, so it didn't take long to raise the pressure inside the hull another ten pounds per inch, just enough to pop the bleeder valves."

Drummer ambled over from the computers and checked off a series of notations on a clipboard. "As near as we can figure, ninety per cent of the ship's compartments are unwatered," he said. "The main problem, as I see it, is that we have more lift than the computers say is necessary. If and when the suction gives way, she'll come up like a kite."

"The *Sea Slug* just dropped her last charge," Curly reported.

"Ask her to make a swing by the *Deep Fathom* before she starts for the surface," Pitt said, "and see if she can make visual contact with Merker and his crew."

"Eleven minutes to go," Giordino announced.

"What in hell is keeping the *Sappho II*?" Sandecker asked no one in particular.

Pitt looked across the room to Spencer. "Are the charges ready to fire?"

Spencer nodded. "Each row is tuned to a different transmitter frequency. All we have to do is turn a dial and they'll go off in their proper sequence."

"What do you bet we see first, the bow or the stern?"

"There's no contest. The bow is buried twenty feet deeper in the sediment than the rudder. I'm counting on the stern breaking free and then using its buoyant leverage to pull up the rest of the keel. She should rise on very nearly the same angle she sank—providing she's agreeable and rises at all."

"Last charge secured," droned Curly. *"Sappho II* is making her getaway."

"Anything from the *Sea Slug*?"

"She reports no visual contact with *Deep Fathom*'s crew."

"Okay, tell her to hightail it toward the surface," Pitt said. "We fire the first row of charges in nine minutes."

"They're dead," Drummer suddenly cried, his voice breaking. "We're too late, they're all dead."

Pitt took two steps and gripped Drummer by the shoulders. "Cut the hysterics. The last thing we need is a premature eulogy."

Drummer dropped his shoulders, his face ashen and frozen in a stonelike expression of dread. Then he silently nodded and walked unsteadily back to the computer console.

"The water must only be a couple of feet from the sub's cabin ceiling by now," Giordino said. It came out about half an octave higher than his normal tone.

"If pessimism sold by the pound, you guys would all be millionaires," Pitt said dryly.

"The *Sappho I* has reached the safety zone at six thousand feet." This from the sonar operator.

"One down, two to go," murmured Sandecker.

There was nothing left to do now but wait for the other submersibles to rise above the danger level of the approaching concussion waves. Eight minutes passed, eight interminable minutes that saw the sweat begin to ooze on two dozen foreheads.

"*Sappho II* and *Sea Slug* now approaching safety zone."

"Sea and weather?" Pitt demanded.

"Four-foot swells, clear skies, wind out of the northeast at five knots," answered Farquar, the weatherman. "You couldn't ask for better conditions."

For several moments no one spoke. Then Pitt said, "Well, gentlemen, the time has come." His voice was level and relaxed, and no trace of apprehension showed in his tone or manner. "Okay, Spencer, count it down."

Spencer began repeating the announcements with clocklike regularity. "Thirty seconds . . . fifteen seconds . . . five seconds . . . signal transmitting . . . mark." Then he unhesitatingly went right into the next firing order. "Eight seconds . . . four seconds . . . signal transmitting . . . mark."

Everyone clustered around the TV monitors and the sonar operator, their only contacts now with the bottom. The first explosion barely caused a tremor through the decks of the *Capricorn*, and the volume of sound came to their ears like that of faraway thunder. The cloud of anxiety could be slashed with a sword. Every single eye was trained straight ahead on the monitors, on the quivering lines that distorted the images when the charges went off. Tense, strained, numb with the expectant look of men who feared the worst but hoped for the best, they stood there immobile as Spencer droned on with his countdowns.

The shudders from the deck became more pronounced as shock wave followed shock wave and broke on the surface of the ocean. Then, abruptly, the monitors all flickered in a kaleidoscope of fused light and went black.

"Damn!" Sandecker muttered. "We've lost picture contact."

"The concussions must have jolted loose the main relay connector," Gunn surmised.

Their attention quickly turned to the sonar scope, but few of them could see it; the operator had drawn himself up so close to the glass that his head obscured it. Finally, Spencer straightened up. He sighed deeply to himself, pulled a handkerchief from his hip pocket and rubbed his face and neck. "That's all she wrote," he said hoarsely. "There isn't any more."

"Still stationary," said the sonar operator. "The Big T is still stationary."

"Go baby!" Giordino pleaded. "Get your big ass up!"

"Oh God, dear God," Drummer mumbled. "The suction is still holding her to the bottom."

"Come on, damn you," Sandecker joined in. "Lift . . . lift."

If it was humanly possible for the mind to will 46,328 tons of steel to release its hold on the grave it had occupied for seventy-six long years and return to the sunlight, the men crowded around the sonarscope would have surely made it so. But there was to be no psychokinetic phenomenon this day. The *Titanic* stayed stubbornly clutched to the sea floor.

"A dirty, rotten break," Farquar said.

Drummer held his hands over his face, turned away, and stumbled from the room.

"Woodson on the *Sappho II* requests permission to descend for a look-see," said Curly.

Pitt shrugged. "Permission granted."

Slowly, wearily, Admiral Sandecker sank into a chair. "What price failure?" he said.

The bitter taste of hopelessness flooded the room, swept by the grim tide of total defeat.

"What now?" Giordino asked, staring vacantly at the deck.

"What we came here to do," answered Pitt tiredly. "We go on with the salvage operation. Tomorrow we'll begin again to . . ."

"She's moved!"

No one reacted immediately.

"She moved," the sonar operator repeated. His voice had a quiver to it.

"Are you sure?" Sandecker whispered.

"Stake my life on it."

Spencer was too stunned to speak. He could only stare at the sonar-scope with an expression of abject incredulity. Then his lips began working. "The aftershocks!" he said. "The aftershocks caused a delayed reaction."

"Rising," the sonar operator shouted, banging his fist on the arm of his chair. "That gorgeous old bucket of bolts has broken free. She's coming up."

48

At first everybody was too dumbstruck to move. The moment they had prayed for, had spent eight tortuous months struggling for, had sneaked up behind them and somehow they couldn't accept it as actually happening. Then the electrifying news began to sink in and they all began shouting at the same time, like a crowd of mission-control space engineers during a rocket lift-off.

"Go baby, go!" Sandecker shouted as joyfully as a schoolboy.

"Move, you mother!" Giordino yelled. "Move, move!"

"Keep coming, you big beautiful rusty old floating palace, you," Spencer murmured.

Suddenly, Pitt rushed across to the radio and clutched Curly's shoulder in a viselike grip.

"Quick, contact Woodson on the *Sappho II*. Tell him the *Titanic* is on her way up and to get the hell out of the way before he's run over."

"Still on a surface course," the sonar operator said. "Speed of ascent accelerating."

"We haven't weathered the storm yet," Pitt said. "A hundred and one things can still go wrong before she breaks surface. If only—"

"Yeah," Giordino cut in, "like, if only the Wetsteel maintains its bond, or if only the bleeder valves can keep up with the sudden drop in water pressure, or if the hull doesn't take it in its mind to go snap, crackle, and pop. 'If' . . . it's a mighty big word."

"Still coming and coming fast," the sonar operator said, staring at his scope. "Six hundred feet in the last minute."

Pitt swung to Giordino. "Al, find Doc Bailey and the pilot of the helicopter, and get in the air like a mad bull was on your ass. Then, as soon as the *Titanic* stabilizes herself, drop down on her forecastle deck. I don't care how you do it—rope ladder, winch, and bucket chair—crash-land the copter if you have to, but you and the good doctor drop down fast and pop the *Deep Fathom*'s hatch cover and lift those men out of that hellhole!"

"We're halfway there." Giordino grinned. He was already out the door before Pitt could issue his next order to Spencer.

"Rick, stand by to hoist the portable diesel pumps on board the derelict. The sooner we can get ahead of any leaks, the better."

"We'll need cutting torches to get inside her," Spencer said, his eyes wide with excitement.

"Then see to it."

Pitt turned back to the sonar panel.

"Rate of ascent?"

"Eight hundred and fifty feet a minute," the sonar operator called back.

"Too fast," Pitt said.

"It's what we didn't want," Sandecker muttered through his cigar. "Her interior compartments are overfilled with air and she's soaring to the surface out of control."

"And, if we've miscalculated the amount of ballast water left in her lower holds, she could rocket two-thirds her length out of the water and capsize," Pitt added.

Sandecker looked him in the eye. "And that would spell finish to the *Deep Fathom*'s crew." Then without another word, the admiral turned and led the exodus from the operations room to the deck outside, where everyone began scanning the restless swells in heart-pounding anticipation.

Only Pitt hung back. "What depth is she?" This to the sonar operator.

"Passing the eight-thousand-foot mark."

"Woodson reporting in," Curly intoned. "He says the Big T just went by the *Sappho II* like a greased pig."

"Acknowledge and tell him to surface. Relay the same message to the *Sea Slug* and *Sappho I*." There was nothing left to do here so he stepped out the door and up the ladder to the port bridge wing, where he joined Gunn and Sandecker.

Gunn picked up the bridge phone. "Sonar, this is the bridge."

"Sonar."

"Can you give me an approximate fix on where she'll appear?"

"She should break water about six hundred yards off the port quarter."

"Time?"

There was a pause.

"Time?" Gunn repeated.

"Is *now* soon enough for you, Commander?"

At that very moment, a huge wave of bubbles spread across the sea and the fantail of the *Titanic* burst up into the afternoon sun like a gigantic whale. For a few seconds it seemed as though there was no stopping her soaring flight from the depths—her stern kept crowding into the sky until she came free of the water up to the boiler casing, where her No. 2 funnel had once stood. It was a staggering sight; the inside air bleeding down sent great torrents of spray shooting through the pressure-relief valves, shrouding the great ship in billowing rainbowed clouds of vapor. She hung poised for several moments, clawing at the crystal blue heavens, and then, slowly at first, began to settle until her keel smacked the sea with a tremendous splash that sent a ten-foot wave surging toward the surrounding fleet of ships. She heeled down as if she had no intention of recovering. A thousand onlookers held their breath as she careened ever farther onto her starboard beam ends, thirty, forty, forty-five, fifty degrees, and there she hung for what seemed like a dreadful eternity; everyone was half-expecting her to continue the roll over onto her superstructure. But then, with agonizing sluggishness, the *Titanic* slowly began the struggle to right herself. Gradually, foot by foot, until her hull reached a starboard list of twelve degrees . . . and there she stayed.

Nobody could speak. They all just stood there, too stunned, too mesmerized by what they had just seen to do anything but breathe. Sandecker's weathered face looked ghostly pale even in the bright sun.

Pitt was the first to find his voice. "She's up," he managed in a barely audible whisper.

"She's up," Gunn acknowledged softly.

Then the spell was broken by the pulsing blades of the *Capricorn*'s helicopter as it headed into the wind and angled over the debris-laden forecastle of the resurrected ship. The pilot held the craft on a level position a few feet above the deck and almost instantly two tiny specks could be seen dropping out of a side door.

Giordino scrambled up the access ladder and found himself staring at the hatch cover of the *Deep Fathom*. Thank God for small miracles: the hull was still sound. Cautiously, he maneuvered his body on top of the rounded, slippery deck and tried the handwheel. The spokes felt like ice, but he gripped firm and gave a heavy twist. The handwheel refused to cooperate.

"Stop dawdling and open the damned thing," Dr. Bailey boomed behind him. "Every second counts."

Giordino took a deep breath and heaved with every ounce the muscles of his oxlike body could give. It moved an inch. He tried again, and this time forced half a turn, and then, finally, it began spinning easily as the air inside the sub hissed out and the pressure against the seal relaxed. When the handwheel halted at the end of its threads, Giordino swung the hatch open and peered into the darkness below. A stale, rancid smell rose up and attacked his nostrils. His heart sank when, after his eyes became accustomed to the darkness inside, he saw the water sloshing only eighteen inches from the upper bulkhead.

Dr. Bailey pushed past and lowered his immense hulk through the hatch and down the interior ladder. The icy water stung his skin. He pushed off the rungs and dog-paddled toward the after part of the submersible until his hand touched something soft in the dim light. It was a leg. Following it over the knee, he felt his way toward the torso. His hand came out of the water at shoulder level and he touched a face.

Bailey moved closer until his nose was a bare inch from the face in the darkness. He tried to feel for a pulse, but his fingers were too numb from the cold water, and he detected nothing that indicated life or death. Then, suddenly, the eyes fluttered open, the lips trembled, and a voice whispered, "Go away . . . I told you . . . I'm not working today."

"Bridge?" Curly's voice scratched through the speaker.

"This is the bridge," answered Gunn.

"Ready to patch in the helicopter."

"Go ahead."

There was a pause and then a strange voice cracked onto the bridge. "*Capricorn,* this is Lieutenant Sturgis."

"This is Commander Gunn, Lieutenant; I have you loud and clear. Over."

"Dr. Bailey has entered the *Deep Fathom*. Please stand by."

The brief respite gave everyone a chance to study the *Titanic*. She looked uncompromisingly utilitarian and downright naked without her towering funnels and masts. The steel plates of her sides were blotched and stained with rust, but the black and white paint of her hull and superstructure still shone through. She looked a mess, like a hideous old prostitute who dwelt in dreams of better days and long-lost beauty. The portholes and windows were covered with the unsightly gray of the Wetsteel, and her once-immaculate teak decks were rotted and cluttered with miles of corroded cable. The empty lifeboat davits seemed to reach out in wraithlike pleading for a return of their long-lost contents. The over-all effect of the ocean liner's presence came across the water like an eerie subject in a surrealistic painting. And yet, there was an inexplicable serenity about her that could not be described.

"*Capricorn,* this is Sturgis. Over."

"Gunn here. Come in."

"Mr. Giordino has just given me three fingers and a thumbs-up sign. Merker, Kiel, and Chavez are still alive."

A strange quiet followed. Then Pitt walked over to the emergency equipment panel and pressed the siren button. The ear-splitting sound whooped across the water.

Then the *Modoc*'s whistle blared in reply, and Pitt saw the normally reserved Sandecker laugh and throw his cap in the air. The *Monterey Park* joined in, and the *Alhambra* and finally the *Bomberger,* until the sea around the *Titanic* was one huge cacophony of sirens and whistles. Not to be outdone, the *Juneau* moved up and punctuated the mad din with a thunderous salute from her eight-inch gun mount.

It was a moment that none of those present would ever live again. And, for the first time in all the years he could remember, Pitt felt the trickle of warm tears on his cheeks.

49

The late-afternoon sun was just touching the tops of the trees as Gene Seagram sat slouched on a bench in East Potomac Park and contemplated the Colt revolver in his lap. Serial number 204,783, he thought, you're about to serve the purpose you were manufactured for. Almost lovingly, he ran his fingers over the barrel, the cylinder, and the grips. Suicide: it seemed the ideal solution to end his flight into black depression. He marveled that he hadn't thought of it before. No more uncontrollable crying in the middle of the night. No more sensations of worthlessness or the gnawing inside his guts that his life had been a transparent sham.

His mind envisioned the past few months as reflected in the cracked and distorted mirror of acute despair. The two things he had cherished most were his wife and the Sicilian Project. Now Dana was gone, his marriage a shambles. And the President of the United States had taken what seemed to Seagram to be a needless risk in leaking his precious project to the sworn enemy of democracy.

Sandecker had revealed to him the presence of the two Soviet agents on the *Titanic*'s salvage fleet. And the fact that the CIA had warned the admiral not to interfere with their espionage activities only served to drive, what seemed to Seagram, another nail into the coffin of the Sicilian Project. Already one of NUMA's engineers had been murdered, and just this morning, the daily report from Sandecker's staff to Meta Section told of the trapped submersible and the apparent hopelessness of rescuing its crew. It had to be sabotage. There could be no doubt of it. The mismatched pieces of the puzzle were forced into unfitting slots by Seagram's confused brain. The Sicilian Project was dead, and he now made up his mind to die with it. He was in the act of releasing the gun's safety catch when a shadow fell across him and a voice spoke in a friendly tone.

"It's much too nice a day to rip off your life, don't you think?"

Officer Peter Jones had been walking his beat along the path beside Ohio Drive when he noticed the man on the park bench. At first glance, Jones thought Seagram was simply a wine-sodden derelict soaking up the sun. He considered running him in, but dismissed it as a waste of time; a booked bum would be back on the streets inside twenty-four hours. Jones figured it was hardly worth the effort of filling out the endless reports. But then something about the man didn't fit the stereotyped lost soul. Jones moved casually, inconspicuously around a large leafing elm tree and doubled back slightly to the side of the bench. On closer inspection his suspicions were confirmed. True, the reddened unseeing eyes and the vacant look of the alcoholic were there, as was the listless uncaring droop of the shoulders, but so were small bits and pieces that didn't belong. The shoes were shined, the suit expensive and pressed, the face neatly shaven, and the fingernails trimmed. And then there was the gun.

Seagram slowly looked up into the face of a black police officer. Instead of meeting a determined look of wariness, he found himself gazing into an expression of genuine compassion.

"Aren't you jumping to conclusions?" Seagram said.

"Man, if I ever saw a classic case of suicidal depression, you're it." Jones made a sitting gesture. "May I share your bench?"

"It's city property," Seagram said indifferently.

Jones carefully sat down an arm's length from Seagram and languidly stretched out his legs and leaned against the backrest, keeping his hands in plain sight and away from his holstered service revolver.

"Now me, I'd pick November," he said softly. "April is when the flowers pop and the trees go green, but November, that's when the weather turns nasty, the winds chill you to the bone, and the skies are always cloudy and dreary. Yeah, that's the month I'd pick all right to do away with myself."

Seagram clutched the Colt tighter, eyeing Jones in apprehension, waiting for him to make his move.

"I take it you consider yourself something of an expert on suicide?"

"Not really," Jones said. "In fact, you're the first one I ever got to watch in the act. Most of the time I come on the scene long after the main event. Now take drownings; they're the worst. Bodies all bloated up and black, eyeballs mush in their sockets after the fish have nibbled at them. Then there's the jumpers. I saw a fella one time who had leaped off a thirty-story building. Lit on his feet. His shin bones came out his shoulders. . . ."

"I don't need this," Seagram snarled. "I don't need a nigger cop feeding me horror stories."

Anger flickered in Jones's eyes for an instant, and then quickly passed.

"Sticks and stones . . ." he said. He took out a handkerchief and leisurely wiped the sweatband of his cap. "Tell me, Mister ah . . ."

"Seagram. You might as well know. It won't make any difference later."

"Tell me, Mr. Seagram, how do you intend on doing it. A bullet in the temple, the forehead, or in the mouth?"

"What does it matter, the results are the same."

"Not necessarily," Jones said conversationally. "I don't recommend the temple or forehead, at least not with a small-caliber gun. Let's see, what have you got there? Yeah, looks like a thirty-eight. It might do a messy job okay, but I doubt if it would kill you proper. I knew one guy who fired a forty-five into his temple. Scrambled his brains and shoved out his left eye, but he didn't die. Lived for years like a turnip. Can't you picture him lying there, his bowels running all over the sheets, and him begging to be put out of his misery. Yeah, if I was you, I'd stick the barrel in my mouth and blow off the back of the head. That's the safest bet."

"If you don't shut up," Seagram snapped, pointing the Colt at Jones, "I'll kill you too."

"Kill me?" Jones said. "You haven't got the balls. You're not a killer, Seagram. It's written all over you."

"Every man is capable of committing murder."

"I agree, murder is no big deal. Anybody can do it. But only a psychopath ignores the consequences."

"Now you're beginning to sound like a philosopher."

"Us dumb nigger cops oftentimes like to fool white people with our smarts routine."

"I apologize for my poor choice of words."

Jones shrugged. "You think you got problems, Mr. Seagram? I'd love to have *your* problems. Look at yourself; you're white, obviously a man of means, you probably have a family and a nice position in life. How'd you like to trade places with me, change the color of your skin, be a black cop with six kids and a ninety-year-old frame house with a thirty-year mortgage on it? Tell me about it, Seagram. Tell me about how tough your world really is."

"You could never understand."

"What's there to understand? Nothing under the sun is worth killing yourself over. Oh sure, your wife will shed a few tears at first; but then she'll give your clothes to the Salvation Army, and six months from now she'll be in bed with another man while you'll be nothing but a picture in a scrapbook. Look around you. It's a beautiful spring day. Hell, think what you'll be missing. Didn't you watch the President on TV?"

"The President?"

"He came on at four o'clock and talked about all the great things that were happening. Manned flights to Mars are only three years away; there's been a breakthrough on the control of cancer; and he showed pictures of some old sunken ship the government salvaged from almost three miles below the ocean."

Seagram stared at Jones with unbelieving eyes. "What was that you said? A ship salvaged? What ship?"

"I don't remember."

"The *Titanic?*" Seagram asked in a whisper. "Was it the *Titanic?*"

"Yeah, that was the name. It rammed an iceberg and sank a long time ago. Come to think of it, I remember seeing a movie about the *Titanic* on television. Barbara Stanwyck and Clifton Webb were in—" Jones broke off at the look of incredulity, then shock, then twisted confusion that showed in Seagram's face.

Seagram handed his gun to the uncomprehending Jones and leaned back against the bench. Thirty days. Thirty days would be all he'd need once he had the byzanium to test the Sicilian Project's system and then see it through to operational status. It had been a narrow thing. If a wandering cop hadn't intruded when he did, thirty seconds would have been all Seagram had left to see anything ever again, forever.

50

"I assume you have weighed the staggering consequences of your accusations?"

Marganin looked at the soft-spoken little man with the cold blue eyes. Admiral Boris Sloyuk seemed more the baker around the corner than the shrewd head of the Soviet Union's second-largest intelligence-gathering network.

"I fully realize, Comrade Admiral, that I am jeopardizing my naval career and risking a prison sentence, but I place duty to the State above my personal ambitions."

"Very noble of you, Lieutenant," Sloyuk said without expression. "The charges you have brought are extremely damaging, to say the least; however you have not produced concrete evidence that indicates Captain Prevlov is a traitor to our country, and without it, I cannot condemn a man on his subordinate's word alone."

Marganin nodded. But he had planned his confrontation with the admiral carefully. Bypassing Prevlov and the normal chain of command to approach Sloyuk had been a risky business indeed, but the trap had been exactingly set and timing was critical. Calmly, he reached into his pocket and produced an envelope which he passed across the desk to Sloyuk.

"Here are transaction records of account number AZF seven-six-oh-nine at the Banque de Lausanne in Switzerland. You will note, sir, that it receives large deposits on a regular basis from one V. Volper, a clumsy anagram derived from the name Prevlov."

Sloyuk studied the bank records and then shot Marganin a very skeptical look. "You must forgive my suspicious nature, Lieutenant Marganin, but this has all the earmarks of trumped-up material."

Marganin passed across another envelope. "This one contains a secret communication from the American ambassador here in Moscow to the Defense Department in Washington. In it he states that Captain André Prevlov has been a vital source of Soviet naval secrets. The ambassador has also included the plans for our fleet deployment in the event of a first nuclear strike against the United States." Marganin felt satisfaction surge through him as the admiral's normally impassive face wrinkled in uncertainty. "I think the picture is clear; there is nothing trumped up here. A low-ranking officer in my position could not possibly obtain such highly classified fleet orders. Captain Prevlov, on the other hand, enjoys the confidence of the Soviet Naval Strategy Committee."

The barriers were down and the road was open; Sloyuk had no option but to acquiesce. He shook his head in perplexity. "The son of a great party leader who betrays his country for money . . . I find it impossible to accept."

"If one takes into consideration Captain Prevlov's extravagant lifestyle, it is not difficult to see the excessive demands made upon his financial resources."

"I am well aware of Captain Prevlov's tastes."

"Are you also aware that he is having an affair with a woman who passes herself off as the wife of the American ambassador's chief aide?"

An annoyed look crossed Sloyuk's face. "You know about her?" he asked guardedly. "Prevlov led me to believe that he was using her to obtain secrets from her husband at the embassy."

"Not so," Marganin said. "In fact, she is a divorcée and an agent of the Central Intelligence Agency." Marganin paused and then drove the point home. "The only secrets that pass through her hands are those provided by Captain Prevlov. It is *he* who is *her* source."

Sloyuk was silent for a few moments. Then he locked Marganin with a penetrating gaze. "How did you come by all this?"

"I would rather not divulge my informant's identity, Comrade Admiral. I mean no disrespect, but I have nurtured and developed his trust for nearly two years, and I gave him a solemn oath that his name and position with the American government would remain known only to me."

Sloyuk nodded. He accepted it. "You realize, of course, that this puts us in a very grave situation."

"The byzanium?"

"Exactly," Sloyuk said tersely. "If Prevlov told the Americans of our plan, it could prove disastrous. Once the byzanium is in their hands and the Sicilian Project is operational, the balance of power would be theirs for the next decade."

"Perhaps Captain Prevlov has not leaked our plan yet," Marganin said. "Perhaps he was waiting until the *Titanic* was raised."

"She has risen," Sloyuk said. "Not more than three hours ago, Captain Parotkin of the *Mikhail Kurkov* reported that the *Titanic* is on the surface and ready to be taken in tow."

Marganin looked up surprised. "But our agents, Silver and Gold, assured us the raising would not be attempted for another seventy-two hours."

Sloyuk shrugged. "The Americans are always in a hurry."

"Then we must cancel Captain Prevlov's plan to seize the byzanium in favor of one with credence."

Prevlov's plan—Marganin had to suppress a grin when he said it. The shrewd captain's colossal ego would be his downfall. From here on in, Marganin thought confidently, the drama would have to be played out very, very carefully.

"It is too late to change our strategy now," Sloyuk said slowly. "The men and ships are in place. We will go ahead as scheduled."

"But what about Captain Prevlov? Surely you will order his arrest?"

Sloyuk looked at Marganin coldly. "No, Lieutenant, he will remain at his duties."

"He cannot be trusted," Marganin said desperately. "You have seen the evidence—"

"I have seen nothing that cannot be manufactured," Sloyuk snapped brusquely. "Your little package comes too neatly wrapped, too meticulously tied with ribbon to be bought at first glance. What I do see is a young upstart who is stabbing his superior in the back in order to reach the next rung on the ladder of promotion. Purges went out before you were born, Lieutenant. You played a dangerous game and you lost."

"I assure you—"

"Enough!" Sloyuk's tone was hard as granite. "I am secure in the knowledge that the byzanium will be safely on board a Soviet ship no later than three days from now; an event that will prove Captain Prevlov's loyalty and your guilt."

51

The *Titanic* lay motionless and dead against the unending onslaught of the waves as they swirled around her huge mass, then closed ranks again and swept onward toward some as yet unknown and distant shore. She lay there and drifted with the current, her sodden wooden decks steaming under the fading evening sun. She was a dead ship that had returned among the living. A dead ship, but not an empty ship. The compass tower on the raised deck over her first-class lounge had been quickly cleared away to accommodate the helicopter, and soon a steady stream of men and equipment was being ferried on board to begin the arduous task of correcting the list and preparing her for the long tow to New York Harbor.

For a few short minutes after the half-dead crew of the *Deep Fathom* were airlifted to the *Capricorn,* Giordino had had the *Titanic* all to himself. The fact that he was the first man to set foot on her decks in seventy-six years never entered his head, and though it was still broad daylight, he shied away from any exploring. Each time he gazed down the 882-foot length of the ship, he felt as if he was staring down into a damp and slimy crypt. Nervously, he lit a cigarette, sat on a wet capstan, and waited for the invasion that wasn't long in coming.

Pitt experienced no pangs of uneasiness when he came on board, but, rather, a feeling of reverence. He walked to the bridge and stood alone, absorbed in the legend of the *Titanic*. God only knew, he'd wondered a hundred times what it was like that Sunday night nearly eight decades ago when Captain Edward J. Smith stood on the very same spot and realized that his great command was slowly and irreversibly sinking beneath his feet. What were his thoughts, knowing the lifeboats could hold only 1180 people, while on the maiden voyage the ship was carrying 2200 passengers and crew? Then he wondered what the venerable old captain would have thought had he known the decks of his ship would one day be walked again by men as yet unborn in his time.

After what seemed hours, but was in reality only a minute or two, Pitt broke out of his reverie and moved aft along the Boat Deck, past the sealed door of the wireless cabin, where First Operator John G. Phillips had sent history's first SOS; past the empty davits of lifeboat No. 6, in which Mrs. J. J. Brown of Denver later achieved enduring fame as the "Unsinkable Molly Brown"; past the entrance to the grand stairway, where Graham Farley and the ship's band had played to the end; past the spot where millionaire Benjamin Guggenheim and his secretary had stood calmly waiting for death, dressed in the finery of their evening clothes so that they could go down like gentlemen.

It took him almost a quarter of an hour to reach the elevator house at the far end of the Boat Deck. Pitt climbed over the hand railing and dropped to the Promenade Deck below. Here, he found the aft mast protruding from the rotted planking like a forelorn stump, ending abruptly at a height of eight feet where it had been cut short by *Sea Slug*'s underwater torch.

Pitt reached inside his jacket and pulled out the package given him by Commodore Bigalow and tenderly unwrapped it. He had forgotten to carry a line or cord, but he made do with the twine from the wrapping. When he was through, he stepped back from the stub of the once tall mast and stared up at his makeshift handiwork.

It was old and it was faded, but the red pennant of the White Star Line that Bigalow had snatched from oblivion so long ago proudly flew once more over the unsinkable *Titanic*.

52

The morning sun was just probing its rays above the eastern horizon when Sandecker jumped from the helicopter's cockpit door and ducked under the whirling blades, clutching his cap. Portable lights still blazed over the derelict's superstructure and crates of machinery were scattered about the decks in various stages of assembly. Pitt and his crew had slaved through the night, struggling like madmen to organize the salvage efforts.

Rudi Gunn greeted him under a rust-cankered ventilator.

"Welcome aboard the *Titanic*, Admiral," Gunn said, grinning. It seemed as if everybody in the salvage fleet was grinning this morning.

"What's the situation?"

"Stable for the moment. As soon as we get the pumps operating, we should be able to correct her list."

"Where's Pitt?"

"In the gymnasium."

Sandecker stopped in midstride and stared at Gunn. "The gymnasium, did you say?"

Gunn nodded and pointed at an opening in a bulkhead whose ragged edges suggested the work of an acetylene torch. "Through here."

The room measured about fifteen feet wide by forty feet deep, and was inhabited by a dozen men who were all involved in their individual assignments and who were seemingly oblivious to the weird assortment of antiquated and rust-worn mechanisms mounted on what had once been a colorful linoleum-block floor. There were ornate rowing machines; funny-looking stationary bicycles that were attached to a large circular distance clock on the wall; several mechanical horses with rotting leather saddles; and what Sandecker could have sworn looked like a mechanical camel which, as he discovered later, was exactly that.

Already the salvage crew had equipped the room with a radio transmitter and receiver, three portable gas-driven electrical generators, a small forest of spotlights on stands, a compact little Rube Goldberg-like galley, a clutter of desks and tables made out of collapsible aluminum tubing and packing crates, and several folding cots.

Pitt was huddled with Drummer and Spencer as Sandecker moved toward them. They were studying a large cutaway drawing of the ship.

Pitt looked up and waved a salute. "Welcome to the Big T, Admiral," he said warmly. "How are Merker, Kiel, and Chavez?"

"Safely bedded down in the *Capricorn*'s sick bay," Sandecker answered. "Ninety-per-cent recuperated and begging Dr. Bailey to return them to duty. A request, I might add, that fell on deaf ears. Bailey insisted that they remain under observation for twenty-four hours, and there is simply no budging a man of his size and determination." Sandecker paused to sniff the air and then wrinkled his nose. "God, what's that smell?"

"Rot," Drummer replied. "It fills every nook and cranny. There's no escaping it. And it's only a matter of time before the dead marine life that came up with the wreck begins to stink."

Sandecker gestured about the room. "A cozy place you've got here," he said, "but why set up operations in the gym rather than the bridge?"

"A break from tradition for practical reasons," Pitt replied. "The bridge serves no useful function on a dead ship. The gym, on the other hand, sits amidships and offers us equal access to either bow or stern. It also adjoins our improvised helicopter pad over the first-class lounge roof. The closer to our supplies we are, the more efficiently we can operate."

"I had to ask," Sandecker said heavily. "I should have known you didn't pick this museum of mechanical monstrosities just to launch a physical-fitness program."

Something in a pile of wreckage that lay in a soggy heap against the forward wall of the gymnasium caught the admiral's eyes and he walked over to it. He stood and stared grimly for several moments at the skeletal remains of what had once been a passenger or crew member of the *Titanic*.

"I wonder who this poor devil was?"

"We'll probably never know," Pitt said. "Any dental records from 1912 have no doubt been destroyed long ago."

Sandecker leaned down and examined the pelvic section of the bones. "Good lord, it was a woman."

"Either one of the first-class passengers who elected to remain behind or one of the women from the steerage quarters who arrived on the Boat Deck after all the lifeboats had been launched."

"Have you found any other bodies?"

"We've been too busy to do any extensive exploring," Pitt said. "But one of Spencer's men reported another skeleton wedged against the fireplace in the lounge."

Sandecker nodded toward an open doorway. "What's through there?"

"That opens onto the grand staircase."

"Let's take a look."

They walked onto the landing above the A Deck lobby and looked down. Several rotting chairs and sofas were scattered haphazardly on the steps where they had fallen when the ship sank by the bow. The graceful flowing lines of the bannisters were still sound and undamaged, and the hands of the bronze clock could be seen frozen at 2:21. They made their way down the silt-coated stairs and entered one of the passageways leading to the staterooms. Without the benefit of outside light, the scene was an eerie one. Room after room was filled with rotted and fallen paneling interspersed with overturned and jumbled furniture. It was too dark to discern any detail, and after penetrating about thirty feet, they found their way blocked by a wall of debris, so they turned and headed back to the gymnasium.

Just as they came through the doorway, the man hunched over the radio turned from his set. It was Al Giordino.

"I wondered where you two went. The Uranus Oil people want to know about their submersible."

"Tell them they can retrieve the *Deep Fathom* off the *Titanic*'s foredeck just as soon as we make dry dock in New York," Pitt said.

Giordino nodded and turned back to the radio.

"Leave it to the commercial business interests to bitch about their precious property on such a momentous occasion," Sandecker said with a gleam in his eye. "And, speaking of momentous occasions, would any of you gentlemen care to celebrate with a touch of spirits?"

"Did you say spirits?" Giordino looked up expectantly.

Sandecker reached under his coat and produced two bottles. "Do not let it be said that James Sandecker ever fails to look out for the best interests of his crew."

"Beware of admirals bearing gifts," Giordino murmured.

Sandecker shot him a weary glance. "What a pity walking the plank became passé."

"And keelhauling," Drummer added.

"I promise never to dig our leader ever again. Providing, of course, he keeps me in booze," Giordino said.

"A small price to pay." Sandecker sighed. "Choose your poison, gentlemen. You see before you a fifth of Cutty Sark scotch for the city slickers, and a fifth of Jack Daniel's for the farm boys. Round up some glasses and be my guests."

It took Giordino all of ten seconds to find the required number of styrofoam cups in their Mickey Mouse all-electric galley. When the liquor had been poured, Sandecker raised his cup.

"Gentlemen, here's to the *Titanic*. May she never again rest in peace."

"To the *Titanic*."

"Hear, hear."

Sandecker then relaxed on a folding chair, sipped at his scotch, and idly wondered which of the men in that soggy room were on the payroll of the Soviet government.

53

Soviet General Secretary Georgi Antonov sucked on his pipe with short, violent puffs and regarded Prevlov with a pensive gaze.

"I must say, Captain, I take a dim view of the whole undertaking."

"We have carefully considered every avenue, and this is the only one left open to us," Prevlov said.

"It's fraught with danger. I fear the Americans will not take the theft of their precious byzanium lying down."

"Once it is in our hands, Comrade Secretary, it will make no difference how loudly the Americans scream. The door will have been slammed in their faces."

Antonov folded and unfolded his hands. A large portrait of Lenin floated on the wall behind him. "There must be no international repercussions. It must look to the world as though we were entirely within our rights."

"This time the American president will have no recourse. International law is on our side."

"It will mean the end of what used to be called détente," Antonov said heavily.

"It will also mean the beginning of the end of the United States as a superpower."

"A cheerful conjecture, Captain; I appreciate that." His pipe had gone out and he relit it, filling the room with a sweet aromatic odor. "However, should you fail, the Americans will be in the same position to say the same of us."

"We will not fail."

"Words," Antonov said. "A good lawyer plans the prosecutor's case as well as his own. What measures have you taken in the event of an unavoidable mishap?"

"The byzanium will be destroyed," Prevlov said. "If we cannot possess it, then neither can the Americans."

"Does that include the *Titanic* as well?"

"It must. By destroying the *Titanic,* we destroy the byzanium. It will be accomplished in such a way that another recovery operation will be totally out of the question."

Prevlov fell silent, but Antonov was satisfied. He had already given his approval for the mission. He studied Prevlov carefully. The captain looked like a man who was not used to failure. His every movement, every gesture, seemed thoughtfully planned in advance; even his words carried an air of confident forethought. Yes, Antonov was satisfied.

"When do you leave for the North Atlantic?" he asked.

"With your permission, Comrade Secretary, at once. A long-range reconnaissance bomber is on standby at Gorki Airfield. It is imperative that I be standing on the bridge of the *Mikhail Kurkov* within twelve hours. Good fortune has sent us a hurricane, and I will make full use of its force as a diversion for what will seem our perfectly legal seizure of the *Titanic*.

"Then I will not keep you." Antonov stood and embraced Prevlov in a great bear hug. "The hopes of the Soviet Union go with you, Captain Prevlov. I beg you, do not disappoint us."

54

The day began going badly for Pitt right after he wandered away from the salvage activity and made his way down to No. 1 cargo hold on G Deck.

The sight that met his eyes in the darkened compartment was one of utter devastation. The vault containing the byzanium was buried under the collapsed forward bulkhead.

He stood there for a long time, staring at the avalanche of broken and twisted steel that prevented any easy attempt to reach the precious element. It was then that he sensed someone standing behind him.

"It looks like we've been dealt a bum hand," Sandecker said.

Pitt nodded. "At least for the moment."

"Perhaps if we—"

"It would take weeks for our portable cutting equipment to clear a path through that jungle of steel."

"There's no other way?"

"A giant Dopplemann crane could clear the debris in a few hours."

"Then what you're saying is that we have no choice but to stand by and wait patiently until we reach the dry-dock facilities in New York."

Pitt looked at him in the dim light and Sandecker could see the look of frustration that cracked his rugged features. There was no need for an answer.

"Removing the byzanium to the *Capricorn* would have been a break in our favor," Pitt said. "It'd certainly have saved us a lot of grief."

"Maybe we could fake a transfer."

"Our friends who work for the Soviets would smell a hoax before the first crate went over the side."

"Assuming they're both on board the *Titanic,* of course."

"I'll know this time tomorrow."

"I take it you have a line on who they are?"

"I've got one of them pegged, the one who killed Henry Munk. The other is purely an educated guess."

"I'd be interested in knowing who you've ferreted out," Sandecker said.

"My proof would never convince a federal prosecutor, much less a jury. Give me a few more hours, Admiral, and I'll lay them both, Silver and Gold, or whatever their stupid code names are, right in your lap."

Sandecker stared at him, then said, "You're that close?"

"I'm that close."

Sandecker passed a weary hand across his face and tightened his lips. He looked at the tons of steel covering the vault. "I leave it with you, Dirk. I'll back your play to the last hand. I don't really have much choice."

Pitt had other worries, too. The two Navy tugs that Admiral Kemper promised to send were still hours away, and sometime during the late morning, for no apparent reason, the *Titanic* took it into her mind to increase her starboard list to seventeen degrees.

The ship rode far too low in the water; the crests of the swells lapped at the sealed portholes along E Deck just ten feet below the scuppers. And although Spencer and his pumping crew had managed to drop suction pipes down the loading hatches into the cargo holds, they had not been able to fight their way through the debris crowding the companionways to reach the engine and boiler rooms, where the greatest volume of water still lay—remote and inaccessible.

Drummer sat in the gymnasium, dirty and exhausted after working around the clock. He sipped at a mug of cocoa. "After almost eighty years of submersion and rot," he said, "the wood paneling in the passageways has fallen and jammed them worse than a path in a Georgia junkyard."

Pitt sat where he'd been all afternoon, bent over a drafting table next to the radio transmitter. He stared out of red-rimmed eyes at a transverse drawing of the *Titanic*'s superstructure.

"Can't we thread our way down the main staircase or the elevator shafts?"

"The staircase is filled with tons of loose junk once you get down past D Deck," Spencer declared.

"And there isn't a prayer of penetrating the elevator shafts," Gunn added. "They're crammed with jumbled masses of corroded cables and wrecked machinery. If that wasn't bad enough, all the watertight double-cylinder doors in the lower compartments are frozen solid in the closed position."

"They were shut automatically by the ship's first officer immediately after she struck the iceberg," Pitt said.

At that moment, a short bull of a man covered from head to toe with oil and grime staggered into the gym. Pitt looked up and faintly smiled. "That you, Al?"

Giordino hauled himself over to a cot and collapsed like a sack of wet cement. "I'd appreciate it if none of you lit any matches around me," he murmured. "I'm too young to die in a fiery blaze of glory."

"Any luck?" asked Sandecker.

"I made it as far as the squash court on F Deck. God, it's blacker than sin down there . . . fell down a companionway. It was flooded with oil that had seeped up from the engine room. Stopped cold. There was no way down."

"A snake might make it to the boiler rooms," Drummer said, "but it's for sure a man ain't gonna. At least, not until he spends a week clearing a passage with dynamite and a wrecking crew."

"There has to be a way," Sandecker said. "Somewhere down there she's taking water. If we don't get ahead of it by this time tomorrow, she'll roll belly up and head back to the bottom."

The thought of losing the *Titanic* after she was sitting pretty and upright again on a smooth sea had never entered their minds, but now everyone in the gym began to feel a sickening ache deep in their stomachs. The ship had yet to be taken in tow and New York was twelve hundred sea miles away.

Pitt sat there staring at the ship's interior diagrams. They were woefully inadequate. No set of detailed blueprints of the *Titanic* and her sister ship, the *Olympic*, existed. They had been destroyed, along with files full of photographs and construction data, when the Harland and Wolff shipbuilding yards in Belfast were leveled by German bombers during World War II.

"If only she wasn't so damned big," Drummer muttered. "The boiler rooms are damn near a hundred feet below the Boat Deck."

"Might as well be a hundred miles," Spencer said. He looked up as Woodson emerged from the grand stairway entrance. "Ah, the great stoneface is with us. What's the official photographer of the operation been up to?"

Woodson lifted a battery of cameras from around his neck and gently laid them on a makeshift worktable. "Just taking some pictures for posterity," he said with his usual deadpan expression. "Never know, I just might write a book about all this someday, and naturally, I'll want credit for the illustrations."

"Naturally," Spencer said. "You didn't by chance find a clear companionway down to the boiler rooms?"

He shook his head. "I've been shooting in the first-class lounge. It's remarkably well preserved. Except for the obvious ravages of water on the carpeting and furniture, it could pass for a sitting room in the Palace of Versailles." He began changing film cartridges. "How's chances of borrowing the helicopter? I'd like to get some bird's-eye shots of our prize before the tugs arrive."

Giordino raised up on one elbow. "Better use up your film while you can. Our prize may be back on the bottom by morning."

Woodson's brows pinched together. "She's sinking?"

"I think not."

Every eye turned to the man who uttered those three words. Pitt was smiling. He smiled with the confidence of a man who just became chairman of the board of General Motors.

He said, "As Kit Carson used to say when he was surrounded and hopelessly outnumbered by Indians, 'We ain't done in yet, not by a damned sight.' In ten hours' time the engine and boiler rooms will be bone-dry." He quickly fumbled through the diagrams on the table until he found the one he wanted. "Woodson said it, the bird's-eye view. It was right under our noses all the time. We should have been looking from overhead instead of from inside."

"Big deal," Giordino said. "What's so interesting from the air?"

"None of you get it?"

Drummer looked puzzled. "You missed me at the last fork in the road."

"Spencer?"

Spencer shook his head.

Pitt grinned at him and said, "Assemble your men topside and tell them to bring their cutting gear."

"If you say so," Spencer said, but made no move for the door.

"Mr. Spencer is mentally measuring me for a strait jacket," Pitt said. "He can't figure why we should be cutting holes on the roof of the ship to penetrate a distance of a hundred feet through eight decks of scrap. Nothing to it, really. We have a built-in tunnel, free of any debris, that leads straight to the boiler rooms. In fact, we have four of them. The boiler casings where the funnels once sat, gentlemen. Torch away the Wetsteel seals over the openings and you have a clear shot directly down to the bilges. Do you see the light?"

Spencer saw the light all right. Everyone else saw it, too. They headed out the door as one, without giving Pitt the benefit of an answer.

Two hours later, the diesel pumps were knocking away in chorus and two thousand gallons of water a minute were being returned over the side to the mounting swells that were being pushed ahead of the approaching hurricane.

55

They had dubbed her Hurricane Amanda, and by that same afternoon the great steamer tracks running across her projected path were devoid of most vessels. All freighters, tankers, and passenger liners that had put to sea between Savannah, Georgia, and Portland, Maine, had been ordered back to port after NUMA's Hurricane Center in Tampa sent out the first warnings. Nearly a hundred vessels along the Eastern seaboard had postponed their sailing dates, while all ships bound from Europe that were already far at sea hove to, waiting for the hurricane to pass.

In Tampa, Dr. Prescott and his weather people swarmed around the wall chart, feeding new data into the computers, and plotting any deviation of Hurricane Amanda's track. Prescott's original predicted track was holding up to within a hundred and seventy-five miles.

A weatherman came up and handed him a sheet of paper. "Here's a report from a Coast Guard reconnaissance plane that penetrated the hurricane's eye."

Prescott took the report and read parts of it aloud. " 'Eye approximately twenty-two miles in diameter. Forward speed increased to forty knots. Wind strength one hundred and eighty plus . . .' " his voice trailed off.

His assistant looked at him, her eyes wide. "A hundred-and-eighty-mile-an-hour winds?"

"And more," Prescott murmured. "I pity the ship that gets caught in this one."

A glaze suddenly passed across the weatherman's eyes and he swung back to study the wall chart. Then his face turned ashen. "Oh Jesus . . . the *Titanic!*"

Prescott looked at him. "The what?"

"The *Titanic* and her salvage fleet. They're sitting right in the middle of the projected path of the hurricane."

"The hell you say!" Prescott snapped.

The weatherman moved up to the wall chart and hesitated for several moments. Finally, he reached up and drew an X just below the Newfoundland Grand Banks. "There, that's the position where she was raised from the bottom."

"Where did you get this information?"

"It's been smeared all over the newspapers and television since yesterday. If you don't believe me, teletype NUMA headquarters in Washington and confirm."

"Screw the teletype," Prescott growled. He rushed across the room, snatched up a telephone and shouted into the receiver: "Punch me on a direct line to our headquarters in Washington. I want to speak with someone who's connected with the *Titanic* project."

While he waited for his call to go through, he peered over his glasses at the X on the wall chart. "Here's hoping those poor bastards have a weatherman on board with uncanny foresight," he muttered to himself, "or about this time tomorrow they'll forever learn the meaning of the fury of the sea."

There was a vague expression on Farquar's face as he stared at the weather maps laid out before him on the table. His mind was so numb and woolly from lack of sleep that he had difficulty in defining the markings he had made only minutes before. The indications of temperature, wind velocity, barometric pressure, and the approaching storm-front all melted together into one indistinct blur.

He rubbed his eyes in a useless attempt to get them to focus. Then he shook his head to clear the cobwebs, trying to remember what it was that he had been about to conclude.

The hurricane. Yes, that was it. Farquar slowly came to the realization that he had made a serious miscalculation. The hurricane had not veered into Cape Hatteras as he'd predicted. Instead, a high-pressure area along the eastern coast held it over the ocean on a northerly course. And what was worse, it had begun to move faster after recurving and was now hurtling toward the *Titanic*'s position with forward speed approaching forty-five knots.

He had watched the hurricane's birth on the satellite photos and had closely studied the warnings from the NUMA station in Tampa, but nothing in all his years of forecasting had prepared him for the violence and the speed that this monstrosity had achieved in such a short time.

A hurricane in May? It was unthinkable. Then his words to Pitt came back to haunt him. What was it he had said? "Only God can make a storm." Farquar suddenly felt sick, his face beaded with sweat, hands clenching and unclenching.

"God help the *Titanic* this time," he murmured under his breath. "He's the only one who can save her now."

56

The U.S. Navy salvage tugs *Thomas J. Morse* and *Samuel R. Wallace* arrived just before 1500 hours and slowly began circling the *Titanic*. The vast size and the strange deathlike aura of the derelict filled the tugs' crews with the same feeling of awe that was experienced by the NUMA salvage people the day before.

After a half an hour of visual inspection, the tugs pulled parallel to the great rusty hull and lay to in the heavy swells, their engines on "stop." Then, as if in unison, their cutters were lowered and the captains came across and began climbing a hastily thrown boarding ladder to the *Titanic*'s shelter deck.

Lieutenant George Uphill of the *Morse* was a short, plump, ruddy-faced man who sported an immense Bismarck mustache, while Lieutenant Commander Scotty Butera of the *Wallace* nearly scraped the ceiling at six feet six and buried his chin in a magnificent black beard. No spick-and-span fleet officers these two. They looked and acted every bit the part of tough, no-nonsense salvage men.

"You don't know how happy we are to see you, gentlemen," Gunn said, shaking their hands. "Admiral Sandecker and Mr. Dirk Pitt, our special projects director, are awaiting you in, if you'll pardon the expression, our operations room."

The tug captains tailed after Gunn up the stairways and across the Boat Deck, staring in trancelike rapture at the remains of the once beautiful ship. They reached the gymnasium and Gunn made the introductions.

"It's positively incredible," Uphill murmured. "I never thought in my wildest imagination that I would ever live to walk the decks of the *Titanic*."

"My sentiments exactly," Butera added.

"I wish we could give you a guided tour," Pitt said, "but each minute adds to the risk of losing her to the sea again."

Admiral Sandecker motioned them to a long table laden with weather maps, diagrams, and charts, and they all settled in with steaming mugs of coffee. "Our chief concern at the moment is weather," he said. "Our weatherman on board the *Capricorn* has suddenly taken to imagining himself as the prophet of doom."

Pitt unrolled a large weather map and flattened it on the table. "There's no ducking the bad news. Our weather is deteriorating rapidly. The barometer has fallen half an inch in the last twenty-four hours. Wind force four, blowing north northeast and building. We're in for it, gentlemen, make no mistake. Unless a miracle occurs and Hurricane Amanda decides to cut a quick left turn to the west, we should be well into her front quadrant by this time tomorrow."

"Hurricane Amanda," Buttera repeated the name. "How nasty is she?"

"Joel Farquar, our weatherman, assures me they don't come any meaner than this baby," Pitt replied. "She's already reported winds of force fifteen on the Beaufort scale."

"Force fifteen?" Gunn repeated in astonishment. "My God, force twelve is considered a maximum hurricane."

"This, I'm afraid," said Sandecker, "is every salvage man's nightmare come true—raise a derelict only to have it snatched away by a whim of the weather." He looked grimly at Uphill and Butera. "It looks as though you two made the trip for nothing. You'd better get back to your ships and make a run for it."

"Make a run for it, hell!" Uphill boomed. "We just got here."

"I couldn't have said it better." Butera grinned and looked up at Sandecker. "The *Morse* and the *Wallace* can tow an aircraft carrier through a swamp in a tornado if they have to. They're designed to slug it out with anything Mother Nature can dish out. If we can get a cable on board the *Titanic* and get her under tow, she'll stand a fighting chance of riding out the storm intact."

"Pulling a forty-five-thousand-ton ship through the jaws of a hurricane," Sandecker murmured. "That's a pretty heady boast."

"No boast." Butera came back dead-serious. "By fastening a cable from the stern of the *Morse* to the bow of the *Wallace,* our combined power can tow the *Titanic* in the same manner as a pair of railroad engines in tandem can pull a freight train."

"And, we can do it in thirty-foot seas at a speed of five to six knots," Uphill added.

Sandecker looked at the two tug captains and let them go on.

Butera charged ahead. "Those aren't run-of-the-mill harbor tugs floating out there, Admiral. They're deep-sea, ocean-rescue tugs, two hundred and fifty feet in length with five-thousand-horse diesel power plants, each boat capable of hauling twenty thousand tons of dead weight at ten knots for two thousand miles without running out of fuel. If any two tugs in the world can pull the *Titanic* through a hurricane, these can."

"I appreciate your enthusiasm," Sandecker said, "but, I won't be responsible for the lives of you and your crews on what has to be an impossible gamble. The *Titanic* will have to drift out the storm as best she can. I'm ordering you both to shove off and head into a safe area."

Uphill looked at Butera. "Tell me, Commander, when was the last time you defied a direct command from an admiral?"

Butera feigned mock thoughtfulness. "Come to think of it, not since breakfast."

"Speaking for myself and the salvage crew," Pitt said, "we'd welcome your company."

"There you have it, sir," Butera said, grinning. "Besides, my orders from Admiral Kemper were either to bring the *Titanic* into port or take out papers for an early retirement. Me, I opt for the *Titanic*."

"That's mutiny," Sandecker said flatly; but there was no hiding the trace of satisfaction in his tone, and it took no great stroke of perception to recognize that the argument had gone exactly as he had planned it. He gave everyone a very shrewd look and said, "Okay, gentlemen, it's your funeral. Now that that's settled, I suggest that instead of sitting around here, you get about the business of saving the *Titanic*."

Captain Ivan Parotkin stood on the port wing bridge of the *Mikhail Kurkov* and searched the sky with a pair of binoculars.

He was a slender man of medium height with a distinguished face that almost never smiled. He was in his late fifties, but his receding hair showed no sign of gray. A thick turtleneck sweater covered his chest while his hips and legs were encased in heavy woolen pants and kneeboots.

Parotkin's first officer touched him on the arm and pointed skyward above the *Mikhail Kurkov*'s huge radar dome. A four-engine patrol bomber appeared out of the northeast and magnified until Parotkin could make out its Russian markings. The aircraft seemed to be crawling scant miles per hour above its stalling speed as it swept overhead. Then suddenly a tiny object ejected from the underbelly, and seconds later a parachute blossomed open and began drifting over the ship's forward mastpeak, its occupant finally dropping into the water about two hundred yards off the starboard bow.

As the *Mikhail Kurkov*'s small boat put away and dipped over the mountainous, wide-spaced waves, Parotkin turned to his first officer. "As soon as he is safely on board, conduct Captain Prevlov to my quarters." Then he laid the binoculars on the bridge counter and disappeared down a companionway.

Twenty minutes later, the first officer knocked at the highly polished mahogany door, opened it, and then stood aside to allow a man to pass through. He was thoroughly soaked and dripping salt water in puddles about the deck.

"Captain Parotkin."

"Captain Prevlov."

They stood there in silence a few moments, both highly trained professionals, and sized each other up. Prevlov had the advantage; he'd studied Parotkin's service history in depth. Parotkin, on the other hand, had only repute and first appearances to form a judgment. He wasn't sure he liked what he saw. Prevlov came off too handsome, too foxlike for Parotkin to grasp a favorable sense of warmth or trust.

"We are short on time," Prevlov said. "If we could get right down to the purpose of my visit—"

Parotkin held up his hand. "First things first. Some hot tea and a change of clothing. Dr. Rogovski, our chief scientist, is about your height and weight."

The first officer nodded and closed the door.

"Now then," Parotkin said, "I am certain a man of your rank and importance didn't risk his life parachuting into a running sea merely to observe the atmospheric phenomenon of a hurricane."

"Hardly. Personal danger is not my cup of tea. And, speaking of tea, I don't suppose you have anything stronger on board?"

Parotkin shook his head. "Sorry, Captain. I insist on a dry ship. Not exactly to the crew's liking, I admit, but it does save occasional grief."

"Admiral Sloyuk said you were a paragon of efficiency."

"I do not believe in tempting the fates."

Prevlov unzipped his sodden jumpsuit and let it fall on the floor. "I am afraid you are about to make an exception to that rule, Captain.

We, you and I, are about to tempt the fates as they have never been tempted before."

57

Pitt could not escape the feeling he was being deserted on a lonely island as he stood on the foredeck of the *Titanic* and watched the salvage fleet get under way and begin moving toward the western horizon and safer waters.

The *Alhambra* was the last in line to slip past, her captain flashing a "good luck" with his addis lamp, the newspeople quietly, solemnly filming what might be the last visual record of the *Titanic*. Pitt searched for Dana Seagram among the crowd gathered at the railings, but his eyes failed to pick her out. He watched the ships until they became small dark specks on a leaden sea. Only the missile cruiser *Juneau* and the *Capricorn* remained behind, but the salvage tender would soon depart and follow the others once the tug captains signaled they had the derelict in tow.

"Mr. Pitt?"

Pitt turned to see a man who had the face of a canvas-weary prize-fighter and the body of a beer keg.

"Chief Bascom, sir, of the *Wallace*. I brought a two-man crew aboard to make fast the towing cable."

Pitt smiled a friendly smile. "I bet they call you Bad Bascom."

"Only behind my back. It's a name that's followed me ever since I tore up a bar in San Diego." Bascom shrugged. Then his eyes narrowed. "How did you guess?"

"Commander Butera described you in glowing terms . . . behind your back, that is."

"A good man, the commander."

"How long will it take for the hookup?"

"With luck and the loan of your helicopter, about an hour."

"No problem over the helicopter; it belongs to the Navy anyway." Pitt turned and gazed down at the *Wallace* as Butera very carefully backed the tug toward the *Titanic*'s old straight up-and-down bows until he was less than a hundred feet away. "I take it the helicopter is to lift the tow cable on board?"

"Yes sir," Bascom answered. "Our cable measures ten inches in diameter and weighs in at one ton per seventy feet. No lightweight that one. On most tow jobs, we'd cast a small line over the derelict's bows which in turn would be attached to a series of heavier lines with increasing diameters that finally tied into the main cable, but that type of operation calls for the services of an electric winch, and since the *Titanic* is a dead ship and human muscles are way undermatched for the job, we take the easy way out. No sense in filling up sick bay with a crew of hernia patients."

Even with the help of the helicopter, it was all Bascom and his men could do to secure the great cable into position. Sturgis came through like an old pro. Tenderly manipulating the helicopter's controls, he laid the end of the *Wallace*'s tow cable on the *Titanic*'s forecastle deck as neatly as though he'd practiced the trick for years. It took only fifty minutes, from the time Sturgis released the cable and flew back to the *Capricorn,* until Chief Bascom stood on the forepeak and waved his arms over his head, signaling the tugs that the connection was made.

Butera on the *Wallace* acknowledged the signal with a blast on the tug's whistle and rang the engine room for "dead ahead slow" as Uphill on the *Morse* went through the same motions. Slowly the two tugs gathered way, the *Wallace* trailing the *Morse* on three hundred yards of wire leash, paying out the main cable until the *Titanic* rose and dropped in the steadily increasing swells nearly a quarter of a mile astern. Then Butera held up his hand and the men on the *Wallace*'s afterdeck gently eased on the brake of the tug's immense towing winch and the cable took up the strain.

From atop the *Titanic*'s vast height, the tugs looked like tiny toy boats tossing over the enormous crests of the waves one moment before disappearing to their mastlights in the cavernous troughs the next. It seemed impossible that such puny objects could budge over forty-five thousand tons of dead weight, and yet slowly, imperceptibly at first, their combined forces of ten-thousand horsepower began to tell and soon a minute dog's bone of foam could be discerned curling around the *Titanic*'s faded Plimsoll's mark.

She was barely making way—New York was still twelve hundred miles to the west—but she had at last picked up where she'd left off that cold night back in 1912 and was once again making for port.

The ominous-looking black clouds rose and spilled over the southern horizon. It was a hurricane bar. Even as Pitt watched, it seemed to expand and strengthen, turning the sea to a dark shade of dirty gray. Oddly, the wind became light, aimlessly changing direction every few seconds. He noticed that the sea gulls that had once swarmed about the salvage fleet were not in view. Only the sight of the *Juneau,* moving steadily five hundred yards abeam the *Titanic,* provided any sense of security.

Pitt glanced at his watch and then took another look over the port railing before he slowly, almost casually, approached the entrance to the gymnasium.

"Is the gang all here?"

"They're getting restless as hell," Giordino said. He was standing huddled against a ventilator in a seemingly vain attempt to hide from the icy wind. "If it wasn't for the Admiral's restraining influence, you'd have had a first-class riot on your hands."

"Everyone is accounted for?"

"To a man."

"You're positive?"

"Take the word of Warden Giordino. None of the inmates have left the room, not even to go potty."

"Then I guess it's my turn to enter stage right."

"Any complaints from our guests?" Giordino asked.

"The usual. Never satisfied with their accommodations, not enough heat or too much air conditioning, you know."

"Yeah, I know."

"You'd better go aft and see about making their wait enjoyable."

"For God's sake, how?"

"Tell them jokes."

Giordino gave Pitt a sour look and mumbled dryly to himself as he turned and walked off into the evening's dimming light.

Pitt checked his watch once more and entered the gymnasium. Three hours had passed since the tow had begun and the final act of the salvage had settled down to a routine. Sandecker and Gunn were bent over the radio pestering Farquar on the *Capricorn,* now fifty miles to the west, for the latest news on Hurricane Amanda, while the rest of the crew was grouped in a tight semicircle around a small and thoroughly inadequate oil-burning stove.

As Pitt entered, they had all looked up expectantly. When at last he spoke, his voice was unnaturally soft in the unnatural quiet that was broken only by the hum of the portable generators. "My apologies, gentlemen, for keeping you waiting, but I thought the short coffee break would reconstitute your sagging sinews."

"Cut the satire," Spencer snapped, his voice taut with irritation. "You call us all up here and then make us sit around for half an hour when there is work to do. What's the story?"

"The story is simple," Pitt said evenly. "In a few minutes, Lieutenant Sturgis will drop his helicopter on board one last time before the storm strikes. With the exception of Giordino and myself, I would like all of you, and that includes you, Admiral, to return with him to the *Capricorn*."

"Aren't you out of your depth, Pitt," Sandecker said in an unemphatic tone.

"To some degree, yes, sir, but I firmly believe I'm doing the right thing."

"Explain yourself." Sandecker glowed like a piranha about to gulp a goldfish. He was playing his role to the hilt. It was an epic job of typecasting.

"I have every reason to believe the *Titanic* hasn't the structural strength left to weather a hurricane."

"This old tub has taken more punishment than any man-made object since the pyramids," Spencer said. "And, now the great seer of the future, Dirk Pitt, predicts the old girl will throw in the sponge and sink at the first blow from a lousy storm."

"There's no guarantee she can't or won't founder under a heavy sea," Pitt hedged. "Either way, it's stupid to risk any more lives than we have to."

"Let me see if I get this straight." Drummer leaned forward, his hawklike features intent and angry. "Except for you and Giordino, the rest of us are supposed to haul ass and ditch everything we've busted our balls to achieve over the last nine months just so's we can hide on the *Capricorn* till the storm blows over? Is that the idea?"

"You go to the head of the class, Drummer."

"Man, you're out of your gourd."

"Impossible," Spencer said. "It takes four men just to oversee the pumps."

"And the hull below the waterline has to be sounded around the clock for new leaks," Gunn added.

"You heroes are all alike," Drummer drawled. "Always making noble sacrifices to save others. Let's face it; ain't no way two men can ride herd on this old tub. I vote we all stay."

Spencer turned and read the faces of his six-man crew. They all stared back at him out of eyes red-rimmed with lack of sleep and nodded in chorus. Then Spencer faced Pitt again. "Sorry, great leader, but Spencer and his merry band of pump-pushers have decided to hang in there."

"I'm with you," Woodson said solemnly.

"Count me in," said Gunn.

Chief Bascom touched Pitt on the arm. "Beggin' your pardon, sir, but me and my boys are for sticking around too. That cable out there has to be checked every hour during the storm for signs of chafing, and heavy grease applied to the fair-lead to prevent a break."

"Sorry, Pitt, my boy," Sandecker said with a marked degree of satisfaction. "You lose."

The sound of Sturgis's helicopter was heard hovering for a landing over the lounge roof. Pitt shrugged resignedly and said, "Well that settles it then. We all sink or swim together." Then he cracked a tired smile. "You'd all better get some rest and some food in your stomachs. It may be your last chance. A few hours from now we'll be up to our eyeballs in the front quadrant of the hurricane. And, I don't have to draw a picture of what we can expect."

He swung on his heels and walked out the door to the helicopter pad. Not a bad performance, he thought to himself. Not a bad performance at all. He'd never be nominated for an Academy Award, but what the hell, his captive audience had thought it convincing and that's all that really mattered.

Jack Sturgis was a short, thin man with sad drooping eyes, the kind women considered bedroom eyes. He gripped a long cigarette holder between his teeth and jutted his chin forward in a show reminiscent of Franklin Roosevelt. He had just climbed down from the cockpit of the helicopter and seemed to be groping for something under the landing gear when Pitt stepped onto the pad.

Sturgis looked up. "Any passengers?" he asked.

"Not this trip."

Sturgis nonchalantly flicked an ash from his cigarette holder. "I knew I should have stayed cuddled in my warm, cozy cabin on the *Capri-*

corn." He sighed. "Flying in the face of hurricanes will be the death of me yet."

"You'd better get going," Pitt said. "The wind will be on us any time now."

"Makes no difference." Sturgis shrugged indifferently. "I'm not going anywhere."

Pitt looked at him. "What do you mean by that?"

"I've been had, that's what I mean." He gestured up at the rotor blades. The two-foot tip of one was hanging down like a limp wrist. "Somebody around here resents whirlybirds."

"Did you strike a bulkhead on landing?"

Sturgis put on a hurt expression. "I do not, repeat, do not strike objects upon landing." He found what he was searching for and straightened up. "Here, see for yourself; some son of a bitch tossed a hammer into my rotor blades."

Pitt took the hammer and examined it. The rubber hand-grip showed a deep gash where it had come in contact with the blade.

"And, after all I've done for you people," Sturgis said, "this is how you show your appreciation."

"Sorry, Sturgis, but I suggest you forget any aspirations of ever becoming a television detective. You sadly lack an analytical mind, and you're prone to leap to false conclusions."

"Get off it, Pitt. Hammers don't fly through the air without a means of propulsion. One of your people must have tossed it when I was landing."

"Wrong. I can vouch for the whereabouts of every soul on board this ship, and no one was anywhere near the helicopter pad in the last ten minutes. Whoever your little destructive friend is, I'm afraid you brought him with you."

"Do you think I'm a dead-brain? Don't you think I'd know if I carried a passenger? Besides, now you're insinuating a suicidal act. If that hammer had been thrown one minute sooner, when we were a hundred feet in the air, you and your crew would have had an ugly mess to clean up."

"Wrong nomenclature," Pitt said. "Not passenger, but stowaway. And, he's no dead-brain either. He waited until your wheels kissed the deck before he made his play and escaped through the cargo hatch. God only knows where he's hiding now. A thorough search of fifty miles of pitch dark passageways and compartments is impossible."

Sturgis's face suddenly paled. "Christ, our intruder is still in the copter."

"Don't be ridiculous. He beat it the instant you landed."

"No, no. It's possible to throw a hammer out and up through an open cabin window into the rotor blades, but escape is something else again."

"I'm listening," Pitt said quietly.

"The cargo compartment hatch is electronically operated and can only be activated from a switch in the control cabin."

"Is there another exit?"

"Only a door to the control cabin."

Pitt studied the sealed cargo hatch for a long moment, then turned back to Sturgis, his eyes cold. "Is this any way to treat an unexpected guest? I think the appropriate thing to do is for us to invite him into the fresh air."

Sturgis became rooted to the deck as he spotted the Colt forty-five automatic, complete with silencer, that had suddenly materialized in Pitt's right hand.

"Sure . . . sure . . ." he stammered. "If you say so."

Sturgis clambered up the ladder to the control cabin, leaned in and pushed a switch. The electric motors made a whirring sound and the contoured seven-foot-by-seven-foot door rose open and upward over the helicopter's fuselage. Even before the locking pins clicked into position, Sturgis was back on the deck and standing warily behind Pitt's broad shoulders.

Half a minute after the door had opened, Pitt was still standing there. He stood there for what Sturgis thought was a lifetime without moving a muscle, breathing slowly and evenly, and listening. The only sounds were the slap of the waves against the hull, the low whine of the steadily building wind over the *Titanic*'s superstructure and the murmur of voices that carried through the gymnasium door, not the sounds he was tuned in for. When he was satisfied there were no sounds of feet scraping, rustling of clothing, or other tones relating to menace or stealth, he stepped into the helicopter.

The darkened skies outside dimmed the interior and Pitt was uneasily aware that he was perfectly silhouetted against the dusk light. At first glance, the compartment seemed empty, but then Pitt felt a tapping on his shoulder and noted that Sturgis was pointing past him at a tarpaulin tucked around a humanlike shape.

"I neatly folded and stowed that tarp not more than an hour ago," Sturgis whispered.

Swiftly, Pitt reached down and dragged the tarpaulin away with his left hand while aiming the Colt as steadily as a park statue with his right.

A figure enveloped in a heavy foul-weather jacket lay huddled on the cargo deck, the eyes loosely closed in a state of unconsciousness that was obviously related to the ugly, bleeding, and purplish bruise just above the hairline.

Sturgis stood rooted in the shadows in shocked immobility, his widening eyes blinking rapidly, still adjusting to the diminishing light. Then he rubbed his chin lightly with his fingers and shook his head in disbelief. "Good lord," he muttered in awe. "Do you know who that is?"

"I do," Pitt answered evenly. "Her name is Seagram, Dana Seagram."

58

With appalling abruptness, the sky above the *Mikhail Kurkov* went pitch dark . . . great black clouds rolled overhead, obliterating the evening stars, and the wind returned and rose to a wailing gale of forty miles an hour, breaking the edges of the wave crests and carrying the foam in well-defined streaks toward the northeast.

Inside the large wheelhouse of the Soviet ship it was warm and comfortable. Prevlov stood beside Parotkin, who was watching the *Titanic*'s blip on radar.

"When I took command of this ship," Parotkin said, as though lecturing a schoolboy, "I was under the impression my orders were to carry out research and surveillance programs. Nothing was said about conducting an out-and-out military operation."

Prevlov held up a protesting hand. "Please, Captain, forget the words *military* and *operation* are unmentionable. The little venture upon which we are about to embark is a perfectly legal civilian activity known in the western countries as a change in management."

"Blatant piracy is closer to the truth," Parotkin said. "And what do you call those ten marines you so kindly added to my crew when we left port? Stockholders?"

"Again, not *marines,* but rather civilian crewmen."

"Of course," Parotkin said dryly. "And every one armed to the teeth."

"There is no international law I know of that forbids ship crewmen the right to possess arms."

"If one existed, you would no doubt discover an escape clause."

"Come, come, my dear Captain Parotkin." Prevlov slapped him heartily on the back. "When this evening is played to the finale, we will both be heroes of the Soviet Union."

"Or dead," Parotkin said woodenly.

"Calm your fears. The plan is flawless, and with the storm which drove off the salvage fleet, it becomes even more so."

"Aren't you overlooking the *Juneau*? Her captain will not stand idly by while we steam alongside the *Titanic,* board her and raise the hammer and sickle over her bridge."

Prevlov held up his wrist and stared at his watch. "In exactly two hours and twenty minutes, one of our nuclear attack submarines will surface a hundred miles to the north and begin transmitting distress signals under the name of the *Laguna Star,* a tramp freighter of rather dubious registry."

"And you think the *Juneau* will take the bait and dash to the rescue?"

"Americans never reject an appeal for help," Prevlov said confidently. "They all have a Good Samaritan complex. Yes, the *Juneau* will respond. She has to; except for the tugs which cannot leave the *Titanic,* she is the only available ship within three hundred miles."

"But if our submarine then submerges, nothing will show on the *Juneau*'s radar screens."

"Naturally, her officers will assume that the *Laguna Star* has sunk, and they will double their efforts to arrive in the nick of time to save the lives of a nonexistent crew."

"I bow to your imagination." Parotkin smiled. "Yet that still leaves you with such problems as the two United States Navy tugs, boarding the *Titanic* during the worst hurricane in years, neutralizing the American salvage crew, and then towing the derelict back to Russia, all without creating an international uproar."

"There are four parts to your statement, Captain." Prevlov paused to light a cigarette. "Number one, the tugboats will be eliminated by two Soviet operatives who are at this moment masquerading as members of the American salvage crew. Number two, I shall board the *Titanic* and assume its command when the eye of the hurricane reaches us. Since the wind velocities in this area seldom exceed fifteen knots, my men and I should have little difficulty in crossing over and entering through a hull loading door that will be conveniently opened on schedule by one of the operatives. Number three, my boarding party will then dispose of the salvage crew quickly and efficiently. And, finally, number four, it will be made to look to the world as though the Americans fled the ship at the height of the hurricane and were lost at sea. That, of course, makes the *Titanic* an abandoned derelict. The first captain who gets a tow-line on her is then entitled to the salvage rights. You are to be that lucky captain, Comrade Parotkin. Under international marine law, you will have every legal right to take the *Titanic* in tow."

"You will never get away with it," Parotkin said. "What you're suggesting is outright mass murder." There was a vacant, sick look in his eyes. "Have you also considered the consequences of failure with the same dedication to detail?"

Prevlov looked at him, the ever-present smile tightening. "Failure has been considered, Comrade. But let us fervently hope our final option will not be required." He pointed at the large blip on the radar screen. "It would be a pity to have to sink the world's most legendary ship a second time, and for all time."

59

Deep in the bowels of the ancient ocean liner, Spencer and his pumping crew struggled to keep the diesel pumps going. Sometimes working alone in the cold, black caverns of steel, with nothing but the pitiful comfort of small spotlights, they uncomplainingly went about their business of keeping the ship afloat. It came as somewhat of a surprise to find that in some compartments the pumps were falling behind the incoming water.

By seven o'clock the weather had deteriorated to the point of no return. The barometer slipped past 29.6 and was still falling steeply. The *Titanic* began to pitch and roll and take solid water over her bows and cargo deck bulwarks. Visibility under the shroud of night and the driving rain dropped to almost zero. The only sighting the men on the tugs had of the big ship came with an occasional bolt of lightning that vaguely silhouetted her ghostly outline. Their main concern, however, was the cable that disappeared into the mad, swirling waters astern. The constant strain on this lifeline was enormous; every time the *Titanic* took the full onslaught from a wave of massive proportions, they watched in ominous fascination as the cable arched out of the water and creaked in agonized protest.

Butera never moved from his bridge, keeping in constant contact with the men in the afterdeck cable house. Suddenly, a voice from the speaker crackled over the howl of the outside wind. "Captain?"

"This is the Captain," he replied into a hand phone.

"Ensign Kelly in the cablehouse, sir. Something mighty peculiar going on back here."

"Would you care to explain, Ensign?"

"Well, sir, the cable seems to have gone berserk. First she swung to port and now she's carried over to starboard at what I must say, sir, is an alarming angle."

"Okay, keep me posted." Butera switched off and opened another channel.

"Uphill, can you hear me? This is Butera."

On the *Morse* Uphill answered almost immediately. "Go ahead."

"I think the *Titanic* has sheered off to starboard."

"Can you make out her position?"

"Negative. The only indication is the angle of the cable."

There came a silence of several moments as Uphill thrashed the new development over in his mind. Then he came back through the speaker: "We're hardly making four knots as it is. We have no alternative but to push on. If we stop to see what's she up to, she may swing broadside into the sea and roll over."

"Can you pick her up on your radar?"

"No can do, a sea swept away out antennae twenty minutes ago. How about yours?"

"Still have the antennae, but the same sea that took yours shorted out my circuits."

"Then it's a case of the blind leading the blind."

Butera set the radio phone in its cradle and cautiously cracked the door leading to the starboard wing of the bridge. Shielding his eyes with his arm, he staggered outside and strained his eyes to penetrate the night gone crazy. The searchlights proved useless, their beams merely reflected the driving rain and revealed nothing. Lightning flashed astern, its thunder drowned out by the wind, and Butera's heart skipped a beat. The brief burst of backlighting failed to reveal any outline of the

Titanic. It was as though she had never been. Water streaming down his oilskins, his breath coming in gasps, he pushed back past the door just as Ensign Kelly's voice rasped over the speaker again.

"Captain?"

Butera wiped the spray from his eyes and picked up the phone. "What is it, Kelly?"

"The cable, it's slackened."

"Is it a break?"

"No, sir, the cable's still paid out, but it's settled several feet lower in the water. I've never seen one act like this before. It's as if the derelict took it in her mind to pass us."

It was the words "pass us" that did it . . . and Butera would never forget the sudden shock of realization. A mental click triggered open a flooodgate in his mind, released a nightmare of images in orderly sequence, images of a mad pendulum, its arc growing ever wider until it turned in on itself. The signs were there, the cable angled badly to starboard, the sudden slackness. He envisioned the whole scene in his mind: the *Titanic* driven slightly ahead and parallel to the *Wallace*'s starboard beam and now the pull from the cable snapping the derelict back in the manner of a line of school children playing Crack the Whip. Then something broke the nightmare inside Butera's head and released him from its numbing thrall.

He grabbed the radio phone and rang the engine room in almost the same movement. "Ahead full speed! Do you hear me engine room? Ahead full speed!" And then he called the *Morse*. "I'm coming at you full speed," he shouted. "Do you read me, Uphill?"

"Please repeat," Uphill asked.

"Order full speed ahead, damn it, or I'll run you down."

Butera dropped the phone and fought his way outside onto the bridge wing again. The hurricane was beating the sea into a froth so savage, so angry, that it was nearly impossible to separate air from water. It was all he could do to maintain a hold on the railing.

Then he saw it, the immense bow of the *Titanic* looming up through the curtain of the thrashing deluge, hardly more than a hundred feet off the starboard quarter. There was nothing he could do now except watch in frozen horror as the menacing mass moved inexorably closer to the *Wallace*.

"No!" he cried above the wind. "You dirty old corpse; you leave my ship alone."

It was too late. It seemed impossible that the *Titanic* could ever swing clear of the *Wallace*'s stern. And yet the impossible happened. The great sixty-foot bow rose up on a mountainous wave and hung there suspended just long enough for the tug's screws to take bite and pull her clear. Then the *Titanic* dropped in the trough, missing the stern of the *Wallace* by no more than three feet, throwing up a surge that engulfed the entire smaller vessel, carrying away both its lifeboats and one of the ventilators.

The wave tore Butera's grip from the railing and swept him across the bridge, jamming his body against the wheelhouse bulkhead. He lay there totally submerged under the billow, his throat choking, his lungs gasping for air, his brain sluggishly taking strength from the strong pulsing beat of the *Wallace*'s engines that transmitted through the deck. When the water finally drained away, he struggled to his feet and retched his stomach empty.

He clawed his way back into the safety of the wheelhouse. Butera, his senses stunned by the miracle of the *Wallace*'s deliverance, watched the great black apparition that was the *Titanic* slide by astern until she disappeared again in the shroud of wind-whipped rain.

60

"Leave it to Dirk Pitt to pick up a dame in the middle of the ocean during a hurricane," Sandecker said. "What's your secret?"

"The Pitt curse," Pitt answered, as he tenderly bandaged the swelling on Dana's head. "Women are forever attracted to me under impossible circumstances when I'm in no mood to respond."

Dana began to moan softly.

"She's coming around," Gunn said. He was on his knees next to a cot they had wedged between the gymnasium's old exercise equipment to steady it from the ship's rolling and pitching.

Pitt covered her with a blanket. "She suffered a nasty tap, but her mass of hair probably saved her from anything worse than a concussion."

"How did she come to be on Sturgis's helicopter?" Woodson asked. "I thought she was babysitting the news people on board the *Alhambra*."

"She was," Admiral Sandecker said. "Several television network correspondents requested permission to cover the *Titanic*'s haul to New York from aboard the *Capricorn*. I gave authorization on the condition that Dana accompany them."

"I ferried them over," Sturgis said. "And, I saw Mrs. Seagram disembark when I landed on the *Capricorn*. It's a mystery to me how she re-entered the helicopter without being noticed."

"Yeah, a mystery," Woodson repeated caustically. "Don't you bother checking your cargo compartment between flights?"

"I'm not running a commercial airline," Sturgis snapped back. He looked as though he was about to hit Woodson. He glanced at Pitt and was met with a disapproving stare. Then, with a visible effort, he reined in his emotions and spoke slowly and firmly: "I'd been flying that bird out there steady for twenty hours straight. I was tired. I easily convinced myself that there was no need to bother with a cargo-compartment check because I was certain it was empty. How was I to know Dana Seagram would sneak on board?"

Gunn shook his head. "Why did she do it? Why would she? . . ."

"I don't know why . . . how the hell should I?" Sturgis said. "Suppose you tell me why she threw a hammer through my rotor blades, wrapped herself up in a tarpaulin, and then clouted herself on the head? Not necessarily in that order."

"Why don't you ask her?" Pitt said. He nodded down at the cot.

Dana was staring up at the men, her eyes devoid of understanding. She looked as though she had just been dragged up from the sanctuary of exhausted sleep.

"Forgive me . . . for asking such a hackneyed question," she murmured. "But, where am I?"

"My dear girl," Sandecker said, kneeling at her side, "you're on the *Titanic*."

She looked dazedly at the admiral, disbelief written across her face. "That can't be?"

"Oh, I assure you it is," Sandecker said. "Pitt, there's a bit of scotch left. Bring me a glass."

Pitt obediently did as he was told and handed Sandecker the glass. Dana took a swallow of the Cutty Sark, choked on it and coughed, holding her head as if to contain the pain that had suddenly exploded in her skull.

"There, there, my dear." It was plain to see Sandecker was somewhat at a loss as to how to treat a woman in agony. "Rest easy. You've suffered a nasty blow on the head."

Dana felt the bandage circling her hair and then clutched the admiral's hand knocking the glass on the deck.

Pitt winced as the scotch spilled. Women just don't appreciate good booze.

"No, no, I'm all right." She struggled to a sitting position on the cot and stared in wonder at the strange mechanical contrivances. "The *Titanic*," she said the name reverently. "I'm actually on the *Titanic*?"

"Yes." Pitt's voice was edged with sharpness. "And, we'd like to know how you got here."

She looked at him, half-uncertainly, half-confused, and said, "I don't know. I honestly don't know. The last thing I recall I was on the *Capricorn*."

"We found you in the helicopter," Pitt said.

"The helicopter . . . I lost my make-up kit . . . must have dropped it on the flight from the *Alhambra*." She forced a wan smile. "Yes, that's it. I returned to the helicopter to search for my make-up kit. I found it jammed between the fold-up seats. I tried pulling it free when . . . well, I guess I fainted and hit my head when I fell."

"Fainted? You're sure you—" Pitt broke off his question and asked another instead. "What was the very last thing you remember seeing before you blacked out?"

She thought a moment, staring as if at some distant vision in time. Those coffee-brown eyes seemed unnaturally large against her pale and strained face.

Sandecker patted her hand paternally. "Just take your time."

Finally her lips formed a word. "Boots."

"Say again," Pitt ordered.

"A pair of boots," she answered as if seeing a revelation. "Yes, I remember now, a pair of sharp-toed cowboy boots."

"Cowboy boots?" Gunn asked, his expression blank.

Dana nodded. "You see, I was down on my hands and knees trying to extricate my make-up kit, and then . . . I don't know . . . they just seemed to be there. . . ." She paused.

"What color were they?" Pitt prodded her.

"Kind of a yellow, cream color."

"Did you see the man's face?"

She started to shake her head and caught herself at the first stab of pain. "No, everything went dark then . . . that's all there is. . . ." Her voice trailed off.

Pitt could see that there was nothing to be gained by further interrogation. He looked down at Dana and smiled. She looked up and smiled back with an anxious-to-please smile.

"We dirty old men had best leave you alone to rest for a while," he said. "If you need anything, one of us will always be close by."

Sandecker followed Pitt over to the entrance to the grand staircase. "What do you make of it?" Sandecker asked. "Why would anyone want to harm Dana?"

"For the same reason they killed Henry Munk."

"You think she got wise to one of the Soviet agents?"

"More likely, in her case, it was a matter of being in the wrong place at the wrong time."

"The last thing we need on our hands now is an injured woman." Sandecker sighed. "There'll be hell to pay when Gene Seagram gets my radio message about what happened to his wife."

"With all due respect, sir, I told Gunn not to send your message. We can't risk a change in plans at the last minute. Men make cautious decisions where women are concerned. We won't hesitate to risk the lives of a dozen members of our own sex, but we'll balk every time when it comes to endangering one of the female species. What Seagram, the President, Admiral Kemper, and the others in Washington don't know won't hurt them, at least for the next twelve hours."

"It would appear my authority means nothing around here," Sandecker said acidly. "Anything else you neglected to tell me, Pitt? Like who those outlandish cowboy boots belong to?"

"The boots belong to Ben Drummer."

"I've never seen him wear them. How would . . . how could you know that?"

"I discovered them when I searched his quarters on the *Capricorn*."

"Now you've added burglarizing to your other talents," Sandecker said.

"Drummer wasn't alone. Giordino and I have searched every one of the salvage crews' belongings over the past month."

"Find anything of interest?"

"Nothing incriminating."

"Who do you think injured Dana?"

"It wasn't Drummer. That much is certain. He's got at least a dozen witnesses including you and me, Admiral, who will testify that he's been on board the *Titanic* since yesterday. It would have been impossible for him to attack Dana Seagram on a ship that was fifty miles away."

At that moment, Woodson came up and caught Pitt's arm. "Sorry for the interruption, boss, but we just received an urgent call from the *Juneau.* I'm afraid it's bad news."

"Let's have it," Sandecker said wearily. "The outlook can't possibly be painted any blacker than it is now."

"Oh, but it can," Woodson said. "The message is from the missile cruiser's captain and reads: 'Have received distress call from eastbound freighter *Laguna Star,* bearing zero five degrees, a hundred and ten miles north of your position. Must respond. Repeat, must respond. Sorry to leave you. Good luck to the *Titanic!*' "

" 'Good luck to the *Titanic,*' " Sandecker echoed. His voice was flat and empty of life. "We might as well raise a flashing sign on the hull that says, 'Welcome thieves and pirates. Come one, come all.' "

So now it begins, Pitt thought to himself.

But the only sensation that coursed through his body was a sudden, overwhelming urge to go to the bathroom.

61

The air in Admiral Joseph Kemper's Pentagon office reeked of stale cigarette smoke and half-eaten sandwiches, and it almost seemed to crackle under the invisible cloud of tension.

Kemper and Gene Seagram were huddled over the admiral's desk in quiet conversation while Mel Donner and Warren Nicholson, the CIA director, sat together on the sofa, their feet propped on a coffee table, and dozed. But they jerked upright in full wakefulness when the strange buzz that was specially tuned into Kemper's red telephone broke the hushed quiet. Kemper grunted into the receiver and laid it back in its cradle.

"It was the security desk. The President is on his way up."

Donner and Nicholson glanced at each other and heaved themselves off the sofa. They had no sooner cleared the coffee table of the evening's debris, straightened their ties and donned their coats when the door opened and the President strode in followed by his Kremlin security adviser, Marshall Collins.

Kemper came from behind his desk and shook the President's hand. "Nice to see you, Mr. President. Please make yourself at home. May I get you something?"

The President scanned his watch and then grinned. "Three hours yet before the bars close. How about a Bloody Mary?"

Kemper grinned back and nodded to his aide. "Commander Keith, will you do the honors?"

Keith nodded. "One Bloody Mary coming up, sir."

"I hope you gentlemen won't mind me standing watch with you," the President said, "but I have a heavy stake in this too!"

"Not at all, sir," Nicholson answered. "We're happy to have you."

"What is the situation at the moment?"

Admiral Kemper gave a full briefing to the President, describing the unexpected ferocity of the hurricane, showing the positions of the ships on a projected wall map, and explaining the *Titanic*'s towing operation.

"Was it absolutely necessary that the *Juneau* be ordered off station?" the President asked.

"A distress call is a distress call," Kemper replied solemnly, "and must be answered by every ship in the area, regardless of the circumstances."

"We have to play according to the other team's rules until half time," Nicholson said. "After that, it's our game."

"Do you think, Admiral Kemper, that the *Titanic* can stand up to the battering of a hurricane?"

"As long as the tugs can keep her bows into the wind and sea, she's an odds-on favorite to come through with flying colors."

"And if for some reason the tugs cannot keep her from swinging broadside to the waves?"

Kemper avoided the President's gaze and shrugged. "Then it's in God's hands."

"Nothing could be done?"

"No, sir. There is simply no way to protect any one vessel caught in the clutches of a hurricane. It becomes a case of every ship for herself."

"I see."

A knock at the door, and another officer entered, laid two slips of paper on Kemper's desk, and retreated.

Kemper read the notes and looked up, his face set in a grim expression. "A message from the *Capricorn*," he said. "Your wife, Mr. Seagram . . . your wife is reported missing. A search party aboard ship was unable to locate her. They fear she was lost overboard. I'm sorry."

Seagram sagged into Collins' arms, his eyes widened in stunned horror. "Oh my God!" he cried. "It can't be true. Oh God! What am I going to do. Dana . . . Dana . . ."

Donner rushed to his side. "Steady, Gene. Steady." He and Collins steered Seagram over to the sofa and gently lowered him to the cushions.

Kemper gestured to the President for his attention. "There's another message, sir. From the *Samuel R. Wallace,* one of the tugs towing the *Titanic.* The towing cable," Kemper said. "It snapped. The *Titanic* is adrift in the center of the hurricane."

The cable hung like a dead snake over the stern of the *Wallace,* its severed end swaying in the black depths a quarter of a mile below.

Butera stood frozen beside the great electric winch, refusing to believe his eyes. "How?" he shouted in Ensign Kelly's ear. "How could it part? It was built to take worse stress than this."

"Can't figure it," Kelly yelled back above the storm. "There was no extreme stress on her when she went."

"Bring her up, Ensign. Let's take a look."

The ensign nodded and gave the orders. The brake was released and the reel began turning, pulling the wire up from the sea. A solid sheet of spray dashed against the cablehouse. The dead weight of the wire acted as an anchor, dragging down the stern of the *Wallace,* and each time a column of water approached, it rose high over the wheelhouse and came thundering down upon it with a shock that jarred the entire tug.

At last the end of the tow cable appeared over the stern and snaked up onto the reel. As soon as the brake was applied, Butera and Kelly moved in and began examining the frayed strands.

Butera stared at it, his face twisted in stunned incomprehension. He touched the burned wire ends and looked dumbly at the ensign.

The ensign did not share Butera's muteness. "Jesus Christ in heaven," he shouted hoarsely. "It's been cut through with an acetylene torch."

Pitt was down on his hands and knees on the cargo floor of the helicopter, sweeping his flashlight under the folded passenger seats when the *Titanic*'s tow cable dropped into the sea.

Outside the wind howled with demonic power. Pitt couldn't have known it, but without the tugs' steadying influence, the *Titanic*'s bows were being forced by the raging sea to leeward, exposing her entire flank to the unleashed furies. She was beginning to broach to.

It had taken him only two minutes to find Dana's make-up kit where it had solidly jammed behind one of the folded front seats immediately behind the control-cabin bulkhead. He could easily see why she had had difficulty retrieving the blue nylon case from its prison. Very few women are blessed with mechanical inclinations, and Dana was definitely not one of them. It hadn't occurred to her to simply unclasp the restraining straps and unfold the seat. Pitt did so and the kit fell free into his hand.

He didn't bother opening it; he wasn't interested. What he was interested in was the recessed compartment in the forward bulkhead, where a twenty-man life raft sat, or where it was supposed to sit. The yellow, rubberized cover was there all right, but the raft was gone.

Pitt had no time to appreciate the implication of his discovery. Even as he pulled the empty cover out of its compartment, a monstrous sea crashed against the flank of the helpless *Titanic,* heeling her great mass over on her starboard side as though she never meant to stop. Pitt made a desperate grab for one of the seat supports, but his fingers closed on air and he was spilled like a sack of potatoes down across the sloping floor, crashing against the partially opened cargo door with such force that he ripped a four-inch gash in his scalp.

Mercifully, the next few hours were lost to Pitt. He was aware of a cold gale sweeping into the fuselage, but not much else. His mind was a vague mass of gray wool and he felt remotely detached from his surroundings. He could not know or even sense when the helicopter shed its triple-lashed moorings and was hurled sideways, dropping off the first-class lounge roof onto the Boat Deck, crumpling its tail section, tearing off its rotor blades, before grinding over the railing and falling toward the tormented sea.

62

The Russians came aboard the *Titanic* during the storm's lull. Deep down in the bowels of the engine and boiler rooms, Spencer and his pumping crew had no chance, not the least opportunity for any resistance. Their total surprise acknowledged Prevlov's dedication to exact planning and detailed execution.

The fight that occurred topside—massacre would have been closer to the truth—was over almost before it began. Five Russian marines, half the boarding force, their faces all but hidden by seaman caps pulled low on top and with huge mufflers wrapped below, were in the gymnasium with automatic machine pistols ready and aimed before anyone could comprehend what was happening.

Woodson was the first to react. He swung from the radio, his eyes widened in a look of recognition, and an expression of pure anger swept over his normally passive face. "You bastard!" he blurted, and then hurled himself at the nearest intruder.

But a knife materialized in the man's hand and he deftly rammed it into Woodson's chest, tearing the photographer's heart nearly in two. Woodson clutched at his killer, then slowly slid downward to the booted feet, shock in his eyes, then disbelief, then pain, and finally the emptiness of death.

Dana sat up on her cot and screamed and screamed. It was that stimulus that finally stung the other members of the salvage crew into action. Drummer caught Woodson's murderer on the cheek with his fist and received the barrel of a machine pistol across his face for his effort. Sturgis launched his body in a flying tackle but his timing was late. A gun butt caught him just above the temple at the same instant he crashed into his intended victim and they both fell to the deck in a heap, the assailant quickly regaining his feet while Sturgis lay there as if dead.

Giordino was in the act of bringing a wrench down on another Russian's skull when there was an ear-splitting crack. A bullet passed through his upraised hand and sent the wrench clattering across the deck. The shot seemed to freeze all movement. Sandecker, Gunn, and Chief Bascom and his men halted in mid-action as they abruptly realized that their unarmed defense of the ship was hopeless in the face of guns held by highly trained killers.

At that precise moment a man strode into the room, his intense gray eyes taking in every detail of the scene. He wasted no more than three seconds—three seconds and no more was all André Prevlov needed to survey any given situation. He stared down at the still-screaming Dana and smiled graciously. "Do you mind, my dear lady," he said in fluent, idiomatic English. "I think female panic inflicts quite an unnecessary strain on the vocal chords."

Her round eyes were stricken. Her mouth closed and she sat huddled in a ball on the cot, staring at the spreading pool of blood under Omar Woodson and shuddering uncontrollably.

"There now, that's much better." Prevlov followed her eyes to Woodson, then to Drummer, who was sitting on the deck in the process of spitting out a tooth, and then to Giordino, who glared back holding his bleeding hand.

"Your resistance was foolish," Prevlov said. "One dead and three injured, and for nothing."

"Who are you?" Sandecker demanded. "By what right do you board this ship and murder my crew?"

"Ah! A pity we must meet under such remote and unpleasant circumstances," Prevlov apologized. "You are, of course, Admiral James Sandecker, are you not?"

"My questions still stand," Sandecker spat angrily.

"My name is of no consequence," Prevlov replied. "The answer to your other question is obvious. I am taking over this ship in the name of the Union of Soviet Socialist Republics."

"My government will never stand idly by and let you get away with it."

"Correction," Prevlov murmured. "Your government *will* stand idly by."

"You underestimate us."

Prevlov shook his head. "Not I, Admiral. I am fully aware of what your countrymen are capable of. I also know they will not start a war over the legitimate boarding of a derelict ship."

" 'Legitimate boarding'?" Sandecker echoed. "The Civil Salvage Service laws define a derelict vessel as one whose crew has abandoned at sea without intent of returning or attempt at recovery. Since this ship still retains its crew, your presence, sir, constitutes a blatant act of high-seas piracy."

"Spare me your interpretation of maritime legalities." Prevlov held up a protesting hand. "You are quite right, of course, for the moment."

The implication was clear. "You wouldn't dare cast us adrift in the middle of a hurricane."

"Nothing so mundane, Admiral. Besides, I am well aware that the *Titanic* is taking on water. I need your salvage engineer, Spencer, I believe his name is, and his crew to keep the pumps operating until the storm abates. After that, you and your people will be provided with a life raft. Your departure will then guarantee our right to salvage."

"We cannot be allowed to live to testify," Sandecker said. "Your government would never permit that. You know it, and I know it."

Prevlov looked at him, calm, unaffected. Then he turned casually, almost callously, dismissing Sandecker. He spoke in Russian to one of the marines. The man nodded and tipped over the radio, and pounded it with the stock of his machine pistol into mangled pieces of metal, glass, and wiring.

"There is no further use for your operations room." Prevlov motioned around the gymnasium. "I have installed my communication facilities in the main dining room on D Deck. If you and the others will be so kind as to follow me, I will see to your comfort until the weather clears."

"One more question," Sandecker said without moving. "You owe me that."

"Of course, Admiral, of course."

"Where is Dirk Pitt?"

"I regret to inform you," Prevlov said with ironic sympathy, "that Mr. Pitt was in your helicopter when it was swept over the side into the sea. His death must have come quickly."

63

Admiral Kemper sat opposite a grim-faced President and casually poured four teaspoons of sugar into his coffee cup.

"The aircraft carrier *Beecher's Island* is nearing the search area. Her planes will begin searching at first light." Kemper forced a thin smile. "Don't worry, Mr. President. We'll have the *Titanic* back in tow by midafternoon. You have my word on it."

The President looked up. "A helpless ship adrift and lost in the middle of the worst storm in fifty years? A ship that's rusted half through after lying on the bottom for seventy-six years? A ship the Soviet government is looking for any excuse to get their hands on? And you say not to worry. You're either a man of unshakable conviction, Admiral, or you're a hyperoptimist."

"Hurricane Amanda." Kemper sighed at the name. "We made allowances for every possible contingency, but nothing in our wildest imagination prepared us for a storm of such tremendous magnitude in the middle of May. It struck so fearfully hard, and on such short notice, that there was no time to reshuffle our priorities and time schedules."

"Suppose the Russians took it into their heads to make their play and are on board the *Titanic* this minute?"

Kemper shook his head. "Boarding a ship under a hundred-plus mile-an-hour winds and seventy-foot seas? My years at sea tell me that's impossible."

"A week ago, Hurricane Amanda would have been considered impossible, too." The President looked up dully as Warren Nicholson sank in the opposite sofa.

"Any news?"

"Nothing from the *Titanic*," Nicholson said. "They haven't reported since they entered the eye of the hurricane."

"And the Navy tugs?"

"They still haven't sighted the *Titanic*—which isn't too surprising. With their radar inoperative, they're reduced to a visual search pattern. A hopeless chore, I'm afraid, in near-zero visibility."

For long moments, there was a suffocating silence. It was finally broken by Gene Seagram. "We can't lose it now, not when we were so close," he said, struggling to his feet. "The terrible price we've paid . . . I've paid . . . the byzanium, oh God, we can't let it be taken away from us again." His shoulders drooped and he seemed to wither as Donner and Collins eased him back down on the sofa.

Kemper spoke in a whisper. "If the worst happens, Mr. President? What then?"

"We write off Sandecker, Pitt, and the others."

"And the Sicilian Project?"

"The Sicilian Project," the President murmured. "Yes, we write that off too."

64

The heavy gray wool slowly began to fade away and Pitt became aware that he was lying in an upside-down position on something hard and in something wet. He hung there long minutes, his mind in the twilight zone between consciousness and unconsciousness, until gradually he was able to pry open his eyes, or at least one eye; the other was caked shut by coagulated blood. Like a man who had just struggled up from a deep dark tunnel into the daylight, he squinted his good eye from right to left, up and down. He was still in the helicopter, his feet and legs curled upward along the floor and his back and shoulders lay against the aft bulkhead.

That accounted for the hardness. The wetness was an understatement. Several inches of water sloshed back and forth around his body. He wondered vaguely how he had come to be contorted in this awkward position.

His head felt as if little men were running around inside it, jabbing pitchforks into his brain. He splashed some water over his face, ignoring the sting of the salt, until the blood diluted and ran off, allowing the eyelid to open. Now that he had regained his peripheral vision he turned his body so that he was sitting on the bulkhead and looking up at the floor. It was like staring at the crazy room of an amusement-park fun house.

There was to be no exiting through the cargo door; it had been jammed shut from the beating the fuselage had taken during its journey across the *Titanic*'s decks. Left with no other choice but to get out through the control-cabin hatch, Pitt began climbing *up* the floor, using the cargo tie-down rings for handgrips.

One ring at a time, he pulled himself toward the forward bulkhead, or what now constituted the ceiling. His head ached and he had to stop every few feet, waiting for the cobwebs to clear. At last, he could reach up and touch the door latch. The door wouldn't budge. He pulled out the Colt and pounded at the latch. The force of the blow knocked the pistol out of his wet hand, and it clattered all the way to the rear bulkhead. The door remained stubbornly closed.

Pitt's breath was coming now in heaving gasps. He was on the verge of blacking out from exhaustion. He turned and looked down. The aft bulkhead seemed a long way away. He gripped a cargo tie-down ring with both hands, swung in a series of ever-widening arcs, and then lashed out with both feet, using all the muscle a man can use when he knows it is his last try.

The latch gave and the door sprung upward at an angle of thirty degrees before gravity took over and brought it slamming back down. But the brief opening was all Pitt needed to thrust a hand over the door frame, using his fingers as a jam. He gasped in agony as the door fell across his knuckles. He hung there, soaking up the pain, gathering the strength for the final hurdle. He took a deep breath and heaved his body through the opening as one would climb through a trapdoor in an attic without benefit of a ladder. Then he rested again, waiting for the dizziness to pass and his heart to slow down to a near-normal beat.

He wrapped his bleeding fingers in a sodden handkerchief and took stock of the control cabin. No problem escaping here. The cabin hatch had been torn off its hinges and the windshield glass knocked from its frames. Now that his escape was assured, he began to wonder how long he had been unconscious. Ten minutes? An hour? Half the night? He had no way of knowing as his watch was gone, probably wrenched from his wrist.

What had happened? He tried to analyze the possibilities. Had the helicopter been blown into the sea? Not likely. It would have been Pitt's coffin in the abyss by now. But where had the water in the cargo section come from? Maybe the aircraft had been ripped loose from its moorings and swept against one of the Boat Deck bulkheads of the derelict. That didn't work either. It couldn't explain why the helicopter was standing in a perfect perpendicular position. What he did know for certain was that every additional second spent sitting around in the middle of a hurricane and playing question-and-answer games moved him one second closer to more serious injury or even death. The answers were waiting outside, so he worked himself over the pilot's seat and stared through the shattered cockpit windows into the darkness beyond.

He was staring straight up the side of the *Titanic*. The gargantuan rusty plates of the hull stretched off into the dim light to the right and left. A quick downward look revealed the angry sea.

The waves were swirling about in massive confusion, often coming together in huge collisions that sounded like an artillery barrage. Visibility was better now; no heavy rain was falling and the wind had slackened to no more than ten or fifteen knots. At first Pitt thought that he must have slept through the hurricane, but then he figured out why the sea was leaping skyward without any sense of direction: the *Titanic* was drifting in the eye of the coil, and only a few more minutes would pass before the full fury of the storm's rear quadrant would fall upon the wallowing ship.

Pitt edged carefully through one of the broken windows over the nose of the helicopter and then dropped onto the deck of the *Titanic*. No sensuous or erotic interlude with the world's most beautiful woman could have come close to matching the thrill he felt at finding his feet on one of the old liner's water-logged decks again.

But which deck? Pitt leaned over the railing, twisted around, and looked up. There on the deck above was the bent and broken handrail still clutching a part of the helicopter. That meant he was standing on the B Deck Promenade. He looked down and saw the reason behind the aircraft's ignominious posture.

Its journey toward the boiling sea had been abruptly halted by the landing skids, which had caught and then wedged into the observation openings along the Promenade Deck, leaving the helicopter hanging in an upright stance like some monstrous bug on a wall. The great swells had then slammed against its fuselage, jamming it even tighter against the ship.

Pitt had no time to appreciate the miracle of his salvation. For, as he stood there, he felt the increasing pressure from the wind as the tail of the hurricane approached. He had trouble getting his footing and he realized that the *Titanic*'s list had returned and she was leaning heavily to starboard again.

It was then that he noticed the running lights of another ship close by, no more than two hundred yards off the starboard beam. There was no way of telling what size she was; the sea and the sky began melting together as the driving rain returned, lashing his face with the cutting power of sandpaper. Could it be one of the tugs, he wondered? Or perhaps the *Juneau* had returned. But suddenly Pitt knew—the lights were from none of these. A shaft of lightning flashed and he saw the unmistakable dome that could only be the *Mikhail Kurkov*'s radar antennae shield.

By the time he had climbed a stairway and staggered to the helicopter pad on the Boat Deck, he was still wet to the skin and panting from the exertion. He paused to kneel and pick up one of the mooring lines, studying the parted ends of the nylon fibers. Then he rose and leaned into the howling wind and vanished into the curtain of water that enshrouded the ship.

65

The vastness of the *Titanic*'s first-class dining saloon stretched under the ornate ceiling far into the dark shadows beyond the lights, the few remaining leaded glass windows reflecting eerie distortions of the bone-tired and defeated people standing under the guns of the unflinching Russians.

Spencer had been forced to join the group. The shock of incomprehension mirrored in his eyes. He stared at Sandecker incredulously.

"Pitt and Woodson dead? It can't be true."

"It's true all right," Drummer mumbled through a swollen mouth. "One of them sadistic bastards standing there shoved a knife into Woodson's gut."

"A miscalculation on your friend's part," Prevlov said with a shrug. He gazed speculatively at the frightened woman and the nine men standing before him, at their gaunt and blood-caked faces. He seemed to enjoy, in a detached sort of way, their struggle to retain their balance whenever the *Titanic* was struck broadside by an immense swell. "And speaking of miscalculations, Mr. Spencer, it seems your men have developed a noticeable lack of enthusiasm for manning the pumps. I needn't remind you that unless the water that is pouring in below the waterline is returned to the sea, this ancient monument to capitalistic extravagance will sink."

"So let it sink," Spencer said easily. "At least you and your Communist scum will go with it."

"Not a likely event, particularly when you consider that the *Mikhail Kurkov* is standing by for just such an emergency." Prevlov selected a cigarette from a gold case and tapped it thoughtfully. "So you see, a sensible man would accept the inevitable and perform his duties accordingly."

"It still beats hell out of letting you get your slimy hands on her."

"You won't get any of us to do your dirty work for you," Sandecker said. There was a quiet finality in his voice.

"Perhaps not." Prevlov was quite unruffled. "On the other hand, I think I shall have the cooperation I require and very soon." He motioned to one of the guards and muttered in Russian. The guard nodded, walked unhurriedly across the dining saloon, grabbed Dana by the arm and roughly pulled her under one of the portable lights.

As one, the salvage crew crowded forward only to be met by four unyielding machine pistols held at gut level. They froze helplessly, rage and hostility seething through their every pore.

"If you harm her," Sandecker whispered, his voice quivering in quiet anger, "you'll pay for it."

"Oh come now, Admiral," Prevlov said. "Rape is for the sick. Only a cretin would attempt blackmailing you and your crew with such a sorry ploy. American men still place their women on marble pedestals. You'd all willingly die in a useless attempt to protect her virtues, and where would that leave me? No, cruelty and torture are crude methods in the fine art of persuasion. Humiliation . . ." He paused, savoring the word. "Yes, humiliation, a magnificent incentive for inducing your men to return to their labors and keep the ship afloat."

Prevlov turned to Dana. She looked at him, pathetic and lost. "Now then, Mrs. Seagram, if you will be so good as to take off your clothes—all of them."

"What kind of cheap trick is this?" Sandecker asked.

"No trick. Mrs. Seagram's modesty will be laid bare, layer after layer until you order Mr. Spencer and his men to cooperate."

"No!" Gunn pleaded. "Don't do it, Dana!"

"Please, no appeals," Prevlov said wearily. "I will have one of my men strip her by force if necessary."

Slowly, barely perceptibly, a strange gleam of belligerence began spreading in Dana's eyes. Then without the slightest hesitation, she slipped out of her jacket, jumpsuit, and underclothing. In less than a minute she stood there in the halo of light, her body supple and alive and very nude.

Sandecker turned his back and one by one the other hardened salvage men followed suit until they were facing away into the darkness.

"You will look upon her," Prevlov said coldly. "Your gallant gesture is touching, but completely useless. Turn around, gentlemen, our little performance is just beginning—"

"I think this stupid, chauvinistic bullshit has gone far enough."

Every head jerked around as if yanked by the strings of a puppeteer at the sound of Dana's voice. She stood there with legs apart, hands on hips, breasts thrust outward, and her eyes blazed with a mocking awareness. Even with the unsightly bandage around her head she looked magnificent.

"The admission is free, boys, stare all you want. A woman's body is no big secret. You've all seen and undoubtedly touched one before. Why all the bashful glances?" Then her eyes changed to shrewd reflection and her lips lifted away from her teeth and she began laughing. She had decisively stolen the stage from Prevlov.

He stared at her, his mouth slowly tightening. "An impressive performance, Mrs. Seagram, an impressive performance indeed. But a typical display of Western decadence I hardly find amusing."

"Show me a Communist, and I'll show you an asshole every time," Dana taunted him. "If you shitheads only knew how the whole world laughs behind your threadbare backs every time you spout your gauche little Marxist terms like Western decadence, imperialistic war-mongering, or bourgeois-manipulating, you might straighten up and show a little class. As it is, your kind is the biggest diabolical farce played on mankind since we climbed down from the trees. And if you had any balls, you'd face up to it."

Prevlov's face went white. "This has gone far enough," he snapped. He was on the verge of losing his very carefully practiced control and it frustrated him.

Dana stretched her long and opulent body and said. "What's the matter, Ivan? Too used to muscle-bound, hod-carrying Russian women? Can't get used to the idea of a liberated gal from the Land of the Free and the Home of the Brave laughing at your sorry tactics?"

"It is your vulgarity that I find difficult to accept. At least our women do not act like common gutter sluts."

"Fuck you." Dana grinned sweetly.

Prevlov missed nothing. He caught the flickered glance between Giordino and Spencer, caught the flexing of Sturgis's fists, and the tiny inclination of Drummer's head. He became fully aware now that Dana's indolent yet continual movement away from the Americans and toward the rear of the Russian guards was neither unconscious nor unplanned. Her performance was nearly complete. The Soviet marines were twisting their necks to gawk; their guns were beginning to droop in their hands, when Prevlov shouted out a command in Russian.

The guards, jolted out of their laxity, swung back and faced the salvage crew, their weapons aimed and steady again.

"My compliments, dear lady." Prevlov bowed. "Your little display of theatrics very nearly worked. A clever, clever deception."

There was a curious clinical satisfaction in Prevlov's expression; a functional chill as if his cunning had been called and he had easily won the hand.

He watched Dana, appraising her fractional show of defeat. The grin had remained on her face, as though painted there, and her shoulders huddled in a slight shiver, but she shook it off and straightened once again, proud and self-assured.

"I don't know what you're talking about."

"Of course not." Prevlov sighed. He stared at her for a moment, and then turned and said something to one of the guards. The man nodded, pulled out a knife and slowly advanced toward Dana.

Dana stiffened and paled, as though turned to salt. "What are you going to do?"

"I ordered him to cut off your left breast," Prevlov said conversationally.

Spencer stared openmouthed at Sandecker, his eyes pleading for the admiral to back down.

"Good God!" Sandecker uttered desperately. "You can't allow—you promised, no cruelty or torture—"

"I am the first to admit there is no finesse in savagery," Prevlov said. "But you leave me no choice. It is the only solution to your obstinacy."

Sandecker sidestepped around the nearest guard. "You'll have to kill me first—"

The guard jammed his machine pistol muzzle into Sandecker's kidney, and the admiral fell to his knees, his face twisted in agony, his breath coming in loud, sucking noises.

Dana clenched her hands at her sides until they turned ivory. She had played her hand down to the last card, and now she looked lost; those beautiful coffee-brown eyes were sick in abhorrence when she saw the guard's eyes suddenly reflect a look of confusion as a steel hand fell on her shoulder and pushed her aside. Pitt walked slowly into the light.

66

Pitt stood frozen in time, like some unspeakable apparition that had risen from the depths of a watery hell. He was saturated from head to foot, his black hair plastered down across a bloodied forehead, his lips curled in a satanic smile. In the light of the lamps, the droplets of water sparkled as they trickled from his wet clothing and splattered on the deck.

Prevlov's face was a wax mask. Calmly, he pulled a cigarette from the gold case, lit it, and exhaled the smoke in a long sigh.

"Your name? May I assume that your name is Dirk Pitt?"

"That's what the fine print reads on the birth certificate."

"It seems you are an uncommonly durable man, Mr. Pitt. It was my understanding that you were dead."

"It just goes to prove you can't rely on shipboard gossip."

Pitt took off his damp jacket and gently draped it over Dana's shoulders. "Sorry, dear heart, it's the best I can do for the moment." Then he turned back to Prevlov. "Any objections?"

Prevlov shook his head. Pitt's offhand manner puzzled him. He scrutinized Pitt as a diamond cutter studies a stone, but saw nothing behind the veil of those sea-green eyes.

Prevlov gestured to one of his men who moved up to Pitt. "Simply a precautionary search, Mr. Pitt. 'Any objections'?"

Pitt shrugged agreeably and held his hands in the air. The guard quickly, efficiently ran his hands up and down Pitt's clothing and then stepped back and shook his head.

"No arms," Prevlov said. "Very wise of you, but then I would have expected nothing less from a man of your reputation. I have read with considerable interest a dossier describing your exploits. I would have liked very much to have known you under less adversary circumstances."

"Sorry I can't return the compliment," Pitt said pleasantly, "but you're not exactly the type of vermin I'd like for a friend."

Prevlov stepped forward two paces and hit Pitt with all his strength with the back of his hand.

Pitt staggered back one step and stood there, a trickle of blood oozing from one corner of his still grinning lips. "Well, well," he said quietly, thickly. "The illustrious André Prevlov finally blew his cool."

Prevlov leaned forward, his eyes half-closed in wary speculation. "My name?" his voice was barely above a murmur. "You know my name?"

"Fair is fair," Pitt answered. "I know as much about you as you know about me."

"You're even cleverer than I was led to believe," Prevlov said. "You've discovered my identity—an astute piece of perception. On that I commend you. But you needn't bluff with knowledge you do not possess. Beyond my name, you know nothing."

"I wonder. Perhaps I can enlighten you further with a bit of local folklore."

"I have no patience for fairy tales," Prevlov said. He motioned to the guard with the knife. "Now if we can get on about the business of persuading Admiral Sandecker to inspire your pumping crew to greater efforts, I would be most grateful."

The guard, a tall man, his face still hidden under the muffler, began advancing toward Dana once more. He extended the knife. Its blade gleamed in the light no more than three inches from Dana's left breast. She hugged Pitts's jacket tightly around her shoulders and stared at the knife, numbed beyond fear.

"Too bad you're not big on fairy tales," Pitt said conversationally. "This is one you'd have enjoyed. It's all about a pair of bumbling characters called Silver and Gold."

Prevlov glanced at him, hesitated, and then nodded the guard back. "You have my attention, Mr. Pitt. I will give you five minutes to prove your point."

"It won't take long," Pitt said. He paused to rub the eye that had caked closed from the hardening blood. "Now then, once upon a time there were two Canadian engineers who discovered that spying could be a lucrative sideline. So they shed all qualms of guilt and became professional espionage agents in every sense of the word, concentrating their talents on obtaining classified data about American oceanographic programs and sending it through hidden channels to Moscow. Silver and Gold earned their money, make no mistake. Over the past two years, there wasn't a NUMA project the Russians didn't have knowledge of down to the tiniest detail. Then, when the *Titanic*'s salvage came up, the Soviet Navy's Department of Foreign Intelligence—your department, Prevlov—smelled a windfall. Without the slightest degree of chicanery, you found yourself with not one, but two men in your employ who were in a perfect situation to obtain and pass along America's most advanced deep-water-salvage techniques. There was, of course, another vital consideration, but even you weren't aware of it at the time.

"Silver and Gold," Pitt went on, "sent regular reports concerning the raising of the wreck through an ingenious method. They used a battery-powered pinger, a device that can transmit underwater sound waves similar to sonar. I should have caught on to it when the *Capricorn*'s sonar man detected the transmissions, but instead I dismissed it as loose debris caused by a deep water current knocking about the *Titanic*. The fact that someone was sending out coded messages never entered our heads. Nobody bothered to decipher the random noises. Nobody, that is, except the man sitting under a set of hydrophones on board the *Mikhail Kurkov*."

Pitt paused and glanced about the dining saloon. He had everyone's attention. "We didn't begin to smell either rat until Henry Munk felt the need for a poorly timed call of nature. On his way back to the head at the aft end of the *Sappho II*, he heard the pinging device in operation and investigated; he caught one of the agents in the act. Your man probably tried to lie his way out of it, but Henry Munk was an instrument specialist. He recognized a communications pinger when he saw one and quickly figured the game. It was a case of the cat killing curiosity. Munk had to be silenced, and he was, from a blow to the base of the skull by one of Woodson's camera tripods. This created an awkward situation for the murderer, so he bashed Munk's head against the alternator housing to make it look like an accident. However, the fish didn't take the bait. Woodson was suspicious; I was suspicious; and to top it off, Doc Bailey found the bruise on Munk's neck. But since there was no way of proving who the killer was, I decided to string along with the accident story until I could scratch up enough evidence to point an accusing finger. Later, I went back and searched the submersible and discovered one slightly used and very bent camera tripod along with the pinging device where our friendly neighborhood spy had, ironically, hidden them in Munk's own storage locker. Certain that it was a waste of time to have them checked on shore for fingerprints—I didn't need a bolt from the blue to tell me I was dealing with a professional—I left the tripod and the pinger exactly as I found them. I took the chance that it would only be a matter of time before your agent got complacent and began contacting the *Mikhail Kurkov* again. So I waited."

"A fascinating story," Prevlov said. "But very circumstantial. Absolute proof would have been impossible to come by."

Pitt smiled enigmatically and continued. "The proof came through a process of elimination. I was relatively sure the killer had to be one of the three men on board the submersible who were supposedly asleep during their rest period. I then alternated the *Sappho II*'s crew schedule every few days so that two of them had duties on the surface while the third was diving below on the wreck. When our sonar man picked up the next transmission from the pinger, I had Munk's murderer."

"Who is it, Pitt?" Spencer asked grimly. "There are ten of us here. Was it one of us?"

Pitt locked eyes for an instant with Prevlov and then turned suddenly and nodded at one of the weary men huddled under the lamps.

"I regret that the only introductory fanfare I can offer is the pounding of the waves against the hull, but bear with me and take a bow anyway, Drummer. It may well be your final encore before you toast in the electric chair."

"Ben Drummer!" Gunn gasped. "I can't believe it. Not with him sitting there all battered and bloody after attacking Woodson's killer."

"Local color," Pitt said. "It was too early to raise the curtain on his identity, not at least until we had all walked the plank. Until then, Prevlov needed an informer to blow the whistle on any ideas we might have dreamed up for retaking the ship."

"He fooled me," said Giordino. "He's worked harder than any two men on the crew to keep the *Titanic* floating."

"Has he?" Pitt came back. "Sure, he's looked busy, even managed to work up a sweat and get dirty, but what have you actually seen him accomplish since we came on board?"

Gunn shook his head. "But he's . . . rather I thought that he'd been working day and night surveying the ship."

"Surveying the ship, hell. Drummer has been running around with a portable acetylene torch and cutting holes in her bottom."

"I can't buy that," said Spencer. "Why work at scuttling the ship if his Russian chums want to lay their claws on her, too?"

"A desperate gamble to delay the tow," Pitt answered. "Timing was critical. The only chance the Russians had to board the *Titanic* with any degree of success was during the eye of the hurricane. It was clever thinking. The possibility never occurred to us. If the tugs could have towed the hulk without any complications, we'd have missed the eye by thirty miles. But thanks to Drummer, the instability of the listing hull made the tow job a shambles. Before the cable parted, she sheered all over the ocean, forcing the tugs to reduce their speed to minimum steerage way. And, as you can see, the mere presence of Prevlov and his band of cutthroats attests to the success of Drummer's efforts."

The truth began to register then. None of the salvage crew had actually witnessed Drummer slaving over a pump or offering to carry his share of the load. It registered that he'd always been off on his own, showing up only to complain of his frustration at not overcoming the obstacles that supposedly prevented his survey tour of the ship. They stared at Drummer as though he was some alien from another world, waiting for, expecting the indignant words of denial.

There was to be no denial, no shocked plea of innocence, only a flicker of annoyance that vanished as quickly as it had come. Drummer's transformation was nothing short of astounding. The sad droop to the eyes had disappeared; they suddenly took on a glinting sharpness. Gone too was the lazy curl from the corners of his lips and the slouched, indifferent posture of his body. The indolent façade was gone and, in its place, was a straight-shouldered, almost aristocratic-looking man.

"Permit me to say, Pitt," Drummer said in a precise tone, "your powers of observation would do a first-class espionage agent proud. However, you haven't uncovered anything that really changes the situation."

"Fancy that," Pitt said. "Our former colleague has suddenly lost his Jubilation T. Cornpone accent."

"I mastered it rather skillfully, don't you think?"

"That's not all you mastered, Drummer. Somewhere in your budding career you learned how to win secrets and murder friends."

"A necessity of the trade," Drummer said. He had eased away from the salvage crew until he was standing beside Prevlov.

"Tell me, which one are you, Silver or Gold?"

"Not that it matters any longer," Drummer shrugged. "I'm Gold."

"Then your brother is Silver."

Drummer's smug expression hardened. "You know this?" he said slowly.

"After I had you pegged, I turned over my evidence, meager as it was, to the FBI. I have to hand it to Prevlov and his comrades at Soviet Naval Intelligence. They laid a phony history on you that was as American as apple pie, or should I say Georgia peach pie, and seemingly as genuine as the Confederate flag. But the bureau finally broke through the false documents certifying your impeccable security clearance and tracked you all the way back to the old homestead in Halifax, Nova Scotia, where you and your brother were born . . . within ten minutes of each other I might add."

"My God!" Spencer muttered. "Twins."

"Yes, but nonidentical. They don't even look like brothers."

"So it became a simple case of one twin leading to the other," Spencer said.

"Hardly simple," Pitt replied. "They're a smart pair, Drummer and his brother. You can't take that away from them. That was my prime mistake, attempting to draw a parallel between two men who should have had the same likes and dislikes, who shared the same quarters or who palled around together. But Silver and Gold played opposite roles to the core. Drummer was equally chummy to everyone and lived alone. I was at a dead end. The FBI was trying to trace Drummer's brother while rechecking the security clearances of every member of the salvage crew, but nobody could make a definite connection. Then a break in the form of near-tragedy burst on the scene and pinned the tail on the donkey."

"The *Deep Fathom* accident," Gunn said, staring at Drummer through cold, unblinking eyes. "But Drummer had no relation with the submersible. He was on the crew of the *Sappho II*."

"He had a very real relation. You see, his brother was on the *Deep Fathom*."

"How did you guess that?" Drummer asked.

"Twins have a curious bond. They think and feel things as one. You may have masqueraded as two totally unrelated persons, Drummer, but the two of you were too close for one of you not to come unglued when the other was on the brink of death. You felt your brother's agony, just as surely as if you were trapped down there in the abyss with him."

"Of course," Gunn said. "We were all on edge at the time, but Drummer was damn-near hysterical."

"Again it became a process of elimination among three men; this time Chavez, Kiel, and Merker. Chavez is obviously of Mexican descent and you can't fake that. Kiel is eight years too young; you can't fake that either. That left Sam Merker."

"Damn!" Spencer muttered. "How could we have been taken in for so long?"

"Not hard to imagine when you consider that we were up against the best team the Russians could field." A smile tugged at Pitt's lips. "Incidentally, Spencer, you previously stated that there were ten of us here. You miscounted: there are eleven. You neglected to include Jack the Ripper there." He turned to the guard who was still standing in front of Dana, still clutching the knife in his hand as if it had grown there. "Why don't you drop your stupid disguise, Merker, and join the party."

The guard slowly removed his cap and unwound the muffler that covered the lower half of his face.

"He's the dirty bastard that knifed Woodson," Giordino hissed.

"Sorry about that," Merker said calmly. "Woodson's first mistake was in recognizing me. He might have lived if he had let it go at that. His second mistake, and a very fatal one, was attacking me."

"Woodson was your friend."

"The business of espionage makes no allowances for friends."

"Merker," Sandecker said. "Merker and Drummer. Silver and Gold. I trusted you both, and yet you sold NUMA down the river. For two years you sold us. And for what? A few lousy dollars."

"I wouldn't say a few, Admiral." Merker eased the knife back into its sheath. "More than enough to support my brother and me in fashionable style for a long time to come."

"Hey, where did he come from?" Gunn asked. "Merker is supposed to be in Doc Bailey's sick bay on board the *Capricorn*."

"He stowed away on Sturgis's helicopter," Pitt said, patting his bleeding head with a damp handkerchief.

"Can't be!" Sturgis blurted out. "You were there, Pitt, when I opened the cargo hatch. Except for Mrs. Seagram, the copter was empty."

"Merker was there all right. After he gave Doc Bailey the slip, he kept away from his own cabin and made for brother Drummer's quarters, where he borrowed a fresh change of clothing, including a pair of cowboy boots. Then he sneaked onto the helicopter, threw out the emergency life raft, and hid under its cover. Unfortunately for Dana, she happened along in search of her make-up kit. When she knelt down to retrieve it, her eye caught Merker's boots protruding from under the life raft cover. Not about to let her screw up his escape, he popped her on the head with a hammer he'd found lying around somewhere, wrapped her in a tarpaulin, and crawled back into his hiding space."

"That means he was still in the cargo compartment when we uncovered Mrs. Seagram."

"No. By then he was gone. If you recall, after you switched open the cargo door, we waited for a few moments, listening for any movement inside. There was none because Merker had already crept into the control cabin under the cover of the noise from the door-actuator motors. Then when you and I played Keystone Kops and entered the cargo compartment, he dropped down the cockpit ladder outside and walked peacefully into the night."

"But why throw the hammer into the rotor blades?" Sturgis persisted. "What was the purpose?"

"Since you flew the copter from the *Capricorn* empty," Merker said, "and there was no freight to unload, I couldn't risk the chance of your taking off again without opening the cargo door. You had me trapped back there and didn't know it."

"You became a busy little beaver after that," Pitt said to Merker, "flitting about the ship, guided no doubt by a diagram provided by Drummer. First, you took your brother's portable cutting rig and burned off the tow cable while Chief Bascom and his men were resting in the gymnasium between inspection tours. Next, you cut the mooring lines to the helicopter, taking great satisfaction, I'm certain, in knowing that it was swept over the side of the ship with me in it."

"Two birds with one slice," Merker admitted. "Why deny—"

Merker was cut short by a muffled burst from a submachine gun that echoed from somewhere on the decks below. Prevlov shrugged and looked at Sandecker.

"I fear your men below are proving difficult." He removed the cigarette from its holder and crushed it out with his boot. "I think this discussion has lasted long enough. The storm will be abating in a few hours and the *Mikhail Kurkov* will move into position for the tow. Admiral Sandecker, you will see to it your men cooperate in manning the pumps. Drummer will show you the locations where he's pierced the hull below the waterline so that the rest of your crew can stem the leakage."

"So it's back to the torture games," Sandecker said contemptuously.

"I am through playing games, Admiral." Prevlov had a determined look. He spoke to one of the guards, a short man with a coarsened toughness about him. The same guard who had shoved his gun into Sandecker's side. "This is Buski, a very direct fellow who happens to be the finest marksman in his regiment. He also understands a smattering of English, enough at any rate to translate numerical progression." He turned to the guard. "Buski, I am going to begin counting. When I reach five, you will shoot Mrs. Seagram in the right arm. At ten, in the left; at fifteen in the right knee; and so on until Admiral Sandecker mends his uncooperative ways."

"A businesslike concept," Pitt added. "And you'll shoot the rest of us after we've served your purpose, weight our bodies, and dump them in the sea so they're never found. Then you'll claim we abandoned the ship in the helicopter, which, of course, conveniently crashed. You'd even provide two witnesses, Drummer and Merker, who would testify after their miraculous survival about how the benevolent Russians plucked them from the sea just as they were going down for the third time."

"I see no need to prolong the agony any further," Prevlov said tiredly. "Buski."

Buski raised his machine pistol and took aim at Dana's arm.

"You intrigue me, Prevlov," Pitt said. "You've shown little interest in how I learned Drummer and Merker's code names or why I didn't have them thrown in the brig after I ferreted out their identities. You don't even seem curious as to how I came to know your name."

"Curious, yes, but it makes no difference. Nothing can change the circumstances. Nothing and no one can help you and your friends, Pitt. Not now. Not the CIA or the whole United States Navy. The die is cast. There will be no more play with words."

Prevlov nodded at Buski. "One."

"When Captain Prevlov reaches the count of four, you will die, Buski."

Buski leered smugly and made no reply.

"Two."

"We knew your plans for taking the *Titanic*. Admiral Sandecker and I have known for the last forty-eight hours."

"You've run your last bluff," Prevlov said. "Three."

Pitt shrugged indifferently. "Then all blood is on your hands, Prevlov."

"Four."

An ear-shattering blam rang deafeningly through the dining saloon as the bullet caught Buski just below the hairline and between the eyes, catapulting a quarter of his skull in a crimson blur of slow-motion, snapping his head upward, and slamming him to the deck in an inert spread-eagle at Prevlov's feet.

Dana cried out in startled pain as she was slammed to the deck. There were no apologies from Pitt for throwing her there and then crushing the breath out of her as he used his hundred and ninety pounds for a protective shield. Giordino dove for Sandecker and hauled him down with all the intensity of a desperation tackle by a linebacker for the Green Bay Packers. The rest of the salvage crew wasted no more than a tenth of a second in demonstrating their fondness for self-preservation. They scattered and dropped like leaves in a windstorm, closely followed by Drummer and Merker, who fell as though shackled together.

The blast was still ringing in the far corners of the room when the guards came alive and began firing bursts from their submachine pistols into the darkness toward the dining-saloon entrance. It was a meaningless gesture. The first was cut down almost instantly, pitching forward on his face. The second flung his machine pistol into the air and clutched the river of red that burst from his neck while the third sank slowly to his knees, staring dumbly at the two small holes that had suddenly appeared in the center of his coat.

Now Prevlov stood alone. He stared down at them all and then at Pitt. His expression was one of acceptance, acceptance of defeat and death. He nodded a salute at Pitt and then calmly pulled his automatic from the holster and began firing into the darkness. He expended his clip and stood there, waiting for the gun flash, braced for the pain that must surely come. But there was no return fire. The room went silent. Everything seemed to slow down, and only then did the revelation burst on him. He was not meant to die.

It had been a trap, and he had walked into it as naïvely as a small child into a tiger's den.

A name began to tear at his very soul, taunting him, repeating itself over and over again.

Marganin . . . Marganin . . . Marganin . . .

67

A marine seal is usually defined as an aquatic carnivorous mammal with webbed flippers and soft fur, but the wraithlike phantoms who suddenly materialized around Prevlov and the fallen guards bore little resemblance to their namesake. The United States Navy SEAL, an acronym of sea, air, and land, were members of an extraordinary elite fighting group, trained in every phase of combat from underwater demolition to jungle warfare.

There were five of them encased in pitch-black rubber wetsuits, hoods, and tight slipperlike boots. Their faces were indistinguishable under the ebony warpaint, making it all but impossible to tell where the wetsuits left off and flesh began. Four men held M-24 automatic rifles with collapsible stocks, while the fifth tightly gripped a Stoner weapon, a wicked looking affair with two barrels. One of the SEALs detached himself from the rest and helped Pitt and Dana to their feet.

"Oh God," Dana moaned. "I'll be black and blue for a month." For perhaps five dazed seconds she massaged her aching body, oblivious to the fact that Pitt's jacket had come open. When shocked realization did come, when she saw the guards sprawled grotesquely in death, her voice dropped to a whisper. "Oh shit . . . Oh shit . . ."

"I think it's safe to say the lady survived," Pitt said with a half grin. He shook the SEAL's hand, then introduced him to Sandecker, who was unsteadily clutching Giordino's shoulder for support.

"Admiral Sandecker, may I present our deliverer, Lieutenant Fergus, United States Navy SEALs."

Sandecker acknowledged Fergus's smart salute with a pleased nod, released his hold on Giordino, and stood ramrod straight.

"The ship, Lieutenant, who commands the ship?"

"Unless I'm mistaken, sir, you do—"

Fergus's words were punctuated by another burst of echoing gunfire from somewhere in the cavernous depths of the ship.

"The last stubborn holdout." Fergus smiled. It was obvious. His white teeth gleamed like a neon sign at midnight. "The ship is secure, sir. My ironclad guarantee on it."

"And the pumping crew?"

"Safe and sound and back at their work."

"How many men in your command?"

"Two combat units, Admiral. Ten men in all, including myself."

Sandecker's eyebrows raised. "Only ten men, did you say?"

"Ordinarily for an assault of this nature," Fergus said matter-of-factly, "we'd have used just one combat unit, but Admiral Kemper thought it best to double our force to be on the safe side."

"The Navy's advanced some since I served," Sandecker said wistfully.

"Any casualties?" Pitt asked.

"Until five minutes ago, two of my men wounded, nothing serious, and one missing."

"Where did you come from?" The question was from Merker's lips. He was staring malevolently over the shoulder of a wary SEAL. "There was no ship in the area, no aircraft was sighted. How . . . ?"

Fergus looked at Pitt questioningly. Pitt nodded. "Permission granted to inform our former colleague the facts of life, Lieutenant. He can muse over your answers while he's sitting in a cell on death row."

"We came aboard the hard way," Fergus obliged. "From fifty feet below the surface through the torpedo tubes of a nuclear submarine. That's how I lost one of my men; the water was rough as hell. A wave must have crushed him against the *Titanic*'s hull while we were taking turns climbing the boarding ladders dropped over the side by Mr. Pitt."

"Strange that no one else saw you come on board," Spencer murmured.

"Not strange at all," Pitt said. "While I was helping Lieutenant Fergus and his team come over the aft cargo deck bulwarks, and then tucking them away in the chief steward's old cabin on C Deck, the rest of you were assembled in the gymnasium awaiting my soul-stirring speech on personal sacrifice."

Spencer shook his head. "Talk about fooling all of the people some of the time."

"I have to hand it to you," Gunn said, "you had us all flimflammed."

"At that, the Russians nearly stole the ballgame. We didn't expect them to make their play until the storm quieted down. Boarding during the lull of the hurricane's eye was a masterstroke. And it almost worked. Without either Giordino, or the admiral or me to warn the lieutenant—we three were the only ones privy to the SEALs' presence—Fergus would have never known when to launch his attack on the boarders."

"I don't mind admitting," Sandecker said, "for a while there I thought that we'd had it. Giordino and I prisoners of Prevlov, and Pitt thought to be dead."

"God knows," Pitt said, "if the helicopter hadn't wedged itself into the Promenade Deck, I'd be asleep in the deep right now."

"As it was," Fergus said, "Mr. Pitt looked like death warmed over when he stumbled in the chief steward's cabin. A hardy man, this one. Half-drowned, his head split open, and yet he still insisted on guiding my team through this floating museum until we located your Soviet visitors."

Dana was looking at Pitt in a peculiar way. "How long were you hiding in the shadows before you made your grand entrance?"

Pitt grinned slyly. "For a minute prior to your strip tease."

"You bastard. You stood there and let me make an ass out of myself," she flared. "You let them use me like I was a cut of beef in a butcher store window."

"I used you too, dear heart, as a matter of necessity. After I found Woodson's body and the smashed radio in the gymnasium I didn't need a gypsy to tell me the boys from the Ukraine had boarded the ship. I then rounded up Fergus and his men and led them down to the boiler rooms figuring the Russians would already be guarding the pumping crew. I was right. First priorities first. Whoever controlled the pumps controlled the derelict. When I saw that I would be more hindrance than help in overcoming the guards, I borrowed a SEAL and came looking for the rest of you. After wandering through half the ship we finally heard voices coming out of the dining saloon. Then I ordered the SEAL to hightail it below for reinforcements."

"Then it was all a great big stalling tactic," Dana said.

"Exactly. I needed every second I could beg, borrow, or steal until Fergus showed up and evened the odds. That's why I held off until the last second to put in an appearance."

"A high stakes gamble," Sandecker said. "You cut Act Two a bit fine, didn't you?"

"I had two things going for me," Pitt explained. "One was compassion. I know you, Admiral. In spite of your gargoyle exterior, you still help little old ladies across streets and feed stray animals. You might have waited until the last instant to give in, but you would have given in." Then Pitt put his arms around Dana and slowly produced a nasty looking weapon from a pocket of the jacket draped on her shoulders. "Number two was my insurance policy. Fergus loaned it to me before the party began. It's called a Stoner weapon. It shoots a cloud of tiny needlelike flachettes. I could have cut down Prevlov and half his men with one burst."

"And I thought you were being a gentleman," Dana said with a contrived bitter tone. "You only hung your jacket on me so they wouldn't find the gun when they searched you."

"You have to admit, that your . . . ahem . . . exposed condition made for an ideal distraction."

"Beggin' your pardon, sir," said Chief Bascom. "But why on earth would this rusty old bucket of bolts interest the Russians?"

"My very thoughts," Spencer added. "What's the big deal?"

"I guess it's a secret no longer." Pitt shrugged. "It's not the ship the Russians were after. It's a rare element called byzanium that sank with the *Titanic* back in 1912. Properly processed and installed in a sophisticated defense system, so I'm told, it will make intercontinental ballistic missiles about as outdated as flying dinosaurs."

Chief Bascom let out a long low whistle. "And you mean to say that stuff is still belowdecks somewhere?"

"Buried under several tons of debris, but it's still down there."

"You'll never live to see it, Pitt. None of you . . . none of us will. The *Titanic* will be totally destroyed by morning." There was no anger in Prevlov's face, but something touching on complacent satisfaction. "Did you really think every contingency was not allowed for? Every possibility for failure not backed up by an alternate plan? If we cannot have the byzanium, then neither can you."

Pitt looked at him with what seemed to be bemusement. "Forget any hopes you entertain of the cavalry, or in your case, the cossacks, galloping to the rescue, Prevlov. You made a hell of a try, but you were playing against an American idiom known as a stacked deck. You prepared for everything, everything, that is, except a setup in preparation for a double cross. I don't know how the scheme was nurtured. It must have been a wonder of creative cunning, and you fell for it hook, line, and sinker. I'm sorry, Captain Prevlov, but to the victor belong the spoils."

"The byzanium belongs to the Russian people," Prevlov said gravely. "It was raped from our soil by your government. It is not we who are the robbers, Pitt, it is you."

"A moot point. If it were a work of historical art, a national treasure, my State Department would no doubt see it off on the next ship back to Murmansk. But not when it's the prime ingredient for a strategic weapon. If our roles were reversed, Prevlov, you wouldn't give it away —any more than we would."

"Then it must be destroyed."

"You're wrong. A weapon that does not take lives, but simply protects them, must never be destroyed."

"Your kind of sanctimonious philosophy simply affirms what our leaders have known all along. You cannot win against us. Someday, in the not too distant future, your precious experiment in democracy will go the way of the Greek senate. A piece of an era for students of communism to study, nothing more."

"Don't hold your breath, Comrade. Your kind will have to show a lot more finesse before you can run the world."

"Read your history," Prevlov said with an ominous smile. "The people whom the sophisticated nations down through the centuries have referred to as the barbarians have always won in the end."

Pitt smiled back courteously as the SEALs herded Prevlov, Merker, and Drummer up the grand staircase to a stateroom where they would be secured under heavy guard.

But Pitt's smile was not genuine. Prevlov was right.

The barbarians always won in the end.

5

Southby

68

Hurricane Amanda was dying, slowly but inevitably. What would long be remembered as the Great Blow of 1988 had cut its devastating swath across three thousand miles of ocean in three and a half days, and it had yet to deliver its final apocalyptic blow. Like the final burst of a supernova before disintegrating into obscurity, it suddenly swung on an eastward track and slammed into the Avalon Peninsula of Newfoundland, lashing the coast from Cape Race north to Pouch Cove.

In minutes, one town after another was inundated by the fallout from the storm's cloud mass. Several small seashore villages were swept out to sea by the runoff that came thundering down into the valleys. Fishing boats were driven onto land and battered into unrecognizable, shattered hulks. Roofs were blown off downtown buildings in St. John's as its city streets were turned into rushing rivers from the deluge. Water and electricity were cut off for days and, until rescue ships arrived, food was at a premium and had to be rationed.

No hurricane on record had ever unleashed such raw fury that its winds would carry it so far, so fast with such terrible velocity. No one would ever evaluate the enormous cost of the damage. Estimates ran as high as $250 million. Of this, $155 million represented the almost totally destroyed Newfoundland fishing fleets. Nine ships were lost at sea; six with no survivors. The death toll behind the storm's wake ran between 300 and 325.

In the early hours of Friday morning, Dr. Ryan Prescott sat alone in the main office of the NUMA Hurricane Center. Hurricane Amanda had finally run her course, accomplished her destruction, taken her lives, and only now was she dissipating over the Gulf of St. Lawrence. The battle was over; there was nothing more the weathermen at the center could do. After seventy-two hours of frenzied tracking and nonsleep, they had all straggled home to bed.

Prescott stared through tired and bloodshot eyes at the desks strewn with charts, data tables, computer readout sheets, and half-empty coffee cups, the floors carpeted with sheets of paper filled with notations and the strange looking symbols common to meteorologists. He stared at the giant wall map and silently cursed the storm. The sudden swing to eastward had caught them all by surprise. A completely illogical pattern; it was unparalleled in hurricane history. No storm on record had ever behaved so erratically.

If only it had given some hint of its impending deviation, some minute clue as to its fanatical behavior, they might have better prepared the people of Newfoundland for the onslaught. At least half, a hundred and fifty lives, might have been spared. A hundred and fifty men, women, and children might have been alive now if the finest scientific sources available for weather prediction had not been swept aside like so much hokum at Mother Nature's capricious whim.

Prescott rose and took his last look at the wall chart before the janitors came and erased Hurricane Amanda out of existence, and wiped clean her confounding track in preparation for her as yet unborn descendant. One small notation out of all the rest caught his eye. It was a small cross, labeled "*Titanic.*"

The last report he'd had from NUMA headquarters in Washington was that the derelict was in tow by two Navy tugs that were desperately attempting to drag her out from under the path of the hurricane. Nothing more had been heard of her for twenty-four hours.

Prescott raised a cup of cold coffee in a toast. "To the *Titanic*," he said aloud in that empty room. "May you have taken every punch Amanda threw at you and still spit in her eye."

He grimaced as he downed the stale coffee. Then he turned and walked out of the room into the early-morning dampness.

69

At first light the *Titanic* still lived. There was no rhyme or reason for her continued existence. She still wallowed aimlessly broadside-on to the sea and wind, trapped in the churning turmoil of the tormented waves left in the wake of the departing hurricane.

Like a dazed fighter taking a fearful beating while hanging on the ropes, she rose drunkenly over the thirty-foot crests, shouldering each one, taking salt spray across her Boat Deck, and then struggling free and somehow staggering upright in time for the next assault.

To Captain Parotkin, as he stared through his binoculars, the *Titanic* looked a doomed ship. Her rusty old hull plates had been subjected to a stress far beyond anything he thought they could stand. He could see the popped rivets and opened seams, and he guessed that she was taking water in a hundred places along her hull. What he could not see were the exhausted men of the salvage crew, the SEALs, and the Navy tugmen laboring shoulder to shoulder deep in the black hell under the waterline in a desperate effort to keep the derelict afloat.

From Parotkin's viewpoint, safe from the elements inside the wheelhouse of the *Mikhail Kurkov,* it seemed a miracle that the *Titanic* hadn't vanished during the night. Yet she still clung to life, even though she was down a good twenty feet at the bow and was listing nearly thirty degrees to starboard.

"Any word from Captain Prevlov?" he asked without taking his eyes from the glasses.

"Nothing, sir," answered his first officer.

"I fear the worst has happened," Parotkin said. "I see no sign that Prevlov is in command of the derelict."

"There, sir," the first officer said pointing, "atop the remains of the aft mast. It looks like a Russian pennant."

Parotkin studied the tiny frayed cloth through the glasses as it snapped in the wind. "Unfortunately, the star on the pennant is white rather than the red of our Soviet ensign." He sighed. "I must assume that the boarding mission has failed."

"Perhaps Comrade Prevlov has had no time to report his situation."

"There is no time left. American search planes will be here within the hour." Parotkin pounded his fist in frustration on the bridge counter. "Damn Prevlov!" he muttered angrily. " 'Let us fervently hope our final option will not be required'; his exact words. He is the fortunate one. He may even be dead, and it is I who must take the responsibility for destroying the *Titanic* and all who remain on board her."

The first officer's face paled, his body stiffened. "There is no alternative, sir?"

Parotkin shook his head. "The orders were clear. We must obliterate the ship rather than let her fall into the hands of the Americans."

Parotkin took a linen handkerchief from his pocket and wiped his eyes. "Have the crew ready the nuclear missile carrier and steer a course ten miles north of the *Titanic* for our firing position."

The first officer stared at Parotkin for a long moment, his face void of expression. Then he slowly wheeled and made for the radio telephone and ordered the helmsman to steer fifteen degrees to the north.

Thirty minutes later, all was in readiness. The *Mikhail Kurkov* dug her bows into the swells at the position laid for the missile launch as Parotkin stood behind the radar operator. "Any hard sightings?" he asked.

"Eight jet aircraft, a hundred and twenty miles west, closing rapidly."

"Surface vessels?"

"Two small ships bearing two-four-five, twenty-one miles southwest."

"That would be the tugs returning," the first officer said.

Parotkin nodded. "It's the aircraft that concern me. They will be over us in ten minutes. Is the nuclear warhead armed?"

"Yes, sir."

"Then begin the countdown."

The first officer gave the order over the phone and then they moved outside and watched from the starboard bridge wing as the forward cargo hatch swung smoothly aside and a twenty-six foot Stoski surface-to-surface missile slowly rose from its concealed tube into the gusty dawn air.

"One minute to firing," came a missile technician's voice over the bridge speaker.

Parotkin aimed his glasses at the *Titanic* in the distance. He could just make out her outline against the gray clouds that crawled along the horizon. A barely perceptible shiver gripped his body. His eyes reflected a distant sad look. He knew he would be forever cursed among sailors as the captain who sent the helpless and resurrected ocean liner back to her grave beneath the sea. He was standing braced and waiting for the roar of the missile's rocket engine and then the great explosion that would pulverize the *Titanic* into thousands of molten particles when he heard the sound of running footsteps from the wheelhouse, and the radio operator burst onto the bridge wing.

"Captain!" he blurted. "An urgent signal from an American submarine!"

"Thirty seconds to firing," the voice droned over the intercom.

There was unmistakable panic in the radio operator's eyes as he thrust the message into Parotkin's hands. It read:

USS DRAGONFISH TO USSR MIKHAIL KURKOV　　DERELICT VESSEL RMS TITANIC UNDER PROTECTION OF UNITED STATES NAVY　　ANY OVERT ACT OF AGGRESSION ON YOUR PART WILL RESULT IN IMMEDI-ATE REPEAT IMMEDIATE RETALIATORY ATTACK
　　　　　　　—SIGNED CAPTAIN USS SUBMARINE DRAGONFISH

"Ten seconds and counting," came the disembodied voice of the missile technician over the speaker. "Seven . . . six . . ."

Parotkin looked up with the clear, unworried expression of a man who has just received a million rubles through the mail.

". . . five . . . four . . . three . . ."

"Stop the countdown," he ordered in precise tones, so there could be no misunderstanding, no misinterpretation.

"Stop countdown," the first officer repeated into the bridge phone, his face beaded with sweat. "And secure the missile."

"Good," Parotkin said curtly. A smile spread across his face. "Not exactly what I was told to do, but I think Soviet Naval authorities will see it my way. After all, the *Mikhail Kurkov* is the finest ship of her kind in the world. We wouldn't want to throw her away because of a senseless and foolish order from a man who is undoubtedly dead, now would we?"

"I am in complete accord." The first officer smiled back. "Our superiors will also be interested to learn that in spite of all our sophisticated detection gear, we failed to discover the presence of an alien submarine practically on our doorstep. American undersea penetration methods must truly be highly advanced."

"I feel sure the Americans will be just as interested in learning that our oceanographic research vessels carry concealed missiles."

"Your orders, sir?"

Parotkin watched the Stoski missile as it sank back into its tube. "Set a course for home." He turned and peered across the sea in the direction of the *Titanic*. What had happened to Prevlov and his men? Were they alive or dead? Would he ever know the true facts?

Overhead the clouds began turning from gray to white and the wind dropped to a brisk breeze. A solitary sea gull emerged from the brightening sky and began circling the Soviet ship. Then, as if heeding a more urgent call to the south, it dipped its wings and flew off toward the *Titanic*.

70

"We're done in," Spencer said in a voice so low that Pitt wasn't sure he heard him.

"Say again."

"We're done in," he repeated through slack lips. His face was smeared with oil and a rustlike slime. "It's a hopeless case. We've plugged most of the holes Drummer opened with his cutting torch, but the sea has battered the hull all to hell and the old girl is taking water faster than a sieve."

"We've got to keep her on the surface until the tugs return," Pitt said. "If they can add their pumps to ours we can stay ahead of the leaks until the damage can be patched."

"It's a damned miracle that she didn't go down hours ago."

"How much time can you give me?" Pitt demanded.

Spencer stared wearily down at the water sloshing around his ankles. "The pump engines are running on fumes now. When their fuel tanks are sucked dry, the pumps will die. A cold, hard, sad fact." He looked up into Pitt's face. "An hour, maybe an hour and a half. I can't promise any more than that when the pumps go."

"And if you had enough fuel to keep the diesels going?"

"I could probably keep her on the surface without assistance until noon," Spencer answered.

"How much fuel will it take?"

"Two hundred gallons would do nicely."

They both looked up as Giordino plunged down a companionway and splashed into the water covering the deck of the No. 4 boiler room.

"Talk about frustration," he moaned. "There are eight aircraft up there, circling the ship. Six Navy fighters and two radar recon planes. I've tried everything except standing on my head and exposing myself and all they do is wave every time they make a pass."

Pitt shook his head in mock sadness. "Remind me never to play charades on your team."

"I'm open for suggestions," Giordino said. "Suppose you tell me how to notify some guy who's flying by at four hundred miles an hour that we need help, and lots of it?"

Pitt scratched his chin. "There's got to be a practical solution."

"Sure," Giordino said sarcastically. "Just call the Automobile Club for a service call."

Pitt and Spencer stared with widened eyes at each other. The same thought had suddenly occurred to them in the same instant.

"Brilliance," Spencer said, "sheer brilliance."

"If we can't get to a service station," Pitt said grinning, "then the service station must come to us."

Giordino looked lost. "Fatigue has queered your minds," he said. "Where are you going to find a pay phone? What will you use for a radio? The Russians smashed ours, the one in the helicopter is soaked through, and Prevlov's transmitter caught two bullets during the brawl." He shook his head. "And you can forget those flyboys upstairs. Without a brush and bucket of paint, there's no way to get a message across to their eager little minds."

"That's your problem," Spencer said loftily. "You always go around looking up when you should be looking down."

Pitt leaned over and picked up a sledge hammer that was lying among a pile of tools. "This should do the trick," he said casually, swinging the sledge against one of the *Titanic*'s hull plates, sending a cacophony of echoes throughout the boiler room.

Spencer dropped wearily onto a raised boiler grating. "They ain't going to believe this."

"Oh I don't know," Pitt managed between swings. "Jungle telegraph. It always used to work in the Congo."

"Giordino was probably right. Fatigue has queered our minds."

Pitt ignored Spencer and kept hammering away. After a few minutes, he paused a moment to get a new grip on the sledge handle. "Let us hope and pray that one of the natives has his ear to the ground," he said between pants. And then he went on hammering.

Of the two sonar operators who were on watch aboard the submarine *Dragonfish,* the one tuned into the passive listening system was leaning forward toward his panel, his head cocked to one side, his mind intent on analyzing the strange beat that emitted through the earphones. Then he gave a slight shake of his head and held up the earphones for the officer who was standing at his shoulder.

"At first I thought it was a hammerhead shark," the sonarman said. "They make a funny pounding noise. But this has a definite metallic ring to it."

The officer pressed the headset against one ear. Then his eyes took on a puzzled look. "It sounds like an SOS."

"That's how I read it, sir. Someone is knocking out a distress call against their hull."

"Where is it coming from?"

The sonarman turned a miniature steering wheel that activated the sensors in the bow of the sub and eyed the panel in front of him. "The contact is three-zero-seven degrees, two thousand yards north of west. It has to be the *Titanic*, sir. With the departure of the *Mikhail Kurkov,* she's the only surface craft left in the area."

The officer handed back the earphones, turned from the sonar compartment, and made his way up a wide curving stairway into the conning tower, the nerve center of the *Dragonfish.* He approached a medium-height, round-faced man with a graying mustache, who wore the oak leaves of a commander on his collar.

"It's the *Titanic* all right, sir. She's hammering out an SOS."

"There's no mistake?"

"No, sir. The contact is firm." The officer paused and then asked, "Are we going to respond?"

The commander looked thoughtful for a few moments. "Our orders were to deliver the SEAL and fend off the *Mikhail Kurkov.* We were also to remain obscure in case the Russians decide to make an end run with one of their own submarines. We'd be in poor position to protect the derelict if we were to surface and move off station."

"During our last sighting, she looked to be in pretty rough shape. Maybe she's going down."

"If that was the case, her crew would be screaming for help over every frequency on their radio—" The commander hesitated, his eyes narrowing. He stepped over to the radio room and leaned in.

"What time was the last communication sent from the *Titanic*?"

One of the radio operators scanned a sheet in a log book. "A few minutes shy of eighteen hundred hours yesterday, Commander. They requested an up-to-the-minute report of the hurricane's speed and direction."

The commander nodded and turned back to the officer. "They haven't transmitted for over twelve hours. Could be their radio is out."

"It's quite possible."

"We'd better have a look," the commander said. "Up periscope."

The periscope tubing hummed slowly into the raised position. The commander gripped the handles and stared through the eyepiece.

"Looks quiet enough," he said. "She's got a heavy list to starboard and she's down by the bows, but not bad enough to be considered dangerous yet. No distress flags flying. No one in sight on her decks— wait a moment, I take that back. There's a man atop the bridgehouse roof." The commander increased the magnification. "Good lord!" he muttered. "It's a woman."

The officer stared at him with a disbelieving expression. "You did say a woman, sir?"

"See for yourself."

The officer saw for himself. There was indeed a young blond woman above the *Titanic*'s bridgehouse. She seemed to be waving a brassiere.

Ten minutes later, the *Dragonfish* had surfaced and was lying under the shadow of the *Titanic*.

Thirty minutes later, reserve fuel from the sub's auxiliary diesel engine was coursing through a pipe that arched across the still thrashing swells and passed neatly into a hastily cut hole in the *Titanic*'s hull.

71

"It's from the *Dragonfish*," Admiral Kemper said, reading the latest in a long line of communications. "Her captain has sent a work party aboard the *Titanic* to assist Pitt and his salvage crew. He states that the derelict should remain afloat, even with numerous leaks, during the tow—providing, of course, she's not struck by another hurricane."

"Thank God for small favors," Marshall Collins exhaled between yawns.

"He also reports," Kemper went on, "that Mrs. Seagram is on board the *Titanic* and is in rare stage form, whatever that means."

Mel Donner moved out of the bathroom, a towel still draped over his arm. "Would you repeat that, Admiral?"

"The captain of the *Dragonfish* says that Mrs. Dana Seagram is alive and well."

Donner rushed over and shook Seagram, who was sleeping fitfully on the couch. "Gene! Wake up! They've found Dana! She's all right!"

Seagram's eyes blinked open and for long seconds he looked up at Donner, astonishment slowly spreading across his face. "Dana . . . Dana is alive?"

"Yes, she must have been on the *Titanic* during the storm."

"But how did she get there?"

"We don't know all the details yet. We'll just have to wait it out. But the important thing is that Dana is safe and the *Titanic* is still afloat."

Seagram hung his head in his hands and sat there huddled and shrunken. He began sobbing quietly.

Admiral Kemper was thankful for the distraction when a very tired Commander Keith entered and handed him another signal. "This one's from Admiral Sandecker," Kemper said. "I think you'll be interested in what he has to say, Mr. Nicholson."

Warren Nicholson and Marshall Collins both eased away from Seagram and gathered around Kemper's desk.

"Sandecker says, 'Visiting relatives have been entertained and furnished with guest bedroom. Got something in my eye during the party last night but enjoyed belting out good old song favorites like "Silver Threads among the Gold." Say hello to Cousin Warren and tell him I have a present to give him. Having wonderful time. Wish you were all here. Signed Sandecker.' "

"It seems the admiral has a strange way with words," said the President. "Just what in hell is it he's trying to get across?"

Kemper stared at him sheepishly. "The Russians apparently boarded during the eye of the hurricane."

"*Apparently,*" the President said icily.

" 'Silver Threads among the Gold,' " Nicholson said excitedly. "Silver and Gold. They've caught the two espionage agents."

"And your present, Cousin Warren," Collins said, grinning with every tooth, "must be none other than Captain André Prevlov."

"It's imperative that I get on board the derelict as soon as possible," Nicholson said to Kemper. "How soon can you arrange transportation for me, Admiral?"

Kemper's hand was already reaching for the phone. "Inside thirty minutes I can have you on a Navy jet that will land you on the *Beecher's Island*. From there you can take a helicopter to the *Titanic*."

The President stepped over to a large window and gazed out at the rising sun as it crept above the eastern horizon and fingered its rays across the lazy waters of the Potomac. He yawned a long comfortable yawn.

72

Dana leaned over the forward railing of the *Titanic*'s bridge and closed her eyes. The ocean breeze whipped her honey hair and tingled the skin on her upturned face. She felt soothed and free and completely relaxed. It was as though she were flying.

She knew now that she could never go back and slip into the painted puppet that had been the Dana Seagram of two days ago. She had made up her mind: she would divorce Gene. Nothing between them mattered any more, at least to her. The girl he had loved was dead, never to return. She reveled in the knowledge. It was her rebirth. To begin again, start fresh with no holds barred.

"A dollar for your thoughts."

She opened her eyes and was greeted by the grinning and freshly shaven face of Dirk Pitt.

"A dollar? I thought it used to be a penny."

"Inflation strikes everything, sooner or later."

They stood for a while without saying anything and watched the *Wallace* and the *Morse* as they strained at the great leash that led to the *Titanic*'s bow. Chief Bascom and his men were checking the tow cable and dabbing grease to the fair-lead to ease the chafing. The chief looked up and waved to them.

"I wish this voyage would never end," Dana murmured as they both waved back. "It's so strange and yet so wonderful." She turned suddenly and laid her hand on his. "Promise me we'll never see New York. Promise me that we'll sail on forever, like the *Flying Dutchman*."

"We'll sail on forever."

She flung her arms around his neck and pressed her body against his. "Dirk, Dirk!" she whispered urgently. "Nothing makes any sense any more. I want you. I want you now, and I don't really know why."

"It's because of where you are," Pitt said quietly.

He took her by the hand and led her down the grand staircase and into one of the two parlour suite bedrooms on B Deck. "There you are, madame. The finest suite of rooms on the entire ship. Cost for a one-way voyage came to better than four thousand dollars. Those were, of course, 1912 prices. However, in honor of the light in your eyes, I'll provide you with a handsome discount." He swept her up and carried her to the bed. It had been cleaned of the slime and rot and was covered with several blankets.

Dana looked at the bed with wise eyes. "You prepared this?"

"Let's just say that like the little old ant who moved the rubber tree plant, I had high hopes."

"You know what you are?"

"A bastard, a lecher, a satyr—I could think of a dozen apt descriptions."

She looked at him with a secret, womanly smile. "No, you're none of those. Even a satyr would not have been so thoughtful."

He pulled her lips to his and kissed her so hard she moaned.

Her performance in bed fooled him. He expected a body that would merely give response. Instead, he found himself merged with thrashing, undulating waves of flesh, piercing screams that he muffled with his hand, nails that dug oozing red trenches in his back, and finally soft, wet sobbings into his neck. He couldn't help wondering if all wives blossom with such abandon when they make love for the first time with someone other than their husbands. The storm lasted for nearly an hour, and the humid perfume of sweating skin began to soak the air of that old rotted, ghostly bedroom.

Finally she pushed him away and sat up. She raised her knees and hunched herself over them, feet crossed. "How was I?"

"Like a spastic tiger," Pitt said.

"I didn't know it could be like this."

"I wish I had a dime for every girl who said those very same words every time she turned on."

"You don't know what it's like to have your guts churning in both agony and delight at the same time."

"I dare say I don't. A woman's release burns from the inside. A man's erotic senses are mostly exterior. Anyway you look at it, sex is a female's game."

"What do you know about the President?" she suddenly asked in a soft nostalgic tone.

Pitt looked at her in amused surprise. "The President? What made you think of him at a time like this?"

"I hear he's a real man."

"I couldn't say. I've never slept with him."

She ignored his remark. "If we had a woman President and she wanted to make love to you, what would you do?"

"My country right or wrong," Pitt said. "Where is all this talk leading?"

"Just answer the question. Would you go to bed with her?"

"Depends?"

"On what?"

"President or not, I couldn't make my gun stand at attention if she was seventy, fat, and had skin like a prune. That's why men never make good prostitutes."

Dana smiled slowly and closed her eyes. "Make love to me again."

"Why? So you can let your imagination run wild and fancy that you're being laid by our Commander-in-Chief?"

Her eyes narrowed. "Does that bother you?"

"Two can play the same game. I'll just pretend that you're Ashley Fleming."

73

Prevlov looked up from his huddled position on the floor of stateroom C-95 as the SEAL guarding the passageway outside turned the newly oiled lock and swung the door open. The SEAL, his M-24 held at the ready, visually checked Prevlov, and then stepped aside to allow another man to enter.

He was carrying an attaché case and wore a business suit that begged to be pressed. A faint smile crossed his lips as Prevlov studied him with a speculative gaze of surprised recognition.

"Captain Prevlov, I am Warren Nicholson."

"I know," Prevlov said as he uncoiled to his feet and gave a very correct half-bow. "I was not prepared to entertain the Chief Director of the Central Intelligence Agency himself. At least not under these rather awkward circumstances."

"I've come personally to escort you to the United States."

"I am flattered."

"It is we who are flattered, Captain Prevlov. You are considered a very big catch indeed."

"Then it is to be an internationally publicized trial, complete with grave accusations against my government for attempted piracy on the high seas."

Nicholson smiled again. "No, except for a few high-ranking members of your government and mine, I'm afraid your defection will remain a well-kept secret."

Prevlov squinted. "Defection?" This was clearly not what he had expected.

Nicholson nodded without answering.

"There is no method by which you can make me willingly defect," Prevlov said grimly. "I shall deny it at every opportunity."

"A noble gesture." Nicholson shrugged. "However, since there will be no trial and no interrogation, a request for political asylum becomes your only escape clause."

"You said, 'no interrogation.' I must accuse you of lying, Mr. Nicholson. No good intelligence service would ever pass up the chance of prying out the knowledge a man of my position could provide them."

"What knowledge?" Nicholson said. "You can't tell us anything that we don't already know."

Prevlov's mind was off-balance. Perspective, he thought. He must gain a perspective. There was only one way the Americans could have gained possession of the mass of Soviet intelligence secrets that were locked away in the files in his office in Moscow. The middle of the puzzle was incomplete, but the borders were neatly locked into place. He met Nicholson's steady gaze and spoke quietly. "Lieutenant Marganin is one of your people." It was more statement than question.

"Yes." Nicholson nodded. "His name is Harry Koskoski, and he was born in Newark, New Jersey."

"Not possible," Prevlov said. "I personally checked every phase of Pavel Marganin's life. He was born and raised in Komsomolsk-na-Amure. His family were tailors."

"True, the real Marganin was a native Russian."

"Then your man is a double, a plant?"

"We arranged it four years ago when one of your *Kashin*-class missile destroyers exploded and sank in the Indian Ocean. Marganin was one of the few survivors. He was discovered in the water by an Exxon oil tanker, but died shortly before the ship docked in Honolulu. It was a rare opportunity, and we had to work fast. Of all our Russian-speaking agents, Koskoski came the closest to Marganin's physical features. We surgically altered his face to make it look as though it had been disfigured in the explosion and then airlifted him to a small, out-of-the-way island two hundred miles from where your ship sank. When our bogus Soviet seaman was finally discovered by native fishermen and returned to Russia, he was delirious and suffering from an acute attack of amnesia."

"I know the rest," Prevlov said solemnly. "We not only repaired his face through plastic surgery to that of the genuine Marganin, but we re-educated him to his own personal history as well."

"That's pretty much the story."

"A brilliant coup, Mr. Nicholson."

"Coming from one of the most respected men in Soviet intelligence, I consider that a rare compliment indeed."

"Then this whole scheme to place me on the *Titanic* was hatched by the CIA and carried through by Marganin."

"Koskoski, alias Marganin, was certain you would accept the plan, and you did."

Prevlov gazed at the deck. He might have known, he might have guessed, should have been suspicious from the beginning that Marganin was slowly and intricately positioning his neck on the headman's block. He should never have fallen for it, never; but his vanity had been his downfall, and he accepted it.

"Where does this all lead?" Prevlov asked bleakly.

"By now Marganin has produced solid proof of your—if you'll pardon the expression—traitorous activities and has also proven, aided by planted evidence, that you intended for the *Titanic* mission to fail from the start. You see, Captain, the trail leading to your defection has been carefully mapped for nearly two years. You yourself helped matters considerably with your fondness for expensive refinements. Your superiors can draw but one conclusion from your actions: you sold out for a very high price."

"And if I deny it?"

"Who would believe you? I venture to say that your name is already on the Soviet liquidation list."

Then what's to become of me now?"

"You have two choices. One, we can set you free after a proper period of time."

"I wouldn't last a week. I am well aware of the KGB assassin network."

"Your second choice is to cooperate with us." Nicholson paused, hesitated, then looked directly at Prevlov. "You're a brilliant man, Captain, the best in your field. We don't like to let good brains go to waste. I don't have to paint you a picture of your value to the Western intelligence community. That's why it's my intention to set you up in charge of a new task force. A line of work you should find right up your alley."

"I suppose I should be grateful for that," Prevlov said dryly.

"Your facial appearance will be altered, of course. You'll get a cram course in English and American idioms along with our history, sports, music, and entertainment. In the end, there won't be the slightest trace of your former shell for the KGB to home in on."

Interest began to form in Prevlov's eyes.

"Your salary will be forty thousand a year, plus expenses and a car."

"Forty thousand dollars?" Prevlov asked, trying to sound casual.

"That will buy quite a bit of Bombay Gin." Nicholson grinned like a wolf sitting down to dinner with a wary rabbit. "I think that if you really try, Captain Prevlov, you might come to enjoy the pleasures of our Western-style decadence. Don't you agree?"

Prevlov said nothing for several moments. But the choice was obvious: constant fear versus a long and pleasurable life. "You win, Nicholson."

Nicholson shook hands and was mildly surprised to see tears welling in Prevlov's eyes.

74

The final hours of the long tow brought a clear and sunny sky with a wandering wind that gently nudged the long ocean swells shoreward and brushed their green curving backs.

Ever since dawn, four Coast Guard ships had been busy riding herd on the huge fleet of pleasure craft that darted in and out vying for a closer look at the sea-worn decks and superstructure of the hulk.

High over the crowded waters, hordes of light aircraft and helicopters swarmed like hornets, their pilots jockeying to give photographers and cameramen the perfect angle from which to shoot the *Titanic*.

From five thousand feet higher, the still listing ship looked like a macabre carcass that was under attack from all sides by armadas of gnats and white ants.

The *Thomas J. Morse* reeled in her tow wire from the bow of the *Samuel R. Wallace* and fell back to the derelict's stern, where she attached a hawser and then eased astern to assist in steering the unwieldy bulk through the Verrazano Narrows and up the East River to the old Brooklyn Navy Yard. Several harbor tugs also appeared and stood by to lend a hand, if called upon, when Commander Butera gave orders to shorten the main tow cable to two hundred yards.

The pilot boat arrived within inches of the bulwarks of the *Wallace* and the pilot leaped aboard. Then it passed on by and thumped against the rusty plates of the *Titanic*, separated only by worn truck tires that hung along the smaller boat's freeboard. Within half a minute, the New York Harbor Chief Pilot had clutched a rope ladder and was scrambling up to the cargo deck.

Pitt and Sandecker greeted him and then led the way up to the port bridge wing, where the chief pilot placed both hands on the railing as though he were part of it and solemnly nodded for the tow to carry on. Pitt waved and Butera punched his whistle in reply. Then the tug commander ordered "slow ahead" and aimed the bow of the *Wallace* into the main channel under the Verrazano Bridge that arches from Long Island to Staten Island.

As the strange convoy probed its nose into Upper New York Bay, Butera began pacing from one side of the tug's bridge to the other, studying the hulk, the wind and the current, and the tow cable with the dedication of a brain surgeon who is about to perform a delicate operation.

Since the night before, thousands of people had lined the waterfront. Manhattan had come to a standstill, streets emptied and office buildings suddenly became silent, as workers crowded the windows in hushed awe as the tow crawled up the harbor.

On the shore of Staten Island, Peter Hull, a reporter from *The New York Times,* began his story:

> Ghosts do exist. I know, I saw one in the mists of morning. Like some grotesque phantom that had been rejected from hell, she passed before my unbelieving eyes. Surrounded by the invisible pall of bygone tragedy, shrouded in the souls of her dead, she was truly an awesome relic from a past age. You could not lay your eyes upon her and not sense pride and sorrow together. . . .

A CBS commentator expressed a more journalistic view: "The *Titanic* completed her maiden voyage today, seventy-six years after departing the dock at Southampton, England. . . ." By noon the *Titanic* was edging past the Statue of Liberty and a vast sea of spectators on the Battery. No one on shore spoke above a whisper, and the city became strangely silent; only an occasional toot from a taxi horn gave any hint of normal activity. It was as though the whole of New York City had been picked up and placed in a vast cathedral.

Many of the watchers wept openly. Among them were three of the passengers who had survived that tragic night so long ago. The air seemed heavy and hard to breathe. Most people, describing their feelings later, were surprised to recall nothing but an odd sense of numbness, as though they had been temporarily paralyzed and struck dumb. Most that is, except a rugged fireman by the name of Arthur Mooney.

Mooney was the captain of one of the New York Harbor fireboats. A big, mischief-eyed Irishman born of the city, and a seagoing fire-eater for nineteen years. He slammed a massive fist against the binnacle and shook off the spell. Then he shouted to his crew.

"Up off your asses, boys. You're not department-store dummies." His voice carried into every corner of the boat. Mooney hardly ever required the services of a bullhorn. "This here's a ship arrivin' on her maiden voyage, ain't she? Then let's show her a good old-fashioned traditional New York welcome."

"But skipper," a crew member protested, "it's not like she was the *QE II* or the *Normandie* comin' up the channel for the first time. That thing is nothin' but a wasted hulk, a ship of the dead."

"Wasted hulk, your ass," Mooney shouted. "That ship you see there is the most famous liner of all time. So she's a little dilapidated, and she's arrivin' a tad late. So who gives a damn? Turn on the hoses and hit the siren."

It was a re-enactment of the *Titanic*'s raising all over again, but on a much grander scale. As the water spouted in great sheets over Mooney's fireboat, and his boat whistle reverberated off the city's skyscrapers, another fireboat followed his example, and another. Then whistles on docked freighters began to scream. Then the horns of cars lined up along the shores of New Jersey, Manhattan, and Brooklyn joined the outpouring of noise followed by the cheers and yells from a million throats.

What had begun with the insignificant shrill of a single whistle now built and built until it was a thunderous bedlam of sound that shook the ground and rattled every window in the city. It was a moment that echoed across every ocean of the world.

The *Titanic* had made port.

75

Thousands of greeters jammed the dock where the *Titanic* was tied up. The swarming antlike mass was made up of newspeople, national dignitaries, cordons of harried policemen, and a multitude of uninvited who climbed the shipyard fence. Any attempt at security was futile.

A battery of reporters and cameramen stormed up the makeshift gangplank and surrounded Admiral Sandecker, who stood like a victorious Caesar, on the steps of the main staircase rising from the reception room on D Deck.

This was Sandecker's big moment and a team of wild horses couldn't have dragged him off the *Titanic* this day. He never missed an opportunity to snatch good publicity in the name of the National Underwater and Marine Agency, and this was one occasion where he was going to milk every line of newsprint, every second of national television, for all they were worth. He enthralled the reporters with highly colored exploits of the salvage crew and stared at the mobile camera units, and smiled and smiled and smiled. The admiral was in his own paradise.

Pitt could have cared less about the fanfare; his idea of paradise at the moment was a shower and a clean, soft bed. He pushed his way down the gangplank to the dock and melted into the crowd. He thought he'd almost gotten clear when a TV commentator rushed forward and thrust a microphone under his nose.

"Hey, fella, are you a member of the *Titanic*'s salvage crew?"

"No, I work for the shipyard," Pitt said, waving like a yokel at the camera.

The commentator's face fell. "Cut it, Joe," he yelled to his cameraman. "We grabbed a bummer." Then he turned and shoved his way toward the ship, shouting for the crowd to keep their feet off his mike cord.

Six blocks, and a whole half-hour later, Pitt finally found a cab driver who was more interested in hauling a fare than in ogling the derelict.

"Where to?" the driver asked.

Pitt hesitated, looking down at his grimy, sweat-stained shirt and pants under the torn and just as grimy windbreaker. He didn't need a mirror to see the bloodshot eyes and five o'clock shadow. He could easily imagine himself as the perfect reflection of a Bowery wino. But then he figured, what the hell, he'd just stepped off what was once the most prestigious ocean liner in the world.

"What's the most luxurious and expensive hotel in town?"

"The Pierre, on Fifth Avenue and Sixty-First, ain't cheap."

"The Pierre it is then."

The driver looked over his shoulder, studied Pitt, and wrinkled his nose. Then he shrugged and pulled into the traffic. He took less than a half hour to reach the curb in front of the Pierre, overlooking Central Park.

Pitt paid off the cabby and walked through the revolving doors and up to the desk.

The clerk gave him a look of disgust that was a classic. "I'm sorry, sir," he said haughtily before Pitt could open his mouth. "We're all filled up."

Pitt knew it would only be a matter of minutes before a mob of reporters discovered his whereabouts if he gave his real name. He wasn't ready to face the ordeal of celebrity status yet. All he wanted was uninterrupted sleep.

"I am not what I appear," Pitt said, trying to sound indignant. "I happen to be Professor R. Malcolm Smythe, author and archeologist. I have just stepped off the plane after a four-month dig up the Amazon, and I haven't had time to change. My man will be here shortly with my luggage from the airport."

The desk clerk was instantly transformed into peaches and cream. "Oh, I am sorry, Professor Smythe, I didn't recognize you. However, we're still filled up. The city is crowded with people who came to see the arrival of the *Titanic*. I'm sure you understand."

It was a masterful performance. He didn't buy Pitt or one word of his fanciful tale.

"I'll vouch for the professor," said a voice behind Pitt. "Give him your best suite and charge it to this address."

A card was thrown on the counter. The desk clerk picked it up and read it and lit up like a roman candle. Then with a flourish he laid a registration card before Pitt and produced a room key as if by sleight of hand.

Pitt slowly turned and met a face that was every bit as worn and haggard as his. The lips were turned up in a crooked smile of understanding, but the eyes were dulled with the lost and vacant stare of a zombie. It was Gene Seagram.

"How did you track me down so fast?" Pitt asked. He was lying in a bathtub nursing a vodka on the rocks. Seagram sat across the bathroom on the john.

"No great exercise in intuition," he said. "I saw you leave the shipyard and followed you."

"I thought you'd be dancing on the *Titanic* about now."

"The ship means nothing to me. My only concern is the byzanium in its vault, and I've been told it will be another forty-eight hours before the derelict can be moved into dry dock and the wreckage in the cargo hold removed."

"Then why don't you relax for a couple of days and have some fun. In a few weeks your problems will be over. The Sicilian Project will be off the drawing boards and a working reality."

Seagram's eyes closed for a moment. "I wanted to talk to you," he said quietly. "I wanted to talk to you about Dana."

Oh God, Pitt thought, here it comes. How do you keep a straight face, knowing you made love to the man's wife. Up to now, it had been all he could do to maintain a casual tone in his conversation. "How is she getting along after her ordeal?"

"All right, I suppose." Seagram shrugged.

"You suppose? She was airlifted off the ship by the Navy two days ago. Haven't you seen her since she came ashore?"

"She refuses to see me . . . said it was all over between us."

Pitt contemplated the vodka in the glass. "So it's hearts-and-flowers time. So who needs her? If I were you, Seagram, I'd find myself the most expensive hooker in town, charge her off on your government expense account, and forget Dana."

"You don't understand. I love her."

"God, you sound like a letter to Ann Landers." Pitt reached for the bottle on the tiled floor and freshened his drink. "Look, Seagram, you're a pretty decent guy underneath your pompous, bullshit façade. And who knows, you may go down in history as the great merciful scientist who saved mankind from a nuclear holocaust. You've still got enough looks to attract a woman, and I'm willing to bet that when you clean off your desk in Washington and bid a fond farewell to government service you'll be a rich man. So don't expect tears and violins from me over a lost love. You've got it made."

"What good is it without the woman I love?"

"I see I'm not getting through to you." Pitt was one third into the bottle and a warm glow had begun to course through his body. "Why throw yourself down the sewer over a broad who suddenly thinks she's found the fountain of youth. If she's gone, she's gone. Men come crawling back, not women. They persevere. There isn't a man alive a woman can't persevere into the grave. Forget Dana, Seagram. There are millions of other fish in the stream. If you need the phony security of a pair of tits making your bed and fixing your supper, go hire a maid; they're cheaper and a hell of a lot less trouble in the long run."

"So now you think you're Sigmund Freud," Seagram said, rising from the john. "Women are nothing to you. A beautiful relationship with you is a love affair with a bottle. You're out of touch with the world."

"Am I?" Pitt stood up in the tub and yanked open the door to the medicine cabinet so that Seagram was staring at his reflection in the mirror. "Take a good look. There's the face of a man who's out of touch with the world. Behind those eyes there's a man who's driven by a thousand demons of his own making. You're sick, Seagram. Mentally sick over problems you've magnified out of all proportion. Dana's desertion is only a crutch to enhance your black depression. You don't love her as much as you think you do. She's only a symbol, a prop you lean on. Look at the glaze over the eyes; look at the slack skin around the mouth. Get yourself to a psychiatrist, and damned soon. Think about Gene Seagram for once. Forget about saving the world. It's time you saved yourself."

Seagram's face was violently flushed. He clenched his fists and trembled. Then the mirror before his eyes began to mist, not on the outside but from within, and another face slowly emerged. A strange face with the same haunted eyes.

Pitt stood mute and watched as Seagram's expression turned from anger to sheer terror.

"God, no . . . it's him!"

"Him?"

"Him!" he cried, "Joshua Hays Brewster!" Then Seagram struck the mirror with both fists, shattering the glass, and fled the room.

76

Pensive and dreamy-eyed, Dana stood in front of a full-length mirror and scrutinized herself. The bruise on her head was neatly covered by a new hair style and, except for several fading black-and-blue marks, her body looked as lithe and perfect as ever. It definitely passed inspection. Then she stared at the eyes that stared back. There were no additional crow's-feet, no new puffiness around the edges. The mythical hardened look of a fallen woman was nowhere to be seen. Instead, they seemed to gleam with a vibrant expectancy that hadn't been there before. Her rebirth as an unfettered woman of the world had been a complete success.

"Care for any breakfast?" Marie Sheldon's voice carried up the stairs.

Dana donned a soft lace dressing gown. "Just coffee, thanks," she said. "What time is it?"

"A few minutes after nine."

A minute later Marie poured the coffee as Dana stepped into the kitchen. "What's on the agenda for today?" she asked.

"Something typically feminine—I think I'll go shopping. Have lunch by myself at an intimate tearoom and then go over to the NUMA clubhouse and scare up a partner for an hour or so of tennis."

"Sounds charming," Marie said dryly; "but I suggest you stop playing Mrs. Rich Bitch, which you aren't, and start acting like a broad with responsibilities, which you are."

"What's the sense in it?"

Marie threw up her hands in exasperation. " 'What's the sense in it?' For one thing, sweetie, you're the girl of the hour. In case you haven't noticed, the phone has been ringing off the hook for the past three days. Every woman's magazine in the country wants your exclusive story, and I've taken at least eight requests for you to appear on nationally televised talk shows. Like it or not, you're big news. Don't you think it's about time you came back down to earth and met the onslaught head-on?"

"What's there to say? So I was the only woman on board an old drifting derelict with twenty men. Big deal."

"You almost died out there in the ocean and you treat the whole episode as though it were just another cruise down the Nile on Cleopatra's barge. Having all those men catering to your every whim must have gone to your head."

If only Marie knew the whole truth. But Dana and everyone on board had been sworn to secrecy by Warren Nicholson. The attempted assault by the Russians was to be buried and forgotten by everyone. But she took a perverse sort of satisfaction in knowing that her performance on the *Titanic* that cold stormy night would linger in the minds of the men who were present for the rest of their lives.

"Too much happened out there." Dana sighed. "I'm not the same person any more."

"So what does that mean?"

"To begin with, I'm taking out papers to divorce Gene."

"It's come to that?"

"It's come to that," Dana repeated firmly. "Also, I'm going to take a leave of absence from NUMA and have a fling at life. As long as I'm the exalted female of the year, I'm going to make it pay. The personal stories, the TV appearances—they're going to enable me to do what every girl yearns to do all her life."

"Which is?"

"Spend money, and have a high old time doing it."

Marie shook her head sadly. "I'm beginning to feel like I've helped create a monster."

Dana took her gently by the hand. "Not you, dear friend. It took a brush with death for me to learn that I had condemned myself to an existence that led nowhere.

"It began, I suppose, with my childhood—" Dana's voice trailed off as the terrible memories came flickering back. "My childhood was a nightmare, and I've carried its effects with me all my adult life. I even infected my marriage with its sickness. Gene recognized the symptoms and married me more out of pity than deep love. Unwittingly, he treated me more as a father than as a lover.

"I can't force myself to go back now. The emotional responses that it takes to build and maintain a lasting relationship just aren't in me. I'm a loner, Marie; I know that now. I'm too selfish with my affections toward others; it's the albatross around my neck. From here on in, I'm going it alone. That way I can never hurt anyone ever again."

Marie looked up, tears in her eyes. "Well then, I guess between us we'll even up the sides. You're folding your marriage and going back to the single ways while I'm shucking the odd-woman-out syndrome and joining the great ranks of the matronly housewives."

Dana's lips parted in a wide smile. "You and Mel?"

"Me and Mel."

"When?"

"It had better be soon or I'm going to have to order my trousseau from the Blessed Event Maternity Shop."

"You're pregnant?"

"That ain't Betty Crocker that's rising in my oven."

Dana came around the table and hugged Marie. "You with a baby, I can't believe it."

"You better believe it. They tried mouth-to-mouth resuscitation and massive doses of adrenalin, but it was no go. The frog still died."

"You mean rabbit."

"Where've you been? They gave up rabbits years ago."

"Oh, Marie, I'm so happy for you. The two of us beginning whole new life patterns. Aren't you excited?"

"Oh sure," Marie said in a dry tone. "Nothing like starting anew with a big bang."

"Is there any other way?"

"I've got the easy path, sweetie." Marie kissed Dana on the cheek lightly. "It's you I'm worried about. Just don't go too far too fast and fall off the deep end."

"The deep end is where all the fun is."

"Take my word for it. Learn to swim in the shallows."

"Too tame." Dana's eyes grew thoughtful. "I'm going to start at the very crest."

"And just how are you going to initiate that little feat?"

Dana met Marie's eyes evenly. "All it takes is one little phone call."

The President came from behind his desk in the Oval Office and greeted the Majority Leader of the Senate, John Burdick, with warmth.

"John, it's good to see you. How are Josie and the kids?"

Burdick, a tall, thin man with a bush of black hair that seldom saw a comb, shrugged good naturedly. "Josie's fine. And you know kids. As far as they're concerned, good old Dad is nothing but a money machine."

After they were seated, the talk kicked off with their differences on budget programs. Although the two men were opposing party leaders and sniped at each other at every opportunity in the open, behind closed doors they were warm, intimate friends.

"Congress is beginning to think you've gone mad, Mr. President. During the past six months, you've vetoed every spending bill sent to the White House from the Hill."

"And I'm going to go right on vetoing until the day I walk through that door for the last time." The President paused to light a thin cigar. "Let's face the cold, hard truth, John. The government of the United States is broke, and it's been broke since the end of World War Two, but nobody will admit it. We go merrily on our way running up a national debt that defies comprehension, figuring that somewhere down the line the poor bastard that defeats us in the next election will pay the piper for the spending spree of the last fifty years."

"What do you expect Congress to do? Declare bankruptcy?"

"Sooner or later it may have to."

"The consequences are unthinkable. The national debt is carried by half the insurance companies, savings and loans, and banks in the nation. They'd all be wiped out overnight."

"So what else is new?"

Burdick shook his head. "I refuse to accept it."

"Damn it, John, you can't sweep it under the carpet. Do you realize that every taxpayer under the age of fifty will never see a Social Security check. In another twelve years it will be absolutely impossible to pay even a third of the people who are eligible for benefits. That's another reason I'm going to sound the warning. A small voice in the wilderness, I regretfully admit. But still, in the few months remaining of my term in office, I'm going to shout doom every chance I get."

"The American people don't like to hear sad tidings. You won't be very popular."

"I don't give a damn. I don't care one thin dime for what anybody thinks. Popularity contests are for egoists. A few months from now I'm going to be on my ketch, sailing peacefully somewhere south of Fiji, and the government can go straight to hell."

"I'm sorry to hear that, Mr. President. You're a good man. Even your worst enemies will concede that."

But the President was not to be stopped. "We had a great republic going for a while, John, but you and I and all the other attorneys screwed it up. Government is a big business and attorneys shouldn't be allowed to take office. It's the accountants and the marketing people who should be congressmen and President."

"It takes attorneys to run a legislature."

The President shrugged wearily. "What's the use? Whatever course I take won't change a thing." Then he straightened in his chair and smiled. "My apologies, John, you didn't come here to hear me make a speech. What's on your mind?"

"The underprivileged children's medical bill." Burdick stared intently at the President. "Are you going to veto that one too?"

The President leaned back in his chair and studied his cigar. "Yes," he said simply.

"That's my bill," Burdick said quietly. "I nursed it through both the House and the Senate."

"I know."

"How can you veto a bill for children whose families can't afford to give them proper medical attention?"

"For the same reason I've vetoed added benefits for citizens over eighty, federal scholarship programs for the minorities, and a dozen other welfare bills. Somebody has to pay for them. And the working class who support this country has been pushed to the wall with a five-hundred-per-cent tax increase over the last ten years."

"For the love of humanity, Mr. President."

"For the love of a balanced budget, Senator. Where do you expect the funds to support your program to come from?"

"You might begin by cutting back the budget of Meta Section."

So there it was. Congressional snoops had finally breached the walls of Meta Section. It had to come sooner or later. At least it was later.

He decided to play it noncommittal. "Meta Section?"

"A superclassified think-tank you've supported for years. Surely, I don't have to describe its operation to you."

"No," the President said evenly. "You don't."

An uncomfortable silence followed.

Finally Burdick forged ahead: "It took months of checking by my investigators—you covered the financial tracks very cleverly—but they finally managed to backtrail the source of the funds used to raise the *Titanic* to a supersecret organization, operating under the name of Meta Section, and then ultimately to you. My God, Mr. President, you authorized nearly three quarters of a billion dollars to salvage that worthless old wreck and then lied by saying that it cost less than half that amount. And here I am only asking for fifty million to get the children's medical bill off the ground. If I may say so, sir, your odd sense of priorities is a bloody crime."

"What do you intend to do, John? Blackmail me into signing your bill?"

"To be perfectly candid, yes."

"I see."

Before the conversation could go on, the President's secretary entered the room.

"Excuse me for interrupting, Mr. President, but you asked to check over your appointment schedule for this afternoon."

The President made an apologetic gesture to Burdick. "Excuse me, John, this will only take a moment."

The President scanned the schedule. He stopped at a name penciled in for 4:15. He looked up at his secretary, his eyebrows raised. "Mrs. Seagram?"

"Yes, sir. She called and said she had traced down the history of that model ship in the bedroom. I thought perhaps you might be interested in what she discovered, so I squeezed her in for a few minutes."

The President held his hands over his face and closed his eyes. "Call

Mrs. Seagram and cancel the four-fifteen appointment. Ask her to join me for dinner on board the Presidential yacht at seven-thirty."

The secretary made the notation and left the room.

The President turned back to Burdick. "Now, John, if I still refuse to sign your bill, what then?"

Burdick held up his hands. "Then you leave me no choice but to blow the whistle on your clandestine uses of government funds. In that event, I fear you can expect a scandal that will make the old Watergate mess look like an Easter egg hunt."

"You'd do that?"

"I would."

An icy calm seemed to settle over the President. "Before you dash out the door and waste more of the taxpayers' dollars on a congressional hearing over my fiscal maneuverings, I suggest you hear from the horse's own mouth what Meta Section is all about and what they've produced in the defense of the country that keeps us both gainfully employed."

"I'm listening, Mr. President."

"Good."

One hour later, a thoroughly subdued Senator John Burdick sat in his office and carefully dropped his secret file on Meta Section into a shredding machine.

77

It was a staggering sight to see the *Titanic* propped high and dry in the huge canyon of a dry dock.

Already the noise had started. Welders were attacking the clogged passageways. Riveters were hammering against the scarred hull, beefing up the temporary repairs made at sea to the jagged wounds below the waterline. Overhead, two sky-reaching cranes dipped their jaws down into the darkened cargo holds only to have them reappear minutes later with mangled bits and pieces of debris clutched in their iron teeth.

Pitt took what he knew would be his last look about the gymnasium and Upper Deck. Like bidding a New Year's Eve good-by to a passing piece of his life, he stood there and soaked up the memories. The sweat of the salvage, the blood and sacrifice of his crew, the fragility of their hope that had in the end carried them through. It would all be left behind. Finally, he cast aside his reverie and walked down the main staircase and eventually found his way to the forward cargo hold on G Deck.

They were all present and accounted for and looking strangely unfamiliar under the silver hard hats. Gene Seagram, gaunt and trembling, paced back and forth. Mel Donner, wiping trickles of sweat from his neck and chin, and nervously keeping a concerned eye on Seagram. Herb Lusky, a Meta Section mineralogist, standing by with his analysis equipment. Admirals Sandecker and Kemper, huddled in one corner of the darkened hold and conversing in low tones.

Pitt carefully stepped around the twisted bulkhead supports and over the rippled deck of warped steel until he was standing behind a shipyard worker who was intently aiming his cutting torch at a massive hinge on the vault door. The vault, Pitt thought darkly, it was only a matter of minutes now before the secret hidden inside its gut was laid bare. Suddenly, he became aware of an icy chill, everything around him seemed to turn cold, and he began to dread the opening of the vault.

As if sharing his uneasiness, the other men in the dank hold became quiet and gathered beside Pitt in restless apprehension.

At last, the worker turned off the fiery blue jet of his torch and raised his face shield.

"How's it look?" Pitt asked.

"They sure built them good in the old days," the worker replied. "I've torched out the lock mechanism and knocked off the hinges, but she's still frozen solid."

"What now?"

"We run a cable from the Doppleman crane above, attach it to the vault door and hope for the best."

It took the better part of an hour for a crew of men to wrestle a two-inch-thick cable into the hold and fasten it onto the vault. Then, when all was ready, a signal was relayed to the crane operator via a portable radio transmitter, and the cable began slowly to straighten out its curves and tighten. No one had to be told to move back out of the way. They all knew that if the wire took it in its head to snap, it would whiplash through the hold with more than enough force to split a man in two.

In the distance they could hear the engine of the crane straining. For long seconds nothing happened; the cable stretched and quivered, its strands groaning under the tremendous load. Pitt threw caution aside and edged closer. Still nothing happened. The vault's stubborn resolve seemed as firm as the steel of its walls.

The cable slackened as the crane operator eased off the strain to work up his engine's rpm's. Then he revved up and engaged the clutch once more, and the cable suddenly went taut with an audible twang. To the silent men who looked anxiously on, it seemed inconceivable that the old rusted vault could stand up to such a powerful assault, and yet the inconceivable was apparently happening. But then a tiny hairline crack made its appearance along the upper edge of the vault door. It was followed by two vertical cracks along the sides and, finally, a fourth, running across the bottom. Abruptly, with an agonizing screech of protest, the door reluctantly relinquished its grip and tore off the great steel cube.

No water came out of the yawning blackness. The vault had remained airtight during its long sojourn in the deep abyss.

Nobody made a move. They stood rooted, frozen, mesmerized by that uninviting black square hole. A musty stench rolled out from within.

Lusky was the first to find his voice. "My God, what is it? What in hell is that smell?"

"Get me a light," Pitt ordered one of the workmen.

Someone produced a fluorescent hand light. Pitt switched it on and danced its bluish-white beam on the interior of the vault.

They could see ten wooden boxes, tightly secured by stout leather straps. They could also see something else, something that turned every face ghostly pale. It was the mummified remains of a man.

78

He was lying in one corner of the vault, eyes closed and sunken in, skin as blackened as old tar paper on a warehouse roof. The muscle tissue was shrunken over the bony skeleton and a bacterial growth covered him from head to toe. He looked like a moldy piece of bread. Only the white hair of his head and beard were perfectly preserved. A pool of viscous fluid extended around the remains and moistened the atmosphere, as if a bucket of water had been thrown on the walls of the vault.

"Whoever it is is still wet," Kemper murmured, his face a mask of horror. "How can that be after so long?"

"Water accounts for over half the weight of the body," Pitt answered quietly. "There simply wasn't enough air trapped inside the vault to evaporate all of the fluids."

Donner turned away, repulsed by the macabre scene. "Who was he?" he managed, fighting the urge to vomit.

Pitt looked at the mummy impassively. "I think we will find that his name was Joshua Hays Brewster."

"Brewster?" Seagram whispered, his frightened eyes wild with fear.

"Why not?" Pitt said. "Who else knew the contents of the vault?"

Admiral Kemper shook his head in stunned wonderment. "Can you imagine," he said reverently, "what it must have been like dying in that black hole while the ship was sinking into the depths of the sea?"

"I don't care to dwell on it," Donner said. "I'll probably have nightmares every night for the next month as it is."

"It's positively ghastly," Sandecker said with difficulty. He studied the saddened, knowing expression on Pitt's face. "You knew about this?"

Pitt nodded. "I was forewarned by Commodore Bigalow."

Sandecker fixed him with a speculative look, but he let it drop at that and turned to one of the shipyard workers. "Call the coroner's office and tell them to come and get that thing out of there. Then clear the area and keep it cleared until I give you an order to the contrary."

The shipyard people needed no further urging. They disappeared from the cargo hold as if by magic.

Seagram grabbed Lusky's arm with an intensity that made the mineralogist start. "Okay, Herb, it's your show now."

Hesitantly, Lusky entered the cavity, stepped over the mummy, and pried open one of the ore boxes. Then he set up his equipment and began analyzing the contents. After what seemed forever to the men pacing the deck outside the vault, he looked up, his eyes reflecting a dazed disbelief.

"This stuff is worthless."

Seagram moved in closer. "Say again."

"It's worthless. There isn't even a minute trace of byzanium."

"Try another box." Seagram gasped feverishly.

Lusky nodded and went to work. But it was the same story on the next ore box, and the next, until the contents of all ten were strewn everywhere.

Lusky looked as though he was suffering a seizure. "Junk . . . pure junk . . ." he stammered. "Nothing but common gravel, the kind you'd find under any roadbed."

The hushed note of bewilderment in Lusky's voice faded away and the quiet in the *Titanic's* cargo hold became heavy and deep. Pitt stared downward, stared dumbly. Every eye was held by the rubble and the broken boxes while numbed minds fought to grasp the appalling reality, the horrible, undeniable truth that *everything*—the salvage, the exhausting labor, the astronomical drain of money, the deaths of Munk and Woodson—had all been for nothing. The byzanium was not on the *Titanic,* nor had it ever been. They were the victims of a monstrously cruel joke that had been played out seventy-six years before.

It was Seagram who finally broke the silence. In the final ignition of madness he grinned to himself in the gray light, the grin mushrooming into a bansheelike laughter that echoed in the steel hold. He thrust himself through the door of the vault, snatched up a rock, and struck Lusky on the side of the head sending a spray of red over the yellow wood ore boxes.

He was still laughing, locked in the throes of black hysteria, when he fell upon the putrescent remains of Joshua Hays Brewster and began bashing the mummified head against the vault wall until it loosened from the neck and came off in his hands.

As he held the ugly, abhorrent thing before him, Seagram's conflicted mind suddenly saw the blackened, parchmentlike lips spread into a hideous grin. His breakdown was complete. The parallel depression of Joshua Hays Brewster had reached out through the mists of time and bequeathed Seagram a ghostly inheritance that hurled the physicist into the yawning jaws of a madness from which he was never to escape.

79

Six days later, Donner entered the hotel dining room where Admiral Sandecker was eating breakfast and eased into a vacant chair across the table. "Have you heard the latest?"

Sandecker paused between bites of his omelet. "If it's more bad news, I'd just as soon you keep it to yourself."

"They nailed me coming out of my apartment this morning." He threw a folded paper on the table in front of him. "A subpoena to appear in front of a congressional investigating committee."

Sandecker forked another slice of the omelet without looking at the paper. "Congratulations."

"Same goes for you, Admiral. Dollars to doughnuts a federal marshal is lurking in your office anteroom this very minute, waiting to slap one on you."

"Who's behind it?"

"Some punk-assed freshman senator from Wyoming who's trying to make a name for himself before he's forty." Donner dabbed a crumpled handkerchief on his damp forehead. "The stupid ass even insists on having Gene testify."

"That I'd have to see." Sandecker pushed the plate away and leaned back in his chair. "How is Seagram getting along?"

"Manic-depressive psychosis is the fancy term for it."

"How about Lusky?"

"Twenty stitches and a nasty concussion. He should be out of the hospital in another week."

Sandecker shook his head. "I hope I never have to live through anything like that ever again." He took a swallow of coffee. "How do we play it?"

"The President called me personally from the White House last night. He said to play it straight. The last thing he wants is to become entangled in a snarl of conflicting lies."

"What about the Sicilian Project?"

"It died a quick death when we opened the *Titanic*'s vault," Donner said. "We have no alternative but to spill the entire can of worms from the beginning to the sorry end."

"Why does the dirty laundry have to be washed in the open? What good will it do?"

"The woes of a democracy," Donner said resignedly. "Everything has to be open and above board, even if it means giving away secrets to an unfriendly foreign government."

Sandecker placed his hands on his face and sighed. "Well, I guess I'll be looking for a new job."

"Not necessarily. The President has promised to issue a statement to the effect that the whole failure of the project was his responsibility and his alone."

Sandecker shook his head. "No good. I have several enemies in Congress. They're just drooling in anticipation of turning the screws on my resignation from NUMA."

"It may not come to that."

"For the past fifteen years, ever since I attained the rank of admiral, I've had to double-deal with politicians. Take my word for it, it's a dirty business. Before this thing is over with, everyone remotely connected with the Sicilian Project and the raising of the *Titanic* will be lucky if they can find a job cleaning stables."

"I'm truly sorry it had to end like this, Admiral."

"Believe me, so am I." Sandecker finished off his coffee and patted a napkin against his mouth. "Tell me, Donner, what's the batting order? Who has the illustrious senator from Wyoming named as the lead-off witness?"

"My understanding is that he intends taking the *Titanic*'s salvage operation first, and then working backward to involve Meta Section and finally the President." Donner picked up the subpoena and shoved it back in his coat pocket. "The first witness they're most likely to call is Dirk Pitt."

Sandecker looked at him. "Pitt, did you say?"

"That's right."

"Interesting," Sandecker said softly. "Most interesting."

"You've lost me somewhere."

Sandecker neatly folded the napkin and laid it on the table. "What you don't know, Donner, what you couldn't know, is that immediately after the men in the little white coats carried Seagram off the *Titanic*, Pitt vanished into thin air."

Donner's eyes narrowed. "Surely you know where he is. His friends? Giordino?"

"Don't you think we all tried to find him?" Sandecker snarled. "He's gone. Disappeared. It's as though the earth swallowed him up."

"But he must have left some clue."

"He did say something, but it didn't make any sense."

"What was that?"

"He said he was going to look for Southby."

"Who in hell is Southby?"

"Damned if I know," Sandecker said. "Damned if I know."

80

Pitt steered the rented Rover sedan cautiously down the narrow, rain-slickened country road. The tall beech trees lining the shoulders seemed to close in and attack the moving car as they pelted its steel roof with the heavy runoff from their leaves.

Pitt was tired, dead tired. He had set out on his odyssey not sure of what it was he might find, if anything. He'd begun as Joshua Hays Brewster and his crew of miners had begun, on the docks of Aberdeen, Scotland, and then he'd followed their death-strewn path across Britain almost to the old Ocean Dock at Southampton from which the *Titanic* had set out on her maiden voyage.

He turned his gaze from the pounding wipers on the windshield and glanced down at the blue notebook lying on the passenger seat. It was filled with dates, places, miscellaneous jottings, and torn newspaper articles he had accumulated along the way. The musty files of the past had told him little.

"TWO AMERICANS FOUND DEAD"

the April 7, 1912, editions of the Glasgow papers noted fifteen pages back from the headline. The detail-barren stories were as deeply buried as the bodies of Coloradans John Caldwell and Thomas Price were in a local cemetery.

Their tombstones, discovered by Pitt in a small churchyard, offered virtually nothing other than their names and dates of death. It was the same story with Charles Widney, Walter Schmidt, and Warner O'Deming. Of Alvin Coulter he could find no trace.

And finally there was Vernon Hall. Pitt hadn't found his resting place either. Where had he fallen? Had his blood been spilled amid the neat and orderly landscape of the Hampshire Downs or perhaps somewhere on the back streets of Southampton itself?

Out of the corner of one eye he caught a marker that gave the distance to the great harbor port as twenty kilometers.

Pitt drove on mechanically. The road curved and then paralleled the lovely, rippling Itchen stream, famous throughout southern England for its fighting trout, but he didn't notice it. Up ahead, across the emerald-green farmlands of the coastal plain, a small town came into view, and he decided he would stop there for breakfast.

An alarm went off in the back of Pitt's mind. He jammed on the brakes, but much too hard—the rear wheels broke loose and the Rover skidded around in a perfect three-hundred-and-sixty-degree circle, coming to rest still aimed southward but sunk to the hubcaps in the yielding muck of a roadside ditch.

Almost before the car had fully stopped, Pitt threw open the door and leaped out. His shoes sank out of sight and became stuck, but he pulled free of them and ran back down the road in his stocking feet.

He halted at a small sign beside the road. Part of the lettering was obscured by a small tree that had grown up around it. Slowly, as if he were afraid his hopes would be shattered by yet another disappointment, he pushed aside the branches and suddenly it all became quite clear. The key to the riddle of Joshua Hays Brewster and the byzanium was there in front of him. He stood there soaking up the falling rain and in that instant he knew that everything had been worthwhile.

81

Marganin sat on a bench by the fountain in Sverdlov Square across from the Bolshoi Theater and read a newspaper. He felt a slight quiver and knew without looking that someone had taken the vacant place beside him.

The fat man in the rumpled suit leaned against the backrest and casually gnawed on an apple. "Congratulations on your promotion, Commander," he mumbled between bites.

"Considering how events turned out," Marganin said without lowering the paper, "it was the least Admiral Sloyuk could do."

"And your situation now . . . with Prevlov out of the way?"

"With the good Captain's defection, I was the logical choice to replace him as Chief of the Foreign Intelligence Analysis Division. It was an obvious conclusion."

"It is good that our years of labor have paid such handsome dividends."

Marganin turned a page. "We have only opened the door. The dividends are yet to come."

"You must be more careful of your actions now than ever before."

"I intend to," Marganin said. "This Prevlov business badly burned the Soviet Navy's credibility with the Kremlin. Everyone in the Naval Intelligence Department is having their security clearances rechecked under tight scrutiny. It will be a long time before I am trusted as fully as Captain Prevlov was."

"We will see to it that things are speeded up a bit." The fat man pretended to swallow a large bite from the apple. "When you leave here, mingle with the crowd at the entrance to the subway across the street. One of our people who is adroit at lifting wallets from the unsuspecting will do a reverse routine and discreetly insert an envelope into your inside breast pocket. The envelope contains the minutes from the last meeting of the United States Navy Chief of Staff with his fleet commanders."

"That's pretty heady material."

"The minutes have been doctored. They may seem important, but in reality they have been carefully reworded to mislead your superiors."

"Passing along fake documents won't do my position any good."

"Ease your mind," the fat man said. "Tomorrow at this time an agent of the KGB will obtain the same material. The KGB will declare it bona fide. Since you will have produced your information twenty-four hours ahead of them, it will put a feather in your cap in the eyes of Admiral Sloyuk."

"Very cunning," Marganin said, staring at the newspaper. "Anything else?"

"This is good-by," the fat man murmured.

"Good-by?"

"Yes. I have been your contact long enough. Too long. We've come too far, you and I, to become lax in our security now."

"And my new contact?"

"Are you still living in the naval barracks?" the fat man replied with another question.

"The barracks will remain my home. I am not about to draw suspicion as a big spender and live in a fancy apartment like Prevlov's. I shall continue to lead a spartan existence on my Soviet naval pay."

"Good. My replacement is already assigned. He will be the orderly who cleans the officers' quarters of your barracks."

"I will miss you, old friend," Marganin said slowly.

"And I, you."

There was a long moment of silence. And then, finally, the fat man spoke again in a hushed undertone. "God bless, Harry."

When Marganin folded the newspaper and laid it aside, the fat man was gone.

82

"That's our destination over there to the right," the pilot of the helicopter said. "I'll set down in that pasture just across the road from the churchyard."

Sandecker looked out the window. It was a gray, overcast morning and soft blankets of mist were hovering over the low areas of the tiny village. A quiet lane wandered past several quaint houses and was bordered on both sides by picturesque rock walls. He stiffened as the pilot made a steep bank around the church steeple.

He glanced at Donner on the seat beside him. Donner was staring straight ahead. In front of him, occupying the seat next to the pilot, was Sid Koplin. The mineralogist had been called back on this one last assignment for Meta Section, because Herb Lusky was still not well enough to make the trip.

Sandecker felt the slight bump as the landing skids touched the ground, and a moment later the pilot cut the engine and the rotor blades drifted to a stop.

In the sudden stillness after the flight from London, the pilot's voice seemed overly loud. "We're here sir."

Sandecker nodded and stepped out the side door. Pitt was waiting and walked toward him with an outstretched hand.

"Welcome to Southby, Admiral," he said smiling.

Sandecker smiled as he took Pitt's hand, but there was no humor in his face. "The next time you take a powder without notifying me as to your intentions, you're fired."

Pitt feigned a hurt expression and then turned and greeted Donner. "Mel, nice to see you."

"Likewise," Donner said warmly. "I believe you've already met Sid Koplin."

"A chance meeting," Pitt grinned. "We were never formally introduced."

Koplin took Pitt's hand in both of his. This was hardly the same man Pitt had found dying in the snows of Novaya Zemlya. Koplin's grip was firm and his eyes alert.

"It was my fondest wish," he said, his voice heavy with emotion, "that some day I would have the opportunity of thanking you in person for saving my life."

"I'm glad to see you in good health," was all Pitt could think of to mumble. He looked down at the ground nervously.

By God, Sandecker thought to himself, the man was actually embarrassed. He never dreamed he'd see the day when Dirk Pitt turned modest. The admiral rescued Pitt by grabbing him by the arm and pulling him toward the village church.

"I hope you know what you're doing," Sandecker said. "The British frown upon colonials who go around digging up their graveyards."

"It took a direct call from the President to the Prime Minister to cut through all the bureaucratic red tape of an exhumation," Donner added.

"I think you will find the inconvenience has been worth it," Pitt said.

They came to the road and crossed it. Then they passed through an ancient wrought-iron gate and walked into the graveyard that surrounded the parish church. They walked in silence for several moments, reading the inscriptions on the weather-worn headstones.

Then Sandecker motioned toward the little village. "It's so far off the beaten track. What steered you onto it?"

"Pure luck," Pitt answered. "When I began tracing the Coloradans' movements from Aberdeen, I had no idea of how Southby might fit in the puzzle. The final sentence in Brewster's journal, if you recall, said: 'How I long to return to Southby.' And, according to Commodore Bigalow, Brewster's last words just before he shut himself in the *Titanic*'s vault were: 'Thank God for Southby.'

"My only inkling, and a meager one at that, was Southby had an English ring to it, so I began by pinpointing as nearly as I could the miners' trail to Southampton—"

"By following their grave markers," Donner finished.

"They read like signposts," Pitt admitted. "That and the fact that Brewster's journal recorded the times and places of their deaths, except, that is, for Alvin Coulter and Vernon Hall. Coulter's final resting place remains a mystery, but Hall lies here in the Southby village cemetery."

"Then you found it on a map."

"No, the village is so small it isn't even a dot in the *Michelin Tour Guide*. I just happened to notice an old, forgotten hand-painted sign some farmer had set along the main road years ago advertising a milk cow for sale. The directions gave the farm's location as three kilometers east on the next country lane to Southby. The last pieces of the puzzle then began dropping into place."

They walked along in silence and made their way over to where three men were standing. Two wore the standard work clothes of local farmers, the third was in the uniform of a county constable. Pitt made the brief introductions, and then Donner solemnly handed the constable the order for exhumation.

They all stared down at the grave. The tombstone stood at one end of a large stone slab that lay atop the deceased. The stone simply read:

VERNON HALL
Died April 8, 1912
R.I.P.

Neatly carved in the center of the arched horizontal slab was the image of an old three-masted sailing ship.

" '. . . the precious ore we labored so desperately to rape from the bowels of that cursed mountain lies safely in the vault of the ship. Only Vernon will be left to tell the tale, for I depart on the great White Star steamer . . .' " Pitt recited the words from Joshua Hays Brewster's journal.

"Vernon Hall's *burial* vault," Donner said as if in a dream. "This is what he meant, not the vault of the *Titanic*."

"It's unreal," Sandecker murmured. "Is it possible that the byzanium lies here?"

"We'll know in a few minutes," Pitt said. He nodded to the two farmers who began shoving at the slab with pry bars. Once the slab was hefted aside, the farmers began digging.

"But why bury the byzanium here?" Sandecker asked. "Why didn't Brewster go on to Southampton and have it loaded on board the *Titanic*?"

"A myriad of reasons," Pitt said, his voice unnaturally loud in the quiet graveyard. "Hunted like a dog, exhausted beyond human endurance, his friends all brutally murdered before his eyes, Brewster was pushed into madness just as surely as Gene Seagram was when he learned that fate had snatched away his moment of success on the very verge of fulfillment. Add all that to the fact that Brewster was in a strange land; he was alone and friendless. Death stalked him constantly without letup, and his only chance for escaping to the United States with the byzanium was moored several miles away at the dock in Southampton.

"It's said that insanity breeds genius. Perhaps in Brewster's case it was so, or perhaps he was simply misguided by his delusions. He assumed, wrongly as it turned out, that he could never make it safely aboard the ship with the byzanium by himself. So, he buried it in Vernon Hall's grave and substituted worthless rock in the original ore boxes. Then he probably left his journal with the church vicar with instructions to turn it over to the American consulate in Southampton. I imagine his cryptic prose grew from the madness that had brought him to the point where he trusted no one—not even an old country vicar. He probably figured that some perceptive soul in the Army Department would decipher the true meaning of his wandering prose in the event of his murder."

"But he made it on board the *Titanic* safely," Donner said. "The French didn't stop him."

"My guess is that things were getting too warm for the French agents. The British police must have followed the trail of bodies, just as I did, and were breathing down the pursuers' back."

"So the French, afraid of an international scandal of gigantic proportions, backed off at the last moment," Koplin injected.

"That's one theory," Pitt replied.

Sandecker looked thoughtful. "The *Titanic* . . . the *Titanic* sank and queered everything."

"True," Pitt answered automatically. "Now a thousand *if*'s enter the picture. *If* Captain Smith had heeded the ice warnings and reduced speed; *if* the ice packs hadn't floated unusually far south that year; *if* the *Titanic* had missed the iceberg and docked in New York as scheduled; and, *if* Brewster had lived to tell his story to the Army, the byzanium would have simply been dug up and recovered at a later date. On the other hand, even if Brewster had been killed before he boarded the ship, the Army Department would have no doubt figured the double meaning at the end of his journal and acted accordingly. Unfortunately, the wheels of chance played a dirty trick: the *Titanic* sank, taking Brewster along with it, and the veiled words of his journal threw everybody, including ourselves, completely off the track for seventy-six years."

"Then why did Brewster lock himself in the *Titanic*'s vault?" Donner asked in puzzlement. "Knowing that the ship was doomed, knowing that any suicidal act was a meaningless gesture, why didn't he try and save himself?"

"Guilt is a powerful motive for suicide," Pitt said. "Brewster was insane. That much we know. When he realized that his scheme to steal the byzanium had caused a score of people, eight of whom were close friends, to die needlessly, he blamed himself. Many men, and women, too, have taken their own lives for much less—"

"Hold on a moment!" Koplin cut in. He was kneeling over an open case of mineral-analysis gear. "I'm getting a radioactive reading from the fill over the coffin."

The diggers climbed out of the hole. The rest clustered around Koplin and peered curiously as he went through his ritual. Sandecker pulled a cigar from his breast pocket and stuck it between his lips without lighting it. The air was cold, but Donner's shirt was wet right through his coat. No one spoke. Their breaths came in small wisps of vapor that quickly dissipated in the subdued gray light.

Koplin studied the rocky soil. It didn't match the composition of the moist brown earth that surrounded the grave's excavation. At last, he rose unsteadily to his feet. He held several small rocks up in his hand. "Byzanium!"

"Is . . . is it here?" Donner asked in a hushed whisper. "Is it really all here?"

"Ultra high grade," Koplin announced. His face broke into a wide smile. "More than enough to complete the Sicilian Project."

"Thank God!" Donner gasped. He staggered over to an above-ground crypt and unceremoniously collapsed on it, oblivious to the shocked stares of the local farmers.

Koplin looked back down into the grave. "Insanity does breed genius," he murmured. "Brewster filled the grave with the ore. Anyone except a professional mineralogist would have simply dug through it and finding nothing in the coffin but bones, would have walked off and left it."

"An ideal way to conceal it," Donner agreed. "Practically right out in the open."

Sandecker stepped over and took Pitt's hand and shook it. "Thank you," he said simply.

Pitt could only nod in reply. He felt tired and numb. He wanted to find himself a place where he could crawl away from the world and forget it for a while. He wished the *Titanic* had never been, had never slid down the ways of the Belfast shipyard to the silent sea, to the merciless sea that had transformed that beautiful ship into a grotesque, rusted old hulk.

Sandecker seemed to read Pitt's eyes. "You look like you need a rest," he said. "Don't let me see your ugly face around my office for at least two weeks."

"I was hoping you'd say that." Pitt smiled wearily.

"Mind telling me where you plan to hide out?" Sandecker asked slyly. "Only in the event an emergency arises at NUMA, of course, and I have to get in touch with you."

"Of course," Pitt came back dryly. He paused a moment. "There's a little airline stewardess who lives with her great grandfather in Teign-mouth. You might try me there."

Sandecker nodded in silent understanding.

Koplin came over and grasped Pitt by both shoulders. "I hope we meet again sometime."

"My sentiments, too."

Donner looked at him without rising and said with emotional hoarse-ness, "It's finally over."

"Yes," Pitt said. "It's over and done with. Everything."

He felt a sudden chill, a feeling of cold familiarity, as though his words had echoed hauntingly from the past. Then he turned and walked from the Southby graveyard.

They all stood and watched him grow smaller in the distance, until he entered a shroud of mist and disappeared.

"He came from the mists and he returned to the mists," Koplin said, his mind drifting back to his first meeting with Pitt on the slopes of Bednaya Mountain.

Donner gazed at him oddly. "What was that you said?"

"Just thinking out loud." Koplin shrugged. "That's all."

Reckoning

"Stop engines."

The telegraph rang in reply to the captain's command, and the vibrations coming from the engine room of the British cruiser H.M.S. *Troy* died away. The foam around the bows melted into the blackness of the sea as the ship slowly lost her momentum, silent except for the hum of her generators.

It was a warm night for the North Atlantic. The sea was glassy-calm and the stars blazed in a sparkling carpet across the sky from horizon to horizon. The Union Jack hung limp and lifeless in its halyards, untouched by even a hint of breeze.

The crew, over two hundred of them, was assembled on the foredeck as a lifeless body sewn in the traditional sailcloth of a bygone era and shrouded by the national flag, was carried out and poised at the ship's railing. Then the captain, his voice resonant and unemotional, read the sailor's burial service. As soon as he uttered the final words, he nodded. The slat was tilted, and the body slid into the waiting arms of the eternal sea. The bugle notes were clear and pure as they drifted into the quiet night; then the men were dismissed and they turned silently away.

A few minutes later, when the *Troy* was under way again, the captain sat down and made the following entry in the ship's log:

H.M.S. Troy. *Time: 0220, 10 August 1988.*
Pos.: Lat. 41°46′N., Long. 50°14′W.

At the exact time in the morning of the White Star steamer R.M.S.
Titanic*'s foundering, and in accordance with his dying wish that he*
spend eternity with his former shipmates, the remains of Com-
modore Sir John L. Bigalow, K.B.E., R.D., R.N.R. (Retired)
were committed to the deep.

The captain's hand trembled as he signed his name. He was closing out
the last chapter of a tragic drama that had stunned the world . . . a
world the likes of which would never be seen again.

At almost the same moment, on the other side of the earth somewhere
in the vast desolate wastes of the Pacific Ocean, a huge cigar-shaped
submarine crept silently far below the languorous waves. Startled fish
scattered into the depths at the monster's approach, while within its
smooth black skin, men prepared to launch a quad of ballistic missiles at
a series of divergent targets six thousand miles to the east.

At precisely 1500 hours, the first of the great missiles ignited its
rocket engine and burst through the sun-danced swells in a volcanic
eruption of white water, rising with a thunderous roar into the blue
Pacific sky. In thirty seconds, it was followed by the second, and the
third, and, finally, the fourth. Then, trailing long fiery columns of orange
flame, the quartet of potential mass-destruction arched into space and
disappeared.

Thirty-two minutes later, while homing in on their down-range trajec-
tory, the missiles abruptly blew up, one by one, in gigantic balls of
flame, and disintegrated while still some ninety miles from their respective targets. It was the first time in the history of American rocketry that
anyone remembered that the attending technicians and engineers and
military officers who held rein on the nation's defense programs had ever
cheered the sudden and seemingly disastrous end to a perfect launch.

The Sicilian Project had proven itself an unqualified success on its
first try.